T0165632

# 90 DAYS OF VIOLENCE

# 90 DAYS OF VIOLENCE

Lyndon Baptiste

iUniverse, Inc.
New York   Bloomington

# 90 Days of Violence

*Copyright © 2009 by Lyndon Baptiste, Potbake Productions*

*Cover design copyright © 2008 by Lyndon Baptiste.*
*Illustrations copyright © 2008 by Martin O'Brien.*
*Editor: Lance Baptiste.*

*All rights reserved. No part of this book may be used or reproduced by any means,*
*graphic, electronic, or mechanical, including photocopying, recording, taping or by any*
*information storage retrieval system without the written permission of the publisher*
*except in the case of brief quotations embodied in critical articles and reviews.*

*All characters in this book are fictitious and any resemblance to actual persons,*
*living or dead, is purely coincidental. The names, incidents, dialogue and opinions*
*expressed are products of the author's imagination and are not to be construed as real.*
*Nothing is intended or should be interpreted as expressing or representing the views of*
*the Trinidad and Tobago protective forces or any other department or agency of any*
*government body.*

*iUniverse books may be ordered through booksellers or by contacting:*

*iUniverse*
*1663 Liberty Drive*
*Bloomington, IN 47403*
*www.iuniverse.com*
*1-800-Authors (1-800-288-4677)*

*Because of the dynamic nature of the Internet, any Web addresses or links contained in*
*this book may have changed since publication and may no longer be valid. The views*
*expressed in this work are solely those of the author and do not necessarily reflect the views*
*of the publisher, and the publisher hereby disclaims any responsibility for them.*

*ISBN: 978-1-4401-2222-4 (pbk)*
*ISBN: 978-1-4401-2223-1 (ebk)*

*Printed in the United States of America*

*iUniverse rev. date: 2/12/2009*

Crows everywhere are equally black
- Chinese Proverb

for my family

# AUTHOR'S NOTE

You might be tempted to attack 90 Days of Violence from three angles: that it depicts Trinidad and Tobago in a negative light, a haven for criminals. Secondly, that the material is libellous, inflamed with racism. Thirdly, on the issue of legislation.

My responses are straightforward.

One: citizens of other countries have already been warned to shun Trinidad and Tobago. Therefore it is safe to conclude that our nation, while a dot on the atlas, is no stranger in the world of terror. Graciously, I have chosen to highlight only ninety days.

Two: 90 Days of Violence is about everyday life and existing interactions among members of our society. The characters, their struggles with ethnicity, gender and religion, and their thoughts are fictitious. Coming from a cosmopolitan background, I would have despised myself had the material been intended as racist.

Three: laws do not remain the same. They are amended in the hope that they can be strengthened through the removal of loopholes. Laws are misused everyday. I have ignored clauses to advance my plot. I acknowledge this.

90 Days of Violence is intended as a literary piece which highlights contemporary social issues and subtly provides highways of action. If you are inclined to believe otherwise then sadly you have been mistaken.

Thanks to Lance Baptiste, my father, for the help; there are countless silken lines and semicolons which I accredit to him. And to Louise Baptiste, my mother, a faithful 'coffee, snacks and food lady.' And to Martin O'Brien who brought my characters, particularly *Bharat*, to life with skilful illustrations. I am indebted to you, Kimberly; And to the countless others who supported.

# 1 The seventh prime minister

HE SAT in the stillness of the chamber, alone, pensive, absorbed by the portraits which decorated the high wall opposite the grand oak desk. When sunlight infiltrated the room, the faces materialised, forefathers of the nation in chronological order. Each expression differed and though the eyes of the Oxford-educated prime minister were hidden behind shaded spectacles, Ambrose felt glared upon. Discomforted, he stood and went to the window.

Separating the curtains revealed a yolk-coloured sun scorching high in the east. From the second floor of his hilltop home in Maraval the office delivered a majestic view of cascading mountains to the north, jade from the December rain. The glass to the southeast, however, revealed what Ambrose considered to be a heartache: Port of Spain. The night usually hid the flaws of the capital, but from where he stood he could see black smoke floating in from the garbage dump. The smoulder was thick, like the exhaust of an ancient coal-powered passenger train. It drifted, then settled like a suffocating blanket upon the city. The real smog, however, was the evil of human nature plaguing the capital. It was an infection for which there seemed no cure. Watching the city, was like observing the deterioration of a loved one's health.

Today the roads were fairly clear. From where Ambrose stood, unseen behind tinted windows, he saw cars darting along the highway, oblivious of the speed limit; the passengers, no doubt, en route to celebrations with family and friends. These were his citizens, his children. There really was no one father of Trinidad and Tobago. It was an accepted responsibility, given to each person selected to bear the mantle of *primus inter pares*. Had he not? Didn't that make him responsible for each citizen? As the appointed leader of the beloved nation it was his duty not only to chair the Cabinet, appoint ministers or act as a spokesperson for government, but to be proactive in the interest of his country.

The people had chosen. As prime minister, Ambrose knew that the citizens were tired of dejection from previous governments which rolled decades backwards. Everyone (Africans, East Indians, Caucasians, Chinese and Mixed races) wanted the same: implementations rather than plans. It was that simple. As a result of empty promises the electorate sank the rivals and Ambrose and his trusted team inherited a nation. A country in dire need of major reform, both at the level of government and the people. Things looked badly broken, irrepairable some said, and slowly consensus grew: it was the crime. Everyone knew it, from the layman to the doctor, the captain to the cook: 'Trinidad sweet yes, but oh *gosh* the crime mashing up we sweet T and T.'

The volumes spoke facts. This year (Ambrose corrected himself – last year) almost had more murders than days, but by the grace of heaven it was a leap year. It wasn't just Trinidad that reported horrendous figures. In separate Christmas courtesy calls to the Jamaican and Guyanese leaders, they echoed the same lamentations. The year hadn't yet finished and the murder toll in Jamaica had already, and once again, exceeded three figures. Guyana to the south bore the same tales of woe, with escalations in gang violence and murders. It was the drugs, Guyana's head of government told Ambrose – in an accent the Trinidadian found difficult to follow – and the trafficking which influenced the growth in crime. There were just too many rivers for the government to manage. The smugglers had unlimited resources. Guyana didn't. The Guyanese resounded the need for assistance from the United States (US) drug enforcement agencies to snuff out transnational crimes in the Caribbean basin. The call ended without pleasantries being exchanged.

Crime didn't happen in isolation, Ambrose thought, as he paced away from the window back to the desk, his hands clasped tight, one manacled to the other behind his back. Even though the twin island had recently entered another economic boom from oil production the cost of manufacturing and utilities had skyrocketed. There had been promises of cheaper goods and services to the citizens, but the cost of basic essentials such as flour and rice soared sky high. National housing was also taking a beating. Yet people weren't experiencing salary hikes. The PM shook his head and, overwhelmed by his thoughts, pushed a series of buttons on a control panel on the desk. The curtains drew automatically. Another button lit the room. *Mark Lloyd really is a sucker for technology.*

It occurred to Ambrose that one day his face would decorate this and other walls. His portrait already hung within government institutions and the homes and offices of patriots. He disliked the photograph enough not to want one in the bedroom, but in some matters Patricia held the final word. Even though he wore slight makeup – much to Ambrose's objection – his cocoa brown complexion shone. Behind spectacles, his eyes appeared to be looking elsewhere, as if there were two photographers at the shoot and he had selected to eyeball the wrong one. There were signs of grey hair cropping his curled locks, which intertwined with each other, even though trimmed short. It was his smile which made his wife select the picture out of fifty-nine options. It said: 'Trust me. Follow me. I will lead you down the safe path. I am your leader. You have chosen me and I have accepted.' His smile made his cheeks look plump, Patricia had said, and Ambrose had blushed. He would be remembered. That was certain. *But as what?*

His decision to enter politics was only because he worried about the direction his country was taking. He believed in Trinidad and Tobago and there were recorded speeches of him stressing his ability to fight harder as prime minister in tackling crime and corruption and providing for the welfare of the people. He thought: *well, Ambrose, you are now in a position to influence change.*

FIFTEEN MILES southeast of the prime minister's office, Navin worked over a shallow grave, a few hours old. He was a short, small man of fair complexion and immense strength although looking at him one would hardly know. The two men for whom the grave was intended had made that mistake and now lay hogtied to each other, not quite dead but wishing they were. Even if their tongues hadn't been sliced off, their screams, now gurgled in blood, would have gone unheard miles inside the canefield. All around cane stalks grew high and leaned mournfully in the hot breeze, as if sensing the impending, inevitable act.

Navin paused. He was tough, but so was the work. He wiped a long blade against his cotton vest, blood stains smearing the cloth. He spat at the immobilised men. *Crapaud* and *Bull* were threats, and menaces had to be removed. There was no other way. If not the foundation of the organisation could not be laid – Mr. Bharat's words. To Navin the building was already complete and in his eyes human pests were to be exterminated. Just like the bats that kept darting and messing up the walls of his house. They were shot.

The problem began when Mr. Bharat, the genius, expanded his empire and overstepped the boundaries of his village into their turf. Crapaud and Bull had ruled with iron fists, but had nothing to show for their efforts. Their flashy cars were wrecked and had become junk used only as dens fit for dogs. They had lacked the vision that Mr. Bharat exhibited and soon their illicit sales in the Borough of Chaguanas declined sharply. Still, they had no right to jeer, to tell The Boss to 'kiss their black bottoms.' Navin wasn't there at the time, but Ricky Lo had reenacted, with the necessary gestures, how the two Africans confronted Mr. Bharat requesting a percentage of profits. Subsequent to their visit The Boss investigated and learnt, from a trusted source known as *Chief*, that the two *Creoles* were police informants. To The Boss the justice on rats was to be delivered swiftly and mercilessly. Navin was just the man for the job. The plan was simple. The henchman was to arrange a meet with Crapaud and Bull and a payment in good faith of one hundred pounds of ganja and a ten per cent of the profits made in their area over the past month would settle all debts.

Behind Navin's house, which he had inhabited since childbirth, were hundreds of acres of sugarcane, green stalks with white blossoms which swayed in the wind. As a child he had run through these fields, hunting and swimming in the surrounding swamp lands. He grew older, forgot his boyhood adventures but remembered the land. Navin knew most of the area intimately. He had prepared the grave then made the call to Crapaud and Bull. The deal was a lucrative one for both men and the choice of location unquestioned. They had roared their way five miles into the fields with loud dirt bikes and came to the rendezvous point marked by a crippled tractor, almost rusted flat into the ground. The clearing was behind that. A bullet to the gut took each man down and severed tongues silenced screams. The skilful butcher would work uninterrupted.

Navin stooped next to the bigger man. "Bull, it was you that tell me boss to kiss your backside?" No answer. Navin sunk his fingers into the man's stomach so that he choked and sputtered to a druggy consciousness. Navin repeated the question. Sweat clung to his body and he pinched the cotton away from his chest. The blood didn't disturb him. The question again, sterner this time, in a voice that didn't falter like the droplets of rain that fell suddenly in the scorching heat.

Bull knew he was about to die; there was something about Navin's cold eyes which made him nod. But that simple word 'sorry' couldn't leave his lips – it was physically impossible. He begged for his life in tearful whimpers. Gurgled blood erupted from his mouth like molten lava. There was another sharp pain as cold steel touched his flesh and the last sensation Bull experienced was choking as all came to darkness and the unknown villain faded from sight. The greater stink of death embraced him and the taste of rain said goodbye.

LOUD ELOQUENT insults darted among the chefs. Aram jousted at another cook in Arabic and the small group erupted into long uncontrollable laughter which finally subsided for the retort. The response was more timid, but still earned itself a few chuckles. After all, everyone gathered was family.

A newcomer joined the group and all in the outdoor kitchen greeted Gregory with hugs, and kisses on his cheeks. Aram did the same, his right hand on his heart, signalling deep affection for his cousin. They exchanged inaudible words, drowned by voices, laughter and classical Arabic music that echoed within the vast expanse of the illustrious backyard bordered by high concrete walls. A famous rendition by a virtuoso singer was playing; a long, elaborately ornamented song of melismatic tunes describing honour among family. When Gregory was finished Aram's features relaxed and the good-natured, comical exchanges resumed.

Lunch came and with it meals, dished into great glass bowls and laid out on fresh, snow-white cloth, starched and pressed for the occasion. The *mezzeh* began. Men, women and children gathered by the swimming pool but remained segregated by gender. With each return trip from the kitchen Aram brought a variety of dishes: *hummous*, *tahini*, *baba ganouj*, *tabouleh*, *falafel* and *pita bread* each in some way garnished with olives, lemon, parsley, onion and garlic.

Everyone praised the host. His thin lips, shaded by a thick, dark moustache, parted into a generous smile. Aram beamed not at the compliments, but at the huge gathering of his family. These times meant everything and all that mattered was his ability to continue building the empire his father had etched as a mere Syrian merchant who once sold clothes from a suitcase.

For the entire day the finest of food and alcohol would flow and as a sign of their appreciation the guests would consume whatever Aram presented. Later in the afternoon the host and the horde of guests would trot to the jetty and sail the Chaguaramas coast on the magnificent *Dolly* until midnight.

IT WAS five in the afternoon when Bharat's cellular phone rang. He was poised before an elaborate fireplace, unused in the tropical climate, waiting, his legs crossed. He answered the call. The job was done. Crapaud and Bull were eliminated.

The news called for a tiny celebration. He dipped into his jacket and extracted a *good times* cigar he always held in reserve. Expertly he lit it and like any spaghetti western cowboy rolled the cigar in his mouth enjoying its taste: strong yet refined. Frank Sinatra's voice added to the ambience of the room, Bharat humming along deeply in his *own way*, which he reflected to be quite superb. Yet, he lacked something. Bharat looked towards the bar. *What I need is ah drink! Where the hell Isabel is?* He shouted for her and confidently she strutted into the room, like an Arabian show-horse, her silicone breasts firm and high on her chest. On command she made him a drink of rum and cola to match his taste. He told her to kiss him and she did. Then he dismissed her.

Bharat looked across at the well-stocked bar complete with a neon no-smoking sign which flickered intermittently. Despite his affluence he couldn't stomach vodka, red wine and the different colours of Scotch. Isabel, however, could drink tequila like water. He admired her and adorned her as a queen and she reciprocated, dues fit for a king. The sense of loyalty Latin women possessed puzzled most, but not Bharat. His Isabel was not different to the countless others he met and enjoyed in the flesh trade. The *mujeres* were '*one-man*' women; there was nothing like another *hombre*. They were loyal, but not timid. That separated Latinas from the East Indian woman. *Yes*, he thought, *that is it.*

Bharat had been married to an East Indian and while she served, as Isabel did, there was a disturbing quietness with which she went about her chores and that irritated him. She was like an animal beaten into submission, cringing whenever the wicked master appeared. Bharat thought himself patient, but his wife aggravated him and he rained licks on her as regularly as money and he was a generous man. Yet she – *that ungrateful witch* – disappeared one day, years ago. She was immediately replaced with Isabel who had been in the picture all along, but left unpainted until then.

In the *Spanish* woman there was a certain fire, a certain defiance which brought thrill to his spirit. She was a lover, a woman, a lady and a whore when *he desired*. She loved sex, yet never demanded it. Bharat always had to initiate the act and that was fine with him. When they made love she would bite his head. *Muy caliente*.

Daily, he overheard men speak of her in low whispers. He observed their glances, the quick flicker of their eyes then the feigned lack of interest when his face, set as flint, turned their way. The Venezuelan, however, would walk with her eyes pitched forward like a prized horse. Bharat smiled. Isabel was an attractive woman who served properly and, as expected, reacted as a woman might at times, but always in the right manner. She was careful not to disrespect him in public or behind closed doors. She had tried once, after she had fed him a beef empanada, and even then she fought valiantly. But a swift left hook took her down for the count bringing the argument to a quick halt. He rocked his head back and laughed.

Bharat's thoughts returned to Crapaud and Bull. With them dead there would certainly be a rush for power; it was part and parcel of the business. Bharat, however, had remedied the situation through lucrative offers to other villains, long before the hit on both men had been orchestrated. Substance abuse brought great monetary gain for suppliers and immeasurable anguish for users. Bharat saw it happen with his father: a selfish man whose unquenchable thirst for vile whiskey had landed him on the pyre. A man whose weekly pay cheque equalled a bottle of rum for himself and a drink for everyone else. The rundown bar was home. Little Chandra had seen the demise of his mother who suffered years of hell as his father's thirst for alcohol increased and his reputation in the village decreased. But the manufacturers of the cursed things profitted even though the government yearly inflated the cost of alcohol and tobacco under the sham of preventing smoking and drinking.

Bharat had long concluded that Trinidadians enjoyed paying exorbitant prices. If the price of chicken went up the queues at fast food outlets lengthened. Cigarettes and alcohol? Smokers increased along with the packs smoked per day. Yet the quantity of marijuana one got for five, ten, twenty or one hundred dollars was still the same. Bharat knew. He had once worked the streets. A long time ago, but he was no longer a *piper* on the corner. No. Not anymore. Now he wholesaled to retailers who bore the risk, and the money poured in.

Bharat considered cocaine. It would afford him further monetary prestige which he craved. He shrugged. *What I need is more marijuana.* He grabbed his cellular phone and dialled a number from memory.

SEVENTY MILES to the southwest a landline rang, disturbing a silence Baljan Balkeran had enjoyed since morning, from the comfort of a potato-sack-hammock. For more than forty years the gallery had served as an office to the man, complete with a secretary – as he sometimes called Lady, the German Shepherd – who liked to have her ears rubbed with her master's bare feet. Business calls came through three phones set on a stool. It was the gold phone that rang, a flashing screen revealing the caller. Only special men had this number.

"Yes, Chandra," he said, his voice a sickening monotone.

The voice was crisp. "*Mamoo*! Crapaud and Bull get put to sleep. More room for me to play with."

Balkeran searched his memory for the names. Crapaud and Bull occasionally called on the black phone. They were *smalltimers*, unreliable, unprofitable, unimportant, their loyalty questionable. But Chandra Bharat? The man possessed a flair for turning drugs into cold cash, no matter the quantity. Small talk had never been his thing. He never made social calls or wasted his time on pleasantries. Only when he wanted product he called. This time he called for marijuana, the biggest order to date. Chandra was unlike other crime bosses. He was brutal, like some Columbian kingpin one heard stories about. A fastidious man, abrupt in his dealings. A good man to have on your side. His usual mood was like a man whose temper was a rock perched precariously on a rusted nail.

There was only one problem: Bharat had not yet graduated to selling the white powder. Balkeran shrugged, removed the handset of the white telephone and dialled his most trusted of men. Seconds later, Icepick came running to receive and perform his orders like a well-trained monkey.

THE COMMISSIONER of Police (COP) travelled in a two-car convoy heading to San Fernando, his security detail leading the way with whooping sirens. His driver had the pedal almost to the floor and was expertly darting past cars which were swerving left and right to clear the path. The COP smiled. Trinidadians regarded the siren. Gridlocks presented no problem for ambulances and security convoys as long as lights flashed and annoying shrills emitted from the vehicles. He would be in *South* (as San Fernando and environs are fondly referred to by locals) in under fifteen minutes, he thought, as the car swung off the westbound lane and turned on to the Uriah Butler Highway. The official grinned.

Ken's rise to COP was swift despite the bureaucracy of the Police Service Commission. It was warranted. He vividly remembered the newspaper headline: "Ken for COP." In his early days he and a four-man team cleared the greater part of Port of Spain and other areas of smalltime druglord wannabes – but not the substance. The toughest of dens were hit, from Laventille and Diego Martin to Chaguaramas. The jobs were usually brutal. Death tolls featured in the newspapers. People liked when thugs could be gunned down, even if they did not know who did the dispatching.

There was something about the acts of violence which pushed newspaper sales.

Ken and his men had acted independently. There was speculation as to the identity of the executioners. Some said the killers were from rival drug gangs and that a major turf war was on. It had to be the Americans, others said, due to the precision and expertise of the operations. Guesses flew but the truth was elusive. Finally the mysterious, savage group became known as *The Wild Bunch*.

The public became aware of Ken Thomas when a simple bust brought him and his men face-to-face with a man armed with a Russian assault rifle. The cook seemed to be expecting the masked men and swung the weapon, firing curses and bullets as rapidly as Spanish sounds to the untrained ear. The den became a war zone and Ken ran for cover. Concrete chipped off the tightly spaced walls as the gas-operated rifle ejected bullets at a muzzle velocity of 710 metres per second. The shooting stopped suddenly. Ken froze, unable to react. In the puffs of dust and smoke he wondered: *what the hell is an AK-47 doing in Trinidad? No doubt a leftover from the Grenada regime, backed by Cuban technicians.*

It was *Chinee* who broke the silence with a slew of curses. "The bastard have an AK-47!"

Ken couldn't see his comrade, but he seemed off to his right. Then he heard Raul screaming. "Steve! You alright?" Ken called desperately. "Steve!" There was no reply. None from *Snake* either.

Behind the wall he heard the operator loading another magazine and the selector lever being lowered. Ken had never used the weapon but knew its mechanics. The charging handle was still to be released, but there was something about going head-on with an AK-47 that made Ken hesitate. Then he thought: *screw it.* He took one bullet to the chest, just above his lungs, and two to his left hand which tore like a paper doll. He lived to tell the story of how he popped the chef with a clean shot, right between the eyes.

11

The Wild Bunch dissolved. Raul and Steve were given twenty-one gun salutes. Snake migrated and enlisted with the Royal Navy, but returned home to train Coast Guard (CG) recruits. Chinee retired from the police service and opened a security consultancy firm which won contracts with two major oil and gas companies on the east coast. The legend that was Ken Thomas became Commissioner.

As the convoy sped past Chaguanas the COP massaged his stomach. Those days were long gone, like earnings from a gambler's pockets, but the game out there was the same. *No.* It was worse. Only time progressed. Society had regressed as sure as the second hand of a clock moves forward. The Wild Bunch's efforts and his attempts had worked for his time. There wasn't a solution only temporary patches. At least, so he thought. Ken sighed as Couva came into view.

Brian checked his boss in the rearview mirror and enquired at the sight of the man's sullen face. Ken nodded. Everything was fine, he assured, just focus on the road; he clapped the driver firmly on his shoulder.

At 100 km/h Couva swiftly sped out of view and the road began to snake steeply. Ken looked outside but saw little. Maybe it was the pomp and glory which changed him, but lives were still being adversely affected by criminal activity and ineffective countermeasures. Even now someone was suffering. Ken felt inadequate. Maybe it was time for him to move on, make way for the new breed who could comprehend the frilly, angry society.

Technology had advanced and some touted it to be the solution, but the crime rate was still steep. Detectives had functioned for centuries without mechanical and electronic assistance. Ken disliked computers and shied away from the typing of reports, leaving any computer-related tasks to Derrick Seales, Deputy Commissioner and a more adept technologist.

For Ken, the mandatory retirement age was five years away, but he wanted to leave with a bang so tales could be told of the great hero who had rescued the nation. He wished two things: that he was young again and didn't have a withered hand to make his job more difficult than it already was.

## 2 The squeaky wheel

BOODOO LANE is a dirt road which turns south off the main road, where Bharat's five-hundred-acre estate ends, and continues for two hundred feet. The residents, originally squatters, were now the legal owners of land they occupied having successfully surpassed a seven-year tenure without eviction. There had been a single serious attempt by the city council a few years back, but The Manager had ironed things out. The dwellers were given lucrative employment in The Boss' citrus production company and now all but the last of the four houses, lined up like jars in a cupboard, were built of concrete.

However the Boodoo family was still an envied household. Separating them from the third house was a great Long mango tree which extended its branches over the family's home providing twenty-four-hour shade and the sweetest mangoes in central Trinidad for most of the year. The wife of the deceased Mr. Boodoo conducted her livelihood, selling heaps of golden mangoes off a crude wooden table arranged every morning at the corner of the lane, much to Bharat's objection.

Mouse was parked beneath the great tree sucking an orange in the idling vehicle. He didn't care for Long mangoes. The ripe ones smelled funny: half-rotted, half-perfumed, a scent that resounds in its taste; they were thread-filled fruits which could take hours to clear from one's teeth. His first contact with the fruit, as a child, had been his last. He thumped the horn a third time.

In the backseat Bharat mumbled while he opened a fresh pack of cigarettes. When the seal was unwrapped and the foil covering the Virginia-blended tobacco removed, he took the first cigarette he laid eyes on, flipped it over then reinserted it into the pack. He pulled another. Before he could put flame to the tobacco he saw Ravi.

"Look the little punk coming," Bharat said, with the cigarette dangling from the corner of his mouth.

Mouse looked up and caught sight of Ravi Boodoo hurrying down the stairs. He didn't look too happy when Bharat signalled for him to move closer.

Bharat didn't look at the youngster when he spoke. "Ravi, where me money?" he demanded.

Ravi closed his eyes, his head bowed like a sinner. He stared at freshly fallen, red-bean-shaped mangoes gathered at his feet, some, their yellow skin blemished with black spots like his own. It was impossible for him to tell this man – of all men – that he had wasted eight thousand dollars in marijuana through riotous living with Frankie The Midget.

"Boss... I could get, let we say, two thousand dollars for you by tomorrow for the latest," Ravi lied lamely, hoping the offer would slide. It had been his cry for the past six months whenever The Manager visited.

"Look at me boy," Bharat said harshly.

Hesitantly the debtor did.

The Manager removed his shades. Ravi's fear mounted. "Your family does live there *ent*?" Bharat asked rhetorically. "If you don't have me money for me in thirty days I coming for your backside. I not joking. I will kill the two of them in front of you. I promising you that. You hear me?"

Ravi understood. The look in Bharat's eye made him. The Manager flicked his cigarette and Mouse pulled off aggressively, the car squashing mangoes as it went. When Ravi crawled back inside, his mother was smacking his sibling for playing with a cigarette lighter. She was adamant that her youngest child would be nothing like the conniving, thieving bastard of a drug addict she had conceived twenty-one years ago.

THE RAMPARTS which hide the roof of the Moorish-styled Whitehall gives it the appearance of an elaborate wedding cake. The structure rests on grounds once lively with stables, horses, coaches and servant quarters. Those days are long gone and only a hitching post and great parasol-like samaan tree remain, its dark colour offsetting the grand structure, an enduring leafy testament. Inside the sweeping house there is a long corridor which leads past a French-styled drawing room decorated in wedgewood blue and a dining room which contrasts sharply through its German layout, a change made possible through the shifting of ownership. Close to the end of the corridor is a marble staircase which leads to the second floor, renovated and modified over time; original bedrooms are now minor offices.

The Blue Room is to the top of Whitehall, an element removed in the '50s but reconstructed under renovations insisted upon by the PM himself, built using the same white limestone imported from Barbados as in the days of the supremacy of the cocoa plantation owner. The Blue Room rests plump in the centre of the roof, away from the balusters which line the crown of the structure to protect any onlooker, wishing to absorb the panoramic view of the Queen's Park Savannah, from falling three stories to the ground.

While the Blue Room looks authentic from the exterior, the interior is a far cry from originality. It is carpeted in green, to the confusion of guests, and divided into two large offices, the smaller serving as the immediate work site of the prime minister. '*The Think Tank*' – as the media dubbed the larger area – is a conference room equipped with a dark, elongated mahogany desk surrounded by black executive chairs. The walls are adorned with pictures which show the evolution of Whitehall and at the northern end of the room an overhead video projector hangs from the ceiling and directs at a projection screen, retractable at the pull of a long cord.

Prime Minister Ambrose Taylor sat at the head of the table, his back to the screen, engaged in rapping his fingers on the desk's polished surface. He had been in the Think Tank early enough to see traffic pile up on the highway separating his office from the savannah. As he stood on the balcony some folks recognised him and waved, others just drove past, too busy to notice anything but the ticking hand of time strapped to their wrists.

The day started beautifully with the slow revelation of an eastern sun, against different shades of peach, that clambered to the top of the sky as quickly as the burning daylight. A slight drizzle had driven him inside where he sat in the room, cold from the raindrops which caressed his neck and disappeared under his shirt. Ambrose was amused at how often he was found in air-conditioned environments. He travelled in air-conditioned cars, slept in an artificially-cooled bedroom and worked in his office and Parliament under the low drone of the units, within earshot, but not loud enough to annoy since it presented luxury and comfort.

Thus, Ambrose enjoyed morning jogs and the steep ascent up the Lady Chancellor Road on afternoons. It kept him in touch with nature, a submissive power able to engulf the beholder with such force that tears could be split at sceneries from high up on lookout points and on the sandy shores of beaches. A natural pleasure provided by an unseen power in whom people could trust, believe and even doubt when circumstances looked dark, then smile again when the rim of light around life's eclipse broke into view.

It was 0900 hours when Lisa Maharaj, the Minister of Finance (MOF), entered. Ambrose rose instinctively, as his father had taught him. He greeted the adorned woman with a handshake – hers was pretty firm – and invited her to sit. He sat opposite her. They engaged in easy conversation which subtly escalated to contemporary national and international economic issues. Talk dissolved as other ministers entered and took their seats.

The Minister of Tourism (MOT), a short, stout man – as Chinese men tend to be – with hair greased into a wicked side-path, was the last to enter at half past the hour. He scanned the room and Ambrose indicated the empty chair at the head of the table. The MOT pardoned his way until he was at the designated seat.

The meeting began: "Who is guilty of kleptocracy, grafting or nepotism?" the PM asked.

The shuffling of papers and clicking of briefcases stopped. Everyone cautiously eyed Ambrose as if guilty of the malpractices. Even the prime minister's secretary, tucked away in a corner, hesitated before transcribing the query.

Ambrose stood and walked alongside the table.

Brows furrowed, eyes followed him, like honest citizens gauging a suspected pickpocket.

He halted opposite *Mister* Tourism. "Folks," Ambrose said, "good morning."

The Minister of Energy (MOE), a plump African man, exhaled loudly, generating a string of nervous chuckles.

"What is our function as government?" The PM wondered aloud. His eyes settled on the Minister of Legal Affairs, a baldheaded Portuguese descendant, decked in a striking Italian suit. His stubby fingers were clasped around his paunch, his thumbs engaged in wrestling.

"Initiating and deciding policy which ensures the provision of security along economic, social, environmental and global lines." The Minister of Sport and Youth Affairs offered the text book definition. Cliff Ragoonan was a lean East Indian with a full crop of white hair. He looked fit enough to run an impromptu marathon. He had a degree in Physical Education and a gold medal in shot putt earned in the '96 Olympics.

The PM acknowledged the minister. "The thing about corruption," Ambrose continued, "is the multiple takes it has regardless of the form of governance, socialist or democratic. What qualifies as unethical in one country may be illegal in another. Take the US, for instance, where a gift to the president, worth more than two hundred dollars, is considered a gift to the office and not to the man himself."

"Much unlike our culture *eh*?" offered the Minister of Trade. "Thousands to millions of dollars are collected in bribes for construction projects and energy contracts. Everyone thinks it's necessary to grease the wheel to get the job done."

The Minister of Energy snapped, like a disturbed rattlesnake: "Are you suggesting that my department abuses governmental powers for illegitimate gain?"

Ambrose interjected. As facilitator it was his duty to address misunderstandings. The meeting's purpose was to set the firm stance which would prevent the party from falling into condemnation. "Gentlemen, please." Ambrose paused until the bickering halted then continued: "Cliff highlighted social and economic security. If our party endorses any form of corruption, be it extortion or bribery, our grand vision for this country would be blurred, legislation would be distorted and the grassroots which are most reliant on public services would be hardest hit. We will not see another term in office."

Kathy Mills, Minister of Science and Technology, spoke in a thick American accent: "In other words we'll be in the shitter?" She had a way with words and no one objected.

Ambrose nodded assent.

"Bureaucracy breeds corruption, Mr. Prime Minister," Lisa Maharaj announced.

Ambrose smiled. The Minister of Finance (MOF) was a radical. To appreciate her, one had to be severely open-minded.

Mrs. Maharaj paused as heads turned to face her and the Minister of Energy, suddenly more involved, prompted her on. "There is a functionalist approach to corruption that suggests the practice aids as a mechanism of conflict-avoidance and modernisation."

Ambrose didn't scoff. "So you're saying that a little application of grease is justifiable since it removes the red tape and puts up a skyscraper or airport more rapidly?"

"Mr. Prime Minister," replied Lisa, "To quote an expert, 'even though public immorality flows like the Mississippi River the US rose to become the world's super power.'"

Kathy bobbed her head at the mention of the great nation. She held a passport of The Republic of Trinidad and Tobago and although she had revoked her American citizenship three years ago, she still loved the great eagle dearly.

Alex Peters stood and politely interjected, causing the prime minister to look at a man he liked and respected. Alex hesitated, his left hand resting contemplatively on his chin. The Minister of National Security (MONS) was a straight-backed, athletic type with stern features, a remnant of his service to country in the army. "Mr. Prime Minister and my esteemed colleagues, a pleasant morning to all," he said in a booming voice accustomed to commanding respect and attention as it did now. "The fortunate thing about corruption is that things indeed can move along smoothly as we've just heard from Lisa. I have seen it with my own eyes."

Around the table heads nodded.

"The unfortunate thing is that the practice cannot be isolated or compartmentalised." He paused, searching for a suitable analogy. "It's a virus that infects and permeates institutions. It is on the constant lookout for new hosts. Corruption really is somewhat like HIV," he said, painting a vivid picture. "This ripple effect, contrary to belief, *does not* encourage efficiency and productivity. It does the exact opposite!"

Ambrose noticed the MOF's lips compress. She shifted in her seat, moved as if to speak, but held her tongue.

Cliff asked: "In other words, progress becomes a costly burden and therefore a barrier to the growth of our nation?" He found the concepts, although outside his academic qualifications, easy to follow.

"Exactly," interjected Ambrose and again the attention reverted to him. "We've seen it with Haiti under the Papa Doc and Baby Doc regimes. Millions of dollars in foreign aid siphoned off by these tyrants and the eventual destruction of the military to strengthen the Tontons Macoute and the VSN." Ambrose elaborated on the paramilitaries' strategies to collect rewards from the suffering population. "What eventually happened?" he asked rhetorically. "This deterioration of social values resulted in a splurge of violence to retain power. Do we want that for Trinidad and Tobago?"

"We have that!" blurted the MOF. "Trinidad has suffered decreased economic performance and distortions in wealth distribution long before we were even elected into power."

"Not to mention," added the Minister of Legal Affairs, swiftly rotating his fingers, "the increasing disaffection and alienation from traditional institutions." He looked to his left at the MONS. "What does this mean for us, Alex?"

"It means that violent conflict could become prevalent in our society."

"Isn't it already?" the Minister of Legal Affairs retorted, leaning forward. His suit rolled up his back into fat clumps.

As MONS, Alex found the question difficult to answer. "Yes it is," he said, with effort. "Everyday the papers report more crime, more hostility toward our police officers who are already held in low esteem by the public." He paused for a big gulp of water. "Not to mention there's no faith whatsoever in the judiciary system which fails to execute justice. At least, that is the population's opinion." He doodled something into a black journal. The MONS was like that. He made notes on important points through illustrations which somehow connected. Something he alone could understand. When he was finished he slapped the journal shut and locked it.

"So you're saying there is a direct link between corruption and crime?" the MOF asked, in apparent disbelief.

"No. No. You're missing the point, Lisa," Alex responded gently, despite her tone. "I'm just saying that the ripple effects in these interrelated areas of economic investments, blurs in wealth distribution and the alienation of the population from public institutions, increase the probability of violent conflict or acts of terror as the US labels it."

The contribution earned him an affirmative nod and thumbs up from Kathy Mills.

"So exactly what is the purpose of this meeting?" Lisa asked, shifting the attention back to the PM.

The question was anticipated. Ambrose recapped the goals of government and plunged into the meat of the discussion. "Corruption is the greatest obstacle to the initiatives we wish to provide. I agree with Alex. There is a link between corruption and crime." He spoke slowly as one does when carefully selecting words, like a lawyer pleading for a defendant. "Corruption will not be tolerated in this Cabinet. That includes grafting, bribery and extortion. Ladies and gentlemen, if we are to clean this country we are to start with ourselves… a top-down-approach which allows for the positive effects to flow into the departments we are directly responsible for." The prime minister looked at the dark East Indian closest to him. "Mr. Grant, as the Minister of Transport you will have challenges with the Licensing Department. And you, Alex–" he addressed the man in charge of security by pointing two fingers in his direction– "you will have challenges with the police and military forces." The prime minister looked around at the faces peering at him. He smiled at the person to the far right of the room, closest to the Minister of Tourism, "And you, Daniel, you are faced with the challenge of combatting corruption within a failing judiciary system probably owned by the drug barons and society's elites." Ambrose stubbed his forefinger to the table (as he usually did at the point of resolve) and declared: "The important thing is that corruption does not make its way into this Cabinet!"

Lisa Maharaj wasn't pacified. "Can the moral values of twenty-four of us abolish corruption like slavery?" Instantly she regretted the simile, but the cosmopolitan Cabinet let it slip.

"No!" the prime minister replied. "There are other factors: political accountability and legislation which ensure the proper management of the public sector. Additionally, a reengineering of institutional restraints within the State, through some degree of the separation of powers."

"Wait," the Minister of Legal Affairs interpolated, grave concern in his voice, "you're calling for constitutional reform where centralised authority on the creation of policies of crime and punishment is removed from the relevant ministries?"

Ambrose confirmed.

*Good luck with that*, the Minister of Legal Affairs didn't say, and resumed his thumb wrestling.

"What about crime and violence?" piped in the MOT, whose industry had been severely injured by an Amnesty International report, released in December. He was soft-spoken, difficult to hear across the table.

The MOE asked him to speak up.

"Carnival is just around the corner," he said louder. "More tourists, more thieves, more guns. How do we deal with this?" he enquired, with small pleading eyes, as Ambrose made his way up the table.

The MONS answered: "Simultaneously with our top-down-approach we tackle crime. Coupled with the alienation of civilians from public institutions, there are other aspects." Alex reflected on Ambrose's words, "The prime minister is right," he said, his eyes shifting to the MOF, "There is a definite link between corruption and violence. Drug barons launder money through corporations and try to sink it into the government with requests for small favours. Then they expect us to turn a blind eye to their transactions." Alex scanned the table until his eyes settled on the Chinese man. "Eventually we will be a puppet government. To answer the question, Mr. Chang, your industry will be supported by my ministry."

"Do you have a plan?" It was a direct challenge, with a harmless tone, from the Minister of Legal Affairs, a colleague Alex found hard to appease.

"Yes. Some were already mentioned by the PM. A body similar to US Congress can significantly decrease the loopholes that crafty lawyers use." The MONS looked at Ambrose who tilted his head in approval. "But even before the judiciary process there are plans of actions we have been toying with. To baseline them at a high level we're looking at police reform, crime detection and management, data collection and retrieval, information retrieval through the use of Computer Information Systems – a project being spearheaded by Kathy Mills – and penal reform and sentencing."

"What about the death penalty?" asked the Minister of Sports, a strong observer of Islam.

"What about it?" Alex replied. "Same nonsense. The Privy Council, along with the Church, has been trying hard to abolish it, but no party is going to cave in to the wishes of lords and bishops. There's no political virtue in getting rid of it since three-quarters of the citizens in the region endorse the practice."

"Maybe we need to start hanging death row criminals?" Cliff asked no one in particular, causing heads to nod emphatically – including the Minister of Legal Affairs and the Attorney General, two devout Catholics.

It was time to end the meeting. "We are the parents of the nation," Ambrose said, "and healthy growth can be nurtured only through careful care."

After the meeting the ministers scattered into small groups and consumed what coffee and goodies (salad) they found on a small folding metal table, brought up from the first floor pantry and covered with a blue cloth. Because it still drizzled, no one ventured onto the roof and the ministers filtered into the depths of Whitehall, leaving the PM and the MONS in the Think Tank.

The room felt too big and both men shifted into Ambrose's office. The blinds were drawn with thin lines of light visible around the window frame. The MONS, finishing his salad, sat at the head of government's desk.

"Alex, how do we inspire change? How do we deflect corruption, crime and violence?" Ambrose took a seat on the leather couch beside the fresh water aquarium – the goldfish, expecting food, zoned in, some thumping the glass noiselessly, in hope of rousing their master's attention. Ambrose had pondered these same questions on countless nights, but no translucent implementation presented itself. Only plans of actions which never materialised into solutions.

"As with any predicament," Alex said, swiping some Italian dressing from the edge of his mouth, "we need to identify and understand the problem, then craft alternative solutions until one meets success. What do you believe *our* problem is?"

"The plague of corruption and drug-related crime," Ambrose said, thumping the arm of the sofa with his forefinger. "The problem is that the removal of corruption is a long-term goal and its merits can be blown to hell by the one inappropriate act of a public servant." He held up his index finger for the MONS to see. "Just one act. Drugs on the other hand?" He scoffed. "Heck, Alex, it's likely that any teen can tell us who the gangsters are. How can we not know?"

"So we're inefficient?" Alex enquired.

It was not what the prime minister meant and he explained this to his colleague. "Criminals are enjoying the incompetence of the judicial system. Each category of criminal, kingpins and corrupt ministers, is raping the land of its pride and resources."

Alex managed a laugh, not a malicious one. "You're suggesting a plan to clean the streets and keep our hands clean. That's almost impossible."

"Yes, Alex." Ambrose rose and emptied some flakes into the fish tank, then walked over to the desk. "We need a renewed vote of confidence in local forces or, as Kathy put it, we're in the shitter."

"We're already in it," Alex said solemnly.

THEY ASKED Mouse only because he was there; not because they cared for his input. His answer was expected: "Woman? I don't know *nah* boy." He was the silent type who had, through his quietness, developed a reputation for being a misogynist. Four of the five men snickered at his response but, unbothered, he continued sucking voraciously on an orange. Patsy, his dog, lay comfortably at his feet.

Ricky Lo, the Rastafarian, was critical of Mouse, "Boy, you is a real *hen* you know that? Always have something bad to say about woman when you do talk." He took a long, hard pull on a marijuana joint and blew a heavy burst of exhaust in Mouse's direction.

"You understand!" Amrit piped in. He agreed with Ricky, and on the topic of women thought himself a specialist. The notepad below his mattress contained enough names to prove the point: from Alana to Zelda, all the way back to Abigail.

Even Raj, his cousin, who fussed over a pot of bubbling dumplings, dismissed Mouse's lack of enthusiasm with a grunt. With each turn of the big, blackened iron pot the scent of curried crab intoxicated the shed.

"Boys, you have to respect women," Lucky said perspicuously. He was closest to Raj, fixing himself a drink. Lucky was the eldest among the group, an old boy from Tunapuna. He continually boasted of high moral values, unaware of the sin of vanity. He was a great card player and had a golden tongue which often landed him in women's beds – and in trouble with their men – so on his comment no one disagreed, except for his preference of black women, which only the Rastafarian endorsed.

"Lucky, tell them what is the best kind of woman!" Ricky Lo exclaimed, jumping to his feet excitedly and upsetting the All Fours game.

Amrit, his opponent, began arguing about the matchsticks which fell off the makeshift table. "Boy, how we will keep track of the points now? Look how you drop the match them!" He looked at his teammate for support, but Navin said nothing.

"Relax yourself *nah* Indian!" Ricky exclaimed.

Lucky staggered over to the table and, with some effort, sat on a bit of wood balanced dangerously on an overturned bucket.

Ricky adjusted his dreadlocks and took a hard drag. The marijuana had burnt out. He flicked the *funk* at the iron bars which secured the structure. The cigarette didn't make it through; Ricky cursed.

Lucky, annoyed at Ricky's language, placed his drink on the edge of the table while a mumbling Amrit shared matchsticks to and fro until his opponents had eleven points and he had seven. He cursed. He took his game seriously, but Lucky was a brilliant card player, a poor gambler, but a wizard with the deck. Involve money and he was certain to lose.

"Buddies," Lucky said, bobbing his head, "let me tell you something. The sweetest woman it have is the African woman, the *darkie*." He spoke from the corner of his mouth, stretching the last word in the sentence, as he always did. He was from the era of Lancaster movies and had long mastered *The Grin*. He was a peculiar man whose full name was unknown to most.

Ricky folded his fist and gave Lucky a *bounce*, but Amrit disagreed adamantly, "*Nah* boy. Spanish is the best!" Placing his cards on the table he shaped an hourglass, the universal outline for sexy women. "They have it here, and here." He motioned towards his buttocks, then cupped his hands like a pair of breasts, all in synch with his description. "Raj, you could speak Spanish *ent*?"

The question was irrelevant, but Raj answered positively. He had a contribution of his own: "Boys, I feel is Indian yes. Them nice *smallies*, them is the best!" He left the pot and walked over. He viewed each player's cards and whistled when he saw Ricky's hand.

Instantly, Navin knew his jack of hearts (trump) was *hung*. With three *days* – as points are called in All Fours – for claiming the card, the opponents would win, having a total of fourteen. He wouldn't wink (the signal for jack) at Amrit though. Of the six cards the game had started with, two remained and his teammate would wish to cheat; he was always quick to. Navin, on the other hand, was indifferent due to the lifeless nature of the game; he played only to accommodate the need for a fourth person.

"No dread!" Ricky said, as Raj walked back to inspect the food. "Spanish and Indian? Them does wear too much makeup on they face, man. I *doh* like that at-all-at-all. Look at Isabel. She does have more foundation plastered to she face than a house."

Navin looked up at the mention of The Boss' woman, but said nothing.

"A little white *thing* now and then is alright," Ricky continued. "They not that bad. Them does be more natural. They does be mount up nice too!" He played a king of hearts on Navin's ten and secured the lift on a pile gathered at his feet.

Navin waited impatiently, not experiencing the spicy tension an avid player would.

Ricky played an Ace, the highest card in All Fours.

Amrit groaned when his teammate casually threw in the jack. Had his partner been someone else, he would have cursed.

Ricky jumped to his feet and gave Lucky another bounce, "I hang a man jack, boy!" He slapped the cards to the table which toppled over.

Lucky was smoking a cigarette, with the entire palm of his hand wrapped around his face, the *cancer-stick* low between his fore and middle finger. He smiled, showing Amrit brownish-yellowish teeth.

"I see that coming," Raj laughed.

"You could of tell me he had jack," Amrit said, annoyed at the cook.

Lucky, who was about to touch a strong drink to his lips, paused. "How the **ass** he go tell you that? That is cheating!"

Ricky flicked his dreadlocks behind his shoulder. Something bothered him. "Talking about Isabel," he said, in a low whisper, "Them breasts... they real or that is implants?"

Amrit scoffed. He knew the answer, but said nothing. Later, when Navin wasn't around, he would tell Ricky.

Navin was about to speak, but Lucky interjected: "Buddy, don't talk about The Boss woman like that..."

"*Fellas*, food ready!" Raj announced. He sat next to Mouse who was adding orange skin to a neat pile and playing with Patsy, the stray dog he had adopted. Raj's plate sizzled with curry-flavoured steam. He had no intention of dishing food. He said so. No one moved to the pot and the cook cursed. He began eating with his hands; the food lacked some flavour. *It missing something, boy*, he thought, hoping the others wouldn't notice.

Navin was weary of cards. He stood and left.

Amrit said something but no one responded.

27

Lucky pointed his cigarette at Ricky. "Buddy, minus the comment on The Boss' woman, what you say is true. Nowadays they so fake you can't tell who is Indian or who is African. Who hair straight, they *curlying* it, who hair curly they ironing it. Not only they looking different they moving real *left*. You not getting any woman to cook and clean for you. Why you feel I is a bachelor all these years? I is a one-shot man. I not greedy. I don't want to get tie up with any woman."

Amrit laughed. "You like to play bachelor *eh* old man?"

Raj hoped the conversation wouldn't swing to him. He was newlywed – *two years must be*? – and had just played chef. Tonight, he was lucky. No one said a word, but Mouse looked at him with small, twinkling eyes.

A brooding Ricky stood and walked to the pot. He dished out. A delinquent vegetarian, he took some of the curried sauce and five large dumplings which he thought were heavy enough to sink a small boat. He reclaimed his seat on an overturned bucket. He dug in, chewed for a while and, still concentrating on the plate, said: "Good food boy Raj, but the curry could have do with a little more salt." A few bites later: "But it have real pepper!" Ricky sucked air into his mouth in an attempt to cool his sizzling tongue. It didn't work; it was milk he needed.

*Salt! That is it!* Raj agreed. It had been hard to detect, eating with hands that had been pinching the ingredient. "It have in the white bag by the pot there. Take if you want *nah*."

Amrit, although not hungry, helped himself to a small serving of food; he loved pepper.

Ricky stopped eating. "Lucky, I telling you, I not taking no *stupidness* from no woman. If is manners they need that is what they go get!" Unlike his father he was a no-nonsense man when it came to commanding respect. "Creole, Indian, Chinese is the same damn thing, put some good licks in they backside and they does boil down nice, like rice in hot water. White woman and all getting licks."

"How it tasting?" Lucky asked, attempting to change the topic. He found Ricky a brash, arrogant fool with a careless tongue.

Annoyed, the Rasta pointed at the pot.

"If I eat I go can't drink again." Lucky slurred, keeping his priorities in order.

"That food real *lash* boy, Raj," Amrit said. He threw the disposable plate into a blue garbage bag knotted around a metal post. "And it have enough salt. I don't know what happen to Ricky. Like he want to get a heart attack or something."

Ten minutes later when everyone except Lucky had eaten, Bharat, dressed in his infamous grey suit and shades, entered with Navin. The discussion on Latinas screeched to a halt. Everyone stood.

"What happen! I look like I a damn woman or what?" The Boss said angrily.

Everyone sat.

Bharat kicked Patsy who had been sniffing his shoes. "Mouse! That damn dog! I will shoot it!"

Mouse retrieved the moaning dog and secured it between his legs.

"Boys!" Bharat said. He patted Lucky, his oldest *acquaintance*, on the back. "Let we don't waste no time. Crapaud and Bull dead, so we go be pushing out more product." He waved at Raj who was signalling from a spot close to the pot. Bharat wasn't hungry. "A set of weed coming in, in a few days. You boys can't shit up. We controlling more territory now. You know what that means?"

"We have to get more people to love us," the Lancaster wannabe said, earning himself another pat from The Manager. Lucky knew it was the primary reason for Bharat's success. Compassion for the weak and brutality for the opposition. It was this motto that drove the man to build temples, churches and mosques for villagers and donate to causes he knew nothing of. His money was not for the Hindus or Muslims, neither was it for the Christians. It was for the people. Mr. Bharat became a manager of central Trinidad; the people built the safety barrier around his mansion. Unknown villagers were even rumoured to report suspicious activity to *The Manager*. If someone farted on Bharat's name, he or one of his lieutenants would know.

"Well that is it! I gone!" Bharat warded off another offer of food (to Raj's disappointment) and exited the shed with Navin.

When he was sure The Boss was out of earshot Ricky cursed. "That is what he had we waiting for all this time?"

Lucky shot up and with The Grin said: "Have some respect for Mr. Bharat, buddy."

Ricky laughed and deposited his plate into the garbage. Without a word of thanks to the cook, he and Amrit left.

Lucky and Raj remained. They had a bottle of red rum to finish ('let wet *bat* it *out*,' they laughed). Mouse who knew he had a long wait ahead of him, settled and peeled an orange. Suddenly, the Lancaster fan began howling *La Bamba* into the night, a sign that the alcohol had begun its work. Mouse thought that the old *test* carried the tune superbly, but didn't comment. Raj didn't care. He only wanted to get as drunk as Lucky, and he did.

## 3  CISTU

IT WAS another early day for Ambrose Taylor. He had received a phone call at home the previous night and after subsequent connections, decided that he must arrive early for the appointment made then. The prime minister hurried up the steps. On the third floor he met Alicia, his secretary, a young woman, way too hefty for her height and age, always in the process of *trying* some fad diet. Early day? she asked, even though her boss had never actually arrived at the office before her. They exchanged pleasantries and after a quick request for coffee he hurried up a few more steps. At the top he pushed opened the entrance to the Think Tank revealing the MONS, the COP and the Deputy COP, both in khaki uniforms, huddled around the table, inspecting a huge chart.

*Heck, they're early.* "Alex?" Ambrose enquired, observing the bloated map of Trinidad and Tobago; another of the Caribbean region was partially hidden below.

"Ambrose–" first name basis suited the PM– "since our discussion I've been investigating conceptual frameworks against which to examine security."

The bubbly secretary entered – the Deputy COP, having never seen her, grimaced at her enormity – with coffee for all then disappeared, her heels resounding on the wooden staircase.

"Did you find a suitable one?" Ambrose asked, his eyes having never left the MONS.

"Yes. It comes in context of post-Cold War and 9/11 realities that previous studies failed to capture. Its central building blocks are: structure, concept and paradigm."

"So what is security defined as?" the COP asked. "Within the context of this framework, that is."

"It's simple. Preservation and protection of people's freedom and rights from external attack," Alex answered. "It doesn't stop there. These ideals include: preventing the erosion of social, political and economic values."

"Exactly," Ambrose interjected. "It would be detrimental for us to limit security concerns to any specific area while ecological disasters, HIV/AIDS and smuggling continue to distress us, not to mention poverty."

"How do we identify and rank these threats?" Ken asked. He scratched his left hand, resting limply at his side, while tilting his head to look at the MONS. Beside him Derrick Seales typed feverishly on his laptop, wishing to capture each word.

"Threats can be thought of as a stack of cards," Alex explained. "If we, the relevant authorities, perceive that in a short term the intensity of a threat can magnify itself, a response has to be invoked by the political party, law enforcement agencies, military or any combination of these."

"In other words if the Jack is stealing Diamonds place him above the King and focus on him?" Ken enquired. "What about the threats below?"

"The reality, Ken, is that resources of any State are limited," Ambrose said. "It's a matter of the ruling heads being able to swiftly analyse and shuffle threats in the internal and external arena and allocate response instruments."

"Does the US suffer this?" the Deputy Commissioner asked, his first input since the meeting began.

"Of course!" Alex declared.

"After 9-11 we saw it," Ambrose contributed. "US troops and agents being extracted from the Caribbean to function in the war against terrorists in Iraq and Afghanistan, and the strengthening of the Mexican border. Minus the use of Guantanamo as a detention staging post America has long relieved the Caribbean of a lot of resources. Helicopters, undercover agents, naval patrols have been reallocated." He looked at Alex for confirmation.

"Ambrose is right," Alex said, "it's been happening over the years. This isn't just a result of the Taliban's attack on the eagle. In the '90s forces were reduced in Puerto Rico, and SOUTHCOM relocated from Panama to Miami. Even the Soviet-Cuban intelligence facility in Lourdes has been ordered closed."

"So?" Ken asked.

"Trinidad is blessed with a strategic location" Alex answered forcefully. "We don't suffer traditional territorial disputes."

"What about fishing woes with Barbados and Venezuela?" Ken asked.

"That's it!" Alex exclaimed. "What this means is that we *should* focus our security efforts on non-traditional aspects."

"But we can't look at non-traditional threats in isolation, Alex. Territorial disputes have affected collaboration in the past with Barbados and Venezuela," Ambrose said. "Geopolitics plays an important role in identifying sources of tourism other than the US and European Union (EU)."

"Once relationships are weakened, the drug-flow in and out of the region is improved," Ken added, tracing his finger along the map.

"What we need to decide is which threat should be placed at the top of the deck," the head of government suggested.

Everyone finally agreed that the king of broken hearts was drug trafficking.

Ambrose helped himself to a drink of water. Ken joined him and the PM poured the man a full glass of the clear liquid, beautiful to look at with the outside light dancing around like fairies in a pool.

"Is there anything else?" Ambrose asked. He replaced his glass – on the *used* tray – and reclaimed his seat.

Alex proceeded to the next urgent matter. He removed photographs from his navy-blue jacket and passed them over the table.

"What the heck!" Ambrose exclaimed. He thumbed through the six photographs twice, as if searching for some element that would deem the colour pictures unreal, clever animations, but they were not.

It had been Alex's exact response. "That's Barry Edwards and Jeremy Gibson, known as Crapaud and Bull to the wider community, notorious drug pushers, womanisers, pimps and gangsters."

"An impressive portfolio," Ambrose scoffed. "What happened?"

"Rally drivers found their remains in the canefield," Ken explained. "Time of death estimated to be around lunch time, New Year's Day."

Still staring at the pictures, The PM asked the obvious question: "That's their penises in their mouths, right?"

"Each man had the other's," Derrick Seales helped.

"That *Sir*–" Ambrose noticed the formality– "is what we have to deal with. It isn't evident in these shots, but their tongues were sliced off." Alex's stomach churned as he thought of the heinous act: the sadists had sawed off hands and legs to fit them into the shallow grave. Hopefully, Crapaud and Bull were dead by then.

The prime minister flipped through the photographs again. The macabre held sway; he repeated the action. The men's arms and legs had been neatly laid, like hot chicken wings at a restaurant. Obviously the persons – *or person? Impossible!* – who had done the job took great pride in this nasty work. Ambrose was silent.

Ken's voice pierced the quiet room. "Mr. Prime Minister?" He shifted, like one uncomfortable – although he wasn't – when Ambrose turned to him. "The community and newspapers know... sorry... knew Crapaud and Bull as drug traffickers but the truth is, they were paid police informants." He waited.

As Alex had warned, the PM was not impressed. His voice had a pinch of anger. "Do you mean criminals are being bargained with?"

"No, Sir. The intention was to allow a small drug organisation, led by some mean SOBs, to reign free thereby raising the barrier of entry for other smugglers. The strategy had worked until the canefield disaster. As it is we now have no underworld contact."

The MONS added: "Mr. PM, there are methods of gathering intelligence which, while not admirable, preserve our nation. To what degree remains indeterminable until some sensitive matter presents itself."

There was merit to what Alex said, but Ambrose wasn't pacified. He shelved his thoughts and addressed the situation. "Who knew they were informants?" His eyes covered the men.

The Deputy COP never looked up.

With a shrug, Ken answered: "A lot of people who shouldn't."

The prime minister exhaled nosily. Intelligence gathering-and-sharing was highly undervalued by most, if not all, of the Caribbean region. The practice condoned corruption. There were assassinations of state witnesses and leaks on tactical operations to preserve big, bad men perceived as modern day Robin Hoods; *wolves in sheep clothing*. The PM helped himself to more water. "Gentlemen," he said, from where he stood, "we must place a higher emphasis on intelligence gathering and the protection of our sources. A hard task," he admitted, "in a culture where neighbours are very aware of each other's dealings." He walked to his seat but didn't sit. "This cannot be reflected in our intelligence services. We'll have people killed. Blood on our hands. If the press gets a hold of these facts, we will be screwed."

"That would be a mess, Mr. PM," the Deputy Commissioner concurred.

"A clear understatement!" PM Taylor exclaimed. He took a seat, the one at the head of the table. "My predecessors have treated intelligence and crime as a game, a daily occurrence which doesn't impact our island because we're third world and too damn carefree!" Ambrose said, his tone bordering vindictiveness. "We can't negate the function of the constitution by disregarding the human rights of our citizens. We've seen this done innumerable times, not just in the Caribbean, but throughout the world. And what happens when someone messes up? The government is restructured. All for personal gain or as favours to financiers. Men assuming roles for which they have no knowledge. People aren't dumb." Ambrose stood again. "Take this red-skinned guy appointed as a security minister a few years back. He didn't know heads from tails. A clear case of patronage! The citizens had cried out and they reassigned him as head of another ministry. It's almost as if poor security, poor health, poor finance and poor agriculture are expected, and governments find men who can't fill the roles." The PM paused for effect. He walked around, returning each man's gaze – including Derrick's - until he was alongside Alex. He placed his palms flat on the table, producing a ghostly, white impression on the dark mahogany.

"So, who are we doing a favour by removing the MONS, the Commissioner or me?" the Deputy Commissioner asked, missing the point.

"Derrick, removing someone doesn't solve the problem."

"Society has created elite classes, even hoodlums, who are untouchable," Seales said. The PM listened with raised eyebrows as the man poised the scenario: "Financiers for instance. If they were involved in racketeering, what can be done?"

The PM fanned his forefinger at the Deputy. "Support during election doesn't mean grants of illegal or unethical post-election favours. No rich kid is going to walk away from a jail sentence because his dad printed one thousand party t-shirts."

"I know, Sir. Previous parties have set such trends in Trinidad and Tobago."

"Not in our government, Derrick. There won't be any misuse of governmental powers for illegitimate private gain. There won't be any facilities for criminal enterprises like drug trafficking and money laundering! Democracy will not be undermined!" the PM snarled. "The French have it all figured out: corporate financing is altogether banned. Candidates have spending caps on campaigning which, once exceeded or ill-reported, invalidates their candidacy."

"Allegiance to none?" Ken enquired.

"None. The key to good governance."

"If you want to tackle crime and corruption you are going to have to get rough. You're going to have to fight fire with fire," Ken suggested. "No Act or public appeal will miraculously deflate these non-traditional threats."

"What do you suggest?" Ambrose asked. "Some CIA type unit? Stiffer penalties?" He became more skeptical: "Some hit squad or public executions? Some Middle Eastern strategy?"

Ken knew the waters were being tested and decided to be cautious. "No, Sir, you need to make the function of key personnel in the various forces more operational than administrative. Pardon my French, but paper-pushing is for *blasted* secretaries. Reallocate the nation's police resources, push incentives that will motivate people with intelligence gathering and analysis capabilities to join the services. In the meantime, we can start taking back the streets by increasing the visibility of the security forces. Shit, put me back on the streets!"

The PM looked at his MONS who shrugged. Ken's words did have virtue.

"I think it's a good plan," Ken continued. "Police presence does have a psychological impact. Involve the Defence Force (DF)."

Alex wanted to confirm his support, but couldn't. Not one hundred per cent. Not yet anyway. There were issues to address. "It isn't so easy. You're going to need legislation for a special unit which operates outside the capacity of the police." The more he thought about it the more complicated it became. "Soldiers aren't trained in policing, they're trained for war. Heck, the culture, jargon and weaponry differ. We can't risk a Galil tearing up the streets in the event of any disturbance. Any bad calls and we'll have soldiers lined up before a Board of Inquiry!" He referred to a case where a Belizean private had been court-martialled after shooting a civilian, on orders from a police constable. "Plus, soldiers don't have the power to arrest. They would become chaperons to police officers who should possess the capacity to upload the law."

"What about giving them the power to make arrests?" Derrick Seales asked.

"And what? Add them to the long list of policemen tied up in court as prosecutors?" A small vertical frown mark appeared on Alex's forehead. "We'll be thinning out our armed forces and, no offence Ken, we'll be exposing them to the same corruption that has our judicial system and police service in grip. However, with the right legislation and directives in place, not to mention the right soldiers, I think joint patrols can be beneficial. The army has already proved itself." He was referring to the '90 coup, Operation Democracy in Haiti and other United Nations tasking.

"Ken, what do you think?" the PM asked.

"I think it could work. Once the roles don't get skewed. We need to sort out some fine points. I'll get in touch with the army in the meantime. The Commanding Officer (CO) and I go way back."

The Deputy Commissioner dissented, but held his tongue. He thought: *my gun isn't big enough to shoot in this town hall.*

"How can existing agencies contribute in fighting crime and drugs?" Ambrose asked, moving the conversation along.

"The current culture is that these units operate as a black box," the COP replied, with reasonable regret, his voice becoming more despondent. "And consider the filth some are involved in. We've had cases, in recent months, where servants from Central Intelligent Unit (CIU) and Criminal Investigation Department (CID) were controlling drug blocks. Officers have been linked to executions ordered by various gangster units."

"Also cases of brutality," the MONS contributed. "There's seemingly an upsurge in the hostility between citizens and the forces." He shook his head.

"Something criminologists link to colonialism where the working social class was policed," Ambrose said. "Alex, did you send the requested report to Amnesty International on allegations relating to human rights violations?"

Alex tipped his head positively. The report had been requested during the reign of the Mark Lloyd administration but was never submitted. It had taken the MONS three weeks to complete.

"Interesting point," Ken reflected. He had never considered the link between colonialism and hostility in police-people relations. *It's similar to why some of us blacks blame slavery on our lack of progress and the disunity that exists among us.*

"Creating another policing or criminal investigation unit isn't going to solve the problem," Derrick Seales said.

*Good grief,* Alex thought.

"How do we increase public confidence?" Ambrose asked.

"We can give them something new to believe in," the MONS suggested. "It can be operated as a Task Force (TF) that supports other agencies using advanced technologies, with the exception that the director reports to the MONS."

Ken looked skeptical. "Won't we be highlighting the failure of the police service?" The COP still had the interest of his men and women in mind. "Such a TF is going to have a bigger, better budget. The Police Association is going to *kick up a fuss.*"

"This isn't about wages or the unions, Ken," Ambrose said firmly. "This is about the people. If you give me a more viable solution we'll consider it."

The COP said nothing and the Deputy looked sorely displeased.

"Alex, what about the human aspect? Or, should I ask, who are the members of the TF?"

"It can be members of the Police Service, the DF and civilians," MONS Peters said. He stopped the COP from interjecting by raising his hand. "Just a second, Ken. Nothing in the Constitution supports the creation of a unit that draws from various agencies. Secondly, the Police Service Act doesn't allow a unit that combines police officers and members who are not. We're going to have to do some juggling. Probably create a new police unit whose members are accountable to the TF only and not to the COP. You're okay with that?"

Ken nodded, looking as if on another planet. He had never been so grossly undermined. His lips quivered, but he held Alex's gaze.

"Additionally," Alex continued, "the Defence Act does not have any aspect that considers the merging of the DF with other bodies."

"Without statutory authority the Opposition is not going to like the idea of this TF," Prime Minister Taylor said skeptically. "They'll see it as a political tool operating in the interest of this government. Especially if it is intended as a clandestine operation."

"They'll lynch the Police Service and DF also," Ken said. "I can see Lance Jones' headline already: '*PM and top officials breaking law.*'"

Alex sucked his teeth, emitting a loud noise – a '*steups*' Trinidadians call it – at the mention of the journalist's name. "Who, that clown?" The men chuckled. Alex disliked the man.

"We can let the people decide," Ambrose said, halting the chuckles. He leaned forward, resting his clasped hands on the desk. "We can issue a non-binding referendum on the matter to the population."

"It isn't mandatory that we do that," Derrick Seales stated.

"At least, the TF will be justifiable in the eyes of the citizens. It also puts the Opposition between a rock and a hard place. Legislation like this is going to need the majority votes in the House of Representatives." He didn't need to mention that the party reaped only nineteen of thirty-six constituency seats. "We need to get cracking on this."

"I'll give the Attorney General and Minister of Legal Affairs a heads up," Alex said. "Ambrose, you'll also have to consult with the President ASAP regarding the DF"

"He has been having some heart trouble recently, but I'll be on it when he gets back from Cuba," Ambrose promised. "One more thing. Let's be wary with the Opposition. It's best we get them to participate somehow in the creation of the Task Force. If they become stakeholders in the project we're more than likely to succeed. What's the long term goal of the TF?"

"Crime management and agency status," Alex said positively.

"And its level of transparency and accountability to the public?" the PM asked.

*Ambrose is a politician.* "Where national security will be compromised it becomes necessary to hold back information," Alex replied. "The unit will work on the same notion of the CIA, but its merger with the DF would expand its capabilities into the tactical arena."

"Time to implementation?" Ken asked.

Alex didn't want to commit an answer; ventures like this took time. It involved collaboration with foreign agencies to take their best practices and tailor them to meet the needs of the Republic. It would mean investments in intelligence and assault equipment, training, and legislation. "A couple of months."

"Months?" the prime minister exclaimed. "As we speak, crime is being committed! We need something, nothing big, but something in place as of now." Ambrose knew it wasn't as easy as he made it sound, but he had read enough books to know that being proactive influenced pace. "Ken, you and the CO arrange a team."

The COP nodded. "I know a good guy. Robert Marco. He worked with the Canadians for a couple of years. Young, intelligent detective. I'll see what I can do."

"Any ideas on a name for the TF?" the Deputy Commissioner asked.

The men looked at each other. Only Alex was prepared. "Central Intelligence and Special Tactics Agency (CISTA)."

"CISTA?" Derrick asked, scorn plastered across his face. "People might think it's a girl group." The statement didn't earn any chuckles.

"I like it," Prime Minister Taylor said seriously. "But remember it's a TF, so we'll work with Central Intelligence and Special Tactics Unit (CISTU) for now. Don't want to rock the political boat with a mere name. Agency status will come with the legislation." Ambrose hated these trivial details but it was necessary to protect his administration from attack and ridicule. He checked his watch. It was 0830 hours and he had another appointment. "Let's get cracking, gentlemen. This is high priority!"

The men shook hands, verbally committing to the project's success.

The intercom buzzed and Alicia announced the arrival of the MOF, a woman with a reputation for being dogmatic. The men stood and Ambrose escorted them to the door where they gave a wide birth for the entry of Lisa Maharaj.

Once alone, Lisa began baselining her ministry's plans for reducing the country's debt.

What about the security budget? Ambrose asked at one point.

There was enough money to purchase a blimp, she said casually, causing Ambrose to ponder the suggestion. He was no intelligence expert, but the device seemed rather inconspicuous for covert operations. But then, if a huge banner was plastered across its belly, people would believe that the whale in the sky was an advertising campaign by a private sector company. Ambrose dismissed the idea and Lisa went on about her ministry's financial plot which sounded feasible, at least in theory.

THE NORM, for as long as Icepick could remember, had always been that he would go to Glen's residence on the first and last Friday of every month. Without failure. Tonight was no different and the puddles of water collected in the dips and crevices of the bumpy path of pitch and stone did not hinder the bimonthly escapade. But Icepick did mutter, like a miserable old man who couldn't get his pipe lit, as he continuously stopped, hiked up his pants and selectively chose points to hop along. The going was slow, but he came to a spot where pitch met sand.

Before him was Glen's home, an eighty-year-old wooden structure which stood four feet off the ground, balanced on pencil-thin wooden staves. When it was humid the outhouse smelled; tonight it was particularly foul. Glen had never fussed over fencing his residence – like most people in the village – and each time Icepick entered the yard he noticed how tidy it was: raked, traces of tines deep in the shell and sand, black charcoal circles evident where rubbish had been burnt. Where there wasn't earth, there was evergreen, trailing periwinkle flowers, hundreds of them, variations of purple and white only. In the yard was a small boat tipped over on its side. It was an oddity. The vessel was last used when it claimed Glen's father's life, off Columbus Bay.

The widow had blamed her only child's sudden introvert nature – she called it '*quietness*' – on the fact that he had no father. A common law husband eighteen months later didn't change anything. Only Glen's age increased. Then his mother died. When his stepfather departed, Glen celebrated with a small drink. It had taken him forty-three years to taste rum, fire water that burned from the back of his throat all the way down to his stomach. A sensation followed by a warm, tingling spike which moved from his waist to the glands of his throat. Icepick, the neighbour, became an acquaintance. Then Glen became his confidant.

Past the periwinkles, Icepick jumped into the gallery, a tiny landing with two low stools for furniture. Further, were two pictures: one of the Lord Shiva, the other of Jesus.

The host appeared with a sealed bottle of rum and a bowl of ice.

"Glen, I tell you about them pictures you know." Icepick slapped a mosquito on the back of his forehead, then smudged at the spot until the blood disappeared. He always wondered if he could contract HIV this way. "When I come to drink rum here, I does feel kind of bad."

Glen said nothing. He felt nothing. Icepick had once described Glen, 'like a ball that leaves a player's bat, but stops short of the boundary because the batsman fielded the damn ball.' When he gave of himself it came as a surprise, like a snake which strikes and coils again, in the face of imminent danger.

Glen passed the rum to his acquaintance, a gesture of honour. "Crack the seal," he said, "is good weather for rum."

Icepick did, then sprinkled a few drops of alcohol into the sand; 'for the spirits,' he would say, each time he did this. He received a glass, some ice, poured himself a drink, then passed the bottle to Glen. Icepick waited impatiently. They knocked glasses. Together, they rocked their heads back and swallowed. The rum slid easily, frictionless, depositing itself into open, willing throats.

"Ahhh!" Glen exclaimed. The firewater was good, the weather conducive.

"Yes boy!" Icepick said, shaking like a wet dog. The earlier rains had left a blanket of cold over the land, a cold which disappeared with the white rum.

Glen coughed. He looked at the boat and had another drink.

One hour later the men had a quarter bottle of rum.

Glen's tongue was loose. "Icepick," he said, almost slipping off the stool, "tell me some stories boy." He enjoyed fantasy. Icepick's tales reminded him of Westerns his father had shared with him as a boy, ones where the old sheriff and two deputies chased the outlaws across Texas. However, Icepick's stories had no good men, not even one. The tales opened a gate in Glen's mind. He could be an Apache or an outlaw, anything he wanted.

"What you want me tell you, boy?" Icepick asked. He scooped up a handful of ice blocks and deposited them into the waiting glass. He knew what Glen desired to hear. "We have some product, coming in by plane tomorrow. I have to make a drive."

"Who you carrying it for?"

"The *fella* I tell you about *nah*... Bharat."

44

"Oh… he." Glen was disappointed. The story was old, a rerun. "He is the boss, no? But them boy does do they thing bad man. You don't find so Sunil?"

"How you mean?" Icepick asked angrily. The insult was for his boss, but he took it as one meant for him. Additionally, he hated when Glen called him Sunil; he would stretch the name the way Icepick's mother did, when irate with him as a child. Icepick sat in the low stool, so that his forearms rested on his knees. He felt intoxicated. The ceiling above began to turn violently, like clothes in a washing machine's swirl.

"Them exposing themselves," Glen said, with the fierce confidence of a good intelligence analyst. "Imagine you know who Bharat is." He hiccupped. "Somebody could sell them out. Like the white man you say Balkeran *liming* with these days."

Icepick contemplated the point, a difficult task in his current state of mind. "That is shit you talking. Nobody not interfering with them fellows." People feared and loved them. There was hate also, but those who despised were too insignificant to compromise. "I mean, look at how many people in Icacos know about Balkeran… You see anybody doing anything about it?"

"You missing my point," Glen said. "I say, if somebody want."

"Well nobody want to!" Icepick was still angry. He took two more drinks, keeping in mind that he was three behind Glen. "Plus, if anybody wanted to, let them go ahead; them men them not afraid of anything. Jake wouldn't dare touch *meh* boss but I still *doh* like he. Man like Bharat and Balkeran? Bad no ass!"

Glen, hunching, laughed, "That is why he put up *ah* big wall around he house and put *babwire* on the top of it? The man can't even get breeze in he hammock anymore!" He downed the little rum which had settled at the base of his glass. "Anyway, that is all the *stories* you have for me tonight?"

Icepick lied. There were more, as much as the sands of the sea, but visits to Glen usually ended sourly. He thought: *maybe it is why we meet twice a month.*

The atmosphere grew still. There was a layer of tension the liquor didn't remove. Glen began drumming his thighs. "So what you think about Prime Minister Taylor?" he asked, when he had had enough of the silence.

"Who, he?" Icepick asked, "Hmmm! He? He is *ah* ass!"

"But how you could say that?"

"And you ask me what I think?" Icepick retorted. "That man don't like Indian at all! Fixing everybody else place but not we own." He pointed at the road to emphasise his point. "Only studying all them Creole and them in the north. Must be bring in a set of Grenadian to voter pad for he."

Glen wasn't impressed by the analysis. "But it have Africans living in Icacos too," he slurred, "and the PM, he is a mixed man. He have all kind of thing in he; a real mix-up breed."

"You mean he mix-up!" Icepick laughed. "The man don't know he ass from he elbow. All kind of stupidness happening in this country and he none the wiser." He muttered something Glen didn't hear.

"Whatever you say yes. The problem with this country is that Creole only killing Creole and Indian only killing *theyself*," the host replied." He rubbed his chin thoughtfully and changed the topic, "You hear they looking for Sonnie?"

Icepick was surprised. "What happen to he now?" Another story: "Sonnie used to work for Balkeran at one time, but he get too big for he own boots. Want to play big '*in-trap-her-near*' and all kind of thing." Icepick didn't care much for the youngster.

"Them boys… Balla and them… I hear them talking on the estate. Apparently Sonnie owing some real big men."

"He is *ah* ass," Icepick said. The pictures on the wall meant nothing now. "He only studying to carry cask wine and cigarette for them Warao and impregnating a set of them. He is no drugs man. Is best he run birds or wild meat. I mean that is *Boxer* son and thing, but somebody should put a bullet in he ass."

Glen disagreed. "You go ahead and talk big so." He gazed at the bottle. It was nearly empty. He took a smaller drink and estimated the remainder in the bottle by tilting his head; *three more*. "God is the one to take life when he ready. You *ent* know that? You does talk too big. Just like Sonnie!"

Icepick swore ambitiously. The pictures looked down directly at him. He gazed back, glass-eyed. "What is your real scene with this Christian thing all of a sudden? Your mother go turn in she grave if she know you going by that white man. He must be tying up your head and taking all your money."

Suddenly, the host became 'Silent Glen' and after three petite drinks, Icepick left.

## 4 The Black Giant

THE NINE runners were tough men, capable of chewing nails and spitting thumbtacks, but the trail was tougher. Three of the nine had passed this way before. It was a path every army recruit knew and dreaded. The soldiers had started off stronger than the rest, but now forty miles into the dense bushes they grew weary.

A skinny, square-jawed sailor, introduced as Leading Seaman Sookram, running as fast as a burdened mule, had overtaken them, spurring Rawlins, an army captain, to send Bob Hope, a promising young private, to follow at the sailor's heels. We'd catch up, he promised the youth, don't worry about George; but the Lieutenant didn't look good. The journey from the east coast to the western peninsula wasn't a race. There was no gold medal, no consolation prize, not even glory at the end. The journey from Matelot to Chaguaramas was a test of wits, the reason unknown.

Rawlins checked his watch. They had started at 0400 hours. The sun burnt mercilessly. The captain was trapped on poor terrain, not far from shelter, but the downed soldier wasn't an easy man for the leaner Rawlins to shoulder. We're going to make it, the captain told the lieutenant, just hold on a bit longer.

REUBEN RODRIGUEZ was a daredevil pilot so the twenty-seven-mile flight from an unofficial airstrip in Tucupita to Icacos was routine. The small, blue Cessna 172 lifted off at

0700 hours, laden with bales of marijuana, rolled like hay for the European winter. The aircraft swiftly ascended to three thousand feet and within minutes the plane approached the Venezuelan coast.

In the distance the pilot saw a familiar coastline: Trinidad. Before the landmass was a smaller, uninhabited island, a popular marker known to Venezuela and Trinidad as '*Soldado.*' The US military had utilised the location as a shooting range and rusty shells could still be found to prove it. Reuben, having never visited the place, was uncertain. *Maybe Icepick's story is fiction.*

Today the sea was ultramarine. From his seat, in the cloudless blue sky, the pilot beheld a litter of rigs and vessels bobbing in the foamy bubble bath. Reuben abhorred the ocean. Its beauty wasn't its own, its colour a favour from the skies; without it the sea would be a pool of murky ink. Offered the same drug task with a seaworthy vessel, he would quit.

Reuben wasn't motivated by money, it was his ability to deny earth's gravity. From a bird's eye view the world was a different place. As a pilot he felt so alive, so large; he could lift an oil tanker, hold it between his thumb and forefinger, and inspect it like a curious child does when wishing to dismantle a toy it must reassemble. Flying was sacred; only gods belonged in the heavens. Reuben smiled at himself. He was alone, in control, a supernatural being; in solitude there was power.

The sea wasn't safe, it was a force to be reckoned with. Only a madman would try and Reuben pitied the souls. Not only was there the element of salt, but the Trinidad Coast Guard and Venezuelan Guardia Naccional had occasionally proven themselves a thorn in the transportation of drugs via the sea. Tons of marijuana and cocaine had been lost. Reuben knew that Trinidad's primary radar was *FUBAR*. Without it the country couldn't *shine* ultrahigh frequency radio waves capable of illuminating objects when energy is reflected.

The only threat was the Venezuelan Air Force. The *Aviacion Militar Venezolana* had recently purchased *Sukhoi*

*Su-30MKK* from the People's Republic of China. Reuben whistled. The plane was a beast. Not only was it powered by two AL-31F engines which provide great thrust and manoeuvrability, and an in flight refuelling probe, but its fire control system integrated the onboard radar and helmet-mounted sight.

The pilot had heard stories of small aircraft being shot down, but none which dictated incidents in the airspace he now flew. Reuben wasn't worried. He was equipped with Inverse Gain Jamming technology capable of fooling radar systems by transmitting copies of the signal generated by the jammer. The technology uses a *strong* replica when the illuminating signal is weak and a *weak* replica when the signal is strong. When the transmitter's signal processor receives and evens out the phases, it is fooled into believing that the radar dish is moving away from the target.

Reuben knew there were countermeasures to Inverse Gain Jamming. In the event of an encounter with a Flanker-G – NATO's reporting name for the Sukhoi Su-30MKK – the Cessna was equipped with small, thin pieces of aluminum metallised glass fibre which, when released, appears as a cluster of secondary targets (Chaff – a technique known to World War Two British pilots as *Window*). Reuben knew he couldn't outrun the air superiority fighter, but for him there was that thrill in being the smaller, smarter bird.

*Why would they shoot me down?* He thought: *it is likely our President wants drugs to leave the country.* Maybe he wanted to piss on the glory of the US and so left his borders unmanned. That way the Columbians had easy entry. Once drugs were dispersed to the Caribbean the issue was out of the hands of the Venezuelans.

Flying low over Icacos – which translates 'Fat Pork' – Reuben saw acres of coconut trees, a sickly brown colour, surrounding large and small houses. He judged size by the expanse of galvanize sheets covering each unit. *Which casa does the buyer own?* Reuben had never stepped onto Trinidad's soil. Below he saw villagers rush onto the streets, shield their eyes, gaze and point at his iron bird which flew low at two hundred feet. Soon he left the village behind and cruised over coconut trees only. There was no sign of road, house and animal life.

Reuben closed in on the drop zone, an earmarked area of five hundred square feet, cleared of coconut trees and high grass. A white van was parked on the perimeter, a man – *sí, Icepick* – standing on its bonnet waving wildly, the prefixed signal for '*make the drop.*' Reuben punched a button on the control panel and, as if anxious, the bales skydived from the plane. The job done, Reuben pointed the plane towards Tucupita. He had more flying to do and for that he was elated.

IT TOOK six seconds for the bales to hit the ground. Blunt thuds. Icepick comically checked the sky. Nothing lingered. He jumped off the bonnet. *Time to wuk!* It was slow, tedious work, a job for three men, but Icepick was used to hard work, a good boy. *Balkeran heself say so.*

The eleven bales were stacked and the engine of the four-by-four grumbled to life, an angry old bull loose among towering coconut trees. Cautiously, Icepick made his way along the weathered trail, wide enough for the van. He thought of Glen, the unbeliever. *Fantasy tales?* Icepick laughed. *Stories? What he feel it is?* After fifteen minutes the winding, bumpy trail led straight to Balkeran's backyard. *Mamoo* was there, but Icepick still had to get out, unlock the gate, park the vehicle and when he was through, secure the entry. The backyard served as a warehouse – for only products beginning with 'c': coconuts, copra, cannabis and cocaine.

Balkeran held the opened driver's door and exclaimed, "Ah boy Icepick! You get the thing!" He wore tattered green pants and a white vest decorated with tiny holes, cockroach chewed. His hair was an oily slick that curled over his forehead. He smelled strongly of coconut oil, but the labourer didn't notice; he too was doused with coconut oil.

"Yes, *Mamoo*," Icepick said subserviently, "eleven bales in all."

Balkeran didn't laugh to show his pleasure; his dark lips parted so that his mouth formed a thin ellipse. He rubbed his hands as if trying to warm himself. When he spoke his voice wasn't excitable; it was the same monotone it had always been. "Good. Good." He wiped his face, an action which left an oily mark. "What you need to do now is get seven of these to Bharat in Central. You could drop them for me."

It was a command and Icepick nodded. He had plans to go home to a movie but: "Okay. *Small thing.*"

"Okay. Well organise," Balkeran said. His hammock, Lady and *Whiteman* were waiting.

IT TOOK two hours to pack, weigh and reweigh, then the crocus bags were thrown, along with coconuts, into the trunk of a big, black sedan ('The Black Giant' was sprawled in white letters across the tinted windshield). Although paid for in cash by Balkeran's Copra Company, the car was in Sunil Harrynarine's name, a smart move by the employer should any unforeseen bust occur.

The car left Icacos at 1013 hours, the diesel engine choking and sputtering clouds of black smoke, like a chimney, for every yard of pitch it covered. After fifteen minutes of winding roads and sharp bends, Icepick came to Columbus junction. When lazing cattle had cleared the road, he turned right and sped along.

He drove one-handed, his right hand hugging the door as if in a headlock, and entertained himself with a chain of cigarettes and Chutney (English songs with East Indian melodies) which blasted on a radio station delivering more static than music. Once in *Bonasse*, a busier fishing village than Icacos, he stopped for a cold beer at one of the many roadside bars. *Glen wouldn't know.* He was on his second when Mrs. Lakhan walked by.

"Aye Icepick," she shouted, "I going Point Fortin. *Gimme* a drop *nah?*"

Icepick beckoned her, *but hurry.* "This is me last beer for the road!"

"Okay I coming back. *Lemme* get the *childrens* them!" She hurried away and returned minutes later with three snotty-nosed youngsters. They looked like they hadn't been showered in ages.

Icepick groaned. They scampered onto the backseat as children do: unconcerned about their shoes on the upholstery. Icepick muttered a curse. He drained the remnants of the beer and signalled to the barman: "Give me a beastly cold brew." The bottle had fat chunks of ice on its rim and base; cold like a glacier. He paid, then joined the Lakhans.

The forty-five-minute drive to Point Fortin was uneventful, except for a roadblock at *Cap de Ville*, a village bordering the Point Fortin borough. It was not the first time, with a trunkload of marijuana, he had encountered police officers, and it would not be the last. Still, Icepick felt a jolt of fear. The Black Giant bore a licence identification plate where the first alpha character was 'H' – a taxi with an old woman and three kids couldn't pose danger. With a wink, the police officer warned Sunil Harrynarine about the faulty muffler – for the fifth time – and waved the car through.

*Policemen and politicians are such a joke*, Icepick thought.

In Point Fortin Mrs. Lakhan, with great effort, clambered out the car, her enormous buttocks twisting and contorting like a wet sponge being compressed and released. The horde of kids – Icepick hoped Johnny would be nothing like them – scampered out.

The driver continued his journey. To him, transporting drugs was as common as a man having a meal. Village after village swooped past until there were no more. Mosquito Creek came next, a long expanse of highway, walled by a sweeping line of grand culverts to protect the road from the ocean's occasional wrath. He slowed, feeling sudden guilt. His father had been cremated under Hindu rites, his ashes cast upon the shores of the Gulf of Paria, whose waters now licked the walls barricading the road. By the time Icepick reached San Fernando his grief had been diluted.

Taking the Bypass, a labyrinth of confusing over- and under-passes, Icepick avoided San Fernando – impossible in the olden days. He took a newly-built road, which snaked its way for one mile, then turned left onto the northbound, Solomon Hochoy Highway.

It was eleven more miles to Bharat's estate, but the traffic was surprisingly heavy for the lunch hour. Icepick lit another cigarette and increased the radio's volume. He pressed into the headrest, enjoying static-free chutney music, hoping that the lady he saw, in the rearview mirror, inching up in the car behind, didn't accelerate and slam into the trunk.

One hour later, the Black Giant swung into Mr. Bharat's estate and drove up a road which danced, twisted and turned until it levelled into a posh compound. Around and before the glamorous castle were citrus trees planted along the hilltop's sea of slopes. The driver had seen the mansion many times but still, it was a wonder to behold the scaled down Taj Mahal. Feeling inferior, Icepick navigated the sedan to a peculiarly high iron shed, adjacent to the grand structure. Mickey 'Mouse' Samaroo and Patsy were waiting.

Icepick appreciated Bharat's driver. He was a talker, a likeable fellow who possessed Glen's serenity, but was different. Mouse didn't drink, neither did he smoke. He was vice free, without vile speech. As *Mamoo* would say: 'he is a good boy.'

Icepick and Mouse talked and laughed. When Icepick realised the discussion wouldn't soon end, he exited the car. Mouse greeted Balkeran's driver with a manly embrace and slapped his shoulder each time they shared jokes. When the conversation dwarfed into chuckles, Bharat's driver enquired on the welfare of the fishing village. Not too good, Icepick answered, it was as if fish no longer fell from the sky. To his confusion, Mouse laughed and slapped his shoulder again.

Icepick noticed that when it came to unloading the crocus bags of marijuana Mouse didn't assist; he never did. *And he does want fish.*

LATER THAT night Sean Brown was hunched over his laptop. He was dressed in a thick sweater to ward off the blistering cold air that hummed into the room. Occasionally, he found himself massaging a steaming cup of coffee. His lower lip quivered, his knuckles grew white. He pulled the sleeve of his overcoat but it didn't help; the university's library was too cold. He glanced around the third floor – s*till alone* – its wide expanse filled with countless books stacked upon shelves twelve feet tall, way too high for most users. In various lanes were small carts filled with books. Tomorrow, the librarian would resume the packing of books which students left idly placed. Sean sighed and resumed work.

At 2000 hours she came. The Beauty glided into the room like a warm current and sat opposite Sean though there were dozens of chairs tucked beneath the long white table. She tossed him a petite smile and slid her long, slender legs beneath the desk. If she was not tanned she would have been a tinge too fair for Sean's taste. He returned a stupid smile – later he would scold himself for that.

Sean closed his eyes and saw her, as when she had first entered. her supple body curved neatly beneath expensive cloth, her straight nose – with its tiny bump – and her brown, curly hair which snaked down her back and lapped at her buttocks. She looked good in pink, like a bunny on an Easter card.

She removed a text book – it might have been on Economics – from a matching pink bag and flipped to a bookmarked page. Sean thought: *it's a bit early in the semester to be studying so hard*. Maybe she wasn't as smart as she looked. He chuckled, hoping she would look up, but she didn't. *She's hot though*.

On a previous occasion he had described her to his father, a man who, like Sean, thought himself a Casanova of exquisite women. On a scale of one to ten, how much? the older man had asked, holding up both hands. Sean shook his head and added his. Twenty is impossible! his father had exclaimed, and resumed hacking on his primordial Staedtler.

There was something about her. The way her eyes remained glued to the big book rendered her unapproachable. Sean wasn't easily intimidated by women, except the beautiful ones, and there was no other way to describe the nameless girl before him. *Maybe that's why beautiful women always end up with scary looking men*. Sean despaired. He noticed the dull, white colour of his laptop. It no longer shone; it was as if stained by curry. Irate, he began typing, cursing the syntax and logic errors which cropped up in software that had been working flawlessly before she came.

IT WAS the time of day when the darkness of night was being pushed back by the gray light of morning, a phenomenon known as dawn which gives the sky a pinkish-peach with spots of red coloured into the background. Leading Seaman Sookram came upon Teteron Bay, Private Hope just behind. Wordlessly, they made their way down the mountainside, Hope hoping to get ahead, Sookram maintaining the lead. To the sailor and soldier it was a race. It had become personal miles ago.

Two hundred feet down, their lactated feet touched pitch. With a gigantic effort Sookram stayed ahead. The mess hall was a mere hundred metres away. Sookram saw the sea, the CG cutters at bay, men walking in light blue shirts with darker pants and berets. He stuck out his tongue, a painful effort, but the smell of rich salt was tasteless. He moved on, conscious that Hope was seconds behind.

Around a steep decline the runners suddenly came upon Alex Peters. In blue tracksuit with white stripes along its seams, the MONS looked fresh, like a daisy basking in the morn's dew. He blocked the runners' path with his arms spread like an eagle's wings. It was only training instinct which made the competitors stop and display disastrous salutes that would have earned them pushups in boot camp. At ease, Alex said, and passed two bottles of water. His invitation to sit, in the army vehicle parked on the road's shoulder, was declined; the men had a race to finish.

Twenty minutes later – Sookram and Hope were still standing, but re-hydrated – a police officer plodded around the corner in a half-walk-half-run.

Mouth opened, Hope looked at Sookram.

Alex Peters was also surprised. He had not expected a single police officer to complete the task and if any, certainly not Nathaniel Pierre. "Let's finish this!" Alex exclaimed and the three men, inspired by the unity and leadership of the ex-military man, jogged to the mess hall.

They finished together.

After lunch Sookram, Pierre and Hope learnt about CISTU. The private almost emptied his bowels. He had seen and heard of such scenarios only in movies. Of course! he declared, when asked, of course he would be honoured to join the assault team. *Why wouldn't I*?

The doors burst open. It was Captain Rawlins, with Lt. George slung on his shoulders, like a great sack of potatoes. The officer was dead.

## 5  Admiral Ivan Lewis

DAN LUCKY began his days without variation. He rose at 0500 hours and within minutes, steam whistled from the kettle. He fixed himself a cup of coffee; it was always half-filled, black with no sugar. It took some manoeuvring but he managed to open the door without spilling coffee or dropping the cigarettes and lighter.

Before he sat on *his* chair, one his grandfather had purchased sixty-odd years ago, he warily slid it away from the flight of steps, the entrance to his home and the exit to a pathway decorated with an inflorescence of carroty-coloured *bougainvillaea*. Then he lit a well-deserved cigarette.

His stretched nerves made him such an anxious wreck that he failed to notice the occasional jogger who would walk up the steep hill, hands gripping at thighs, for the extra push. Jogging would resume when the road flattened, just before the school. Lucky stretched out his hands. They quivered. He needed a drink. He finished the coffee, stubbed out the cigarette in the dregs of the black liquid and threw the remnants into the yard. With short, excited shuffles he entered the small kitchen, a gambler's kitchen; bare.

Flipping *The Spot* open, a counter decorated with a grimy – it might have been flower-patterned – curtain, he was shocked: the rum was gone. *That blasted child*. Lucky cursed loudly, causing a light to ignite in his daughter's bedroom. He abused her verbally, lifting his hand in mock pretence – he did this more than once – as if to hit her.

Eventually, she returned the bottle she had hidden in an empty shoebox beneath her bed. Her father chased her back inside and helped himself to rum, glorious rum, toasting the day's first drink to his grinning drinking partner – himself. He no longer felt the burn that rum gave, but his initial craving was gone. Left only was the desire for more.

Inside the bedroom, Davie Lucky wept bitterly into her pillow, its fabric long softened by tears. Her father had forgotten her birthday for the eighteenth consecutive year. She hated him, and herself, for hoping differently. *Maybe it's because of me he's like that.*

JOE HARDIN & Associates is a Private Military Company (PMC) located on forty-five hundred acres of swampland in the state of North Carolina. The firm, one of the top five contractors in the United States, is heavily involved in the Iraqi war and its consultants have not only engaged with, but killed insurgents in the name of freedom in dozens of official 'low intensity conflicts.' An additional aspect of the firm's portfolio is the training of personnel in specialised operations and tactical skills. For the first time, the company was training Trinidadians and a Tobagonian, a fact that had made its way into the powerful corridors of Washington, in a manila folder labelled 'Top Secret.'

A MORNING operation. Captain Rawlins and his three-man team were making their way through a room-clearing exercise in the Military Operations on Urban Terrain (MOUT) Centre, a man-made area that looked like a small war-torn city. The current structure was a two-storied building with a wide landing onto which they had rappelled from a helicopter.

The team stood outside the doorway of the *shoot house*. The leader shook his thumb and *pinkie*, at Nathaniel Pierre, using his weak hand, his leftie. Inside were men, like them, armed to the teeth, not with MP5s, but with mean little guns that shot nasty rubber bullets. Oxy, as Pierre had been nicknamed, shook his head. He had seen his share of welts and didn't care for more. This time he wouldn't *muck* up.

The men gathered in a stacked position on opposite ends of the entry, each clothed in full Close Quarter Battle (CQB) kit, including modern vests with combined armour protection and modular pouches. The only intelligence Rawlins accessed was: the entry to the house, a small room, was unlocked. The orders were simple: clear the building, neutralise any perceived threats, bearing in mind the presence of hostages, genders unknown; the *insurgents* expected them.

Sookram waited, looking almost comical in his bulletproof helmet and goggles which hung on his wiry frame.

The number one man twisted the door knob. "Pull and go," Rawlins barked.

Bob Hope – as door-opener he carried a Remington shotgun – on command, stepped out from his position behind the captain and placed himself before the door. Rawlins nodded thrice and the Tobago-born army private pulled the door.

The captain and the sailor hustled aggressively into the room, using *Buttonhook* formation, clearing the *fatal funnel*, the doorway, and manning positions in the corners of the room.

"Clear!" Both men reported that their Area Of Responsibility (AOR) was secure.

"Coming In!" Oxy shouted and entered on Sookram's signal.

"Room clear!" Rawlins barked.

Hope, who had been manning outside, entered.

The exit was an open door against a wall to the far corner of the room.

"Stack up," the leader barked and the men assumed a line formation. Rawlins took three *quick peeps* before he had an idea of what lay ahead. The exit led to a corridor, blocked by a door which swung outwards and was decorated with a gaping hole at its base. The hallway was wide open to artillery fire from downstairs. It had to be assumed there were *insurgents* waiting – trainers who had proven anxious to pop caps on the third world, military personnel. To the left of the exit was a solid wall.

*What next?* Rawlins jogged his memory, recapping software simulations they had been shown. *This situation hadn't been depicted.* His stomach was a tight knot of despair. Pulling the door back to access the corridor would render the point man blocked off from support and leave him wide open to assault. The area was too cramped for a pre-slice. *Shit.*

The captain waved three signals to Sookram and the sailor, crouched, moved slowly into position against the wall with the door hinges. Sookram signalled back; the blocked portion of the corridor was 'All Clear.' The sailor straightened until he could see downstairs. Another 'Okay' gesture. 'Cover this area' the captain signalled back.

Rawlins pointed at the man behind him. Conventional and customised hand signals followed. *We're moving too slow.*

Bob Hope – glad to be rid of Oxy who had been stuck to him like chewing gum – exited the stack. Hope was '*shitting bricks*' as his old drill sergeant would say. He felt fear gush into him, as rapid as a waterfall filling a cup. This happened each time the captain tasked him. The Systematic High-Lowe Crossover was a slow, safe approach and with Leading Seaman Sookram covering downstairs through the cross-sights of his MP5, the private still didn't feel safe. The hole in the door worried him.

The sailor nodded three times – the signal for 'Go' – and swiftly, *but not* aggressively, the Tobagonian used the Buttonhook to enter the corridor. No shots were fired. The team still held the element of surprise. A quick peep. His heart leaped; he had seen something, something to the northern wing. Hope made eye contact with Sookram. The private pointed upwards with his forefinger then indicated to his gun hand. His final signal was a crooked, trembling square – one person behind a window, friend or foe he wasn't sure, but on the topic they had been drilled: assume all were enemies since insurgents sometimes camouflaged as friendlies.

Sookram relayed the message to the man in charge.

Behind the wall, Rawlins was having a hard time; behind the gear it was hard to see his face. *The damned door.* He sensed Oxy's hot, irritating breath through the flame retardant undergarments. The captain made a decision. He gave brief verbal orders to the sailor who, in turn, signalled to a fidgeting Hope.

The next move started slowly then erupted. It began by Hope pulling the door then bursting around it – the 'L' shaped corridor was clear. Sookram swiftly took the Tobagonian's place. Hope swore. The man he had seen was a life-sized picture of a turban-clad terrorist behind bars.

At the next door, Rawlins was anxious. So far, his team had failed every mission. The routine was always the same: he would crack and his men would follow. As they stacked up against the wall, on his command, he noticed that no one manned the rear. They weren't operating in harmony. The pistons weren't firing right, unlike the Navy Seals they had seen on video. The Americans knew urban warfare, *but so far so good.*

Rawlins signalled and Hope front kicked the door. Sookram and Oxy – the big man carried a Level IV ballistic shield – knew they had to filter in fast.

A few steps into the room and Oxy's pistol exploded.

Before Rawlins could react, kinetic energy expelled into his bulletproof vest. He looked at the red splatter on his chest. He had been marked as dead. The shooter had appeared at the elbow of the corridor.

Rawlins cursed. *It was a blasted 'T' shaped corridor.* Rawlins cursed again. His grandmother detested foul – the old woman spelled and pronounced it *'fowl'* – language, but the captain had picked up the habit from Oxy who was swearing also; he could curse from one's dog to mother in a couple of different languages. Despairing, Rawlins walked away.

Later, after training, the team would, with four ex-Navy Seals analysts, review videos of their shortcomings. The leader, however, wouldn't get to eat until midnight. The consultants would drill him on the value of leadership and controlled violence. Not only that: his men had gear they weren't utilising.

THE RAIN which threatened to ruin the game never came. Instead, the mass of clouds hovered over the hilltop hotel like a fluffy grey ghost. A high chain-linked fence encompassed the tennis courts and when dry leaves from the tropical foliage shuffled over the clay, a sharp cackling sound emitted, like a rake's tines on concrete.

Ambrose and Alex were on their second game. On the outskirts stood three bodyguards in their dark threatening shades, their MP5-Ks (the bodyguard's weapon of choice because of its compact size and ease to conceal) hidden below black jackets. They had placed bets; Mr. Peters was the favourite.

The MONS had won the first set demolishing the prime minister six games to two. Alex played hard, especially against Ambrose. He smashed a ball down *no man's land* to win the second set.

Ambrose was drenched, to his white, ankle-high cotton socks. His game had improved, the MONS highlighted, but his forehand was still weak. The men walked to a bench on the perimeter. The ministers' wives were playing a hopeless game on second court.

As Alex sat, Angela skied a ball over the fence. He flapped his lips, emitting a horse-like sound.

Ambrose laughed. "At least Patricia is winning one for the team."

Alex passed a bottle of water and towel to his friend who graciously accepted, then proceeded to wipe big beads of sweat off his face. The liquid was sweet to his lips, like a drink of water after being in the ocean for hours.

"What's the word?" Ambrose asked, using slang he had picked up from the Commissioner.

"Ken arranged some joint patrols with the army. The CO was happy to get his boys out of the barracks. It has been a while since they've seen some action." Another big gulp, then: "I've been thinking about our approach. It isn't long-term. These patrols are going to become sporadic and the hostile divide may extend to our DF. The media is pounding the topic of legality since the incident." A soldier's weapon had discharged as police tried to remove an illegal vendor from Charlotte Street. The woman had jerked the barrel of the private's Galil. No one had been hurt but Mark Lloyd, the Opposition leader who had privately endorsed the joint efforts, openly criticised the venture. Lance Jones, the nosey reporter, was having a field day.

"Suggestions?"

"Other avenues," Alex replied. He continued after Ambrose shrugged. "I've been in contact with Admiral Ivan Lewis of the Jamaican DF." Alex waited for a reaction, but was encouraged to continue. "Like Trinidad, Jamaica is an ideal transit location. The drugs come in from San Andreas just off Honduras, probably thirty hours by boat. Dons are accepting payments in drugs. These transits and spill-over drugs contribute heavily to crime and trade in illegal arms and ammunition. Money laundering, more addicts, even narcoterrorism. We are very *potential* targets."

Alex was right, Ambrose reflected. Trinidad was rich in petroleum and liquefied natural gas, resources which attracted the United States. "What did the Jamaicans do?" he asked, his curiosity spiked. He knew the MONS held a surprise.

Alex looked around like a kid stealing cookies. He was satisfied that the tennis players and bodyguards – one was receiving money – were out of earshot, but he leaned closer to Ambrose. "The State took care of some Jamaican dons. I'm beginning to feel that maybe we should too." Alex shrugged.

Ambrose reclined and exhaled sharply. He had not realised how dark it had become. "Do you know what you're suggesting?"

"It's working for the Jamaicans." Alex leaned back. He watched the ball duel until his wife foiled the shot. "We have to play a bit rougher," he said, not looking at the prime minister but at Angela. She had proper tennis form, but lacked aggression.

Ambrose was ready. "When old men die, new ones rise. These successes only serve to drive threats underground. Or they lie dormant. For example: the Cortez cartel." His voice was firm

"Are you saying we bargain with the criminals, Sir?"

"Ouch!" It was a low blow from the MONS. "No... no. Things must be done in accordance with the supreme law. We can't live below the Constitution. What example would we set?"

"But everyone else can, and we can't do one heck about it?"

"That's enough Alex! Anything else?"

"Angela is suggesting an anonymous call centre for tracking criminal activity. I think it's a good idea."

"You're discussing security matters with your wife?" Ambrose asked hastily.

Alex shook his head. "No, she suggested it. People might act if they believe they can anonymously report crime to an automated system or agent." When he said *anonymously*, he quoted the air.

Ambrose was reluctant. "Privacy issues?"

The MONS dodged the question. "Maybe Lance Jones will offer free full page adverts."

Ambrose laughed.

"Sir, regarding Jamaica. I think it's worth considering. Slowly, we're pulling the pieces together. We have four guys training with the Private Military Company as we speak."

"How's that going?"

Alex filled him in. Last he had heard, Nathaniel 'Oxy' Pierre had blasted a male hostage with yellow paint. The armed female *insurgent* had confronted three members single-handedly, swooping past the ballistic shield and *killing* everyone. "Guy goes head-on with an unarmed man and there is a gun-toting woman." *Trust a Trinidadian*. "From what I hear he is a terrific shot, a bit unorthodox. Urban warfare? The training is new to the men, so it could get pretty rough. What's important is that when the captain and his men return, the facilities and tools to train are available." Training was the key.

"On that note," Ambrose said, "*The Tabloid* is continuing to make a fiasco of Lt. George's death."

Alex began to speak but Ambrose stood – the wives were coming. The ladies were laughing like schoolgirls and patting each other, the way good friends do. It wasn't bad light that ended the game, they admitted, it was the loss of the third ball.

The group, bodyguards in tow, walked to the parking lot where more armed men awaited. Typically the group would chat, but tonight Alex, Angela and his men left hurriedly.

What's wrong? Patricia asked. She always knew when Ambrose was frustrated.

Ambrose shrugged and signalled to Wayne: they were ready. The vehicles left the hotel's compound and sped away, flashing lights temporarily lifting the city's gloominess.

## 6   Chip Rivers

JAKE PIPES was a tall bloke whose muscular frame wasn't built in the gym but from rugby. Ambrose felt the power in the man's handshake and as Alicia Sylvester left the room – her clumsy buttocks wriggling as she walked – the prime minister noticed the secretary's eyes lingering on the Drug Enforcement Agency (DEA) agent. Trinidadian women were more pert than they were fifteen years ago, something Ambrose still had trouble accepting.

"Thanks for meeting on such short notice, Mr. Prime Minister," Jake said graciously in a Trinidadian accent that Ambrose had to congratulate him on. On the leader's invitation the American sat.

"Please, Jake, call me Ambrose." A nod from the agent. Americans were amicable to first names; the British were ticklish.

Jake cut straight to the chase: "We've wind on a huge shipment of illegal drugs en route to Trinidad. Half a ton of narcotics."

Ambrose whistled; *1120 lbs is a lot of cocaine*. "Any idea who's behind it?"

"We're looking at a street value of over two hundred million dollars," the agent evaded. Confirming suspects could compromise his informant. There was plenty the prime minister wasn't cleared for – especially a *Trini*. "Whoever is behind it, would have a great deal of financing."

*The Syrian mafia?* Ambrose wondered. When it came to the big bucks, *supposedly* those were the fat ducks. Ambrose wished Alex hadn't flown to Tobago earlier that morning. "Is there something you wish to propose, Jake?"

The agent alerted the PM: an American cutter was on the outskirts of Bajan waters. "It's imperative that the US and Trinidad CG coordinate activities." Jake knew that The Maritime and Over-flight Agreement permitted the foreign vessel to operate in Trinidad waters.

"Jake, there is a lot of sea out there," Ambrose said, sweeping his hands, as if the ocean was before the Blue Room.

"The shipment is coming into a Chaguaramas boatyard. Which one we can't say." He paused, then admitted: "We don't know."

"Okay," Ambrose said. "Alert your forces. I'll do the necessary."

"It's already done," Jake said, placing his hand on the PM's desk. He leaned forward, like he was about to share the secret of eternal youth. "Keep a tight lid on this. The DEA has reason to believe... unfortunately... that some of your forces are in collaboration with the local mafias." Jake paused to gauge Ambrose's reaction, but the PM's face was like a room swept clean. "We want this order to come from the top. Not even from the CO. We want you to make the call."

Ambrose nodded.

After the meeting, Jake abruptly excused himself. Alicia happily escorted the American out.

The PM, from a secure line, punched in Alex's cellular number. As he waited for the call to connect he wondered if the Americans had ever attempted to bug the Blue Room. *I'll have to remember to ask Alex about that.*

LEAH WASN'T looking for love, but love was sometimes found by those not searching. She had long – fourteen days ago – barricaded the door to her heart; love couldn't knock. What she didn't know was that love could enter through a window and was often disguised as a new friend.

She stood in front of the gizmo, a stout black plastic case, a machine the height and shape of a mini refrigerator with instructions and selectors for rookies. Each time she inserted a crisp five dollar bill the device spat out the money noisily, like a baby does to food when it's filled. She thought: *maybe coffee isn't for me.*

She gave up on the sixth attempt and turning for the library, bumped into *him*. Books sprawled across the cafeteria floor. They apologised, paused, and laughed at how often they said sorry. Then, they stooped and began gathering papers and books. They were like mimes.

Leah thought: *I am in a hopeless, cheesy British comedy.*

He thought: *thank goodness she wasn't holding coffee.* Then, looking at Leah: *she really likes pink.*

Leah wondered if her underwear was exposed as she stooped on the floor. She stood; a few seconds later he did too. Grateful, she took the offered items, dusted and huddled them below her arms, as if to pacify the belongings.

He pointed to the dispenser: "The price raised yesterday. It's eight dollars for a cup of French Vanilla." He twisted his face. "Something is screwy though. The machine only accepts tens or twenties." Then, with a mischievous grin: "I'm not brave enough to try a hundred."

Leah liked the smile. Concealing the thought, she asked in disbelief, "Eight dollars for a cup of coffee?" She hadn't meant to speak loudly. Pitch decreased, she repeated the question.

He smiled: a nice smile, a spontaneous smile, more pleasant than the rehearsed ones she had seen him deliver in the library. His teeth were yellow and he had a paunch, but his height, plump lips and manner of dress softened the defects nicely. Tonight, he wore black jeans and an earthy, orange-coloured shirt decorated with hibiscus flowers. *He has something for funky shirts.*

"Let me get you one," he said. The twenty was in the machine and the French Vanilla in Leah's hand, despite her adamant refusal.

*He didn't even ask my choice of flavour.* "I'm sorry, I can't have this," she said, as they began walking to the library.

He was cooling his coffee, but stopped. "Why not?"

"I can't pay eight dollars for something and enjoy it when other people can't afford it. The best things in life are free, not man-made pleasures slapped with hefty price tags." Leah gestured at the coffee. "But there are things we can enjoy. Magical peaceful places with a reverence and appreciation for a higher being."

"You're emotional," he said incredulously and continued walking.

Leah was appalled at the stranger's bluntness. He seemed different, not the quiet person who sat opposite her in the library. She wanted to storm off and never see him again, but she was entitled to her opinions. "I am a crusader against what I believe to be unjust."

He looked unimpressed. "Oh. A crusader? And how do you determine what qualifies as *unjust*?" Before she could retort he waved her silent. "I understand your sentiment but please enjoy the coffee. I bought it for you, Leah." He took her books without asking. "Let me help. Don't worry, I'm not trying to impress you. I'm just being nice."

He walked off but she remained grounded. Dumbfoundedly, she asked, "Wait, how do you know my name?" When he told her, she felt pretty silly. Her name was scribbled – in a handwriting she wasn't proud of – on the papers he had helped retrieve. She didn't bother to ask his name. She didn't want to appear interested but quickened her pace until she caught up.

In silence they walked across the quadrangle bustling with student life that accommodated group gossip, card playing and the consumption of alcohol from soft drink bottles. Leah hustled to match his long strides. He sat on the library's steps, illuminated by a neon sign boasting the university's logo.

"Have a seat *nah*." He was gently patting the concrete, like a baby he was skeptical to touch.

Without hesitating Leah sat, even though her business belonged on the library's third floor, behind her books and notes which now separated *her* from *him*.

"So, what's the problem with paying eight bucks for a cup of coffee?" Sitting with the beautiful girl and the ice broken, he was comfortable as the warmth his insides received with each sip of the hot, creamy liquid. Leah's lips hadn't yet touched her cup. Starved for conversation, and desiring to remain in safe territory, he recapped the question.

Leah was still peeved at his bluntness. She didn't look at him. "I told you. I'm uncomfortable paying exorbitant prices, especially when others are denied the privilege. It's better that I refuse myself."

He pointed at a sign, flickering brightly against a long glass pane, to the left of where they sat. "Have you ever been to Fidel's?"

She stared at the crowded café. She hadn't.

"You will *bawl*! The cheapest latte is twenty dollars." He quoted 'latte' with his fingers.

"Wow," Leah said, so softly that her companion didn't hear. She counted seventeen customers lounging in the brightly-lit venue.

"Trinidadians are like that," he said, and with a gulp he finished the drink which had grown too cold for his liking. An overhead throw and the cup was in the bin at the foot of the steps. *Thank goodness.* He wiped his lips with the sleeve of his shirt. "Decorate the place lavishly, slap a big fee tag on the product and you've got a seller. Trinidadians don't *brakes* from price."

*His speech is peculiar.* "That's it!" she exclaimed, rather upset. "No one stops when prices skyrocket. No one says: 'I will not buy.' If that's done then the seller doesn't have a choice. Who can afford, buys, and who has to go without, does just that." Her gaze left the store and in the semi-darkness of the cool night their eyes met. She felt comfortable to share a bit of herself, "That's why I don't pay more than I think is reasonable. I cannot if other people can't."

He nodded in agreement and shared a Venezuelan experience. "When I was there sometime ago… '99 I believe it was… the price of gasoline went up by what we might consider a negligible amount. *Eh heh*? The country literally shut down! Three-day fiesta." He chuckled, "We remained stuck in the airport. You know what? The price of gasoline slid right back."

"Thank you!" Leah congratulated the Venezuelan spirit by tapping her fingers against the wrist of her hand holding the coffee. Some of the creamy liquid spilt onto the lid. The conversation paused. They looked around at students bustling on the stairs, in and out of the library. A group of four boys had gathered and were practising stunts on two skateboards. Each time someone fell or failed to impress they would pass it along to the next person.

"I'm a bit of an activist myself," Leah's companion said. "I can't say I'm the best role model, but I've had *doubles* once since the price went to four dollars."

Leah couldn't tell if the look on his face was one of shame or regret. She had a confession: "Do you know I have never had *doubles*?"

Her companion, obviously startled, stood. "You is *ah* Trinidadian?"

She giggled and shook her head, amused by his character, his speech. He was different, not the quiet one she had perceived him to be, so uncultured.

"You can't be for real!" He laughed. "Girl, you have to be the first Trinidadian I meet that never had a hot, tasty *doubles*. I must take you for one." Then mischievously: "*Doh study it I go pay.*"

"Is it nice?" Leah asked. She was still laughing.

"If it nice!" he exclaimed. "Leah–" she felt a chill. She looked up and their eyes met lingeringly– "my mouth watering." He exploded into a vivid description of the silky dough and curried channa which could be decorated with spicy East Indian condiments.

"Calm down," Leah joked. *He is crazy.* She patted the concrete.

The *doubles* fanatic sat and for a long time remained still, his gaze shifting to Fidel's, the skateboarders and Leah. Each time he looked at her, she folded her lips and lifted her eyebrows. He knew she waited on him to say something, anything.

Leah broke the silence. "You know what?"

He looked at her.

"I don't feel too bad about this eight dollar cup of coffee. Fidel's on the other hand..." She laughed then grew serious. She sipped the coffee. Her face took on the frown people reserve when deciding whether or not they like something. She exhaled. French Vanilla was the most superb drink she had ever tasted, on the sweet side, but still, perfect. It smelled great too. She had another confession. "Can you believe I've never had coffee?" She laughed when some trickled down the corner of her mouth. She didn't feel ashamed, just ridiculous.

He seemed genuinely surprised. "You for real?" A burst of laughter disrupted their conversation. A skater had fallen hard and was trying to redeem himself by holding on to the skateboard.

Another sip. The taste was exhilarating. "Yes! I love it!"

"How old are you?" he asked. Before she could answer, he blurted: "I took your virginity twice tonight!"

He erupted into scandalous laughter that reminded Leah of a pack of cackling hyenas she had seen on Discovery Channel. Had it not been for the inherent humour, she would have sorely disapproved of the comment; the way he said it that made it okay. Leah wondered if she would have been as forgiving to her ex-boyfriend. She frowned, eyebrows knitted tight; to be unalarmed was peculiar.

The night wore on, with the moon never showing its face against the starry sky. Student activity slowly declined. Suddenly, the library's neon sign flicked off.

Leah, appalled at the hour, stood but showed no sign of being anxious to close the topic: oxygen, heat and time, enemies of coffee's freshness. They had spent the night discussing all she didn't know about coffee and *doubles*, but it was time to leave. She was sure a scolding awaited her at home. "Maybe I will see you again, Sean," she said, and gathering her books, ran off to a carpark beyond Fidel's, leaving the bewildered man behind. He hadn't introduced himself; she hadn't asked, but somehow she knew his name.

He watched her go then flung his bag over his shoulder and began hunting for an open classroom. He had work to do.

HUEVOS ISLAND – titled by the Venezuelans – or Egg Island, is one of five that form the Bocas Islands. The captain had expected to arrive at nightfall, but the sheet of sea was made for smooth sailing and the *Amity* moored against the jetty at 1600 hours.

Chip Rivers, dressed in cargo shorts and a t-shirt, stood on the landing stage, hands on hips. The yachtie ignored the grand yellow house two hundred feet away, choosing instead to admire his sailboat. He was passionate about it, a love that didn't bob as the boat did, but fizzed and bubbled over. It was an adoration he did not feel for his wife.

The woman hated the sea, the itch of fibreglass, the freckles the Caribbean sun had given her. She complained and remained hidden in the cabin, a woman given to the seductive, crazy nightlife the tropics boasted. A few days ago she had issued a threat: she would leave and never return.

Chip didn't despise her but he had grown weary of the nag's whining. She blamed Chip for every discomfort. It wasn't her will, but her husband's hunger for the sea which had resulted in the sale of their Oregon home, purchasing the *Amity* – with a bank loan in Angie Rivers' maiden name – and sailing halfway around the world. They arrived in Trinidad broke. They couldn't even afford the cheapest marina.

That was before Paul Headley, a man who had given Chip hope, the promise of a luxury to sail the seas again. Chip had listened to the man – outside an Automated Teller Machine (ATM) – waiting for the clincher. The tanned tourist was no fool; nothing in the world was free, not anymore.

Angie had made friends, especially among the local blacks in Tobago; she could now exchange American dollars for good times, parties, alcohol and drugs, but first they needed to do a job. Chip had been skeptical, but in a bind had little choice. *Amity's* hull was refitted and remodelled so that it could transport contraband from foreign waters into Trinidad. The jobs had increased; now they were talking cocaine.

"Chip, you made it!" Paul Headley hailed out, as he walked the path from the yellow mansion.

Chip greeted the tall, black man with a powerful handshake – Headley's was more impressive. "Good weather," the yachtie said, pointing to the orange sun.

"Shall we start then?" Paul Headley was dressed like a scholar, a man who should be in academics rather than drugs. He looked good in his pinstriped suit. He wore no tie, the two top buttons of his white shirt unhooked, the collar stiff with starch.

"Not too early?" the American asked, with some concern. Sea traffic was busy, too busy.

Paul checked his watch and shook his head. Timing couldn't have been better. He asked for Angie.

Halfheartedly, Chip thumbed over his shoulder. "In the boat, with the product."

"She still leaves as planned, come Friday?"

"Yeah, she'll be going back to Oregon to her parents," Chip said. He wasn't sure why but he added, "I'll still be around if you need anything."

Paul smacked Chip roughly on his shoulder. "Of course! Of course! We expect nothing less."

Rubbing his shoulder, Chip looked towards the house, "Just the two of us?"

"No, we've got some guys inside the house," Paul said, and left to summon help.

Chip looked at *Amity*. Soon he would be alone, alone with his boat. He smiled briefly. He had been yearning to do repairs on her hull. With the money earned and Angie gone he could then do as he pleased. He didn't care for *BiteInn's* craftsmanship; *they do crude work*. He had seen vessels from other marinas. Once the big bucks came he had promised himself to look at the competition. Not only was *Marina Ideal* cheaper but the craftsmen worked better with fibreglass.

It didn't take long for Paul to return with four hardcore caucasians whom he didn't introduce.

Chip solemnly acknowledged the men. He thought it better not to introduce himself like a Ms. Universe contestant. They followed the captain onto his boat and they, like his wife who wordlessly sulked into a corner, didn't help as he shifted items in the cabin. It was tense work. Even after the secret compartment was revealed, Chip felt that he would be killed and his body dumped into the sea. It was Satan's work; he tried to see it as survival, but couldn't. The job was a means to an end. *Not end of life*, he hoped, as he stepped back, allowing the men to view the compartment.

"It goes down nine feet," Chip said. He sounded boastful, but wasn't.

Paul smiled at him then looked again into the darkness.

"How many packages?" the smallest white man asked. He sounded Arabic, but behind shades didn't look it.

"One hundred and sixty-eight," Chip said hastily.

"You're two packages short," the small man said, extracting a pistol.

Chip went cold. He cringed, but his wife was indifferent to his ordeal. She held a book and was propped against a tiny refrigerator which chilled drinks nicely. Chip looked at Headley for support.

Paul rescued Chip: "It's okay, *Greg*, it checks out."

Gregory, replacing the weapon, smiled wickedly at Chip. Showing chrome to inject fear was necessary; necessary to keep the goon in check. The yachtie wasn't a good player. He would adhere to any rule. Gregory clapped. "Let's get to work," he barked. "You in the hole," he said, pointing to Chip.

The compartment had been stuffed by Guyanese nationals. It was slow, tedious work for Chip, bending and lifting the packages out of the depths. He didn't wear a watch and had no idea of time. Neither did he request it of Paul who, his jacket removed, collected the packages. Chip's arms ached. He was a rough man but this was different to sailing. Harder, more dangerous work. There was no rest. Chip sank deeper into the bowels of the vessel with each heave and hoist of the twenty-pound packages. He was in hell. Time passed. One more package to go. Suddenly there was a shout, fear, panic. The yachtie's head jerked up at the noise.

Paul was peering into the gaping hole. "It's the bloody Coast Guard," he said, his voice a dry whisper. Droplets of sweat fell from his face landing with a 'plop' on the package Chip held pressed against his chest.

"Shit!" Chip almost dropped the cocaine. He wasn't ready for this mess. "What's happening?" he asked, but Paul had disappeared.

A long silence. Chip strained his ear. He thought he heard talking. Was his partial deafness playing tricks on him? He stood frozen, tearful that if he moved he would alert some faceless personnel – *good or bad?* – who might be trigger happy. *Where's Angie?* He hadn't heard her whining since he went into the hole. *Who the hell is up there?* Chip felt faint. Time crept. Suspense. Suddenly the grate was dragged over the cocaine den. Darkness. *Shit.*

More silence, like a priest in prayer. Nothing. Only the emptiness of the darkened hole which threatened to squeeze Chip into the sea. No drips, no noise, just the dip of the rocking boat, the smell of rusted metal mixed with what might have been salt. *Shit.* Then, directly overhead, he heard footsteps, heavier ones than Paul's. It sounded like heavy boots on *Amity's* decking. Chip became angry. The footsteps faded. He waited.

A boat's roar, then the grate screeched. Chip froze. He was still clutching the *twenty-pounder* against his chest.

Paul's bald head smiled down at him. "That was a close one, buddy."

Chip just wanted out. He passed the last package and with great enthusiasm escaped the hole with the help of Paul's strong arms. Chip was slapped hard on the back.

Paul, high on adrenaline, laughed. Chip had hoisted 168 packages, the equivalent of 1.5 tonnes of cocaine. *Amity* was no longer worth eighty three million American dollars. The yachtie didn't care.

He arrived on deck in time to see three CG cutters speeding away, leaving a hefty spray in their wake. In the distance was a fourth military vessel flying the American flag.

From the bow, his wife smirked. *Shit.*

## 7   Baby and Betsy


IN 1582, Pope Gregory XIII made a decree which would have a significant impact on Trinidad and Tobago. Easter is determined by the ecclesiastical moon. This holy moon is defined by permanent church-constructed tables, for calculating the phase of the moon. The full moon is not the same as the astronomical full moon: Easter isn't necessarily the Sunday after a full moon, but rather the Sunday following the holy moon. Because of these calculations, Easter can fall anywhere between March 22nd and April 25th. The significance of Easter to a lot of islanders is its link in determining Ash Wednesday. Because a mass of Roman Catholics participate in Carnival, the event must end forty days before the time of hiding and sharing bunny eggs. The holy church had determined that Easter would fall in late March, creating an early Carnival season for Trinidad and Tobago. Ultimately this meant warm-up parties in January.

Amrit was looking dapper in a blue pants ironed into sharp seams, and in an orange shirt that faded violently into white and blue. He wore alligator-skin shoes, decorated with a three-inch blue stripe that ran from the tip, across the laces, to the heel.

When Ricky saw the shoes he said, "*Eh* boy, like you going to moonwalk across the stage." The shoes looked like those a flamboyant homosexual singer would wear, a comment to which Amrit didn't react lightly. Ricky Lo was dressed in different shades of green which failed to match, and sneakers, a size too large. His dreadlocks were open, their thick clumps stretched, like fat anacondas.

Together, the pair did not blend, *chalk and cheese*. Oblivious to most stares, both jibbed easily to *Fox Company*, the soca group performing a smash hit on the big stage. Trinidad's star performer, *Sugar Boy*, was prancing around like a madman, waving a miniature flag attached to a stick, his image projected onto huge screens scattered across the venue. Nothing escaped the cameras, not even the large droplets of sweat on his face. The performer's antics were infectious, spawning the waving of hands, flags, cigarette lighters; beer flew into the air at the frenzied shake of bottles. Frequently, female fans would be pulled from the thick, cosmopolitan crowd onto the stage and *Sugar Boy* would gyrate like a grater working a carrot. Then, much to their displeasure, they would be dismissed.

"Boy, them men have it sweet yes," Amrit said enviously, over the loud music. "Them have the best-of-the-best to choose from. Thousand girls!"

"True. True." Ricky said. He enjoyed himself, but a marijuana joint would have made the fete tiptop. Some scantly-clad girls passed, causing him to nudge his companion.

Amrit elbowed confirmation – *they hot boy*. "Horse, you see the shorts the little red *thing* wearing?" he asked, as the females filtered through the bumper-to-bumper crowd. "She give me a little eye contact, you know."

Ricky adjusted his crotch. "Boy, don't let them girls slip," he said. He lit a cigarette and took a pull; it smelled awful lit. Cigarettes weren't good. *Weed? Ital!* An unprocessed herb, the natural high. He passed the cigarette to Amrit who smoked and drank only at parties.

"You know what I want," the Rasta said, as the act on stage simmered down. He wasn't aware he was speaking loudly, but it didn't matter. *I and I is Ricky Lo*. On stage, *Sugar Boy* was attempting to seduce a reluctant female to dance. "I want a white *thing* like that one on stage there now. She looking good. That is one good thing about them white woman; them natural and they have nice legs." He pointed at a screen to his right. The camera focussed on an appalled blonde. *Sugar Boy* was having a hard time winning her affection and was obviously upset. Take it down bass man, the performer said, and the guitar died.

Amrit scoffed. "Like *Sugar Boy* meet he match! The white *thing* don't want to *whine* with the man yes."

Ricky's eyes were glued to the screen, but he was trying to catch the action on stage using peripheral vision. *Sugar Boy* was not giving up. As the entertainer's luck would have it, the cameras showed the female leaving front stage, the crowd booing her. *Who the hell that white woman feel she is to diss we star boy like that?*

The show had to go on. *Sugar Boy* burst into *Road Rage*, a frenzied soca song *mashing up* the airwaves since mid-December.

"That is Road March you hearing there!" Ricky exclaimed.

Amrit disagreed.

Ricky *steupsed*. His East Indian friend didn't know good soca.

Minutes later – when Amrit had gone to the crowded bar for two black-bottled brews – Ricky saw the caucasian who had rejected *Sugar Boy*, standing alone, her arms crossed, her face likewise. She stood about arm's length away and when their eyes made contact Ricky nodded.

She twisted her face.

*Maybe she doh like Rastas.* Ricky moved nearer. *Who the hell she think she really is?* Someone in the crowd bounced him and he cursed. When Ricky was closer she turned, flashing a fierce, stubborn eye. Ricky laughed. *Freckled face backside.* Hostilely: "You know what we does do white people in Trinidad?"

She didn't reply (aware of the tense atmosphere, people began to slink away).

The lady's silent defiance antagonised Ricky. Had his threshold been higher, he would have ignored her. "You want me to hold you down and put some licks on you?" he asked suggestively.

The white lady understood the implication. She said defiantly: "Two asses can't fit in one pants."

*Sugar Boy* had just ended his performance. People heard the comment and laughed at the low punch aimed at the Rasta.

"You taking that from a white woman?" one man exclaimed. He darted away when Ricky cursed.

Amrit, who had returned with two stouts, stood, fazed at the exchange. Ricky was shaking a fist at the woman, cursing, parading so close to her face that his hair rubbed against hers. The white lady was unmoved. She stood, unafraid of Ricky's hollow eyes which burned into hers. Ricky inched away, a move which robbed his pride. He snatched the drink from Amrit.

Fireworks erupted as another performer bolted onstage, but Ricky stood like a mannequin to the melody of *Empress*, the sexy Bajan superstar he had paid especially to see. He took small, angry sips, glancing menacingly at the *White Trash* as he had dubbed her. After *Empress'* third song Ricky bent over and whispered to Amrit. The music suddenly didn't matter, only the *White Trash* who hadn't budged.

ISABEL HAD just fixed a drink of rum and cola and rejoined Bharat when the telephone rang. He answered loudly. Brief exchanges. He became more engrossed in the conversation; his forehead parted into lines and his eyebrows sank behind his shades. He began massaging his crown. She didn't understand everything, but deciphered the most common words; his English was terrible, not English at all, but some horrendous language – 'Trinidadian,' he called it – which she too was adopting. She listened. He was planning to meet with someone.

Noticing her curiosity, Bharat pointed to the kitchen.

Isabel left quickly – as she had learnt to do on Bharat's command – but once past the staircase and inside the kitchen, flattened herself against the wall, like a *roti* pressed onto a hot platter. She heard his anxious voice, booming loudly. He wanted to know where, when, how. Then the call ended. *Was it another woman?* Isabel checked her watch.

*¿A altas horas de la madrugada?* Women came to her *novio* like she had; he didn't go to them. Isabel decided that she was safe.

Bharat called for her and promptly she returned. He was more agitated. He slicked his hands by running them through his hair then rubbed them lightly against his pants. He behaved like someone who looked for keys no longer in a familiar spot. "Where my shades?" he barked, and proceeded to upset the cushions.

Isabel froze. She observed him ploughing mechanically, scattering her English notes and overturning her textbooks. She felt moved, in a strange way, which would prompt another woman to say Isabel was mad for loving Bharat – but such a woman would not know of South American passion. He stopped and looked at her, his hands spread wide. Isabel looked into his eyes, sad violent eyes which betrayed nothing but spoke wonders to her. It had taken her a long time to see those eyes.

In the early days he had insisted on sex with shades on. One morning Isabel had crossed the line, removing the peepers as he slept. His hand was heavy. Isabel had bled, but the blows were warranted. She saw him nude, his eyes a beautiful brown, except for the left pupil, a translucent, cloudy, white bead. He thought himself loathsome, but she had wrapped her legs around him and pressed her lips into his face. He softened, he shivered, then they made love; animal love. His world opened; he spoke of the condition he bore since childhood. 'Retinoblastoma,' the village doctor had called it, blindness of the eye which he had suffered on the eve of his fifth birthday. It was a delicate morning, one Isabel had experienced long ago and never again enjoyed, one she wished for even if it meant his anger. *Mi papi chulo.*

"Where me damn shades, woman?" Bharat asked, as if Isabel had misplaced it.

She began toppling cushions and seats in the lush room

Minutes later he found it on the inside of his jacket, after patting his chest. "Go and get *Baby* for me," he snarled. "That is the big one. Bring *Betsy* too."

*¡Madre de dios!* The ex-prostitute hurried upstairs muttering Spanish. He spoke like a man speaking to a whore, a low life, a no good, someone less than a woman, interested only in making a quick, dirty dollar. Isabel thought herself different, a lady compared to the Trinidadian woman who seemingly enjoyed the flesh trade. The islanders spoke of hard times, the slums, but what did they know of the – *¿Cómo se dice?* – ghetto? *Ha!* Caribbean prostitutes were a disgrace. They didn't have children living on some hillside in Caracas where it's impossible to identify any one house because the galvanised rooves are pinned together, like a gigantic metallic lasagna. *Latinas knew hard times.* Learning English was a bonus, a way out of poverty, but like everywhere else, education came at a cost. The price had been Isabel's body. Her Manager was the way out.

Isabel found the heavy gun pinned to the underside of an ironing board. Guns made her sick. She held the weapon perilously by the trigger and holding it at arm's length went to Bharat. Isabel wasn't sure what type of handgun it was. However, she was certain that in the bedroom were firearms scotchtaped to every imaginable location.

She went to the storeroom and got *Betsy*.

He stuck *Baby* into his waist when, cringing, she passed it. *Betsy* he held in his hands. Upstairs, Bharat commanded, and Isabel went.

*¡El coño é la madre!* Five minutes later, from the master bedroom, she watched Amrit's car speed down the hill. *¿Estar sin ánimo?* Yes, her spirits were low. She felt sick to the core. Isabel went to the bathroom and vomitted violently.

MICKEY 'MOUSE' Samaroo loved driving, but tonight he was weary. He had been dragged, like a fishnet, out of bed, ordered by Ricky and Amrit to collect one of the *hot cars* from Bharat's garage and bring it to the outskirts of the golf course in Chaguaramas. Half an hour later – after Ricky and Amrit had shoved a white lady into the backseat and Mouse had driven four miles into a forested area – Bharat had called to deliver new orders.

Mouse, driving Amrit's car, had to return to The Manager's mansion where he picked up The Boss and sped out of the compound. The shades hid the anxiety in Bharat's eyes, but his tone highlighted his roused appetite. He wanted to know everything. Mouse told him. Ricky had tussled with the lady in the back seat of the *hot car* while Amrit followed in his car. She was a tough woman, hard like coffin nails. Ricky had cried out when she scratched his face.

The return to the location seemed longer. *Why were they so interested in the white woman?* Mouse leaned against the automobile and watched Bharat walk into the darkness, *Baby* and *Betsy* in hand. Through the dark sheath of forest Mouse could see the spot where the three men stood. There were loud moans of distress. *Is she being raped or tortured?* Mouse reminded himself that being raped was being tortured. *What I doing here? That could be my sister.*

He opened the trunk noisily in an attempt to shut out the cries, magnified in the still forest. He heard Bharat speaking, demanding something. Futilely, Mouse tried to erase the sinister distractions, but they did not fade like chalk beneath a teacher's duster. They remained like a wall smeared with painted words of hate. He felt sheer pain when the woman screamed.

Vigorously, Mouse searched the trunk. His flesh tore when his hand brushed against a wheel spanner. He cursed. Then he found it, nudged in a corner: a plastic bag filled with oranges. He extracted one and using a blade – a New Year's Day gift from Navin – peeled away the rind. He was halfway through when a gunshot boomed, followed by the wave-like sound of a person exhaling. Mouse cringed. Then came a sickening, thumping sound, like a cricket bat pounding a crease. *What they doing?*

Mouse bit into the orange he hadn't yet sliced. The fruit was sour in his mouth, as if salt had been rubbed into its pulp. He spat and, disgusted, threw it angrily in the direction of the men, still wondering but not wanting to know what had happened. He never wanted to know. For this reason he shunned newspapers and radio. It was simpler to drive, not ask questions, and be handsomely paid. No one could whisper: 'he is a real killer you know'; neither could Mouse do the same about his *friends*.

The three men appeared from the darkness like aliens from a science fiction movie – covered in blood. Mouse pretended it was ketchup. Misattributing negative visual and auditory facts made driving The Boss and his gang easier.

Amrit opened the trunk and Ricky tossed some items inside, the rectangular metal pieces banging loudly on the wheel spanner.

The men were ecstatic. Mouse associated their excitement with love. It was difficult to tell that something very wrong had possibly been committed in the forests of Chaguaramas. In the rearview mirror he saw Ricky Lo attempting to wipe ketchup off his moss green jersey. It was a good jersey, he said, but the white woman had ruined it. Mouse squeezed off a chuckle, but everyone else managed scandalous laughter, particularly Bharat.

## 8   The Transporter

RICKY LOVE was an unpleasant looking fellow with thin long hands which brushed against his knees when he walked and nappy hair that hung over his sallow, skeletal face. He was like a dirty old mop hung out on a fence to dry and forgotten. The only claim to good looks were two gold caps which covered his incisors with the letters 'L' and 'o' molded into them. There had once been a 'v' and an 'e', but a motorbike crash had knocked both teeth bearing those inscriptions out of his mouth, gaining him the nickname *Ricky Lo*.

At midnight, dressed in tattered clothes and quietly stumbling through Port of Spain, Ricky Lo was just another vagrant. He played the part, stepping first with his left leg, then dragging the right behind. Street after street he walked, a restless soul, hunting. The streets were uncomfortably quiet, a far cry from what they would be in a few hours when people came to the city to commence another week of labour. The neon signs of stores lining the sidewalks flickered as if someone was adjusting the switches from the inside. Here and there dogs, the only other beasts brave enough to travel the streets, fought each other and tore at garbage long emptied by madmen. Ricky Lo was heading north on Frederick Street when he found it.

The open end of the forty-foot container faced north. From where he stood he was uncertain of events and since he had to be sure, he hobbled along, coming up on the transport equipment faster than he had anticipated. Suddenly two men, burdened with a bale of pink cloth, cut across his pathway. They stiffened, then chased the vagrant with simple curses, as if threatening a bothersome dog.

Ricky's eyes followed as they disappeared into a narrow corridor. *The Transporter* was parked inside. Ricky hopped into the *pissy*-smelling alley. *Shiny* appeared, as a ghost from the shadows. His hands were suspiciously close to his hip.

Ricky begged, "Boss, spare me some change. A red go do. Father go bless you."

The man muttered something in an unfamiliar language and roughly shooed Ricky away. The vagrant mumbled some choice Trinidad curses and continued north. Looking back, he glimpsed someone within the hollow depths of the container.

Ricky, convinced he had found the right scene, hurried away, limp free. He turned left on Park Street and walked west. Hastily, he looked around and once certain the streets were empty, extracted a cellular phone and punched in seven digits. The call was answered on the first ring. Ricky reported his find.

Was he certain? the voice asked.

Irritably, the Rasta confirmed. The white woman hadn't been lying. Her promise of plenty cash, drugs and weapons in exchange for life had been 'the real deal.' The story hadn't saved her life but had rewarded Raj, Ricky and Mouse with a fishing trip, along with The Boss, on his pirogue *Limer*.

Raj didn't find the boat spectacular – 'Lamer' he called it – for a man of Bharat's calibre.

The Rastafarian had objected; he thought it great. The chance to go fishing, for the first time, had temporarily dispelled his *aqua-phobia*. He carried a caster, hook and five pounds of shrimp bait, held in a black, plastic bag packed so tight that it had burst with tiny holes and leaked pink water.

They had spent the weekend hiding, fishing, with Raj cooking the day's catch at dusk, the big yellow house always in proximity. It had been 0500 hours when Raj, creeping to the property's picket fence, had seen a speed boat skimming up, almost noiselessly, to the jetty. Two men had disembarked from the craft and soon they, along with the house's four occupants, had formed a daisy chain and were passing along healthy-looking packages.

Bharat had removed his shades but still could not discern the activity – the movements were blurs, like a photograph taken from a speeding car.

Mouse had described the scene to The Boss.

"You jackass! You really think that is salt they packing?"

"Boss, what you think?" Ricky had asked.

"I feeling it boy Ricky... I feeling it! I getting the vibes!"

Ricky had never heard Bharat speak so benevolently. "But Boss, how we getting the product? We do not even know where them men going from here?"

"Well, we will take them at sea!" Bharat had exclaimed loudly, causing the sixth man in the chain – the one they had codenamed 'Shiny' – to shield his eyes and stare in their direction.

Raj, who had made his way back to the group, didn't like the plan. Teteron Bay was too close for comfort. There would be a gun battle at sea. Not only were they outnumbered, but the *Limer* was a slow boat with over four hundred times less horsepower than the rivals' vessel. *Six against three?* He didn't like the odds, neither could he count on Mouse; his cousin wasn't a hen as Ricky had declared, but a pussy.

Mouse didn't like the plan either. His two dozen oranges had finished and the spot they had sneaked up on was cold and damp, the smell of bat – *or some other kind of animal, maybe a manicou* – dung evident. He kept his mouth shut.

Bharat had, with his shades on, looked thoughtful as he massaged his chin; the stubble made him irritable. "Raj, you did see the name of the boat?"

Raj had not.

The Manager's unseen eyes had darted angrily among the men – to Mouse he looked like a puppet on a string. None had. Bharat swore. If they followed with *Limer* they would certainly be detected. He cursed. The group had stood in silence, each man, waiting on their leader. He had extracted his cellular and made a call.

Amrit, posing as a fisherman before the entrance of the military base, had stayed on the call for six minutes and recognised the boat described by The Boss. The six men on board had gazed in his direction, only briefly, none choosing to return his wave.

From the shore he had seen the vessel pull into Bitelnn, the same boatyard which housed Bharat's *Limer.*

Ricky Lo had doubted, but at the street corner he decided that something valuable was being stuffed into the container. They had almost missed the heavily-tinted panel van when it pulled out of the boatyard but '*The Transporter*' was plastered at the top of the windshield, as it had been inscribed on the boat's bow. It was the same van which brought them to Port of Spain.

The *vagrant* made two more calls.

Ricky identified Amrit before he arrived. He had been in Lord Harris Square and ran south along Pembroke Street when Ricky called. He was dressed like the Rasta, but not as persuasive, the expensive cologne foiling his disguise. The scent disgusted Ricky, but he said nothing. He asked about Raj and Navin.

Amrit sketched the plan. He and Raj would stay at the intersection of Park Street with Navin planted further south where Duke intersects Frederick Street. He told Ricky his part and after two more telephone calls the men eased to the corner. Crouching, they saw Raj peeping south. He had a better view than they did. In the semi-darkness they saw him give the thumbs up signal. The coast was clear.

Ricky Lo stepped out and walked the streets, performing again. *That container empty, boy?* He wasn't certain. The cellular phone vibrated in his pocket but he ignored it. Adrenaline pumped. He was back at pissy-alley.

This time, Shiny pointed a gun straight at Ricky.

GREGORY WASN'T a careless man, especially with guns, but the intensity of the night's operation and the vagrant's boldness had unnerved him. The second time the filthy Rastafarian showed his face, Gregory unleashed a menacing, dull, black Beretta 92 from his waist and pointed it at the crackhead's stomach. There was something about a gun which made people flee, but the vagrant didn't run as the Syrian had hoped. Lowering his weapon, Gregory stepped closer to the gold-toothed man, feeling that a solid slap would do the trick. It was a bad move for a well-trained ex-soldier of the Ba'ath regime.

RICKY LO wasn't particularly fond of Navin, but tonight he was glad to lay eyes on him. Skilfully, Navin penetrated Shiny with a treacherous blade as long and wide as a child's arm. Ricky rushed in and covered the man's mouth. A quick flick of the wrist sent the gun flying from the Syrian's big hands. The weapon skated and disappeared below *The Transporter*.

Gregory was strong, accustomed to fistfights and military engagements where he had been outnumbered and wounded. His attackers were nowhere as skilful. Holding onto Navin, Shiny deliberately stumbled backwards, ramming Ricky into the wall behind. Navin, his centre of gravity upset, stumbled forward and crashed into concrete. As fluid as a ballerina the knifed man turned with Ricky hooked to his back. A quick elbow to the Rastafarian's head nearly knocked him unconscious and a strong right hand brought him over Gregory's shoulder. Jagged concrete waited to absorb Ricky. Shiny fought to get to the van where a tap on the vehicle's windshield would trigger an alarm, a signal to his friends inside.

Navin, who had recovered, rushed Gregory, sinking the blade deep into his back, missing the spine by inches. The extra weight and momentum generated by the cheap attack propelled the ex-soldier forward and he fell flat against the van with a loud bang. No alarm sounded.

Navin twisted the knife free and he and Ricky hurried behind the van. The double doors were open.

"Shit! Check coke!" Ricky couldn't count beyond ten, but he knew there were more than twenty packages – he compared what he saw to the number of cigarettes in a *full pack*.

Then a shout. Navin turned to see two flashing muzzles hustling towards them, light reflecting as bullets slammed into the vehicle. Flashes as big as Independence Day fireworks jumped from the barrels, complete with instant booms. A bullet crashed into the open door. Ricky ducked for cover. Another loud noise and a sharp jolt of pain in his lower right arm caused him to scream. *Where the hell were the others*?

As if sent by Satan's angel, Amrit appeared and several abrupt shots choked the darkness, from whence the opposition had come, into silence.

Ricky felt hands lifting him into *The Transporter*. As the van rumbled to life, Gregory stood and desperately squeezed past the closing doors. The vehicle screeched down Frederick Street, slowing only at the police station at the corner of Duke Street, a fight for life in progress between Ricky and *Shiny*. Then *The Transporter* was gone, leaving Port of Spain and the smell of rubber behind.

DAVID ALFONSO'S life was spared by hunger that night. As the presiding customs officer it was his responsibility to oversee the stuffing of the container; but the fat man's desire for food had overruled. An hour after monitoring the manual labour, he had boarded his new, purple, luxury car and headed west where he hoped to find food at Ariapita Avenue. He had come up empty-handed. St. James also proved foodless.

Back at Frederick Street, he noticed the unusual silence. Armed with a torchlight David walked to the alley. *The Transporter* was gone. He stumbled over a lump and the flashlight revealed a man – *was it Brian*? – clutching his stomach, his black clothes sticky with blood. His legs appeared to be crushed by some weight. *Jeesanages! Did something run over him*? David vomitted.

Brian wasn't dead; he just lay there, his head stirring, his eyes rolled back. David saw the sharp rise and fall of the man's stomach as he fought for air, each exhale followed by the bubbling sound one makes when gargling. *Where were the others*? David flashed around and saw another unmoving body. *What's going on?*

The customs officer hesitated. He should call the police. Instead, as instructed, he reached Paul Headley. David stooped beside Brian, wanting to comfort the injured man but not knowing how to. David had never seen death; he wasn't certain what he should say. *Should I share good times? Should I cradle this man?* He knew nothing of Brian. David repeated the word 'Aye' loudly, like a stuck record. It didn't help.

The customs officer was shocked when a reputable police officer responded to the call and gruffly told David to scram, like a barman tells a drunk. David objected. He had a manifest to complete, his ass to cover, but the lawman, with backup, insisted so forcefully that David had to sourly slink to his car. He was paid handsomely to ignore a lot of things. Oblivious to his hunger he drove his dream car east on Park Street as Frederick Street had been cordoned off.

Never in his life had David seen the police respond so quickly and efficiently. It seemed they were being paid much more extravagantly than he was. He thought: *how unfortunate that some police officers collected bribes*. David had never considered it before but now that he did, he felt sorry. His car purred into the night, leaving the capital behind.

The next day, there would be no scoop, no editorial, nothing in *The Tabloid's* pages concerning the shootout. David would be surprised and upset at the police; he said as much to his wife.

CAPTAIN RAWLINS consulted his watch – 0450 hours – which didn't have to be adjusted on arrival in North Carolina. From the top bunk he could see mist, as thick as wool, hugging the swampy land, hurry to go nowhere, threatening to blind everything. Outside was cold, inside too, so cold that his nostrils burnt with each breath. It was the Sabbath, a day of rest and the team had been promised a break after gruelling exercises which had run past midnight each night for the past week.

Saturday night had been different. Not only did they finish in time for supper – they had been fed and given alcohol to their hearts' content in celebration of a minor victory over Nancy and her one-man team. But Rawlins felt disappointed, they were still losers. He had politely declined the celebratory drinks.

Below his bunk he could hear Hope snoring loudly, wheezing like a pig when he inhaled, whistling like a kettle when the carbon dioxide exited. The private had been beaten to a pulp by Nancy, the same woman who had *killed* them ten days ago. Staring at the ceiling, hands clasped behind his head, Rawlins grinned. The brunette was good. Her fighting style was *Krav Maga*, and she had disarmed and disfigured the Tobagonian's nose using eclectic techniques associated with the Israeli hand-to-hand combat system. In spite of the beating, Rawlins felt satisfied. He had seen growth in his team, not much, but enough to make him grin. He had good men.

Oxy was a crackshot with pistol and sniper rifle, a bit oafish in movements, but the man to count on when it came to the needed accuracy for a kill.

Sookram was a quick little bastard, built for speed, lean as a stick and as quick as a dean's whip. Slowly they were moving away from being individuals, integrating more as a system, one properly designed and built.

Bob Hope, so far, was the weakest link. The trainers constantly picked on the private who gradually was growing more courageous.

Rawlins knew that he was gaining respect by making the right calls. Command was coming naturally. The captain was motivated by the team's progress.

His thoughts shifted home. His wife was a great cook and an ardent church-goer. Diego Martin, a once serene place, had seen its demise but had reincarnated into a Wild West town where bullets punched up the murder rate. Rawlins looked at his hands. He missed his ring, his wife, his quiet life. Off duty, he would tend to his kitchen garden which yielded enough vegetables to share with the neighbours. The military was a hard place for a Christian, but duty had called and he had honoured the obligation. He had trophies in swimming, shooting and running to prove this. He thought of his son, Phillip, a youngster who felt himself a man, his wish: to be a soldier – '*just like dad.*' Rawlins smiled and thought of his father, a military man also. *It is the love for a parent which promotes a child's desire to be like them. It is the love for a child which makes a parent reciprocate the feeling.*

Suddenly, the doors to the dormitory burst open. Rawlins sat upright. There was a deafening explosion of light and sound – a *Flash Bang*, something the soldier had never experienced. By the time he had shielded his eyes it was already too late. The room seemed to have been sucked into his head; the illumination, a crazy flash, intoxicatingly worse than a drunk experience. The four highly-disoriented *Trinbagonians* were dragged out of their beds by Nancy and three large men – 'they had hell to pay,' she threatened.

Oxy cursed as he outfitted himself. A sullen Sookram scowled, a movement which caused his hard, square jaw to fold into tight lines. Bob Hope sobbed openly, loudly. Minutes later they were in full CQB gear. They had work to do, a building to clear, Rawlins barked.

Today they would train with Flash Bangs.

## 9  The detective and the analyst

ROBERT DROVE four clicks into the forest until he came to the spot he was told he couldn't miss. He silenced the Ford's engine and exited the van, leaving the high beams shining bright, like a pair of spotlights, into the dense forest which grew from the edge of the road. The flashing blue and red lights of three unmanned police cars and an ambulance cast a disco-like effect on the chilly woods. In his blue denim Levis jeans and festive short-sleeved shirt which boasted coconut trees and silhouettes of shapely girls, Robert felt smack at home. He cursed at the view his headlights displayed and briskly rubbed his hands together, suddenly craving a cigarette. He mastered his vice and left the Marlboros in his worn pocket. *Now isn't the time.*

In the woods was a faint smell of the ocean, too far away to be heard, and overpowering it was the pungent scent of rotted leaves. A whisper of breeze wafted through the forest, revealing the unmistakable odour of death. It took forty-three careful steps along the trail to the crime scene. There were curious cops, bustling firefighters and paramedics in the core area; enough to contribute to an entire season of extras to a crime scene investigation flick.

"Who's in charge here?" Robert scowled.

A stocky East Indian who looked angry to be in the woods at 0115 hours, crawled around the driver's side of the vehicle and stopped uncomfortably close to the newcomer. Robert flashed his identification and the chubby-faced policeman snatched it like a greedy kid stealing candy. The badge said CISTU. Based on recent directives from the MONS and the COP, Detective Robert Marco was in charge.

"Ladies and gentlemen," Robert declared.

The splinter groups, huddled around the car, looked up, flashlights aimed in the direction of the voice.

Robert shielded his eyes and the beams dropped to his chest. "Please vacate this crime scene!" he ordered.

No one moved.

"Now!" he snarled.

Everyone looked at the boss – the same officer who had greeted Robert; he merely shrugged, and defiantly slid past the CISTU agent. Twigs snapped as the others angrily trounced on the trail back to the road where a viscous conversation ensued. In passing, a firefighter flicked a cigarette stub at the showstopper's feet.

Robert stood in the darkness listening to the night creatures. Someone was sure to use *jurisdiction*, but who cared? He was paid to work, not bullshit. He ambled to the group, hearing his name mentioned above hoarse whispers. Conversation ceased when he reappeared.

"Good morning," the CISTU agent said.

No one responded.

"My name is Robert Marco and I, like you, represent the protective services. I'm here to work with and not against you." He made this crystal clear.

*Rubbish*, the group thought. Sure, they had read about CISTU in *The Tabloid* and heard about it in the grapevine, but who the hell needed American help in solving national crime? they argued.

"I'm Canadian trained," Robert corrected, then pointing at the man who had greeted him: "What's your name?"

The man told him.

"Okay Sergeant Singh, I'm going to look around the crime scene. No one comes or goes until I'm through."

The lawman nodded lethargically and stood at the entrance of the trail, a gunslinger, hands stuck behind his belt.

Robert retrieved a CSI field kit and a camera from his vehicle. Everyone stared. He ordered the area taped off. They looked at each other stupidly. Robert cursed under his breath and threw fifty feet of yellow tape, retrieved from his van, to a constable. Just enough to seal off the entrance, Marco saw, as he headed to the crime scene.

*Ken's description of the victim was clearly underplayed.* Robert, on the driver's side of the vehicle, uttered a single stretched obscenity at the sight of the corpse, slumped halfway out the window.

It was 0130 hours when Robert began his work. Visually, he inspected the exterior of the '97 model vehicle, careful not to upset any evidence. The torchlight revealed no bumps, damages or impressions to the body of the car. The licence plates were missing. The windshield and hood were smeared with dry red prints; the trunk and bonnet spotless with blood spatters on the front bumper – *throw-off spatters?* Robert worked the camera from varying angles, the digital Nikon D100 lighting up the woods like a brewing Toronto storm.

Thirty minutes later, Robert was back at the spot where his kit lay. The vehicle still had to be dusted for prints and the *morons* who had contaminated the scene would have to be fingerprinted. He could hear Sgt. Singh refusing entry to someone.

He looked around. *What happened in these woods?* Among the boot prints he noticed the pear-shaped outline of sneakers. Before it, closer to the car, were barefooted impressions. Robert measured and photographed the sneaker prints and the clearest of the bare soled prints, jotting the results on a pad. Later, he would transfer these to forensic software.

The victim's face was smashed, unrecognisable. Neck tissue was torn and the jaw drooped. The victim had been brutally restrained: the window on the driver's side had acted as a vise on the neck.

Robert shone the light at the ground and cursed. There was a large footprint in a pool of blood that had collected and dried below the door. *No doubt the rubber sole of a fireman's boot. Blast it! Are there any policies for crime scene protection in this country? Do these people value evidence?* Contaminated evidence made the difference in a criminal walking free or being put behind bars. Robert had seen it happen. He had even messed up big-time during the murder investigation of a Hell's Angels biker in *Hogtown*, something he tried hard to forget.

A few more clicks of the camera. The scene was falling into place. *Was this an abduction and rape case?* The deep impression of the toes and blood smears suggested that the victim had been forced against the vehicle. Robert focussed on the car. There were splashes of blood spilt in a horizontal direction on the rear window. *Peculiar.*

When the fingerprints had been secured Robert would later measure the blood spatters. Medium Velocity Impact Spatter (MVIS) is generally between the length of 1 mm and 3 mm; this type of pattern includes blunt force trauma, suspected in *Jane Doe's* case. Another measurement of a spatter at a sharper angle to the victim's head would reveal the same results. Variations of the angles of impact suggested that she had been hit repeatedly.

*Something is missing. The point of origin.* Robert flashed his lights into the woods as if searching for someone. Sgt. Singh called and Robert answered; everything was fine. The detective walked to the passenger side. The window was up. Jane Doe *must* have been beaten, forced into the car and beaten further on the head with a blunt instrument.

*Why not the back seat? It would have been far easier.* The job would have required at least two men. *Maybe three.* One to restrain the victim from the outside, one to navigate her from the inside and one to push her from behind. With two it would have been difficult. *There were three.* Someone had to lift the manual window.

When Robert finished two hours later it was still dark. Eighteen paces away from the roadside, he stopped in his tracks. He bent and bagged an item.

Sgt. Singh waited, his eyes hungry for details. Marco simply said that he had dusted the car and raised latent prints off the dashboard. The victim was female and showed signs of decay evident after three days of decomposition. The sergeant twisted his face as Robert described the foul smell of the car and the unsightly blisters which decorated the woman's greenish-blue skin. Singh became more alert when he heard that the woman had been forced into a kneeling position.

Robert, disgusted at the man, confirmed that her anus and vagina were ruptured. He omitted the contents of the tagged paper bags which held vital evidence. Keep the area secure, he ordered firmly.

Sgt. Singh watched the van disappear then called his favourite journalist. He was promised one hundred dollars for the information and an additional four if Lance Jones could walk the crime scene. Hurry up, the police officer said, rubbing his stubby fingers in glee.

ARAM HAMAD wasn't the loud, gesticulating man he had been on New Year's Day. Rather, his mood was pensive. He was a tall man who carried a couple extra pounds, with broad shoulders, and the facial structure of a rounded horseshoe. Although his moustache had streaks of grey his hair, which had begun to recede at the forehead, was jet black. Thin brows hung low over green eyes, short ellipses in his head. His most distinguishing features were a broad forehead and straight nose, the tip of which hooked over the whiskers above his mouth. The deep lines around high cheekbones signalled growing confusion, like a child lost in the plaza.

The Syrian had been pacing the luxurious Persian-styled bedroom since the wee hours of the morning. His wife was still asleep, wrapped between expensive sheets which hugged her body, like spandex, hiding nakedness which held little appeal to the faithful husband.

Aram had been analysing the scenario, but hadn't arrived at a conclusion. It was impossible that anyone could have known about the shipment. *Was it*? The men on that job were trusted family, loyal as Syrians are expected to be. Everything was now in a mess. Three men were dead, Brian having succumbed to his injuries. *And Gregory*? Was it he who had masterminded the theft? *Impossible!* Gregory was the backbone of covert operations for the family's empire. He knew everything. His service in the Ba'ath regime attributed him with the expertise required to function as the underworld contact for the family. Aram ordered, but it was Gregory who efficiently executed. It was the way things worked. No other way was suitable. *Was it Gregory who had betrayed the family? Impossible! Cops maybe, but not Gregory.*

Paul Headley. *Could he be trusted?* Gregory had thought so. The African had alerted Aram of the robbery, a direct breach of rank, a good move, but unacceptable. Aram had been shocked, then scared at the news. Now he was angry at the lack of information, a new twist. Answers were needed. When half a billion dollars in cocaine belonging to the Cortez cartel goes missing, questions would arise. As the local transshipper Aram would be expected to have answers and the cartel didn't consist of compassionate men.

The Syrian left the comfort of the bedroom and from his basement office dialled Paul Headley.

THE LOCATION is Mount Hope, the first forensic lab built in the Caribbean, a facility equipped with the latest technology that money could import. Few people knew the one hundred and fifty square foot lab existed, mistaking it for another abandoned section of the hospital. The facility was built based on the advice and design of a US consultancy firm and implementation cost exceeded twenty million dollars under the Mark Lloyd administration. The building is zoned into six different departments, the biggest being Serology and DNA, and a conference room. The lab is strategically located next to the mortuary, should a coroner wish to share facilities with the hospital.

Robert had earlier dropped off the Jane Doe crime scene evidence and a four gigabyte memory stick filled with pictures. It had taken Ernie eight minutes to process the one hundred and thirty-seven high resolution photographs.

Ernie had just finished lunch – fish and chicken pies, his daily delight – and was on his way back to the lab when he met Robert again. The detective looked unhappy and reeked of cigarette smoke.

In the conference room Ernie sat behind a laptop while Robert helped himself to coffee, swirling the contents like red wine, his free hand removing and replacing photographs from the three neat piles laid out on the table. He scowled at the imagery.

"Did you find the bullet?" Ernie asked softly, catching Det. Marco off guard.

*The kid is good.* "I'm wondering the same thing," Robert replied, sounding more relaxed than when they had first met in the corridor. He picked up a scaled picture from the *Close Up* column and showed Ernie the hood from the interior.

"Exactly," the analyst said. "That's HVIS. Unlike the medium velocity spatters on the outside."

"Which explains its mist-like appearance," Robert added.

Ernie nodded.

"So she was shot, then beaten?" Robert wondered aloud.

Ernie eyed him like the dumb blonde from a lame joke.

"Why would they do that?" Robert sighed. He sipped his coffee.

"I checked the photographs of the interior. No sign of the bullet," Ernie said. "Petal Clarke is working on Jane Doe and promised to call when finished. It doesn't make sense to shoot then bash someone." *Every crime scene really is different.* There was no one approach to solving crime, only suggested best practices. The African analyst had learnt this in school and proven it on the job.

"Unless they wanted to disfigure her," Robert guessed.

"And the semen samples on the passenger seat?"

Robert placed his coffee away from the pictures and began sorting through the close-ups. "Take a look at this," he said, passing a photograph to the analyst.

"Bloody prints on the back of the driver's seat." He looked at Robert who was shaking his head.

"Yes. The point of origin isn't in those woods. She was bleeding before she arrived at the murder scene," the detective said confidently. "That explains the bloody handprints on the vehicle."

"Why take her out to put her back inside?"

"Beats me."

Robert's cellular rang. It was Petal Clarke, the pathologist. The call was placed on loud speaker. *Jane Doe* had been shot through the mouth where gun-shot residue (GSR) was found, but it had been a blunt instrument that displaced the jaw. Semen deposits were in the anus. No bullet, the coroner reported; probably it was lodged in the car. The cadaver's last meal had been baked ham and pastel.

Robert thanked Petal for the heads up. "Vital piece of information," he grimaced, "but she could have eaten that meal anywhere."

"Or, she could have eaten it at an all-inclusive fete."

Robert lifted a brow.

"Sure," Ernie added, "they serve such meals at expensive parties."

"Can you get a list of Carnival fetes for the past two weeks?"

"Done," Ernie said. After a few keystrokes the high-end printer came to life. He passed the printout to the detective.

*The World Wide Web is something*, Robert concluded and Ernie was definitely the greatest Internet Detective he had ever met. "Three to four nights ago?" Robert went to the man behind the laptop, "Look at this," he said, hitting the paper with his knuckles, "Super Soca's fete was located on the golf course."

"So Jane Doe was at the party, later raped and killed?" Ernie concluded prematurely.

"There's more to it," Robert said. His mind was working overtime. "The nature of the killing suggests that the killer or killers wanted... I don't know... revenge?" It was like trying to produce a painting without paint, not challenging, but impossible, at least so far. This woman had been raped. That was fact. *Why disfigured?* A bullet to the head or strangulation would have sufficed. Rapists were stupid, egoistic people, but there were other ugly signs consistent with gang-related murders. *I'm jumping the gun.* "The way I see it, she had been to the party... she probably met someone and decided to go home with them... however she was beaten, raped and... for some perverse reason... her head was stuck in a car window. At this point she realised she was about to be killed..." Robert's voice trailed off. Nothing seemed plausible.

Ernie interjected: "In addition, the killers removed the documents and license plates from the vehicle."

"Which suggests that they don't want us to know who she is."

"Hence *Jane Doe*," Ernie said sarcastically. "But why?"

"Because... because she told them something of high value and the longer it takes *us* to find out who she is, the better for *them*." Robert was stumped again. Someone with high value was an ace in the pack. He was feeling like a rookie. "Anything on the cellular phone found under the driver's seat?"

"Nothing," Ernie replied. It had been cleared of numbers. "It's registered to Lewis Clark, a yachtie, supposedly on his way to Grenada as we speak." The American's address was linked to a marina in Chaguaramas. Ernie knew the place. He had been to BiteInn on a date, he said, emphasising *date* to impress the divorced Robert.

"Make sure it's powered," Robert indicated.

Ernie gave two thumbs up; it was already done.

"Good work," the detective said to an expressionless Ernie – so different to the puppet after whom he had been nicknamed. "I'm going to check out the golf course."

AMBROSE TOOK the call in Washington, during the lunch break of the Caribbean Community (CARICOM)/US Summit.

"How's it going?" The MONS voice was crisp over the cellular.

"Same-story-different-day," Ambrose said, removing himself from the proximity of the dessert line, his plate half-filled with American sweets as addictive as cocaine. "The

St. Lucian and Bajan prime ministers didn't attend. They didn't even send a single foreign representative," Ambrose said regretfully, his shoulder and tilted head supporting the phone, his spoon attacking the black forest cake. "Otherwise the event is big. Over nine hundred people from the Caribbean and a couple score of US personnel." *And the cake is great*, he didn't mention to his tennis partner.

*No surprise there*, Alex thought. St. Lucia was nursing wounds from their denial of entry to the American online gambling market, an action taken by the US President, which the islanders claimed breached World Trade Organisation (WTO) policy. The Bajans' grouse was that the Free Trade Agreement had flooded the local market with foreign products. However, as a Barbados Manufacturing Association director had declared: 'There is no one in the great USA who wants the natives' goods.' Central American exports were hurting the island, but the Bajan population and other CARICOM member states didn't care. The North America Free Trade Agreement (NAFTA) meant American products which Caribbean people were partial to. "What's CARICOM's stance?" Alex asked.

"We're holding our ground. We learnt our lesson in '94 when Mexico joined NAFTA. Our duty free exports under the movie star's administration couldn't compete with the Mexicans'. We are not going to make a move this time until a solid agreement is in place with the EU. Only then we'll negotiate with the US. No doubt they would want similar, favourable agreements."

"Not my job," Alex said, with some relief. On to security matters: "We have one more cadaver."

Silence.

Ambrose, suddenly filled, dumped the cake in a nearby bin. A man – *Secret Service?* – turned at the noise and stared at the foreign diplomat. Ambrose needed more privacy. Feigning the need to take a leak he followed an array of bilingual signs which measured the distance to *Los baños* every few feet. *America was the land of signs*, he thought, as he locked himself in the single compartment unit: an exquisite room, deodorised with aerosol tangerine. "Okay," the prime minister said, "I'm back." He leaned against the sink.

Alex described the crime scene, flipping through photographs as he spoke. The beaten woman had been stripped and her body lay contorted in the white sedan. Once trapped by her neck she had been brutally sodomised then killed. Or vice versa. *There were sick people out there*, the MONS thought.

*What the heck is going on at home?* "Any leads?"

"Robert, the fellow with CISTU, thinks it's drug related. He's managed to unearth some semen samples and fingerprints which might have been useful had Kathy's CARICOM team implemented the Automated Fingerprint Identification System (AFIS) which Mark Lloyd spent a crown and a pound on from Japan; a system which his administration failed to make operational. We're going to end in a bind if we keep these bloody, excuse the pun, fingerprints stored without lexicographic order at our police stations."

Ambrose calmed his MONS. "I'll talk to Kathy," he promised. "It's a new system but she knows it is priority. Anything else?"

"Robert found a cellular phone in the car, but it has been swiped clean of contacts," Alex announced. "We checked the phone company. We are on to a yachtie, guy by the name of Lewis Clark. The boatyard confirmed he left for Grenada. Customs verified. I'm guessing he gave the phone away before he left. Additionally, the registration plates were removed from the vehicle."

Ambrose scratched the back of his head. "Why the care in removing these items?"

"This isn't any average homicide, rape or robbery. Whoever did this wanted to make sure we took a long time to determine Miss Doe's identity."

"And the media? What's their take?" *The Tabloid* never ceased to worry Ambrose.

"Same old grumbling from Lance Jones," Alex scoffed. "The story broke at 0400 hours Trinidad time, a leak we're investigating." In summer, Washington observed Eastern

Daylight Time which meant clocks were in sync with the island, but mid-January qualified as winter and Eastern Standard Time placed the US one hour behind. The MONS glanced at the headline: '*Put Your House In Order.*' The article, written by Jones, launched a brutal attack on the prime minister. Alex didn't mention the article; they would deal with that when Ambrose returned tomorrow.

"Okay, fine," Ambrose said. "Be sure to follow up with Grenada's Customs."

"We've been trying for the past two hours," Alex said hastily. "I'm guessing their phones are still whacked." Six months ago Hurricane Marvin had distressed the island's infrastructure.

"Okay, Alex, I've got to go. We'll be in touch." The call ended and the prime minister exited the washroom. On his way back the dessert line was empty, but his sweet tooth desire had vanished.

In the conference room he met Admiral Ivan Lewis and they chatted about effective crime management in the Caribbean. Later, Lewis would be speaking on the topic, immediately after the US Secretary of Defence. Good luck, Ambrose wished, wondering if in the Admiral's presentation he would allude to Jamaica's black operations.

THE TREES in the orchard were void of grapefruits and oranges, but planted so close together that moisture remained trapped, cooling the men huddled together, engaged in a heated discussion. The earth was littered with leaves, different shades of green and brown mixed with yellow in some areas. Rays of sunlight filtered through the foliage casting a setting similar to the one seen in motivational Christian art. The bitter smell of citrus was prominent and tantalisingly refreshing.

Each member of the group glanced occasionally at Shiny who sat, his back to a tree, his head toppled onto his chest as if drunk. There was no need for him to be tied, his legs being broken in three places, but he was. He was a tough fellow, hard – 'like a common fowl,' Raj acknowledged

– more brute than human, more abominable than the snowman.

Navin indicated The Boss' arrival.

Bharat came on a Four Wheeler. He was dressed in an expensive grey suit – Amrit didn't miss that it was new and stopped shy of his ankles and wrists.

To Ricky Lo the man looked like ten million bucks.

Bharat never glanced at the incapacitated Shiny as he approached the group. He retrieved a cigarette from his jacket and Ricky gave fire to it.

Lucky spoke for the group: "Boss, big shootout last night. Is Syrians you know!" He looked bothered.

Bharat looked unfazed.

Ricky Lo supported: "Yes Manager, three of them dead but that one by the tree there–" he pointed– "that bastard have fire in him. But if you see *coke eh* man. The wheel touching the ground." Pausing for breath, Ricky outstretched his hand and boasted, "Look, Boss, I even take a bullet for you."

"That is a scratch boy!" Bharat exclaimed impatiently. "*An* where the product?"

It was Raj who spoke: "In the shed. We transfer the goods and dump *The Transporter* in the Caroni River." He answered the next obvious question: "Mouse guarding the shed."

"That is damn good work!" A rare compliment from The Boss. The men's brief smiles ceased when Bharat nodded at Shiny. "What he doing here?" *Why the ass he not dead*? his face depicted.

A stillness overcame the group and The Manager fingered the inside of his shirt collar, as if the tie was strangling him.

Ricky Lo, Raj and Amrit fidgeted uncomfortably. Navin looked steadily into Bharat's shades. Lucky grinned.

"Is he who shoot me," Ricky explained. "That Syrian bad like crab."

"That is nothing!" Bharat exclaimed.

A voice hollered from along the trail The Manager had just travelled.

Ricky's hand dipped to his waist but Raj stalled him. "Relax, that is the *fellah* from Icacos. Mouse partner *nah*! I forget he name yes. He have something for you, *ent* Boss?"

Icepick came into view and seeing the gun-toting group, was reluctant to approach. His whizzing eyes found the unconscious man. He turned to leave, rolling his hands over his head like a gun barrel, implying that the men should meet him when finished.

The Boss beckoned. He threw his hand around the newcomer and in machine gun dialect concocted a story: the Syrian had attempted to violate Bharat's niece.

Icepick was not convinced. His face didn't say it, but his voice revealed his doubt. The story had too many holes. He pointed at the slumped body: "Mr. B, a white man try that stunt? And all you sure he not dead?"

"So what, white people don't rape?" Bharat retorted. "You is *ah* ass or *ah* marble?"

Icepick swung his arm in a wide arc which began at Raj. "Well, why he not dead yet? If I was all you he done dead!" he declared. The semi-circle ended at Navin.

Chandra Bharat smiled. Icepick was falling nicely into the trap. He grappled the visitor closer, careful not to stain his sleeve on Icepick's oiled hair, and walked away from the group. When The Manager spoke his voice was low and dangerous. "Icepick, this man threatens the foundation of we organisation. I not asking you, I telling you: this man *have* to dead!!"

Icepick felt Mr. Bharat's grip tighten and suddenly he understood. "Wait, you want *me* to kill him?"

"Yes, Sunil, I want *you* to kill him."

Icepick looked over his shoulder. The gang was smiling. He said: "Boss, I is no killer. Transport work is my thing."

Bharat, anticipating refusal, reminded Icepick of his declaration. "Do this and I know *we* is friend," he said convincingly. "How else *we* could trust each other?"

Icepick wanted to disappear, to awaken from the nightmare, but it was day. He had sniffed the bait, bitten, and caught in the hook there was no escape. Poor timing had walked him straight into an execution. He had brayed and now his saltiness was being tested. There had to be a way out, but he saw none.

The threatening whip-like crack of a nine millimetre being loaded scattered Icepick's thoughts. Bharat shoved a Smith and Wesson into his hands. The gun was cocked, the safety disengaged, The Manager cautioned.

Icepick faced the intended victim, lifted the weapon and after a trembling minute, squeezed the trigger. The orchard went silent. Icepick opened his eyes. His shot had gone wide of the nameless man staring at him.

Icepick looked around and saw Navin's weapon trained on him. Bharat's lieutenant nodded in the direction of the intended victim. *Finish the job or join him*, his face warned.

Shuddering like an old woman, Icepick stepped closer to the Syrian. He wondered: *are there enough bullets to shoot all these bad men? No.* He also knew he wasn't handy with a gun. He stooped, inserted the weapon into the man's mouth – Shiny was his name, Bharat had said – and with the bawl of a madman he squeezed the trigger. The deed was done.

Bharat patted the *killer's* shoulder. "Good boy, Icepick… good boy."

The murderer looked up. A fat cigar rolled around The Boss' mouth. Icepick sprinted away. He needed to escape. He needed a drink. He needed Glen.

"Feed the Syrian to the pigs," Bharat ordered.

The subordinates began working on the body. The job was simpler once Shiny was in pieces.

MOUSE, WHO had been waiting patiently, swung open the doors of the van when Bharat appeared. Cocaine packages were stacked neatly, like salt parcels in a grocery.

*Unbelievable*, Bharat thought. He removed his shades then opened his eyes. The packages had not disappeared. *Impossible*. He laughed, hugged Mouse, then struck his driver hard on the shoulder.

Mouse flinched at the pressure of his boss' fingers digging into his flesh. The Manager was a rough man who had a strange way of displaying his pleasure. Mouse managed a laugh, a nervous chuckle of pain and fear.

Bharat couldn't believe it. The sight was mind boggling. For years he had avoided the white powder choosing instead to *deal* marijuana. He now had enough cocaine to comfortably supply all the *pipers* in Trinidad. Bharat's eyes grew wide; he saw what was his and suddenly became greedy to *own* more. "Where the guns and ammo? Where the US dollars the woman talk about? *¿Dónde están? ¿Dónde están?*" Bharat addressed Mouse. "And all this damn blood on the packages! All *yuh* could have clean that!" Bharat scowled. He donned his shades and looked at his driver.

"I don't know, Boss. Is only powder them boy find. That is Ricky and the Syrian own," he said, indicating the blood.

"*Dem* bastard blood thick boy!" Bharat looked around the shed. "I have to find somewhere to hide all this."

The men entered the shed. Lucky, a bloody mess, was in the lead.

"Boss, real cocaine *eh!*" Ricky exclaimed, approaching The Boss, expecting a high five.

Bharat scowled at the Rasta's bloodstained hand. "Lucky, where the *jail* we going to put all this cocaine? All this thing here could get all *you* kill."

"Why you don't use one of your other property?" Raj asked.

"What, and have somebody rob me?" Bharat said angrily. "This thing have to stay close to me. It cannot go too far."

"Well, dig some hole and hide it in the ground," Ricky suggested.

"The cocaine will get wet you damn fool," Bharat chided. "You know what moisture does do to drugs?"

"No Boss."

"*¿Por qué no te callas?*"

The Rastafarian shut up.

"All you understand how big this thing is, right?" Bharat asked. He did as if to remove his shades, but stopped. "If any word get out all *yuh* dogs dead!"

All nodded emphatically. After working together for nine years, experience had taught them the value of silence. Bharat was good to them. Squealing on a heavy, satisfied stomach was difficult, unlikely. The concept worked with these thugs.

"We safe," Raj said for all.

Navin nodded.

"Okay, good!" Bharat became more serious: "This–" *robbery wasn't suitable–* "reallocation of product going to cause a tidal wave in we world, the underworld *nah*. We have to keep it low. Real low." They would wait and when the time came they would push out the drugs internationally via contacts in the airport. To do otherwise would be hazardous. Bharat The Shrewd thought: *the right time would come!*

"I have an idea," Lucky said. "I know where *you* can hide it."

Where? Bharat enquired and the grinning man explained.

Later that night, on the quiet compound, the group would hide the cocaine packages, under the disapproving eye of an angry god.

ROBERT MARCO saw the reflection of light on metal on his fifth journey along the stretch leading to the golf course, a road still littered with paper cups and beer bottles. He stopped the vehicle and walked to the edge of the road. There he found it: the twisted frame of a bicycle lying in the bushes, its handles bent and pointing away from the golf course. He kept instinct at bay, but the skid marks alongside the bike did seem suspicious.

The CISTU detective retrieved his gear and photographed the scene. Later, the tyre marks would be compared to those of Jane Doe's car. With gloved hands he placed the twisted frame of the mountain bike into the Ford's tray. More photographs of the scene ensued. As he secured the potential evidence he noticed blood smears along the bicycle's top tube. Robert grimaced. Coincidence was a myth. He swabbed the evidence then drove east to the forensic lab.

SEAN ANSWERED the telephone on its first ring. "Hello goodnight," he said, and chuckled at the oddity: most Trinidadians incorrectly greet with 'goodnight.'

"Hi, it's me." It was Leah's raspy voice. She had picked up a lousy flu earlier in the day. "Are you busy?"

"No, no. I'm not," Sean lied.

"I can hear your keyboard."

"Nothing I can't handle," Sean said quickly. "Our contractor came down on us today. Apparently they're in a rush for the application."

"What do you do exactly?" Leah asked, her influenza disguising the caution in her voice. She didn't want to appear forward. It was her first phone call to him since he had sprawled his number across a coffee cup the day after they first spoke. She had thought it a smooth move, almost as sleek as with the French Vanilla. She had wondered whether or not he was a *player*.

"I'm working on a software application for the government. The idea is to have a centralised database system and pluggable modules which the health, police and other sectors can hook into."

The girl on the line coughed but not because she was impressed. "That's cool." Leah was more confused than enlightened. "So they contract that work out? Isn't that sensitive data?"

"If I tell you I'd have to kill you," Sean said with a British accent. "Our team... three of us... is designing the schema and the GUI. We don't touch live data."

Leah changed the topic. "Do you actually study at the university then?"

"I'm employed with a private firm. We bid on government projects and so have access to the best facilities in the world," he said with a grunt.

Leah detected the sarcasm and laughed; a dry, painful sound. "You're smarter than you look."

They laughed.

Leah was amused. She thought: *we suit each other*. She was a pacified child clasping a bottle; Sean, warm milk.

It seemed they had known each other for ages. "My birthday is in two days," she said abruptly.

Silence.

Leah enquired into the hollowness of her bedroom telephone.

"I'm here." Sean was wondering if he should go out on a limb and ask her out. He hated doing that; there was the possibility of rejection. True, there was a potential reward, but with *potential* there was room for failure. He decided to play it safe. "So what are *your* plans?"

Leah wasn't sure. Earlier her dad, furious as a cornered dog, lectured her on her recent splurges of late coming. His word was final. "Maybe my family is planning a surprise," she said. "I don't know... I guess I'll just be at home."

"So you mean I won't be seeing you?" Sean asked, sounding disappointed without meaning to.

More silence.

"Would you like to, Sean?"

Sean thought Leah sounded indifferent. Maybe she played the same game. Maybe it was worth a try. "I go real like that," he said, lapsing into dialect he had avoided since the conversation began.

Leah was relieved. It didn't seem right for a girl to ask a guy out, especially on her birthday.

"I'll tell my dad I have tutorials to attend," she whispered. "We will have to meet early in the day." She paused then admitted: "I've never lied to my parents, Sean." A nervous laugh.

He joked – it included the word 'virginity.'

She pursed her lips and giggled. What a silly boy he was. Talk turned to petty chit-chat about music, flowers, movies and places. She detected each time Sean attempted to sound her on her birthday wishes. She revealed nothing. Finally, after a string of goodbyes, Leah hung up without telling Sean how she had known his name.

Alone in the darkness she wondered: *is there another girl? There must be!* In the wee hours of the morning, she fell asleep.

## 10   Sean Brown and Bharat


BHARAT TOLD himself he wasn't annoyed, he was *damn mad*. He got into the car cursing. "Take me for a drive!" he ordered Mouse. "I *hadda* cool off."

Mouse swung out of Boodoo Lane and drove a short distance to the highway. He thought: *a drive to the Santa Rosa Race Track would make The Boss more better*. He drove north while Bharat grumbled in the backseat. The traffic flowed lightly until they caught a red light at a busy intersection. Bharat swore. The driver scanned The Manager in the rearview mirror, not quite appreciating what it was about Ravi Boodoo that ticked Bharat off. A car horn shrieked. *Blast it*, Mouse thought. He hadn't seen the green light. He felt Bharat's hand on his shoulder.

"Wait!" The Boss told him, "*doh* drive off as yet."


THE PRINCESS Margaret Highway was constructed in '58. After its extension in '88 it was renamed in honour of the Grenada-born labour leader, Tubal Uriah 'Buzz' Butler. The road, which intersects Churchill-Roosevelt Highway, is infamous for its twenty-four-hour traffic and is relentlessly notorious for accidents when drivers challenge red and amber signals.

Sean was usually a patient motorist, but he had been waiting long. When the car behind honked, he fisted the steering wheel repeatedly, the horn tooting like an annoying time bomb.

The back door of the executive car ahead opened and a splendidly attired occupant strode across, with laconic indifference to the jeering horns and curses around. He wore a grey suit and dark shades which cast him as a comical mafia boss from a Bollywood remake. He bent over, staring into the car at the couple.

Sean saw the gun and felt the coldness of its steel. Fear crippled him. Leah breathed heavily, her throat all knotted. Sean heard the hammer cock and saw the cylinder revolve and align with the barrel.

"What the ass you only blowing *yuh* horn for?" the man asked slowly. His voice was rough, like a grater's body, his breath stink of tobacco.

Sean opened his mouth on the man's orders and the gun was roughly stuck past his teeth. The gun smelled used; the odour, acrid gunpowder. There was a warmth between his legs and cross-eyed he looked up the barrel. Sean wanted to cough but the man's finger was precariously close to the trigger.

The gun was still in Sean's mouth when Bharat spoke: "You want six of this in *yuh* ass? Learn to wait! Okay?"

Sean nodded cautiously.

"I not hearing you, boy!"

"Yes. Yes. Yes!" Sean said awkwardly. The gun choked his answer.

"You see this face?" Bharat said. "Don't forget it." He tilted his shades. "Don't ever screw up again."

Sean shook his head violently. He was good with faces. He wouldn't forget.

The man in the grey suit and dark shades walked away.

The light was red once again.

Fumbling, Sean raised the power windows, feeling like a fool for not doing so earlier. But the man might have blown the windows away. He looked crazy enough.

Sean looked at Leah, frozen like a popsicle. Not knowing what to say, he placed his hand on her leg and rubbed it. She blinked at him then turned her blank gaze to the car ahead. Sean stared with her, hoping she hadn't noticed the tiny spot of liquid fear on his crotch.

Five minutes later the light turned green. Sean waited nervously. He thought: *you never know who's who*. He had heard his dad say it and when the executive car screeched off, he lingered. The light turned red. *To heck with the honkers*, he thought, hoping another Bollywood gangster was not behind.

The drive to the university was painful. Leah's birthday had been foiled and there was nothing he could do to rectify that. He should have settled for *doubles* only. She had enjoyed the delicacy immensely. She even laughed about having it for the first time, a virginity joke which was peculiar coming from her.

Sean had wanted to outdo himself. She had professed her love for nature and, unwisely, as he realised now, he had decided to take her to the Temple in the Sea. She had fun. She loved the place. She had never been there. If he hadn't done that they would not have been by the Uriah Butler Highway. The incident would not have occurred. *How was I to know*? Sean wondered about the emotional meter: the additive effect of fun times and the subtractive nature of fear. *A day of fun plus two minutes of panic and he was in the negative.*

Cautiously, Sean pulled into the university's carpark. They sat in silence. Leah stared elsewhere while he propped himself against the driver's door and gauged her.

Leah felt unsure, unsafe, even in his presence.

Sean checked his watch. Twenty-five minutes ago they had been laughing, talking, smiling. Now they sat, uncertain of what to say.

Time elapsed.

"What the *jail* is this boy?" Sean said finally.

Leah had never heard the expression and, hesitantly, she asked what it meant. He explained. She saw his noble attempt to win back her jovial mood but she didn't have the heart to succumb. Rather, she had to leave. *I must*, she convinced herself, and in a strained manner departed from

Sean, not with a peck on the cheek, but with an awkward handshake which she erased on her jeans skirt.

There would be no birthday party for her that night. Everyone would be glum. Not even the memory of the majestic temple in Waterloo, basking in a bleeding sunset, would calm her troubled spirit. Tears would flow. Her pillows would become wet. Her spirit would not be cheered by photographs of Sean and herself. Instead, Leah would worry that her father would learn about the altercation.

## 11  I love you not

A LIGHT comes on and inside the Charged Coupled Device a sensor system (similar to that found in digital cameras) uses light sensitive diodes to generate an electric signal of the thumb. The machine then compares specific features of the fingerprint (known to professionals as 'minutiae') to data stored on file. Finding a significant number of pattern matches, it allows the Syrian entry to his basement office. The entire process takes milliseconds.

Aram collapsed into an executive chair behind an ornate glass desk. The effect of a disturbance in the drug trade was similar to a rock being violently tossed into a stream. In the military, crap flows down the ranks, as it is expected to, but Aram Hamad felt as if he had nostrils on his feet, fingertips and head.

Paul Headley wasn't proving to be as effective as Gregory had suggested. Aram understood that gathering information took time, but *none* of his extravagantly paid arms and legs yielded results. Not one. Though the Syrian objected, Paul acted as a buffer and executed commands on request. Aram, however, was cautious.

On the desk was a Secure Terminal Equipment (STE). The device looks like a high-end office telephone, but when a KSV-21 Enhanced Crypto Card is inserted into a special slot, encrypted calls can be made to identical sets, using speeds of up to 128 kbps, which the Integrated Services Digital Network (ISDN) allows. The STE is the latest technology for secure fax and telephone communications used by the US Federal Government and Aram had one in his office; so did Paul Headley.

"Any word?" a synthesised voice asked when a secure connection was established.

"None yet," Paul replied, wondering if his voice also sounded like something from a science fiction flick. "I've made contact with my people. We have listening ears out there." It was true. Paul had links in the underworld, the police service and the media. The word was out, but none came in.

"And the importers? Anything?"

No luck, Paul reported. He would make connections, he promised, having little more to offer. Patience was the game yet he knew that time wasn't on the Syrian's side. The cocaine shipment should have arrived in Puerto Rico today, where it was guaranteed secure passage through the container x-ray scanners.

"If you hear anything let me know," a faltering robotic voice said.

Paul guaranteed. The call ended and he removed the KV-21 Enhanced Crypto Card.

From his basement office, Aram made a further secure call, an overseas to South America.

THE VIOLENT sunset by the seaside, candlelight dinner completed, and his date in a crimson dress, made the moment seem right.

"I love you," Sean whispered. His eyes said it also.

Leah shifted uncomfortably and looked around the restaurant. They were in a popular seafood joint in Chaguaramas, where the food was rumoured to be the best. Today, the shrimp and fries tasted strange – like custard. *Was it butterflies?* She whispered his name, sighed and looked away. Words failed. *This is wrong.* They had not known each other long. *Why then does it feel the only other way it could*?

He leaned forward until his elbows rested on the edge of the table. "It isn't as you say. It's how I feel about you. I'm not

120

patronising you." It had been two days since their encounter with the Bollywood menace and they had decided that the subject remain closed. Sean signalled for Leah's hands and after a moment's hesitation, she locked fingers with his as lovers do. Sean was relieved.

Her hands were cold; they shook violently, not from fear, but custard. Leah tilted her head, her curls twisting to the right. "Sean, I'm sorry."

He tugged his hands away and drooped in his chair like a dejected sportsman, a sore loser. His fear had materialised and shattered his ego in moments.

"How can you love me, Sean?" she asked, hoping he would tell her, but wishing he wouldn't. "Why would you?"

Sean sat up abruptly as if shocked. "Why would I not, Leah?"

It was the way he said 'Leah.' That custard taste again.

He paused to wave at a couple and a dog passing on a sailboat just off the jetty, "Strange how tourists always wave *eh*?"

Leah implored him to continue; the way he was often distracted aggravated her. When Sean explained his love for her, she huffed and pushed her unfinished fries and shrimp away – she had heard the same ballad from Adam.

Sean finished her food.

She smiled. She liked him for that. He had no shame, sometimes no class, yet he could be the perfect gentleman. *Strange.* She wondered what her father would think. Leah relaxed and when Janel, their waitress, returned for the tenth time they both refused her hospitality. Leah thought Sean flirted a bit, but couldn't be sure. It was difficult to tell. *Strange.* They sat in silence, watching the waitress attend to the thickening crowd of diners. When Janel returned, the plates and glasses vanished in one swift, skilful motion.

"Why should I trust you, Sean?" Leah asked. "What makes you different?"

"Because if you don't we'd probably miss out on something great." Sean placed his napkin on the table to hide the cloth, soiled from his eating. "I'm no different to other guys. No one says that I'm the one for you."

Leah was confused. *He's good.* "Then why would I even consider being with you?"

"We never will know for sure, Leah." He pointed at her as if about to make an accusation, but his voice was calm: "Have you ever had a boyfriend?"

"Of course!" Leah exclaimed, laughing. "Two and a half."

"Have you been with a midget?"

They laughed

"No you *imp*. You didn't *catch* it."

Sean laughed. Then she laughed at his laugh, scandalous enough to turn the heads of other patrons. She behaved as if ashamed of him. He roared. Suddenly he became serious and without a smile corrected her, as a passionate teacher does a promising student: the word was '*imps*', even when referring to someone in the singular. Secretly, Sean felt that he and Leah were close to achieving a common realisation of emotion, but still he threaded cautiously, like a city dweller would when walking in wild, impenetrable jungle. It was time to tell her: "In the end we will have only one true boyfriend or girlfriend." When she gave a questioning shrug he said to her with a soft smile, "The one we end up with forever and ever."

Leah tasted custard the entire drive back to the university where she left Sean, not wanting to, and without revealing how she truly felt. *What the jail going on boy?* she wondered, as she pulled out of the university, giggling at the phrase. *At least we could laugh now*, she thought, as she sped west, hoping that no one was yet at home. She prepared her lie. She would tell her father – or family – that a tutorial session had run late. *They could be such imps.* She scolded herself. She had learnt that an *imp* wasn't a goblin or an elf, but a person who qualified as a grand idiot. She sighed. *Was it 'impses' for two or more?* Leah wasn't sure. She would have to ask, then changed her mind and dialled Sean's mobile phone.

## 12  The confessional

GLEN AWOKE with a brutal hangover, one that churned his stomach, spiralled up his spine, stopped at the nape, and throbbed. The alarm clock − his stepfather's − had failed him again. He was late for confession. In a flash − or so he thought − he straightened the room, dressed and minutes later the African/ East Indian (*dougla*) stumbled to church.

When he arrived, a large crowd had gathered. Glen hated being among country folk; someone always had something *wise* to say. His faith however did not allow him to turn away. He met *Bat* first, a jet-black fellow with long arms and unusually large ears. The only other name he answered to was *Battyman*.

"Glen, boy, you hear the latest? Sonnie get kill in Tucupita," Bat said. He had first heard the news from an excitable *Rat*. "Like he owe them *Spanish* them real money and they pass him out yes."

Beyond the crowd, inside the church, Glen heard wailing, a low mournful sound which died into sputters.

"That is Shirley," Bat reported unnecessarily. "Poor woman, she taking it real hard *eh*? I mean that is she only child and thing, *eh* boy." He looked at Glen and thought: *what an unexcitable ass*. In the distance he saw Lily approaching. Battyman left without excusing himself.

Glen lurked on the edge of the crowd for ten minutes then decided that today he wouldn't be attending confession. It had been ritual for the past six years, without fail, on the last Saturday of every month. There was no Hindu temple in Icacos and Glen's shyness denied him the pleasure of travelling twelve miles to the nearest temple. Walking was no longer in the equation; he tried it once and reaped blisters as big as Fat Pork.

He thought the crowd to be faithless. It was the nature of the countryside: boredom. simple trade. simple lives. *Fishing? Husking coconuts? Ha! Emptiness! Church? What is that? Rum and sex? Bring thing!* Country folks wanted the tangible, something with substance, something they could see and believe in. Something they could wrap their fingers around, a woman or a bottle of rum. Excitement that infected their minds and delivered good and bad times, at the end of a hard week's labour. Boredom was the reason for hordes of naked children who wandered the dirt roads aimlessly, like stray cattle searching for good grass. Glen *steupsed*.

He thought: *I am different*. He knew it. Silently, he began walking home, away from the senseless commotion that was death. Briefly, he thought of his father, but he erected a wall which deflected the memory. Yet the memories persisted and the wall disappeared.

Glen had been the sole child. God had seen it necessary to reclaim his father – the Catholic priest had said so and *he is a smart man*. He had exposed Glen to more sensible teachings than the Hinduism his mother had practised. Glen had seen his father's passing as unnecessary, but he had been a boy then. He was grown now, he thought, more connected to the world in his subtle way – able to connect the dots.

Minutes later he was back at home, in a clean bed which embraced him. He thought of his mother. She had always wanted the best for him. She had tried to replace his father with a sober individual who evolved into a drinking man. Glen had shied away from the bottle, choosing instead to daily disconnect himself from his mother's affairs.

He could not accept the term 'stepfather.' In primary school the tease – *'Yuh mammy like plenty man'* – offended him and as a young man it made him morose and angry;

bitter toward society and country folk. In the country a man was a stud – or *ram goat* – if he slept with countless women. A widow was expected to mourn for the rest of her days, not remarry.

Glen tossed in bed. He was stale drunk and weary, but couldn't sleep. He needed to confess. He thought of *Rabbit*, the man who died without an heir, without being called 'father.' Glen had been beaten soundly by his stepfather to utter the word. Rabbit's dutiful common law wife eventually joined the fray. Blow-after-blow, time-after-time didn't help. *What else was a child who had just lost his father expected to do?* It was wiser to say nothing. Having one bedroom had made things worse.

Glen's faith had weakened. Hinduism held little appeal. His father, mother and Rabbit were cremated. Glen preferred burial. The promise of the resurrection which the priest – with his peculiar accent – spoke of seemed more credible. Still there was conflict. Glen had placed the picture of the dying Messiah on the left of his home's entrance, but did not remove the picture of Lord Shiva which his father had nailed to the wall years ago. It was a struggle Father Dugan knew nothing of; the priest knew other stories.

Glen drifted into a troubled sleep. He dreamt he was eight years old, at sea with his father. They had fished all night and caught nothing. A man soared down from the heavens. He had giant wings and a round blue face which belonged to a child. His voice was loud, commanding as the ocean which swayed the small boat. In one hand he held a bow, in the other, a sword. He told them to fish, and they would reel in a whale and Glen's father, despite his son's pleas, cast the net into the water. When the man flew off, the sea became agitated. The boat rocked violently: Glen's father had caught the whale. Suddenly, the net burst and the boat tipped over.

Glen awoke gasping, drenched in sweat. He coated the sponge mattress in clean linen but ignored himself. He entered the gallery and looked southwest where the sun was falling like a giant, metal ball into the depths of the ocean. The sky was deep red. *Had Sonnie's blood been that colour?*

In the foreground, people were gathered at Shirley's residence. In Icacos, deaths were more celebrated than weddings and definitely more recognised than new-born babies. Glen *steupsed.* Weddings lasted a day: only one good serving of food and rum. A wake on the other hand could go on for days, especially if friends and family were expected from abroad. Glen laughed.

He had been surprised when he learnt that Sonnie was an only child; *Reshma must be they niece. And Sonnie was so unlike me?* A drug mule, womaniser and most likely a cocaine user, Glen thought. *He had the look.* It was sad, the boy's mother being such a pleasant woman, a key figure in Icacos' history: school teacher for decades, principal for years. *Icepick was right, Sonnie was a fool. He mother nice, but he was ah idiot.*

Glen perched on a stool and watched the activity. He could see Bat arguing with another man – it looked like Rambo – regarding the depth of a hole in which bamboo would be placed to support a shed to cover the midnight card-playing, coffee-drinking and random bursts of wailing. Glen thought of his father. He thought about the slender limbs of bamboo expected to bear the weight of the galvanise sheets. He compared the pillars to the support of the risen Christ and smiled at the simile. His perceived spiritual growth thrilled him. He thought of Father Dugan. *Speak of the devil.* The priest was walking down the lane to Glen's residence. *What he doing here?*

Glen looked at the picture of Lord Shiva then at Dugan. The priest drew closer. Another quick look. Dugan waved and stopped to admire the static beauty of the periwinkles. Glen jumped up and removed both photographs. He stacked them together and after some darting around on the creaking, wooden floors he hid them under the mattress.

The priest was standing outside the gallery when Glen returned. "Father, what you doing here?" His tone was like a beatific parent encountering his innocent son at a gentleman's club.

126

Glen's tone didn't dampen the priest's spirit. "How are you?" After the softening of vowels and hardening of consonants associated with the Irish accent, the greeting sounded: *Ha-ware-ya*? "My son," he said delicately, noticing Glen's facial twitch, "I missed you at confession."

Glen paused. He fidgeted. He stuttered.

"My child, a priest is never too busy to conduct the Lord's work. Death–" he waved at the commotion yonder– "an unpredictable event, much like our lives, but something we must all face." The plump, baldheaded Irishman looked at the budding Catholic standing in the gallery. "Are you prepared for death, Glen? For it would come like a thief in the night."

Glen thought of the money hidden inside the slits of his sponge mattress. He thought of the pictures beneath the bed. He had placed them facing each other. He fidgeted and scolded himself for the waves of profanity which invaded his thoughts. The priest looked up at him and Glen felt like the rich man in hell. Shyly, he invited the priest in, pondering whether the floor could bear the hefty man's weight.

"My legs," the Irishman said, patting his stomach rather than his thighs, "Arthritis has gotten the better of an old man's joints. I cannot step so high."

Glen nodded. He sat on the stool he had consumed rum on the night before.

"So?" the priest enquired.

"I not comfortable here Mr..... Father Dugan." Glen couldn't confess to the priest eye-to-eye. With deep shame he admitted this.

After a very slow walk – the priest's pace coupled with the impression he seemed to know everyone – the Trinidadian and the Irishman were engulfed in the darkness of the confessional, a crudely built booth within the entrance of the church. To enter, the priest and the penitent slipped past black, floor length curtains. Inside, they were separated by a sheet of varnished ply.

Glen slid to a diagonal kneeler and clasped his hands. He shut his eyes tight and envisioned his connection to heaven. With rocking effort a screen was pulled back and the repentant could see the shadow of the lattice imposed on the priest's round head. A crucifix hung against the grill, shifting with each breath in the confined space. A short candle burnt in the priest's compartment, its flame licking high for the oxygen above the open booth. There was enough darkness, a shroud of anonymity Glen enjoyed, despite the compartment's musty odour, like that of a cupboard filled with dry, soiled clothes.

"Forgive me father for I have sinned," Glen whispered, like a child speaking to another in the presence of a stern headmaster.

Dugan cleared his throat. In the stillness the sound reverberated. "What have you done, my son?"

A long silence then Glen spoke, "Father, forgive me for I have killed a man." He opened his eyes and looked up, hoping to see the priest stir, but the Irishman didn't. Glen wasn't sure if it was the way the grill's shadow fell on his face, but it looked as if the man's eyes were closed. "I did not want to, but I was forced to do it else I was a *dead man walking*." The penitent paused. He expected the priest to speak. When he didn't, the sinner proceeded to give more gruesome details. In the confessional Glen felt alive, he could pour out his soul and no one would jeer. He could entrust his dreams, his fears, his ambitions to *this* father and be assured they would never be repeated to the outside world – the crude villagers.

Glen knew his life was not really exciting. A few months ago Dugan knew everything about him. But Glen began to claim Icepick's juicy stories and the confessional became vibrant.

Dugan's eyes weren't closed. They were wide open yet his voice carried the same low monotone: "And how do you feel about this?" The candle's flame, fanned by his breath, danced.

"Guilty father! *Wha'happen?* Is why I here confessing it to you."

The Irishman shifted but not from the discomfort of the wooden stool. It was a worrisome confession. He had never, in forty-five years of service to the holy church, heard an admittance to murder. An older cardinal had once shared a similar experience but it had never been the Irishman's; a novel, troublesome issue. His mind turned to Sonnie, a promising adult whose future had been snapped from life's branch in an unfortunate incident.

"I will pray for you, Glen. Should your heart be earnest you will be forgiven." There was heavenly, then earthly rule. State law hinged on God's holy will. Crime and punishment were inseparable. "Do you plan to surrender to the local authorities?"

Glen stumbled off the diagonal kneeler. He steadied himself and pressed his lips against the grill. Father Dugan's face became darkened. "No father!" the repentant said in a coarse whisper, "You must not speak of this to anybody… Nobody at all!"

"Your confession is confidential," Father Dugan guaranteed.

"*Or haw.*" Glen retracted from the lattice.

"Man can only harm the body. If the holy father has forgiven you and you are prompted to do the right thing, do not fear for no harm will come to you, my child."

Glen was uncertain whether it was fear or anger he felt. His hands shook, his blinking increased. He doubted, but knew that the priest was bound by *some* law; the clergyman couldn't reveal secrets. Still, Glen was worried by the magnitude of his so-called revelations; he had borne false witness within the confessional. He felt himself grow calm, his fear subsiding.

He switched the topic to bales of marijuana which had come into Icacos airborne; this was a far lighter affair.

ONE OF the requirements – omitted from the prime minister's portfolio – was that a landline telephone would always be handy. Patricia had been adamant and it was removed from the room. They weren't used to the vice, she had told Ambrose flatly, and night was made for sleep. However she appreciated his role as the head of government and the need for his cellular phone to be handy, as long as its vibrations woke him only.

The cellular phone buzzed twice before he grabbed it. Ambrose hurried upstairs into the dimly lit office. 'Alex Peters' flashed rhythmically, on the digital display and the prime minister answered.

"Ambrose, we've got a shitty problem."

Obscenities; this had to be serious.

"We've got a cadaver in Port Fortin; a twenty-five-year-old male. Shot twice in the chest at point blank range."

The prime minister stiffened. Another murder. *Couldn't this have waited?* "What's special about it?"

Alex hesitated. "Sir, the incident occurred on Venezuelan soil."

Ambrose came wide awake.

Alex explained that the victim and two witnesses had left Icacos without clearing Customs, in what was described as a high-end pirogue; they got to Tucupita through the river mouth where the incident occurred. Alex didn't have all the details but suspected that it was a contraband operation. Drugs was a pretty good guess.

Ambrose massaged the knotted lines on his forehead. Citizens were playing Cowboys and Indians, making mad dashes across the border like Mexicans escaping the peanut plantations. Obviously people were unconcerned about the cold relations existing between Trinidad and Venezuela. A recent newspaper article had described the relationship as 'lukewarm' – as the few miles of water which separated both nations – over the island's refusal to join petrol initiatives set up by the South American socialist leader.

"Are the Venezuelan authorities aware of the incident?"

"Not that we know," Alex shrugged.

"Okay, we must utilise the appropriate diplomatic channels to alert them" Ambrose cautioned. "I'll have Alicia contact the Venezuelan Consulate. Their ambassador is fairly agreeable."

"Ambrose, about the school opening ceremony in Icacos," the MONS said. "Maybe you should cancel it. You know what these villages tend to be like during bereavement." He didn't say that there was an ugly mood regarding the PM.

"It depends," Ambrose said. "I'll have my secretary call the principal who is coordinating the event."

"Sir," Alex said sadly, and premonition told Ambrose it was Shirley's son who had been executed.

Speculation confirmed.

"I'll be keeping my appointment, Alex. Make sure it's on the day of the funeral. I'll be attending it." There was a hint of anger in his voice.

Ambrose had met Shirley once, a pleasant woman whose picture was often featured in the media. She was the leading force in the fight for a new school and improved public utilities. After a decade she had won, and on the eve of what was to be a jubilant ceremony, her Sonnie was killed. According to the press her teaching career spanned thirty-odd years. Shirley was the first citizen Ambrose had met who had suffered the death of a loved one by murder, and as he told Alex a weary goodbye, he was horrified to think: *very soon, everyone in Trinidad might know the family of someone who had been murdered.*

Despondently, Ambrose returned to the bedroom and slipped beneath sheets that had gone cold. Patricia was resting peacefully, but sleep escaped him. His anger welled. Nothing seemed to work. The police-army patrols were being heavily criticised by the press, the public appeals he made to curb violence went unheeded, and the Opposition was doing exactly that – opposing legislation in the interest of the people. *Maybe Alex is right*, he thought, *maybe the Jamaicans did have the right approach to gangsters*: grab the bastards by the nuts whenever they pimpled on society's sacred surface. *It is my duty to make the people smile again*, Ambrose swore. Patricia woke.

## 13  Paul Headley


PAUL HEADLEY, ex-security-guard-turned-gangster, knew scum who knew scum, but the trail had gone cold. The tall, baldheaded, African man who had the physique of a bodybuilder, had spent the last week hinting on a quantity of missing drugs. How much, he didn't say, but not a single contact in the underworld had a response. Not even the crooked cops. If they did, their lips were tightly pursed. Paul had hired and fired, bashed and bruised. He had sunk over a dozen heads into toilets and thrown five *bad eggs* off roofs; because of Paul three men had checked into Casualty with kneecaps blown-off. Still, no one had information.

Paul adjusted his jacket and walked the short pathway to a scorned home. He was in Central Trinidad and Frankie – the crook, the *piper*, the midget – who had sold everything except the blistered paint on the walls, was waiting. Paul refused the offered chair, more corroded than white.

Frankie's drug addiction added to his appalling figure, with its huge head and long arms which stretched past his knees, like the crooked extension of a modern excavator. Tight patches of black clumps stuck to his head like a scattered colony of ants. To Paul he looked like a gibbon, hardly human.

"What news you have for me, Frankie?" Paul removed a white kerchief and mopped sweat from his shining forehead.

"Not a damn thing!" The stout man had a booming voice that compensated for lack of height.

Paul swore. He had driven far to hear this; just this. He had been to BiteInn, a great way off and hadn't found Chip Rivers. His frustration showed.

"It have them Indian and them up the road from here," Frankie contributed. He lit the end of a cigarette. Exhaling, he continued: "But them *doh* do hard stuff, just *weed*. That is Mickey Samaroo and them." If they were doing cocaine Frankie would have known. "How much you say it was again?"

"Ten kilos," Paul said. He knew the hooked-nose midget saw through the white lie. *Conniving little bastard*. Druggies had a sixth sense. "Anybody else you could tell me about?"

Frankie shook his head. "But if I hear anything I will call you." He flicked the stub into the yard where it hung for a moment atop the bushes, then disappeared beneath the thick greenery. Frankie eyed the spot.

Paul turned to leave.

"Big man... handle me a five bucks?" Frankie preferred '*bucks*' to '*dollars.*' Somehow it made the amount seem less.

Paul gave the surprised beggar one hundred dollars and quickly left – the addict's abode was a depressing reminder of where he himself had lived as a child.

Aram's henchman had two more drug dens to visit in the area.

Frankie hobbled to Boodoo Lane as fast as his stumpy legs allowed. There, Ravi exchanged the blue note for marijuana, the buyer's substance of choice. Ravi didn't know anything about the missing cocaine. The weather conducive, the two men smoked in the shade of the mango tree.

One hour later, Frankie would point out Paul Headley to Ravi, when the tall man stopped to purchase Mrs. Boodoo's mangoes.

"IT'S POSITIVE," Ernie said, holding two hardcopies.

"The tyres and the hair samples?" Robert asked. They were in the conference room.

Ernie nodded. "Not just that. We have a pair of matching prints on the bike and car and it doesn't belong to the victim." He paused, like a priest about to tell an off-colour joke, then added: "Hair recovered off the bike exhibits the same microscopic characteristics as a *manicou*. Be on the lookout for a killer rodent." He gave Det. Marco the prints and left the room, disgust written on his face.

Robert scanned the results. Jane Doe's trail so far was brambly. As quickly as things turned up they were slashed and burnt. The bike had been rented, for the weekend, from a partially blind entrepreneur whose office was a wooden shed on the Chaguaramas coastline. He maintained no written records of his clients. Bike four, said the old man who wore bottle-thick lenses, had been rented by a caucasian female but he didn't know her name or address.

The glass doors swung open and CSI Frank Marshall stuck his head in and asked for Ernie. Robert pointed towards Serology and DNA.

Five minutes later, an annoyed Ernie returned. "You know what ticks me off?" the analyst asked. "We have all this evidence but nothing to compare it to. Our databases are active, waiting to be fed data... but out there," he said, his hands rotating, "there is no system to collect and share information. We have enough hair samples to go into the weave business and sufficient sperm to impregnate a nation. Yet, we have no corroborative link."

"Aren't they putting something in place?" Robert asked. He had heard something, but nothing solid.

Ernie scoffed. "Supposedly. I've seen the prototype. A web solution can't do squat for us except collect data and display tabulated results. Kathy Mills' ministry has outsourced the work to some hot shot firm, as far as I know. Hopefully, the system would be designed to facilitate integration with our software, else we would just be a modern evidence collection centre unable to crunch data."

"Well, let's keep our fingers crossed," Robert said, trying to broadcast hope he did not feel. "Any luck with Jane Doe's cellular?"

"Nothing," came the uninspired reply.

SEAN LOOKED up from his laptop at his father hacking away at his Staedtler, the type hammers cracking like a whip against the paper. *Ting!* A bell signalled the end of a line and his dad dragged the carriage return lever. He was good on the machine and one of few who still used the old-fashioned, finger-powered typewriter.

Sean helped himself to coffee from the stove and beckoned to his old man. Dad, who never looked up, wanted his coffee without sugar and black, the way he liked his women. Sean laughed. The man had a sense of humour. The software engineer passed the cup to a grateful hand and resumed his work. The coffee was strong, the way it should be when one has to work beyond midnight.

Sean's mood slipped. "I'm not even sure Leah likes me, dad."

"You're a desperate, hopeless boy, Sean. You're in love with a girl whose middle name you don't know." His father's tone was crucial yet kind and as coarse as the typewriter's metal slugs which struck the paper but left fine print. He removed his glasses and rested them on the table, pinching his nose to release work tension. "You fall in love too fast, young man," his father scolded. "You can't be my son." They laughed at the wisecrack.

"But, it feels right," the son replied, pleading weakly.

"Love isn't a feeling you can lay claim to in... what is it, a few weeks? It's something that is nurtured, built each day. Take your mother and I, that didn't just happen overnight."

"What you talking about? *Allyuh* get married in six months!" Sean retorted.

"Those times were different, son." He didn't want to get into the *then versus now* argument. He changed the topic, his tone gentler: "I'm not saying that you aren't in love, but maybe you need to be careful that you're not experiencing some magnificent, euphoric high that can cloud your judgment." He knew how the boy felt. He had been there before. He had experienced the heartache that fickle love brought. He had purchased it retail on numerous occasions. In matters of the heart there were unpredictable winds. The father didn't want to compound Sean's emotions. Times were different; a parent had to be a friend, anything else would result in rebellion. But Sean had already said to Leah 'I love you.' *What the heck is wrong with him*? Father waited for son. He was an impatient man, except for his children, but now, after midnight, his left foot pumped anxiously, like a jack hammer. He shook the empty cup at his son and got a refill.

Then, wordlessly, Sean returned to his work. His father watched him browsing the Internet or *whatever the heck he alone did or understood. Those damn computers; such nuisances and distractions*. The Staedtler resumed its banging.

## 14 The country funeral


WHEN THE prime minister is being escorted, the official state car is a *BMW X5 Security*. The armoured vehicle has 20 mm thick safety glass coated with polycarbonate that acts as splinter protection. The glass is reinforced and bullet resistant to a calibre of a .44 magnum travelling at 440 m/s. The vehicle's additional weight is compensated by an adapted shock and spring absorber and in the event of a blowout, by bullet or sharp object, the run-flat tyres guarantee that the vehicle can be driven – approximately – a further 50 km up to a maximum speed of 80 km/h, the speed Ambrose was being driven at.

The landscape glided by, but not fast enough for PM Taylor to miss the dry beauty of the land. In some places it looked like a prairie with giant lotus distributed over flat, brown terrain. Other than that, there were only coconut trees: tall trees, short trees, bent trees, needle-straight trees, greenish-yellowish trees, old trees, young trees, yellowish-greenish coconut trees.

They were two miles from Icacos. The four-car convoy had departed from the prime minister's residence before dawn and as they sped along the recently paved country road, already showing signs of deterioration, rays of sunlight peaked through the foliage to be embraced by the earth, damp with dew and glistening like shiny dust on a masquerader's costume.

Wayne, the driver, felt they could have been in the village at least twenty minutes ago, if not for the cows which patrolled the roads. Was the vehicle cow-proof? he joked, as they entered the rural village, but Ambrose did not chuckle, not today. *Strange.*

Icacos was sombre. A day of celebration had been overturned by death. Villagers walked the road, heads bent, oblivious, unenthused by the prime ministerial convoy. The loss was evident, bereavement a wet heavy cloak.

The convoy crawled past the rainbow-coloured government primary school, decorated in vain anticipation of the prime minister's visit, and continued along the shoddy road until it came to a wooden church, its front steps almost arm's length from the pavement. Villagers had gathered en masse, many decked in their best funereal clothes. Stragglers gave way for vehicles to park.

Ambrose, not waiting on his driver, exited the armoured van, ironed out the front of his suit with his hands and stepped briskly towards the old building, equipped with a retired-looking tenor bell. The crowd blocking the double-door entrance parted swiftly, reminding Ambrose of sardines scattering when a pebble is tossed into a stream. The PM exchanged handshakes. A drunkard began cursing and he was hustled away.

Unpainted pews and a mournful congregation greeted Ambrose. The air was stale and as he moved up the aisle, he was conscious of frowns and checkered smiles that followed.

The congregation eased into comments. 'Shirley really know big boys,' someone remarked.

Ambrose felt pained as he approached the grieving family. *I have failed honest citizens.* A seat was reserved for him in the first row next to Shirley, dressed in white, the colour of purity, of hope. Ambrose guessed that the man – he looked like a pugilist – seated in the same pew was her husband. Shirley looked old, more fragile than Ambrose could recall. She had the same wise face, a principal's trademark, but looked as though an artist had drawn thick, bold lines into her forehead, channels of grief. Her eyes

138

were spider webs of red veins. *Boxer* – her husband who managed a choked introduction – attempted to be strong, but at the task he broke. Ambrose added his to the couple's clasped hands and audibly, they wept.

The deep sound of the tenor bell boomed, its sad toll echoing through the village, spawning fresh cries. The PM looked around. There was a priest, dressed in a black cope. He sprinkled holy water on the casket and muttered Latin intonations which the prime minister knew as the 50th Psalm, and another he couldn't recall. The coffin moved towards the altar. Some, their curiosity pricked by the proceedings, tiptoed for a clearer view as the pallbearers squeezed past wooden benches lined like dominoes.

The six men burdened with the casket stopped before the priest who, clasping the bible against his chest, directed proceedings. Had Sonnie been a layman, his feet would have been placed towards the altar. Fr. Dugan, an advocate of *traditional* Catholic doctrine, removed his cope and the service continued. Stimulated by the congregation's size – his biggest yet – and the presence of the prime minister, the priest pressed on, quoting from Thessalonians and the Gospels of Christ, stressing Martha's belief in the resurrection of her brother Lazarus, and the reunification of spirits.

How much the Christian word meant to the majority of Hindus present, was anybody's guess, but Ambrose was moved to tears.

In keeping with *traditional* Catholic funerals no eulogy and high praise were offered on Sonnie's behalf. Dugan was an advocate of the conviction that eulogies detracted from the Mass itself and were often seen as the centre of the liturgy; in the process the Christian meaning of death was obscured.

After a run of mournful hymns led by an imported, intermediate organ player, the priest donned his black cope and, standing at the foot of the coffin, pleaded for grants of the departed's absolution. '*Liberia Me. A Kyrie*' was chanted and the *Pater* followed, during which the priest walked around the coffin twice, flickering holy water and incensing it with smoke that rose in wisps from the thurible, its sweet odour irritating Ambrose's sinuses. The censer swung perilously from a rope in the priest's hand; coughing pockets of the congregation filtered out of the building.

A prayer, then the priest signalled the pallbearers. As the body was escorted out of the church the organ began *Antiphon in Paradisum* and the loud sobs of villagers erupted, like a dam which waited on the cue to burst.

"*DEPONATUR SACERDOS qui peccata p nitentis publicare præsumit,*" the priest said slowly. He was in the back seat of the BMW X5 Security.

The convoy was in Fullerton, a village in every way like Icacos; it had taken over an hour to get to it with the cars en route to the ceremony. As the sunset sprouted waves of crimson across the sky, the wailing continued. It had been painful to leave Shirley, kneeling before the fresh mound of soil, piled higher with the lonely coffin inside, but it was necessary. Time stood still for no one.

Ambrose gauged the priest sitting beside him in the parked vehicle. Fr. Dugan, the Irishman with a plump, round head and matching pink body, showed signs of sweat through his priestly garbs. He was no longer the commanding figure he had been during the funeral ceremony. He appeared agitated. He scanned the van like a man in a zoo observing swinging monkeys. His accent sounded more English than Irish. *From Northern Ireland*, Ambrose thought.

"A principle of Church Law," the Irishman reiterated, shuffling his feet. "Let the priest who dares to make known the sins of the penitent be deposed. Not even under the threat of death is a priest to operate as a–" he groped for the word– "snitch. You do appreciate the consequences of a priest divulging the confessions of a sinner, Mr. Prime Minister?"

"I do, Father" Ambrose said gently. His knitted eyebrows said: *but come on priest, spill your guts.* The priest-penitent privilege rendered it impossible for the government to force open whatever the priest hid, but it had to be something *pertinent*, Ambrose thought. Maybe something Sonnie had mentioned. *Was there a loophole that allowed priests to reveal the confessions of a deceased person?* Ambrose decided to wait. He saw the priest as a man who bore a great burden, some closely-guarded secret. He considered the man's mind to be a vault full of dark treasure to which there was no key. Ironic that the priest should appear to require confession. The *Decretum*, legislation written by Gratian, a 12th century canon lawyer, bounded the Irishman to secrecy. *Yet, why would he have requested a private word?*

"I cannot betray my penitent," Dugan said unconvincingly.

"What do you fear, Father?" Ambrose asked cautiously. There was so much he wanted to know. "*Latae Sententaie*, is it?" A new Latin term and coming from his lips it sounded strange.

The priest stared at his knees. He thought of Jesus in the garden; the Messiah had triumphed over the flesh. *But am I not combatting evil by now aiding as a Christian should?* There were things he knew; had he acted he could have saved Sonnie's life. He had seen the decline of the boy who had assisted as an altar server, always anxious to ring the bell. This made Dugan smile. He could see the wee lad in his dark-brown cassock, a big clerical smile on his face. *He would have been a fine priest.* As he grew older his gifts to the church were generous, perhaps too generous for a lowly fisherman. Alas, earthly treasures meant nothing to the dead man. Sonnie would never smile again. *Is his death my fault?* He thought of Glen. *Can I wash more blood off my soiled hands?*

"Father?"

"I cannot betray this lad," Dugan said firmly. "Let's-not-misunderstand-each-other. This is my faith, my life. I'm sorry having wasted your time." He was anxious to leave, but didn't know the exit button.

Ambrose sighed. He signalled to his driver and before the clergyman left – with the help of the prime ministerial aide – Ambrose slipped him a contact card. Wordlessly, the priest departed and PM Taylor watched as the heavyset man hobbled along the darkening path to the hillside grave where Shirley still wept.

The convoy was back on the road. It had been a long, sad day and Ambrose was hungry. Step on it, he said, much to the Wayne's delight; it was the opportunity to *eat up* the road in BMW style.

ABOUT MIDNIGHT, Patricia Taylor knew something was wrong. It was part of her intuitive reward as a wife: to know that when her husband hadn't yet fallen asleep, on his side, facing her, his hand embracing her stomach, that something was amiss. She slid up behind him, propped herself up on her elbow, and looked into his opened, burdened eyes.

"What's wrong, Honey?" she asked gently, stroking his temple.

He didn't answer. He appeared confused, like a fly trapped between a curtain and glass. Ambrose turned onto his back.

Patricia smiled. She knew her man: brief silence existed when questions were tumbling through his mind.

Finally, Ambrose's voice penetrated the darkness: "With each day there is more death, more crimes that are unsolved." He paused.

Patricia waited.

"Do you know who the people look to?"

"They look to their leader," Mrs. Taylor said earnestly.

She had seen it before, teachers and students whispering – *shoo-shooing* – as she walked the corridors. They would scowl if something negative appeared on *The Tabloid's* front page and ignore her otherwise. The prime minister's wife was famous for one reason: being the wife of the head of government. Should she ever take up a position in parliament she would never be acknowledged as the Minister of Education (MOE), just the wife of Ambrose Taylor. Thus, she had declined being principal at a primary school, an offer which surprisingly came only after Ambrose was elected leader. Patricia knew she was a simple woman, one who preferred working with the future of the nation – first year students – at a practical level.

Ambrose lapsed into further silence and after a spell, spoke: "I spend each hour of a day anxious to rectify things. I dream of it... I thought I would be able to stretch my hand to the poor and offer financial and emotional help. Yet, things are deteriorating. I despair more. I feel like I am being lowered into a well with mossy walls." He regretted the negatives.

"You can't teach old dogs new tricks, Honey. You know that. I know that."

"Then what?"

"We must appeal to the young ones," Angela responded. She ceased rubbing his arm.

*She sounds as if scolding a child. Teachers!* They never relinquish concern for their students, even when they meet twenty years later. *Pat* had projected her ideas to him a long time ago. If the schools trained the *children* then they should grow right, but the hypothesis had a fatal flaw. The majority of West Indian students lived at home with their parents, even after university. Home was where the foundation of good character was built, Ambrose knew. Poor parenting had everything do with society's decay. *How can a poor tree bring forth good fruit?* Fr. Dugan had mentioned something to the effect during Sonnie's sermon. Again, Patricia was right. "Our schools can only do so much," Ambrose said, swinging the conversation to his wife's highway of thought. "What do our children need?"

Pat sat up, her legs folded under her like a yoga swami. She clapped the lights on and when the room lit up her husband's eyes were on her. "What do they need? They need prayers. Prayers that can turn their minds off of Hollywood and the music industry." She shook her head. "Today, every role model is a *pimp rapper*, or *gangster*. Imagine, eyewitnesses have reportedly seen *Sugar Boy* smoking weed." She held her hands up to the ceiling. "Not even sports heroes are clean. Olympians are being stripped of gold."

"I wonder how much can be done for the community," Ambrose stated sadly. "People can only address their individual lives." He thought of the Chinese proverb: *If there*

143

is light in the soul, there will be beauty in the person. If there is beauty in the person there will be harmony in the house. If there is harmony in the house, there will be order in the nation. If there is order in the nation, there will be peace in the world. Yet, nasty evils were more contagious, easier shared.

An idea dawned on Patricia. "It is possible, very possible," she said confidently, "that actively involving public servants in the lives of children, at an impressionable age, can have a tremendous impact on youngsters. Come on! Most children have respect for police officers. Every boy wants to be a fireman and every little girl, a school teacher. I did! Years ago!" She laughed. "This can be channeled positively if the *right* people act as public relations officers, throughout primary and secondary schools." It was a heavy conversation at that late hour but her interest and excitement overshadowed her husband's sombre spirit.

"Respect dissolves," Ambrose said cautiously, not wanting to rain on his wife's parade. Her idea sounded feasible, but there were other factors that could cause a showstopper. Gently, he told her so.

Patricia left the room. He heard her clapping as she went down the corridor. She returned shortly with a tall glass of cranberry juice. Drink it, she told him, it was good for the prostate and had a reputation for making one relax, even smile. Ambrose, not quite sure if he had been bribed, grinned and promised to convey his darling wife's idea to the Minister of Education.

MIDNIGHT. THE prime minister has fallen asleep. Elsewhere in Trinidad: an abandoned two-storey administrative building; four men hunting one. Captain Rawlins engages his Night Vision Device (NVD) and the dark room adopts a fluorescent green skin. He signals and Sookram leaves the stack. They have been training relentlessly for the past ten days since their return from the PMC in North Carolina.

The building has been prepared for them, modified into a shoot house. Training does not stop, but no one complains. Minds are being taxed to the limit; bodies are expected to respond easier, oiled, in unison. They are shaped to kill, born to win, human machines against flesh and blood. But the man they hunt is a deadly assassin, a killer: Snake. Hidden within the three hundred square feet of concrete, Snake is a slippery little devil, mountain man and ex-royal naval officer.

Hope sees a blur as the man zips past, a crafty bastard, old enough to own a walking stick – Oxy's words. A man, *probably* quicker than Sookram.

The team reacts. Oxy, with the ballistic shield, assumes a forward position, and Rawlins and Sookram spread out along the walls, weapons lifted, fanning, perfectly balanced and ready for the kill. Their eyes miss nothing. Suddenly, the NVD overloads with a flash of light that makes each man hesitate and pull wildly at the devices. Within seconds, Snake *executes* each man with his bare hands. Again, Snake barks, and the exercise resumes.

Training will not cease, not for the next few months.

146

## 15 One drink for the killer

A BOWL of ice, two glasses, a soft drink and a bottle of rum. Icepick cracked the seal, fixed himself a drink, passed the bottle and waited while Glen poured. There was the careful knock of glasses and the drinking began. Time was measured by the amount of drink remaining and tonight, in silence, the alcohol diminished rapidly.

"Where Shiva gone?" Icepick looked at the periwinkles, as if he expected to see the picture tossed there.

Glen downed a drink. "*Eh, eh*! You alive?" He gazed at the rum. "It have about two more drink and that is the first thing you say. Like you really kill that Syrian man you talk about or what?"

Icepick frowned, lines of sorrow. He felt more of an introvert than Glen. "Why you don't believe me?" he implored.

"Sunil, you have a big mouth but you can't kill nobody," Glen taunted. "Look at your arms how skinny and your belly how big. You does look like you have a stroke. You really expect me to believe that you, Sunil, kill a man? Ha!" Glen scoffed and goaded by rum, continued talking dangerously, "Look at you, your arms does flap like a pelican when you walk and your head? *Lawd!* Your hair and hand always greasy. A gun will slip out your hand."

The more Glen taunted, the angrier Icepick became. He clutched the glass tightly. "And you does play this big Christian," he countered bitterly, poison to the host's ears.

148

"Who are you to judge me?" Glen asked, fuming, incensed more than his guest. "Judge not less you be judged!"

"What nonsense you talking?" Icepick stood. "You babbling all this stupidness that white man teaching you. You is an embarrassment to everybody, especially to your father."

Glen tried to rise, but stumbled. The low stool tipped over and he fell flat on his face.

Violently, Icepick flung his glass against the spot where Shiva once graced. He cringed as the glass barely missed the Catholic Messiah and shattered. He cried. He had killed a man and the one person – not counting Balkeran – he had entrusted his emotions to didn't console him as he had hoped. Icepick looked down at the slobbering Glen who was cursing. Icepick knew little about Glen except his father's unfortunate death, the widow's remarriage, her death and Rabbit's passing. Glen had never shared his secrets, his dreams. Their friendship was a one-way flow in which Icepick told all – *bust his files* – only to have his life viewed as grossly funny tales.

Icepick concluded: *it is the spirit of the village*. Icacos was a family with good and bad children who could depend on each other when the going got tough. When Icepick was out of sugar or salt he could go to Bat. When Bat needed a ride into Bonasse he could depend on the Black Giant. Icepick thought: *but Glen is a miserable outcast. Why then am I here*? *Is it sympathy*? He jumped from the landing and walked away angrily, promising never to visit Glen again. He could hear the *dougla* cursing in the background.

## 16　The Boodoo Lane fire

IT WAS 0500 hours Ash Wednesday when Lucky stumbled into his yard singing *La Bamba* lustily. He stopped at the base of the stairs. He had wobbled home from a Carnival Tuesday party, from where, he couldn't remember. *I walk or somebody drop me?* He wasn't certain but it didn't matter. He wanted only to safely ascend the stairs, a difficult task for his inebriated mind.

Lucky's residence was obliquely opposite the Anglican primary school where he knew the prime minister's wife taught. The Lucky family had inhabited Tunapuna since the era of his grandfather, an erect, rigid man with a weakness for the bottle and who was once rumoured to be the founder of the Tunapuna vegetable market. His grandpa wasn't destined to be credited as such, but rather as the one who had succumbed to alcohol and who eventually broke his neck on the front steps. Years later the same fate overtook Lucky's father; a giant cockroach had been chasing him, he swore, up to the moment before his death.

Lucky burped and stumbled against the wall, grinning at the thought of the old man. *That backside*. His forefathers had died as drunkards. *Now them was alcoholics who had real hallucinations.* Propped against the wall, he manoeuvred up the stairs, eyeing the edge cautiously, as if standing on the brink of a treacherous cliff. His journey to the kitchen was without mishap. *I could use ah drink before*

*I fall asleep.* He flipped the grimy flower-patterned curtain. *The Spot* was bare.

Lucky's anger soared. He burst into his daughter's room, grabbed her hair and yanked her off the bed. *The wench have good hair, like she mother.* He tugged hard. Repeatedly his hand came down on her with the fury of a judge's gavel on a sound block. He swore. "Where the rum?" He cursed.

The eighteen-year-old stumbled into the kitchen, blood gushing from open wounds in her head. The sot saw this, became concerned, but couldn't stop. Mrs. Lucky, screaming, ran into the kitchen, hands stuck to her bawling face like they had been super glued there. Lucky silenced her with a devious uppercut that landed squarely on her jowls, cracking her jaw. A ceramic plate, to the skull, sank the big lady.

Lucky cursed his wretched life, his misery. He needed a drink – *no, I want to dead.* He turned all five burners on the stove; a low hiss followed, then the foul smell of gas. Lucky craved a smoke, but more urgently, he wanted to die. He saw himself in the casket, fresh as a rose, smiling, his wretchedness, his sins, erased. *I need to dead clean.*

A cigarette consumed and body cleansed, Lucky returned to the kitchen. The ladies were still unconscious. *Where the box of matches is?* He looked around the kitchen, kicked fragments and pans out of the way and felt frustration growing again. He was uncontrollable. He searched relentlessly for a fire source. *Where me damn lighter? Maybe I leave it on the bus I take home. Or in the bathroom?* The matchbox was drenched.

Lucky slipped, fell to the floor and was fast asleep.

Two days later, he would emerge from an *en bloc* category blackout. It would take his daughter seventeen days to emerge from a coma. Mrs. Lucky would say that the girl had fallen.

*MARINA IDEAL* was as quiet as the still emerald water that skirted lazily past the jetty. The ocean was calm, with tiny wrinkles on the surface, like a beautiful woman who had begun to age gracefully.

Paul Headley parked and walked along the pier where yachts of varying sizes and costs bobbed monotonously. At the third vessel he found a barebacked Chip Rivers, grinding at the *Amity's* hull with a disc sander.

Chip stopped when Paul's shadow shielded the sunlight. "How's it going old buddy?" he asked, more cheerfully than he felt. He and Paul weren't friends, they were business acquaintances. Low whispers, then the yachtie invited him on board. Sound carried easily over warm, open water. Paul stepped onto the yacht, left foot first. *A bad omen*, thought Chip. He washed fibreglass off his skin – using cold water – and rejoined Paul in the cockpit.

"Where's your wife?" Paul demanded.

"Angie? Oh, she flew back to Oregon as planned… As you do know. Right?" His golden tan and broad, white smile said: *it is good to be alone.*

Paul wasn't smiling. "Have you been in contact with her?"

The yachtie erased his smile and shook his head.

Paul leaned forward and propped his elbows on his knees. Nothing made sense. A ton and a half of cocaine had simply vanished, like a bunch of house keys, and remained as skilfully hidden. He displayed his frustration openly. It wasn't loyalty that kept him going, but rather his failure to succeed when he should so easily have conquered. Any news would be good news – better than no news. "Give your wife a call," he ordered.

Chip was jolted. He was paid only to shut up and get the job done. However, he accepted the cellular and dialled Oregon. After the call, Chip was as confused as Paul. "Her mother said she never came home." There was concern in his voice. *Has she really left me?*

"When did you last see her?" Paul asked. He did some quick calculations when Chip told him. It could be another dead end, but Aram's henchman felt that he finally had a lead.

The thought of Angie fleeing with a local struck Chip. He dove into the cabin and reappeared, holding a notoriously cheap phone (nicknamed '*Me-2*'). He found Angie's mobile number, looked at Paul and dialled.

SEAN BROWN was in a hurry. *Just my luck to get stuck with a product deadline on Ash Wednesday.* If he finished the job, he would be able to keep his dinner promise to Leah. He uploaded the last of the software scripts through Secure Copy (SCP), then checked the designated Uniform Resource Locator using a web browser. The hit was a success, the software working as it did on his local machine: like a charm. He dialled Kathy Mills and left a recording, recapping the web address twice, a letter at a time. The next call was to Leah. She would soon be ready, she promised. Sean ignored a bath; he was in a hurry.

THE SUN was six hours hidden below the horizon when the black car turned onto Boodoo Lane and parked below the mango tree. Like the others the last house was in darkness. It was a still night. Not even nocturnal creatures chirped. Death was coming and everyone knew. Even the moon hid behind fat grey clouds.

Bharat exited the car, *Baby* and *Bang* in hand – *Betsy* he had left at home. Tonight, a lesson would be taught. The Manager reminded himself that he was a kind man, good enough to alert the neighbours that he was paying the Boodoo family a visit. 'There was hell to pay,' he had warned, and everyone knew that Bharat was a man of his word. He sighed, disappointed that he had to be hard to be respected.

Raj kicked in the wooden double door and Navin burst into the house. It was a small room, the only furniture being a bed, ferruginous stove and chest of drawers used as a pantry.

Before Mrs. Boodoo, on a low metal bed in the corner, could scream Navin was over her. The pillow which had provided comfort was thrust over her face.

Bharat and Raj cornered Ravi who, in his mad dash for the only door, had crashed into the stove, dislodging a heap of mangoes which rushed along the oil-stained wooden floor.

"What I tell you, Ravi?" Bharat said nastily to the trembling man pinned against the stove by Raj. The Manager lit a cigarette from the flame of a kerosene lamp which burnt atop the pantry. He took a hard drag, tasting the oil in the cigarette, then blew the smoke down at his captive. "*Ent* I tell you I will come for you and what I will do?" He extinguished the cigarette on Ravi's face and choked him when he screamed. Bharat looked questioningly at Navin. "*Wha'happen* to *tantie dey*?" The old lady had stopped wriggling.

Navin moved the pillow. "She dead yes."

"How?" The Manager asked.

Navin shrugged. "How I go know?" He examined her, keeping the pillow close to his chest. "Is not like I stab she up."

Raj cursed. His night wasn't super. He needed a drink. *Where Lucky anyway*? The Lancaster fan was supposed to be on the beat.

Bharat grunted. He clouted the debtor who had begun to sob at the news of his mother's death. "Ravi, you see what you do? You kill the poor woman." Then, addressing Navin: "Boy, you sure she didn't faint?" He was hoping she hadn't. She was to die, but not by suffocation. "Try to revive she yes."

"How you mean revive she?" Navin asked. In the flickering light the confusion of the assertive butcher showed.

"Wait, you want to give she CPR to wake she up to shoot she?" Raj asked in disbelief.

Bharat lifted his hands in equal shock. *What else I go mean?*

Navin changed the topic. "Where the boy?" *Ent* he have a little brother?"

"Answer The Boss!" Raj exclaimed, whacking Ravi across his face with a gun butt.

Navin joined the group. "Answer we."

With four guns to his head, the captive was tempted to talk but didn't. His time had come. He knew it. Even as the curses grew faint in his ears, his tongue kept still. His final act would be an honorable one.

*Baby* and *Bang* pumped Ravi Boodoo full of lead.

OUTSIDE, MOUSE cringed at the shots. He saw Bharat emerge, followed by Navin and Raj who accepted a Cuban cigar. They talked then Raj stepped inside the house. He returned moments later then the house burst into flames.

A small movement caught Mouse's eyes. He leaned over the steering wheel, peering. A low, almost inaudible scream punctured the sickly air. The men observing the bonfire had not heard it. Then, the sight registered. *Shit!* Mouse burst from the car and slid to the spot where he had seen the child under the house.

Aroused, Bharat and company followed.

"Grab my hand, boy!" Mouse bawled.

RANJI WAS confused. His brother had let him down through a fissure in the flooring, just before the bad men had burst into the poor abode, telling him not to show his face no matter what. Now, as fire licked at his backside, he was desperate. He tried to move, to reach out to this bad man despite his brother's advice, but he was pinned. The spot where he lay, on his stomach, provided enough space to lie, not leopard crawl. He could see other faces peering at him. He could see the man's mouth moving, but could not hear his words. Ranji was deafened by the roar of the growing inferno.

RAJ SAW it first: a huge branch crashing down on the structure. Instinctively he grabbed Mouse's feet and pulled him to safety. Mouse screamed like a banshee gone mad, his strength almost sufficient to pull a cursing Bharat into the flames. Bharat slapped Mouse hard. The three men bundled him into the car. With Raj at the wheel, The Boss rapped the dashboard to indicate haste. The car lunged. Tomorrow, the Boodoo's residence and the mango tree would be history.

## 17  The Boodoo Lane massacre

WHEN AMBROSE Taylor took the oath to serve his country he knew he would become a busy man, way busier than he had been during the party's campaigning, but not even that knowledge could have prepared him for his hectic schedule. At lunchtime he was still without breakfast and when he finally sat to read the daily paper he realised meals would elude him altogether.

The ashen face of a youngster, long overdue for a haircut, greeted him. The headline told Ambrose it wasn't some academic success, but a fiery death for Ranji Boodoo and family. Ambrose thumbed to page three; any article by Lance Jones was worth reading, often distressing but still, valuable. The story was gruesome. An anonymous eyewitness described the fire that had engulfed the home on Boodoo Lane around midnight.

Ambrose looked at the aquarium where two goldfish pecked at something between the coloured stones decorating the tank. *Boodoo Lane and Mark Lloyd. What was it?*

The eyewitness described the death of Mrs. Boodoo as untimely. She was a lady quick to share her mangoes and offer a hot meal from her menial supplies. '*No doubt! she and lil boy, the young one nah, Raj, them go be missed, but the bigger one? Lawd Father. He is the worst piper the village see for over thirty years.*'

Ambrose sighed. He closed the paper. It was unfortunate when life was lost, especially by murder or mishap. He wondered if freak accidents, like the suggested oil lamp falling over, could be avoided.

Lance Jones, who had mercifully excluded the prime minister's name from the article, had once described murder as a plague of unrighteousness which the government could prevent, given that the proper measures were in place. However, the journalist had never suggested a game plan. It wasn't his job, he had declared.

Ambrose was disturbed. The Boodoos had been deemed responsible for the mishap. *Why were there still people without electric power to their homes?* Somehow the journalist had failed to elaborate the point. The PM wondered about the luxuries he enjoyed, the meals he had at his fingertips. *Is my pay cheque too steep*? Something had to be done. Ambrose punched seven digits into his cellular phone. The Minister of Public Utilities answered.

"HAVE YOU seen this?" Ernie was in the conference room, hunched over *The Tabloid*.

Robert sipped his coffee then placed the cup on his desk. "The kid?" He had a little girl of his own. He didn't want to imagine what it would be like to lose a child. "No parent should suffer such loss."

"Well, at least the mother is dead too, so no worries."

Ernie said the strangest things, Robert thought. "It is an unfortunate accident," he sighed.

Ernie straightened. "The *eyewitness* described Ravi as a *piper*. Don't you find it's strange that the Boodoos' house burns down, his mother and brother end up dead, and just down the road lives a major druglord?"

Robert Marco wasn't aware of that fact. He had lost track of the list of *knowns* since migrating to Canada as a boy. He walked to his co-worker and began reading over his shoulder. Part of the story read: '*Mr. Boodoo was gunned down three years ago. He had worked in a neighbouring estate in Central Trinidad. Police closed the case one year ago without anyone being apprehended for the murder.*'

"I've heard people speak of a kingpin in the village," Ernie said flatly. "People love him. But oranges can't have all that money in it." He shrugged. "Come on *nah* man."

"What's his name?" Robert asked.

"How should I know? *Mr. Big*? You know how these things work." To compensate for his inadequacy, he added: "I can point out the road to his house."

"So you don't think it's an accident?" Robert asked, ignoring the sarcasm and reclaiming his coffee cup.

"The firefighters say so, blaming the oil lamp for the fire. The villagers say so. The papers say so. But the barbequed bodies in the morgue could tell us for sure. Something is fishy. It was a wooden house. You know country homes, they tend to have big windows. One person *should* have made it out, even if it meant being badly burnt."

Robert was thoughtful. He was trained to follow instinct and part of having a successful team was allowing equal opportunity. Plus, it was likely post mortems on the victims could be overlooked. The detective gave the all clear.

"On it," Ernie said and speed dialled Petal Clarke who was wrapping up lunch. She invited Robert and Ernie over.

## 18   iCitizen

"*MICKEY*, YOU know where your cousin is?" Radica asked.

Mouse shook his head. He didn't give a damn where Raj was.

"Imagine, that man gone to drink rum!" Radica walked over and sat beside her cousin-in-law. "You know what today is?" she asked, straddling the two-year-old Randy against her hip; he clung to her like a young monkey. From Mickey she got no reaction. "What is the matter with you, boy?" she asked, and before he could answer she said, "For the past few days you moving *cargo-cargo*. Real *poohar*. Like you half dead or something?"

The problem was sprawled before Mouse in big black letters, across the newspaper lying on the coffee table. *The Tabloid* had initially reported the Boodoo Lane fire as accidental, but further investigation revealed mass murder of the family of three. Lunch time news on television and radio said the same.

Radica embraced her child, then began bouncing him on her knee. "Yes. Them men who do that real sick. Imagine a little boy like that. *Oh gorm man!* I don't know what I go do if I lose Randy, especially like that." She blew a kiss at the grinning child who begged for a faster rhythmic beating of her knee. "Here boy, go by your uncle, let me check the pot." She got up, switching off the television. "And since when you does watch TV?" she asked scandalously.

A stillness engulfed the room permeating Mouse and the toddler. The boy looked at him through innocent, fearless eyes. Mouse did not smile. The scent of cindered wood filled his nostrils. The fear in Ranji's eyes lingered in his memory. The boy on the front page would never smile, play or go to school again.

Randy began crying and his mother returned, wiping her hands against her dress. She took the toddler, informing Mickey that lunch was ready.

Mouse declined. She was a great cook but he wasn't hungry. Since the incident he had eaten only soup. His insides were tormented. His stomach felt as if a powerful hand had slid into his mouth and punished his intestines. The smell of oranges was nauseating. The smell of anything cooking or burning sickened him; cigarettes made him choke.

The Manager had given him some days to *cool off*. "Take your time," The Boss had advised, "and when *yuh* ready come back." Bharat had been nice about it, too nice.

The newspaper articles worried Mouse. He wasn't a reading man but the transfixed mood of the nation bothered him. He wanted to know what they knew. Lance Jones documented the story and *The Tabloid* had become Mouse's paper of choice. The earlier articles were tame but the journalist now lashed openly and shamelessly at the prime minister. Mouse didn't count himself a learnt man, but the tone of the articles suggested that Ambrose Taylor was directly responsible for the wrath of evil unleashed upon innocent citizens.

*But*, Mouse thought, *Lance Jones is wrong*. There was nothing the prime minister or Alex Peters could have done to prevent the random act of violence instigated by Bharat. Each man was responsible for his own actions and no one should be condemned for another's evil deeds. Mouse sighed.

Mickey heard his name being called. He walked towards the master bedroom, large and vacant with unpacked boxes stacked high in one corner.

It was a day of love and so he romanced Radica who was dressed in red lingerie. Randy, *their son*, slept peacefully in a crib at the other end of the room.

"IT'S A pretty nifty solution," Ernie admitted. "This is good work, a far cry from the prototype I had seen."

*The software had to be good*, Robert thought, *Ernie isn't easily impressed.* The analyst had been assigned a pin and password to the online system and had insisted on being in office on Valentine's Day to toy with the application. Robert's ex-wife was with their daughter and given the history of the day – even for old *firesticks* – it was best to be away from home. So, he was in office, stuck with the geek.

"How do we benefit?" Det. Marco asked, his mind on Jane Doe and the Boodoos rather than the software. He was a hands-on man.

"The cool part," Ernie said hurriedly, "is that the programmers constructed an Application Programming Interface (API) which we can use to connect to their system. It's called *iCitizen*. Cool name *huh*? There's something called a cron job which can run at programmer specified intervals. We can use these technologies to update our internal solution automatically." Ernie saw the confusion on Robert's face and simplified the explanation.

"So we're finally moving away from recording data in giant ledgers at police stations and hospitals?" Robert asked.

Ernie was puzzled that despite his extensive account Robert had deciphered little. "That's not all. When the police fingerprint a suspect our system can download this image and compare it to evidence *we* have on file here at the forensic lab."

Robert whistled.

"That's great news!" Ernie exclaimed. "All I have to do is bridge the CSI software and iCitizen and we have access to all the data we need. Know what that means? We can compare fingerprints from the police and hospitals against our internal records."

Robert looked worried. "Is this secure?"

"Sure. To access the system participants must be assigned keys. Only then can they run queries. The forensic lab has already been assigned one. Actually, we're the first participant." Ernie was elated. Minutes later, Ernie walloped the glass table. He had triumphed; he had established a bridge between the two systems.

Robert looked at the grinning analyst. *At least he's making headway*, he thought sourly.

## 19  The suspect

THERE IS a spot on Caura Royal Road, just before the hospital, where on a clear day one can see far south, all the way to the Central Range, resting on the inset of the horizon. Today, a slight haze distorted the landscape, as scattered puffs of cloud, shepherded by a gentle wind, blew west.

Sean Brown sipped in the view. He was propped against a car which also supported Leah's weight, nestled against his body, his hands stuck deep into her pockets. Her hair had been tied but the wind prevailed, making her curls dance across Sean's face. If it wasn't for love it would have been annoying, but today he was tickled at how the *snakes* brushed against his nose.

Leah relaxed so that her head nestled against Sean's chest. She felt safe. She loved Caura. It was her first visit and it was peculiar to behold the landscape, brown in some places, green in others. She commented on the dryness of the terrain around Central Trinidad.

'Chaguanas' Sean corrected, then squeezed her.

His hands felt good, strong, safe. An onslaught of cars, blasting loud chutney music, hustled along the road. Men whistled and hooted: *'Best thing! Friend! Family.'* Someone, recognising Sean, stuck his head out the car window and commented: 'Ah boy you pick up a white thing.' Then the cars were gone.

Leah laughed. It puzzled her that she did. She should be scolding herself and despairing at such obnoxious behaviour. *Is it Sean?* His personality was influential but she doubted it. She was endeared to him and thought she might even love him. But she couldn't be certain so, on the matter, her lips remained sealed. *Did love make people look and behave the same way?* Leah knew spouses who looked like siblings. Sean wasn't exactly a role model, yet his sometimes inane acts were sincere. He delivered love in a strange manner: unwrapped, unpackaged yet affectionate.

Sean interrupted her thoughts. "Do you know what I like most about Caura?" He pointed over her shoulder at six large national flags (hoisted high on poles over seventy feet tall), a choppy sea of red, white and black in the plains below. "It was a good move by the PM to have them erected throughout the country. There are twelve in all, located as far as Cedros and Mayaro."

Leah had seen the flags before but knew nothing of their origin. There was one to the left, more than seven miles away, yet quite visible.

"The banners remind me that I am a Trinidadian," Sean said proudly. "I'm not claiming to be captain patriot, but there is something in the lifelike movement of a flag which generates self respect within me. It stirs my soul to be a better citizen. I guess it's Prime Minister Taylor's hope that everyone feels inspired by our freedom."

"Freedom is fragile if there is disunity, Sean," Leah added, working her digital camera. She zoomed (12x) to the fluttering symbol in Chaguanas and clicked. Then she took more pictures of Sean and herself.

They turned as another line of cars passed. More whistles and heckles.

"Where are they going?" a confused Leah asked. She knew there was a hospital a few metres off. She could see its boundary from where they stood, but the joy-seekers certainly didn't look and behave like they were about to visit dying souls. Besides, it was after lunch; visiting hour was over.

Sean enlightened her: Caura River. The river which originates in the northern range drains the Caura Valley and passes through Tacarigua. Eventually it flows into the Caroni River.

Sean pointed at a flag, indicating where the rivers met.

"Is it good to swim in?" Leah asked. She didn't care for a dip; she just wanted to know.

"Caura river? Yeah, it's decent enough, but it could get nasty… you know, litter: discarded cups and broken rum bottles, stew, curry and cooking oil floating in the river."

Leah, busy laughing, didn't see the twisted face he made. There was nothing in his voice to indicate he was serious.

Sean continued, "I don't know *nah*. Plus when people drink they rum they does turn Apache and the place could get rowdy, even rough." He added seriously: "It's an interesting place though. The Hindus use it as a site for shavings and other rituals. Some people aren't really comfortable with that aspect, but it is a historical place." He shrugged, Leah moving gently with his body. "A toll should be introduced to preserve the valley. People wouldn't mind paying a dollar."

"Are you part East Indian, Sean?" Leah asked. She had always wondered.

"Of course I am!" Sean exclaimed. "I'm what people will call a *Callaloo*. Real mix up *nah*. My mom's father was from Scotland and my grandmother was pure Indian, real dark, what Trinidadians call *Madras*. My father's parents are French Creole, the aristocratic kind, the ones who real *uppity*, *nah*." Sean stopped. He felt he was talking too much. "What about you?"

Leah, her head pressed into Sean's chest, turned and grinned at him. "Me *dread*? I is a white *thing*."

Sean laughed raucously. It was amusing to hear Leah speak like that.

A plane was arriving from the West, descending rapidly. It was low in the sky, like a giant iron bird about to touch down at Piarco International Airport.

"There's a plane, baby," Sean pointed.

Tasting custard, she blushed, the spider web capillaries in her face awash with blood. She savoured the love she tasted.

Little did Leah know that on the same plane was one of the most dreaded men she would ever encounter.

NIGHTTIME FOUND Mouse driving along the Chaguaramas coastline. The past few days had seen a steady decline of peace at the Samaroos' residence. Raj was drunk more often, hitting his madam quite frequently and Randy was always in tears. It was peace of mind Mouse longed for and it was peace of mind which lurked just out of reach, like Ranji Boodoo's hands.

Before, the only pain Mouse had ever felt was the surge of guilt that came from sleeping with Radica, but that had vanished. He had his justifications: Raj's love for whores, rum and cigarettes. Radica deserved far better than her husband could give and Mouse thought himself worthy of filling in the blanks. Tonight, it wasn't this that bothered him. He couldn't determine if he also was responsible for Ranji Boodoo's murder. *But I is only the driver.*

His hands turned the steering wheel as if guided by some force, the car taking him down a faintly familiar road, one he recognised only when at the end of it. It was here they had brought the white woman. Had he come to make peace? *Can peace be made with the dead*? He exited the vehicle and seeing yellow caution tape slung around the trees, stopped. *What am I doing here?*

Then he heard a rumble and saw a van approaching. The vehicle stopped, but the flashing red and blue lights throbbed on authoritatively.

DET. MARCO had been burdened by a hunch the entire day. The thought caused his temples to ache. Commitments to personal duties had kept him busy, but his ex-wife had pulled him out, agreeing to keep their daughter Tracey on this night when the child was Robert's responsibility.

So far, he thought, he had been lackadaisical concerning the terrain surrounding Jane Doe's murder, having focussed primarily on the car. They had found the victim shot in the car, windows up, the glass intact. As an experienced CSI it was an oversight to assume that the windows had been *up* when the gun was fired.

Robert met Mickey 'Mouse' Samaroo at the boundary of the abandoned crime scene. He parked so that the car was blocked and kept the high beams on the man. At midnight one should not be careless. He noted that the stranger had no visible company. The detective exited the vehicle and called out to the wiry man who made no attempt to shield his eyes from the blinding lights. Robert kept a safe distance in a low hands – palms downward – ready position.

Det. Marco engaged communication with the stranger, identifying himself and issuing short authoritative commands. Mouse turned and placed his hands behind his head. Robert didn't want to, but had to treat the man as a hostile. He was alone, but dispatch already knew his location. "What's your name, Sir?" Robert asked authoritatively.

Mouse squeaked.

"Sir, you're going to have to say that again," Robert said assertively.

Mouse shifted his weight. He breathed rapidly. "Mickey Samaroo."

"Ok Mr. Samaroo, I'm going to have to ask you to do a complete 360-degree turn. Slower than that, sir."

Mouse did as commanded, his manner displaying his desire to run.

Robert noted this. "Okay sir, I want you to drop to your knees, lie face down with your hands outstretched at your sides, and legs crossed at the ankles." The detective thought he had seen a bulge in the man's back pocket.

The inner Mouse wanted to defy the officer and flee. He thought: *if I cooperate maybe I go get the upper hand.* He wasn't sure what the *hot car* had in its trunk – *it might have ah gun* – and didn't want the officer identified as Robert Marco to search the vehicle, but Bharat's driver had never confronted the law and didn't want to now. In his current position he would have to make a few moves before he could dart into the bushes, by which time he would definitely be brought down. All he could hope for was a quiet escape through cooperation. He answered random questions and concocted a story: he was waiting on a married woman who hadn't shown up. *Her name?* He fumbled, then confirmed, "Jane Smith."

"Sir, are you carrying any sharp objects?"

*Blast it.* Mouse admitted to possession.

Robert Marco removed the switch blade from Mr. Samaroo's back pocket and continued the search, feeling, twisting, crushing Mickey's clothing. The man was a frightened little man. The detective stepped back, still maintaining a safe distance and stance, and ordered Mr. Samaroo up.

"Don't worry about it," Mickey said, relieved when Robert thanked him for his cooperation, "You're just doing your job."

Mouse walked to his car. In it was a bag. "You want any orange?"

It was Mickey Samaroo's offer that reverted him to crossed ankles. Then Det. Marco searched the vehicle.

Sgt. Smith and Constable Brown of the Chaguaramas Police arrived six minutes later and arrested Mickey Samaroo after reading him his Miranda Rights. At the station the man's data and gun charges were keyed into the iCitizen System. The *hot car* was impounded.

AT MIDNIGHT a *cron* job was executed and the forensic lab software established a connection with iCitizen. All offenders flagged as new were queried. There were thirty-six including Mickey Samaroo. After the update, the forensic software searched the new data against evidence already logged. When case *5263* was encountered the forensic software logged a likely positive fingerprint match and queued the find to an area which the assigned crime scene analyst could access via a graphical interface.

ABOUT THE time the cron job executed, Robert Marco found what he had been looking for – a bullet lodged in the bark of a tree. In the forest's darkness he smiled. *No such thing as coincidence*. The passenger window *was* down when she was shot.

THEIR MOVEMENTS are easy. Like a greased wheel the assault team moves fluidly from corridor to room. They reach the stronghold, locked with a heavy industrial fire safety door, but Private Hope is ready, his hands steady, his aim confident. The Remington blasts the hinges off and pulverises the lock. A solid front kick topples the door.

Rawlins, point man, enters simultaneously with a Flash Bang tossed in by Sookram. The sound is deafening, the flash blinding, but the filters over goggles offer protection.

The Flash Bang, also known as the Stun Grenade, does not burst into lethal fragments, but raises the pressure in a room. It can distract even the most determined terrorist. When the non-fragmenting aluminum body – earlier versions were made with cardboard – detonates, it can achieve up to 180 decibels, the relative loudness of a jet engine.

Sookram had been experiencing the most difficulty working with the device, but now moved eel-like into the room alongside the captain. Oxy followed, taking up his AOR, the centre of the room, an eye to any threats the others might have missed or become disadvantaged to when reloading or experiencing weapon jams. Outside, Hope waited, manning the corridor.

Inside the stronghold Snake looms up and Rawlins brings him down with a quick *double tap*. It is the way they had been trained: to work the MP5 on single shot rather than automatic to avoid spraying bullets, a practice which can kill terrorists – and hostages. The double tap rectifies the situation should the first shot go wide or prove to be insufficient in incapacitating the immediate threat.

Snake, a good sportsman, but better winner, drops in mock pretence. Sookram binds the man. The combat simulation had lasted seven seconds, excluding the covert approach. Speed, surprise and violence of action fuse with the members. For them, Close Quarter Battle has become a way of life.

The assault team trains into the night.

## 20   The Reid interrogation technique

TO THE back of the conference area was a small, soundproof, almost claustrophobic room. Ernie sat behind the desk. Robert sat facing Mickey, nothing between them, an observation mirror to the suspect's left. On the table were Robert's coffee and the handcuffs which had bound Mouse. The conversation had slipped past casual happenings and although it had started off slowly the man seemed anxious to talk. It was time to confront the suspect.

"Where were you the night of January 17th, Mr. Samaroo?" Robert asked. He leaned into the suspect's personal space.

Mickey, sweating, shifted. The room was cramped. With both hands outstretched he could touch the walls opposite him. He wanted out of the compartment, a box, a sardine can of terrifying hopelessness.

"I was at a party," Mickey lied, running his hands through untidy hair.

"Super Soca Fete?" Robert asked, with a frown.

No answer.

The detective smoothly presented his scenarios: "So you and some friends are coming home from the party. You see an attractive lady on a bike. She's alone. What happened? Were you the drunken one who decided to stop the car, pull her off the bike and rape her, twice, in the forest? Was it a random act or did you meet her at the party? Maybe she embarrassed you and you're not one who takes lightly to insult."

Mouse remained silent for awhile, unconsciously nodding. He was about to deny his involvement when Robert interjected: "Let me finish. You'll speak in a moment... You couldn't have been alone. To trap her head in the window would have required at least two strong men."

Mouse spoke: "I could never rape a woman. That could have been someone's wife." He looked at the African analyst who seemed more focussed on the wooden desk.

"That's good Mickey," Robert said, patting the man's leg. "You're telling me that you couldn't have planned this, that it was out of your control. You're telling me that it was a mistake, only a random act."

Mouse was frustrated. He thought of Bharat, Amrit and Ricky Lo. He felt that to be free he had to whistle.

The detective moved closer and placed his hands on the suspect's shoulder. They were one now. Robert was here for him. Their eyes held for a long time then he asked: "Mickey, did you kill the woman?"

Mickey's eyelids blinked rapidly, like a humming bird's wings. He hunched over and began crying into his palms.

"Was it a crime of passion, Mickey, or was it for money?" Robert asked, presenting two alternatives as the Reid technique suggested. He massaged the man's shoulders.

No answer.

Robert repeated the question softly, the way he would if asking his ex-wife whether or not she still loved him. The sobbing man maintained silence. Robert thought he had lost connection with the suspect.

Mickey looked up and said: "But I is just Mouse the driver." Then he began squealing, selectively choosing which beans to spill.

Behind the one-way mirror a digital camcorder recorded the confession.

When the nerve-racking ordeal was over Mickey agreed to have Ernie take a sample of his saliva. Back in handcuffs, Mouse began to worry about Bharat – a name he hadn't mentioned. *What I do*?

Outside, Robert called the MONS and told him about the canary.

ALEX WAS in the Think Tank with the prime minister when he ended the call. "Good news," he told the man behind the desk. "We have an accomplice to Jane Doe's murder."

"That is good news," Ambrose echoed, looking up from his laptop.

"The bad news is the guy isn't revealing the names of his *compadres*."

"Oh," Ambrose said simply. His mind was elsewhere, despite the intelligence. He had been working on a speech for the past three hours, but hadn't advanced. The Minister of Education had approved Patricia's project and Ambrose had been scheduled to deliver speeches across the nation, starting with primary schools. He had not anticipated that it would have been so difficult to address children.

"It's drug-related by the way," Alex said, filling in the prime minister on the core details, withholding only the most sensitive information.

"You're saying there's one tonne of cocaine floating around?" Ambrose asked loudly. He was distracted now. "Any leads?"

"Huevos Islands, a big yellow house. I'll have Rawlins see to it. I'll liaise with Jake Pipes from the DEA, maybe there's some connection we can establish. In the meantime we'll try to push the canary into a corner," Alex said hopefully. "If he feels trapped maybe he will even testify for the State."

"What do we know about him?"

"Not a damn thing. He's as clean as a whistle. It seems he's scared of his gang. We can use this to push him into the witness stand."

"Okay. Keep me posted," PM Taylor said.

After a solid handshake Alex Peters left.

After a call, CISTU's assault arm had work to do.

## 21  Merv the pervert

MERV'S PREFERENCE had always been for boys, young African boys. He had been deported from the US for crimes involving a six-year-old. He had also laughed at the Americans on the plane ride home. Despite their sophistication, they could pin only one assault on him. He had enjoyed countless bodies.

With the foreign exchange he had purchased a decent flat in a quiet, upscale neighbourhood in west Trinidad, where he was unknown. Neighbours loved the flamboyant stranger, especially women and children. He was a hip man with the coolest toys, latest gadgets and game consoles from America and best of all he had a swimming pool.

The deportee's eyes were on Phillip. He had been waiting, since his arrival, to invite the eight-year-old (a bit too old for the pervert's taste, but workable) over for a splash in the pool. Merv would wait. Patience was a grand virtue of the sex offender.

"MR. SAMAROO, is there something you aren't telling us?" Det. Marco's voice portrayed disappointment. "If you don't cooperate with us, how can we help? You still haven't given us a single name."

A bewildered Mouse stared between both men who had interviewed him two days ago. "I told you all. Everything!" he exclaimed exasperatedly.

"What about the Boodoo family?" Ernie asked.

It was the first time Mouse had heard the young, black analyst speak; his words landed like a bombshell. *How did they know?* Mouse quivered.

"Mickey, through ballistic fingerprinting we've been able to match the bullets from Ravi's – is that his name? – corpse with the one found at Jane Doe's murder scene."

"Is that her name?" Mouse asked.

Ernie cleared his throat, stifling a laugh.

"Does any of your associates own a Smith and Wesson .38-calibre revolver?" Robert asked.

Mouse froze. Bharat owned such a gun. It was called *Baby*. The driver remained silent. He wasn't planning on cooperating in this interview.

"Not only that," Ernie interjected, on cue, "there aren't a lot of knife crimes in this country and the blade in your possession–" he held up the bagged evidence– "was used in the murder of Barry Edwards and Jeremy Gibson. You might have known them as Crapaud and Bull."

Mouse bowed his head. *Navin, that bastard. But that can't be the only knife like that in Trinidad.*

Robert held up a bagged orange. "Also, there's a positive match with your saliva sample and evidence collected at Jane Doe's crime scene."

Mouse was appalled. He stared at the orange, recalling his disgust. He was in trouble and knew it. He could swim, but the weight was too heavy.

"Things aren't looking good for you, Mickey," Robert said sorrowfully, as if offering condolences to a widow. He paused to allow the suspect's despair to deepen.

"What can I do?" Mouse asked. His exits had been blocked. He needed a way out. "I didn't commit any of these crimes. An accomplice, maybe, but not a killer." He had a flashback of Ranji. "I tried to help the boy. I tried to stop him from burning, but his brother owed The Boss money."

The detective scribbled 'The Boss' into his notepad. "We can help you, if you help us," Robert said using a more authoritative than sympathetic tone. He knew he had to be cautious. "If you are willing to testify for the State against your associates, I'm sure you can qualify for immunity from prosecution. You can start over your life." He shied away from offering the State's protection programme; citizens usually had little faith in it.

"And what happens after that?" Mouse asked, thinking more about Radica than Bharat.

Robert patted Mickey's leg. "Let's take it one day at a time, Mr. Samaroo. One day at a time... now, tell me what happened."

Mouse told the men he knew the Boodoo family, but had nothing to do with their death. He didn't kill Crapaud and Bull, he insisted; the knife was a New Year's Day gift. He mentioned a corrupt official codenamed *Chief*; it was rum shop gossip, he claimed. He never named The Manager and his death squad.

Two hours later, when Mickey was through, Robert tried to make a connection: "Tell us about Mr. Chandra Bharat. How is he linked to all this?" Robert had been investigating *Mr. Big* who Ernie had mentioned.

Mouse didn't flinch, neither did he say another word.

When the interview was over and Mickey was taken away, Ernie met Robert by the coffee dispenser. "Do you think he'll break?" the analyst asked. "He's a conniving little creep, skimming the surface but excluding the names of his employer and associates."

Robert nodded.

"And Mr. Big?" Ernie asked.

"I'm not sure. Chandra Bharat appears to have a legitimate operation. I checked the records. He's done time, but he's cutting it clean, filing his taxes and aiding the community. I scouted his spread and he's quite a gentleman and an idol to his workers. Maybe, he's just *Mr. Big Heart*. We'll be keeping an occasional eye on him though." The detective looked at the analyst. "Anything on the house?"

"Oh I forgot." Ernie apologised to his superior. "Whoever was the legitimate contact for the shipment was running a smart operation. The big, yellow house Mickey spoke of is registered in the name of a woman, deceased years ago. When the assault team raided, the location was abandoned, clean as a whistle. However, there was a campsite in close proximity and, get this, peels of dried orange skin."

Another promising lead had morphed into a dead end. Robert swore. Each time he found a walking stick it was broken. Mickey had betrayed no sign of knowing Chandra Bharat; he hadn't even flinched. Maybe Bharat's status as a crime lord was only *Trini* hearsay. Robert checked his watch. *Blast it.* He would have to review Mickey Samaroo's interview later. He hoped that his ex-wife would be able to keep Tracey again. Robert nodded in the direction of the interrogation room. "I feel sorry for the guy."

"Why? Because he was a driver? Mickey Samaroo has aided and abetted in death. His hands are as dirty as any of the SOBs he is linked to," Ernie chided. "Let us concentrate on getting names. I'm an analyst not an interviewer." He walked off, leaving the detective with a cheerless cup of coffee.

"MOUSE! THAT blasted rat!" Bharat was upset. Chief had let the cat out of the bag. Since then The Manager had been cursing the *ex*-driver and parading wildly with *Baby*.

"I say he dead yes," Ricky Lo admitted. "I never would of think he go turn rat. Informer *haffe* dead!"

"Wait, you mean to say he in police custody and squeal on all of we?" Raj was still in disbelief.

Navin, who had said nothing since entering the shed stated: "He have to dead, yes."

Bharat appeared to settle. "If he have to *flipping* dead? No two ways about that! He done dead! Is just a matter of when. I don't care how or who or how much just make sure that rat get some good bullet in he ass." Manically, he swung *Baby* in a wide arc, causing Amrit and Ricky to dodge the .38-calibre's barrel. "*Wha'happen*? All you is two girls or what?"

"Where they keeping him?" Raj asked.

"You shut your mouth," Bharat ordered. "That is your family. You bring he in here. I give he *wuk* to drive for me. Good pay, good salary. You should be answering for him. Police asking all *kinda* question and thing."

Raj saw Navin shift his weight.

"That is not Raj fault," Ricky Lo piped in unexpectedly.

Bharat looked at the Rastafarian.

Amrit backed his friend. "Raj is a good boy. He could real cook. This is not he fault" He looked for more support but got none from Navin.

"They keeping the little ass in Teteron," Bharat revealed, his eyes still on Mouse's cousin.

Ricky Lo did the math. "It go be hard to get he there," he said needlessly.

"It will have to be an inside job," Raj helped. He was still licking his wounds.

Bharat paced the room. "Yes, an inside job." He stopped and looked among the boys. "All you have any partner inside there?"

Lips drawn tight, the men shook their head. None did.

"Where Lucky?" Bharat asked suddenly.

No one knew the drunkard's location.

"You," Bharat said, pointing to the *rat's* cousin, "Mouse was with your wife *eh*." The Manager left the shed. He had a plan. Money could buy anything. Even a uniform.

## 22  Edmond Belfast

THE FIRST thing a stale drunk Raj did when he entered his home, the following morning, was hit Radica a backhand smack across her face. In the crib, Randy began crying but Raj didn't care.

"What you do that for?" Radica bellowed from the bed onto which she had fallen.

Raj didn't hear her, neither did her screams register as he brutally pounded her body. Then, when an incoming blow missed its mark and Raj went sprawling, Radica escaped. Grabbing her son, she fled the room. *Had he found out about Mickey?* She doubted it. Only two persons in the whole wide world knew the truth: Mickey and Radica's cousin. *He go never sell me out. I could put meh head on a block for that.* Bharat was first blood and, she knew, blood was thicker than water. *Especially Bharat. He blood must be thicker than grease.*

Radica fled.

FR. DUGAN slid back the screen, a nuisance to operate. It had been poorly designed and being gifted with stubby fingers the priest's attempts to repair the partition always rendered it worse. The outline of Glen's face was visible behind the lattice. The weight of Atlas' burden descended on the Irishman, the burning candle contributing to the nausea he had been experiencing since the penitent's last visit.

Glen, the village's sole soul who attended confession, had once tried to hide this from everyone, but upon his mother's demise he had become more involved, more open – perhaps too open. His confessions toyed with the priest's conscience. They were sinister and they grew more so.

Fr. Dugan, however, hadn't expected the confession of murder. Even as he listened to Glen's sorrows, a breath away from the violent man, the killing played on his mind. A priest could listen, but it was God who had to forgive. Dugan's joints ached. He heard but didn't listen. Sonnie's death still weighed heavily on his heart. The priest knew he should have done more, especially when the family had grown distant from the church. He had tried, but probably not enough, he told himself.

Glen confessed nothing new. He spoke of his guilt, then after he had droned on about his repentant spirit he unexpectedly spoke of negotiations *being made* to transport a huge quantity of cocaine for a new buyer, a contact – he said 'guy' – in Toco, not something of the past, but something due to occur; a bothersome matter. I don't trust *Jake*, Glen whispered through the lattice. He grew silent, a cue for the priest to speak.

Fr. Dugan's shoulders drooped. "My son, you know these things are wrong, yet you persist." He felt the Trinidadian was deaf to his Irish accent. "Premeditated sin, my son. We speak of the risen Christ… the work he has done and can do in your life." He wanted to recommend that Glen converse with the authorities. He hesitated, then did so. His heart was grieved at the man's carnal response.

In the confessional Glen was a different man. Dugan had seen him on the village road – a quiet, unassuming, introvert who shied away from barking dogs and neighbours whom he treated like strangers. It was difficult to imagine Glen pulling a trigger, even if forced. However, none had expected Doug Dugan for priest. God had willed it and judgment was reserved for the Almighty.

Glen droned on, and the priest found himself responding with low groans of despair. His heart ached, his joints probed. He found himself cracking his knuckles, a habit he avoided.

He smote his chest and pleaded with the penitent to end his wicked ways, but Glen plodded further into the realms of darkness. It was like a confession from hell. Inspired by a burning stump of wax, shadows danced, casting a horn-like appearance on Glen's head. Fr. Dugan cuddled a crucifix and began the Lord's Prayer. Glen waited, then continued his ill-natured lies.

When Glen was gone Dugan retreated to his tiny room at the back of the building. There, despite his arthritis, he knelt and prayed. He pleaded for Sonnie's soul and Glen's deliverance from evil.

EDMOND BELFAST despised Trinidad. When his Tobago-born parents died in an accident in Scarborough, he was shipped to the larger of the twin islands and lived with his grandmother who had migrated years ago. He hated the old lady's home. It was a damp musty place with crochet magazines in every nook. Regardless of what was cooked it smelled the same way: like boiled rice and unseasoned chicken.

Edmond wasn't happy when his guardian died, but she had been generous enough to give him the house which, so far, he had been unable to sell. He had advertised the property in *The Tabloid* as 'a nice flat nestled in the fantastic lowlands of Chaguaramas, no more than fifteen minutes drive from the capital.' But everyone turned their noses at the place. Edmond was upset; he needed money, the key to escaping his dull life.

Edmond Belfast hated Trinidadians. To him they were a pushy, snobbish lot with no appreciation for heritage, quick to anger, unlike their more laidback relatives in the sister aisle. Trinidadians joked a lot and when gathered they bullied and bashed anyone who was different. Edmond had never learnt to adapt to the faster pace of life and the unquestionable mark of hopelessness on his broad face made him an easy target for ridicule among his peers. In primary and secondary school Edmond suffered yet he had never returned to his motherland. He had tried once but life in Tobago had been a trifle too slow for his liking. What he craved now was a way out of the army, a way into luxury.

Edmond Belfast was on sentry duty when the phone rang, two loud bursts.

The voice on the other end was coarse, like army canvas. "Who is this?" it demanded.

Private Belfast gave his rank, number and name. He figured it was the fat, idiotic sergeant who had successfully pinned the nickname *Dumpling* to him.

"Listen, Belfast," the voice continued, "I have one million dollars for you if you could kill a man. You could do that? He name is Mickey *Mouse* Samaroo, a little Indian *fellah*. He have a kind of rat face."

Edmond was shocked but interested. He knew Mickey. The army was keeping him sequestered in the old administrative building – *the one where CISTU trained*. "Go on."

"What else you want me tell you?" the unidentified caller asked hostilely.

"How I know you will give me the money when I get the job done?" Edmond asked skeptically, excitably. Mentally, his uniform was already shredded. The call sounded genuine.

"A quarter of the cash up front," the voice offered, "The rest later when the job done."

"Hold on." Edmond went outside. Lifting the barrier he allowed five army trucks (nicknamed *Rat Dogs*) loaded with baldheaded recruits to exit the Base. He felt sorry for the youngsters, remembering his horrible, lonely experience in boot camp. *One million isn't enough*. The caller was waiting. The private said with his best bargaining voice, "He will be a hard man to get to, you know."

"Two million. And that is it. No more." A long pause followed. Then: "Once you collect, you guaranteeing the *wuk* go get put down."

Private Belfast's hands shook. Things had escalated too fast for him. He tested the waters. "How does a pickup today sound? You will have what you want in… two days."

"Excellent!"

Edmond wished he had said three million.

181

The caller described the details of the pickup, with the private modifying the plan. Then the call ended. Edmond checked his watch: *four long hours to pickup*. He had nothing to lose. There was a promise of crisp, blue hundred dollar bills waiting in a like-coloured vehicle. *Five hundred grand large.*

RICKY LO was filled to the brim. "*Jah*! Chinese food real filling *eh*?" he said to Amrit who leaned beside him on an old model car. "What does make it so filling? The amount of oil they does use?"

Amrit, the dapper, laughed. "No boy. Something call MSG, I think. That does fill you faster. Plus it have more carbohydrates than protein. You ever realise you does be hungry soon after you eat Chinese?"

Ricky shook his head half-heartedly. He wasn't listening. People were filtering onto the streets, many striding along quickly, each with a concerted attempt to exit the city ahead of others. "Real ladies in *town*, boy," he commented and the talk veered from food.

UPSTAIRS, IN a food court, Belfast observed both men. He had been doing so since their arrival an hour ago. Like the anonymous caller had promised, the men would be a Rasta and an East Indian – 'a pretty boy.'

From where Edmond sat he could not see the duffle money bag. He waited until both men scoured Frederick Street and when the *pretty boy* consulted his watch, the Tobagonian donned enormous shades.

In minutes Edmond faced the men. In seconds the transfer was made and Belfast was just another uniform walking the streets, save for the five hundred thousand dollars stuffed into the standard military issue backpack.

Two taxis later Belfast was safe in his musty home thumbing through stacks of crisp blue notes. *It would be easy to run now*, he reasoned, but he wanted *all* the money. The private knew that to claim the rest of the cash he would have to hire help which unfortunately meant that he would have to share his newfound wealth. *But not much*. He dialled the second of two numbers stored on his mobile phone.

"BOB SPEAKING," a strong Tobagonian voice said when the call connected.

Edmond offered his childhood classmate and only friend in boot camp a hearty greeting. He thumbed through the money as he spoke. "Hope," he said, counting a fresh pile of bills, "I have an offer for you. It worth some good money."

"Serious?" Bob Hope exclaimed. He excused himself from Captain Rawlins who was again casually discussing the mechanics of the Separator (a breaching device with a 20 tonne cutting force and 4 tonne separating force, able to could cut through steel like butter). "Talk to me."

Edmond was cautious. He could trust Bob, but one had to thread carefully when life was at stake. "Is regarding the Trinidadian fellow all you minding. Somebody call about him today."

*Now how did Edmond know about Mickey?* Bob entered the kitchen where the sequestered man sat on a stool looking intently into the dimly lit yard at the declining activity of recruits and Rat Dogs. Private Hope read between the lines. "How much?" Bob asked. He waved when Mickey turned.

"One million," Edmond lied. "Half for you and half for me."

Hope gagged. He accepted a glass of water from Mickey. *Five hundred thousand dollars is a lot of money.* "I'm in!" he exclaimed, to his comrade's delight. Hope smiled at Mickey, the gentle gentleman, and returned the glass. People wanted the man dead and they were anxious to dish out cash. *Belfast should have asked for plenty more.*

WHEN AMBROSE dozed off the cellular phone vibrated loud enough to wake Patricia. It was Alex Peters at the front door. In minutes they had coffee and were in Ambrose's office.

"Well?" Taylor asked. "You aren't here for a game of tennis?" They had not played in ages.

Alex gingerly placed the roasting cup on a coaster, careful not to spill the contents onto the oak. "We have a problem," he said. "Someone wants our witness dead."

The words did a better job than the coffee in waking Ambrose. "What?"

Alex quickly recounted the story. "Coincidentally, Belfast tried to collaborate with one of our CISTU guys." He didn't mention that Oxy had manhandled the traitor.

Agitated by the news of the soldier's treason, Ambrose paced the floor. No wonder Alex had come over. "So once the caller has proof of death they'll pay the difference?"

"Belfast doesn't have means of contacting them, so we're going to have to wait for them to call."

"I don't like that plan," Ambrose admitted.

Alex concurred. He too didn't like waiting.

"What time is it?" Ambrose asked.

"2300 hours."

They had time. Taylor told MONS Peters the plan.

"The imbecile fell for it," Alex scoffed, after the call to Lance Jones. "One more thing. There's also the issue of a mole."

This was news to the prime minister. "A mole?" he queried.

"Codenamed *Chief*," Alex said bitterly. He was bothered. "We are on the hunt for a man high up the ranks."

"The Commissioner?" Ambrose asked skeptically.

"My initial guess," Alex admitted. He leaned forward and whispered, "I'm hoping not, but I have a couple of eyes and ears on him." He slumped into silence.

Their conversation became repetitive and the MONS excused himself. At the door Ambrose promised to relay Alex's apologies to Patricia.

## 23  The Dustbin Bomber


THE BOMB rocked the capital at 0800 hours. *Scratcher* died first; the vagrant had been sifting through a dustbin. Cathleen Fate died next. The electronics store manageress was at the time opening the doors to her workplace. Hart Weekes, a pensioner who hadn't been hit by shrapnel, succumbed to cardiac arrest. Screaming men, women and school-children scampered along Frederick Street as horrified faces stared from behind store windows. Despite the chaos, those brave enough hurriedly dragged amputees over shattered glass and away from danger. Tension dripped in the capital. The second bomb exploded five minutes later.

IT WAS Ken Thomas who called the prime minister and told him to switch on the television. Three minutes into the live footage, Alex Peters burst into the office. He looked dishevelled, like he had just lost a fight.

"I feel like I'm watching something in Baghdad," Ambrose said, still in shock. He was standing before the projector, one hand folded, the other to his face, his forefinger massaging his lower lip. The screen showed a female amputee being dragged away in the darkening stain of her blood. Part of a butchered leg clung to her knee by a thin thread of flesh. The PM wasn't happy. He was not seeing as much uniformed officers and ambulance personnel as he expected. "What's going on, Alex?" he demanded roughly. "Do you know the average response time of the US Air Force?"

Alex knew but didn't fall into the obvious trap. "As we speak CISTU, the police and the army are controlling the situation," he said reassuringly. Then pointing to the screen: "What you're seeing is footage from the second blast site. Our resources were initially dispatched to lower Frederick Street. Robert Marco is on the ball at the first site. CISTU agents Frank Marshall and Stanley Bishop are being escorted to the second location."

The explanation didn't console the PM. He motioned wildly at the screen where the camera was panning a crowd that should have long fled the city. Alex pointed out the arrival of two men in white forensic suits, accompanied by soldiers and police officers who addressed the people. The crowd fell back with each forward step of the armed men, forming a haphazard semicircle, too close for comfort around the bomb site.

The appearance of the authorities still didn't pacify Ambrose. He paced around his desk in restless circles. "What are we dealing with, Alex? Terrorists?"

The MONS didn't know and wasn't afraid to say so. He would have a better idea when the forensic team reported in. "Obviously, someone is trying to send a message."

"A message? To whom? Me?"

"We're gathering evidence to establish that, Sir." Alex nodded at the screen. "The objective of a bomb is to injure, maim and destabilise." The curious Trinidadians huddled together on the projector's display suggested that they were not *destabilised*. At least not yet.

Suddenly, another loud explosion, then the screen went blank.

In the capital a third bomb had detonated.

Ambrose swore.

Using his forefingers Alex traced a square. The nation had to be addressed.

PAUL HEADLEY, avid tea drinker (preferably lukewarm and made with powdered milk clumped into tight round balls around the brim), was dressed in a blue bathrobe. Cup in hand, he sat on a wicker chair, one of a set of four that came with a smoked glass-covered table. On it was a copy of *The Tabloid.*

Paul flipped open the newspaper and skimmed its pages. He whistled at the page three story. Reporters often had more valuable information than even cops and crooks; this never ceased to amaze him. *Mickey Samaroo.* The name was familiar. The State witness was linked to two murders, the first of which interested the reader.

There had been an earlier account of an unidentified woman's murder. Jane Doe, they called her. *Angie Rivers had disappeared around the same time* and the poisoned Mickey Samaroo had been linked to her murder. *Interesting.*

Paul had made key calls and gained access to a manifest of flights out of Trinidad. Angie had never left the island. Not even her half-assed husband was aware of this. *It is possible that Jane Doe is Angie Rivers.* It made sense, Paul thought, sipping his tea and rolling the milky clumps in his mouth before swallowing. So far he had been blocked at all avenues, but Frankie had mentioned a Mickey. He would visit the midget but first he needed to contact Alan, the old timer who worked at the *Rose Cottage.*

THE BENEDICTINE abbey is located on a high hill northwest of Tunapuna. The array of red-roofed buildings and its landmark tower, accented by the magnificent northern range, is visible for miles around, but the view which people have of the monastery, church and yogurt factory does not compare to the view the monastery has of the landscape before and around it.

Lucky finished a late breakfast, and a nurse – dressed like a maid – charmed away the used utensils with a returned smile. He grinned to hide his disgust: the food was bad, especially for a rehabilitation centre.

Raj Samaroo entered the ward armed with a newspaper.

With a rejuvenated smile, Lucky waved the visitor over and signalled to a chair near the bed.

Raj sat.

"Who put a *spoke in your wheel*?" Lucky asked, then remembering his manners, "Morning."

"You could smoke here?" Raj asked hopefully.

Lucky shook his head, he hadn't smoked in twenty-two days. Neither drank. "Drying out is what they call it," he told his friend. "I cry and beg for drinks in here, but them lady nurses not giving me a chance. I even consider messing myself to get one," he joked, "but they not giving me anything to help the shakes." Lucky wanted to change the topic. "How them boys going?"

"Them good man... them good," Raj replied. Obviously Lucky wanted the spicy news. Raj signalled to the sleeping man behind him, and when Lucky waved indifferently at the patient, Raj told him all he had missed. "Bombs going off in the city and thing. Last I hear two went off today, but is not we." He laughed reassuringly then showed the patient *The Tabloid's* headline: *Mouse poisoned*.

Lucky was more shocked at the driver's betrayal than his death. "I sorry to hear he get pass out though. But all you fellows not easy, boy! Best I was still drinking rum!" He frowned after he said this.

"No, boy. Don't do that. I real glad for you," Raj said earnestly, recalling the motive of his visit. He thought Lucky looked super. A glow had erased the dark folds beneath his eyes. "So what make you decide to check into rehab?" All of we was wondering where you gone. I happy you tell your family to call and tell me where you is."

Gloomily, Lucky recapped the Ash Wednesday story he had heard from his wife.

"Shit boy, you really have *ah* alcohol problem you know," Raj said seriously.

"Is called an *in block* category blackout. To people you does look like you functioning *normal-normal* but you does *cyar* remember a damn thing that happen." Lucky stuck his hand under his green robe and began scratching his chest. He gauged his friend. "What about you, Raj?"

"Who me?" Raj looked shocked. He shook both palms and his head at the sick man. "Not me partner. I is not *ah* alcoholic. I is a drinker. I could control it. The only thing I can't control is my wife," he moped.

Lucky stopped smiling. "*Wha'happen* to you, pal? Something looking wrong."

Raj told him everything. "You know what does hurt me the most? The woman can't even come clean and say what she do wrong. Imagine some soldier called Belfast poison my cousin, the little bastard, and she still not talking the truth. She just pick up *sheself* and my child and gone by she mother and *ain't* come back yet."

Lucky lifted his lean frame by pushing down firmly on the bed. "Raj, I can't tell you what to do. What I will say though is try to decide things on a clear head. I mean, what happen with my wife and I certainly could be blamed on the drinks. I can't say that I expect she to *horn* me with another man just because I is *ah* alcoholic. That *doh* make sense." He searched for a likely comparison. "That is like me going and have sex with another woman because my wife seeing she PMS."

"You understand!" Raj exclaimed. A passing nurse signalled for them to be quiet. "You sounding like a thinking man, Lucky. Real different. I glad for you."

Lucky ignored the compliment. "Pal, I not saying you responsible in any way, but try and drop the alcohol. Clear your mind and try to make some good decisions. Mickey was your cousin. What he did, if he did it, was dishonest, but sometimes as men we could foster bad habit. No young, married man should have a next man home in they house, even if is family. You have a good looking wife and Mouse was not any *limer* or drinker. As a matter of fact, he was home more than you! Remember he was your cousin; she don't always have to be your wife."

"Sense. Sense. That is me *child mother*, although I real beat she the other day. Four-letter word for so! She *coulda* get pregnant again!"

"What that have to do with you making amends?" an appalled Lucky asked. "You made a crucial mistake. With a clear head you can do better. You know what *murder* spell backwards is? Don't get tie up, buddy."

The visitor looked up and with a shrug said: "I guess you right."

"And Raj," Lucky cautioned, "believe in the God of your understanding. It real hard, buddy but I drinking years before your father dream about making you. Restore your sanity. The body will follow."

Raj shrugged. Lucky's sober preaching had begun to irritate him. "Besides my drinking, she is a hard woman to deal with."

Lucky prepared to make his admission. "Buddy, you have not realise that since you married I don't come by you so often? That Radica. I mean what else you expect? You see the family she come from? I never uses to see them thing. The alcohol had make everything fuzzy for me. Right now I on step eight of the Twelve Steps and I trying to make amends to all the people I harm. It not easy." He showed Raj a notepad. "It have three hundred and eighty names in here." His spirit was willing but his mind was weak. "That Radica really not easy."

Raj eyed the patient.

"You can't expect to get apples from a sour lemon tree," Lucky said with a yellow toothy grin. He sighed and added Radica's name to the book.

Raj had heard enough. He smiled to hide his disappointment, and parted from Lucky, wishing he had never visited, promising he never would again. He stopped at the first bar he saw and had a couple drinks too many. *Tomorrow is another day*, he concluded in his drunken stupor.

*Dan* Lucky's sobriety deserved applause and Raj pounded the table, startling the barman and patrons in the dingy bar.

BHARAT, ELATED at the news of Mouse's death, lit a hundred dollar and ignited a Cuban cigar. He made arrangements with the Tobagonian – Ricky had said the man looked like a dumpling – and then at the appointed hour, Amrit and the Rasta departed to deliver two million dollars to Belfast who deserved a bonus for his quick, brutal work.

Ricky Lo was sour the entire drive to the drop-off. It would have been better to have the soldier gunned down, he thought, but the man was an asset. The Boss recognised the value of people in high and low places. These he reserved for the pockets of his expensive suits, next to his cigars.

The early morning bombings had caused Bharat to change the drop-off location and time. At 2300 hours Amrit and Ricky were waiting outside the national stadium, west of the capital. No activity brewed and no football equalled no stadium lighting. The arena was a big dark disc.

Ricky Lo pointed at Belfast, walking towards them, wearing big goofy shades.

"He looking small, *jed*," Amrit noticed.

"*Nah*, that is the man," Ricky said confidently. "Is how it dark! Leave the engine running and keep the bright lights on him in case he try something stupid."

BOB HOPE decreased his pace. It was unlikely the men had discerned the switch. The driver worried the private, but he knew the sailor would be moving into place. Oxy was in the bushes, off to the car's right, the driver's head plump between the crosshairs.

Leading Seaman Sookram tossed a Noise and Flash Diversionary Device (NFDD) into the car. When it detonated, a flash momentarily activated the photosensitive light in the eyes of the confused passengers, blinding them. The disruption of fluid in the semicircular canals of the ear disoriented Amrit and Ricky.

In seconds, CISTU had the suspects face down on the pitch and the vehicle searched. These special prisoners were not processed as criminal offenders, but were taken to an undisclosed location somewhere in the northern range.

LEAH LAY in bed thumbing through digital photographs of Sean and herself, her attention shared with the television. She found it strange that Sean, although handsome, wasn't photogenic. Maybe one day she would have pictures of their lips locked together. She smiled.

Her father entered and she slipped the camera under her pillow. He noticed the movement but ignored it. The weary man stood at the foot of her bed. "Doll, you've heard of the bombings?"

Leah nodded. Her lecturer had broken the news during sociology.

"I need you to be careful," he said. "I don't want any harm coming to you."

There was pain in his voice but Leah couldn't see the wound. She knelt and crept across the bed to her father who embraced her. "I'll be okay Papa," she said earnestly. She was her father's angel. She meant him no pain but news of Sean would pierce his heart, like a bayonet to a soldier's chest.

Papa felt the hug and returned the squeeze. Her hugs felt as they always did. He remembered the day when she took her first steps and clasped her hands around his neck. His Doll had said, "Papa." He felt guilty. His life had gotten busy. So many things had changed. He jogged his memory: he last hugged his daughter twenty-five days ago. Leah seemed different. She walked strangely, smiled more. Even her speech was strange; colloquial. He stepped back and looked at her. "Doll, how are you?"

She was surprised, like someone given an opportunity to cross on a busy road. "Everything is great," she reported truthfully. It wasn't the question but his tone, his faltering voice, which puzzled her. "How you going, Papa?"

It took awhile for him to speak. Her name came to his lips then fizzled. He tried to distract himself with the television – India featured on the travel channel. He consoled himself. *She is still fascinated by intriguing places. She is still my Doll.* "I need you to stay close to home for awhile," he pleaded. "It's important. I don't like it one bit the way things are out there. I know it's hard what I'm asking but it's necessary. I wouldn't if I didn't have to." He didn't need to ask again. He smiled weakly and left.

Sobbing, Leah called Sean and broke the news.

Don't worry, he comforted, everything would be okay. He hung up.

Suddenly, the documentary on India was cut and a distressed Prime Minister Ambrose Taylor greeted the nation. Leah switched off the tube and resumed her tearful slideshow.

ARAM USED the remote control to activate the 50' widescreen LCD flat panel television hanging on the basement's wall. Ten minutes into the address, Aram smirked. He had heard enough garbage. Men in high places had big egos and Ambrose Taylor was no different. He lacked fore and hindsight. Three attacks on the city in a single day, eight persons dead and forty injured. The politician was brave – *or mad?* – enough to claim there was a list of likely suspects and leads that were being followed. Aram's thoughts drifted. Ambrose, like Mark Lloyd, was a fool. The Syrian laughed, but didn't feel better. He had his problems. Hamad was worth one hundred million dollars. *Could insurance cover the cost?* he wondered.

## 24   The Melbourne connection

VLASTA, CITIZEN of the Czech Republic, sat chatting with her fiancé. It wasn't coincidence but love's urge which brought her to the Internet café. Every Wednesday for the past six months she had dutifully established a virtual conversation with her man. She was realistic. For men, a relationship meant contact and the Internet allowed her such a facility while she toured the world. Prior to Trinidad she had stopped in Cuba, the only place where she had missed her weekly conversation with the charming Michelangelo. She had no intention of disappointing him a second time. Not even the Port of Spain bombings could stop her. After all, she was born and bred in Semtin, the suburbs where the explosive Semtex originates.

It took seconds to download the Instant Messaging (IM) software and once Vlasta's credentials had been entered, the software connected to a server in Melbourne, Australia. Michelangelo was already online. She sent an invitation and in seconds his cherry face popped up on the video stream.

The Internet café had no microphones; she typed and blew her man kisses, sending other cute gestures. She yearned to hear him, to speak to him. She signalled for him to wait; she would ask the sour-faced attendant for a microphone and speakers.

On the other end of the stream the Aussie waited. From Melbourne to Trinidad the connection was surprisingly good, he thought. Beyond the café's glass window he had a clear view of people walking the streets. The island was busy, not quite as festive as he expected, but rather a place deep in the machinery of life.

Suddenly, a bright flash startled Michelangelo. On the screen debris was tossed everywhere and the glass of the café shattered. *Bollocks*. His vision became obscured then he saw people scampering on the littered pavement. He panicked for his fiancée.

Minutes into the chaos Vlasta reappeared. She was alright, she typed, more excited than scared. She pointed to her lips and mouthed silent words. The Australian typed: '*of course I still record our conversations.*'

IT TOOK fifteen minutes for Michelangelo to edit the tape – it involved removing Vlasta and adding the punk rock song, *Smash Up*. Then he tagged and uploaded the video clip to *bloodyTube*. Within two hours the recording had five hundred thousand hits. Username *jamaicanchick18* viewed the video and uploaded it to *caribbeanMeetUp*. When *Cyberduck*, flagged as a Trinidadian, saw the video he phoned a familiar journalist. Then he emailed the footage. That evening *The Tabloid* released a page one story accompanied by a picture of the suspect believed to have planted the bomb in the dustbin.

"WHERE THE ass them two is?" Bharat wasn't in the best of moods. "Anything on Lucky yet?"

Raj was driving. He lied about Lucky but on Amrit and Ricky told the truth. The dynamic duo hadn't called.

"You mean to say them two little asses run off with *my* money? I will scrape the gold off Ricky Lo teeth!" Bharat slammed the driver's headrest and an irritable Raj rocked in his seat. Bharat wondered: *I losing my mettle? Impossible! Mouse dead cause of me!*

Raj slowly navigated the car into The Boss' compound, parking clumsily in the shed. The Manager was upset by the bucking vehicle. Suddenly a voice shouted and Raj imagined he saw Bharat flinch.

"Who's that?" Bharat asked. There was no fear in his voice just anger at being startled.

"It sound like that fellow from down the road... the midget man *nah*," Raj said, exiting the car to support The Boss in case he was wrong.

"Is Frankie!" The voice was more agitated.

Bharat stiffened. "Come in, boy." When the junkie stepped inside Bharat slapped him hard on his big, round head. "Don't ever do that again! You hear me?"

Frankie nodded, a reminder nod for himself, rather than the big man. "Manager, I have some news for you."

"And what is that?" Bharat barked. He had little patience for *pipers* – an abstract label for any person who would place a *For Sale* sign on anything to secure the next hit.

Frankie wanted to exchange the information for marijuana, but wasn't certain how to eloquently word the request. Humility stepped in; Bharat was a hard hitter. "Boss, it have a man I know only asking around about you. He check me up to yesterday." *So far so good.* He paused and looked at Raj who, like Bharat, was waiting for more details. The junkie wasn't sure if the encounter was proceeding smoothly, but Bharat had long-term profit which Paul Headley couldn't offer. If the African was willing to pay out hundred dollar bills for information, Bharat would certainly be more entertaining. *Would he?*

"And? What kind of man? Come on midget, speak!" Bharat's tone was convincing.

Frankie described Paul Headley. "A big strong *Creole*, Boss. He think you *mighta* thief some cocaine. I cannot remember how much he say, but like is plenty... a ten kilos, he say... nothing much." Frankie shrugged apathetically as if quoting the price of a menial lollipop.

Raj and Bharat exchanged glances. Neither knew of such a man.

Bharat showed more confusion than he cared to and so corrected the situation by flaring his lips angrily. "You feel Amrit and them playing up?"

"No, I don't feel so," Raj said. It was a dangerous thing to guess, especially since Mouse had betrayed the Samaroo name.

Bharat cursed and kicked an overturned bucket – the one Ricky favoured as a seat. He walked over and grabbed Frankie by the back of his jersey. He looked at the *piper* the same way a customer does when checking an item for a price. "And what you tell this Paul Headley, Frankie?"

"The truth Boss... the truth." Frankie cried like a child pleading pardon from the rod. He didn't want to share Ravi Boodoo's fate. "I tell him that all you is only small fries."

"Small fries? What the ass?" Bharat slapped Frankie hard. "So what? You come to hunt we out?"

Frankie avoided another slap. "No Boss! No!" Then he told Bharat when Paul Headley would return for information.

Frankie didn't think that his night had turned out that bad. After his brain was picked clean, Bharat sent him home with an ounce of top notch ganja. The midget smoked as he walked past Boodoo Lane and in honour of his dead friend, *took a pull*.

IT WAS the room which maddened Amrit most. In it he had lost track of time. *How long*, he wasn't sure. The flickering light hanging low from the ceiling of the concrete room irritated him, but fear kept his eyes open. Fear kept him awake. Through the black hood he saw the silhouette of Ricky Lo who, like him, was bound to a chair with his hands manacled behind his back. So close, yet so far. They could not speak. They had tried but the cloth, stuck thick into their mouths, muffled sound. There was only the occasional grunt to acknowledge that blood still coursed through their veins.

Suddenly, the door creaked causing the prisoners to jerk their heads at the light which filtered into the room. Amrit saw the silhouette of the man moving towards him. Then his hood was lifted, his lips revealed. Roughly, his mouth was freed of the gag. A synthesised voice enquired on the identity of his boss.

Amrit cursed, breathing deeply with the gag removed. He wanted to break. He wanted to crack, but even under pressure he admitted nothing. Bharat had ordered a hit on Mouse for his betrayal, Amrit recalled. Maybe this was a test of loyalty. *Maybe Belfast had always been inside Bharat's pocket.* The Manager was capable of anything. *Maybe The Boss is taking inventory of his stock.* The Syrians worried Amrit. *Had they found out?* Amrit reasoned: *they couldn't know.* He and Ricky would have been dead already. *Police? Nah!* He spat, and despite his resistance the gag and hood were replaced.

The man moved towards Ricky. The gag removed, the Rasta began cursing Jamaican style. The silhouette slapped Ricky Lo and left the room.

Amrit's pride was in for a nasty jolt: for the first time in history the dapper gangster emptied his bowels on himself. *Shit!*

IN THE adjacent room Oxy was eating a sandwich and staring at one of four monitors. "Look's like he's messing himself," he commented casually.

"Who do you think will crack first?" Bob Hope asked.

Oxy shrugged. "Either one, just give me a few more minutes with them." He laughed and finished his meal with one bite. "Seriously? The Indian will cave in first. Them boys in forensics say the Rasta do time already, so he seasoned."

"For what?" Sookram asked. He was looking away from the monitors.

"Weed, and stealing tyres from a government compound," Oxy said. "Why the ass somebody will steal tyres? In that kind of work you have nowhere to go." He alone laughed at his joke. "The other guy, he's a bachelor, quite an eligible one," Oxy said with a lifted eyebrow, "but I'm not so sure about now."

"What about their families?" the sailor asked.

"Not sure about that." Oxy extracted another sandwich from a big bag. "It's safe to guess they wouldn't be contacted."

Bob Hope betted on it but Sookram said nothing.

## 25 The early incident

ICEPICK'S BEHAVIOUR had worried Glen. He had never left before the bottle of rum was finished, but when he did there were ten big drinks left. Glen had downed them and went to bed.

Now, as he entered the confessional, Icepick flooded his thoughts. Life had seemingly left the *dougla*. He no longer argued but his tales were darker, less fantastic. In essence, great for the confessional. The screen slid back. It was early, bright enough so no candle was necessary. "Forgive me, Father, for I have sinned."

The priest, surprised at the sight of the repentant – *indeed, it is the first Saturday in March* – responded with the usual words.

There was an emptiness in the priest's voice which Glen resented; he sounded like Icepick. The sinner whispered a tale about drugs he must transport to Jake, the white man in the north.

"Father, to be honest I don't trust the man," he said rapidly. "But my boss... he want me to do it so I have to do it."

"You are responsible for your actions, my son," Dugan said wearily. The Christian in him made him plead. Divine patience was in control, he reminded himself, and thanked the holy mother.

"I know Father... I know." Glen mimicked Icepick: "My boss find out I kill a man, or at least I was forced to. He angry like hell, but can't do nothing. He say it will start a war that he do not want. Plus he say he sick, suffering with diabetes and *portrait* cancer." He paused. No response. "He playing it out on me, like a nasty old man, is like he trying to blackmail me. I confide in he, Father, and look what he doing me."

"Your burdens are for the Lord, my son," the priest murmured. He leaned forward and his fleshy cheeks pressed against the lattice. "Have you begged for forgiveness, my child?"

"Yes Father, yes. I tell you so already. I don't want to make this drop, but I… no choice Father… no choice. I don't know when it is though. I feeling trapped… like I in confessional–" a poor comparison which Glen didn't recognise. "The boss going too! He say is a big order and he want to watchman the operation. You know how it is, no?"

Father Dugan didn't. "Pray Glen and let the hand above guide and direct your life. Speaking of it is one thing, lad, but doing the right thing is another." He clutched the crucifix to his chest, struggling with the inner man. His voice laboured, "I will pray for you."

With these words Glen departed.

Doug Dugan steadied himself. Labouring, he exited the confessional and went to his room. "Give me a sign, Lord," the Irishman cried out to the heavens. He fisted his heart, "I beg it of you." His mind ran to scripture where Jesus cast out the money changers from the temple. Father Dugan had no such authority. It wasn't his lot to be the guardian of church doors. Catholic law conflicted with his morals. He had already failed Sonnie and the boy's family. *Am I failing Glen?*

He found his bible on the bedside table and opened it: Mark Eleven. Within the crease of the pages was the call card the prime minister had given him. *A sign?*

BY MID-MARCH the sporadic rains that graced the nation, and explosions which bombarded the capital, had ceased. The dry season was in full swing; its heat hovered between the sticky spaces of skin and cloth. The nation, however, wasn't safer. Tension hung in the air like an incomplete magic trick, and each day *The Tabloid* reported more murders, more suicides. CISTU agents Frank Marshall and Stanley Bishop had succumbed to injuries brought on by the capital's third bombing. It was a time of death. Ambrose knew the tension; *it is synonymous as facing the eye of a hurricane*.

All else had ceased to matter. To his citizens the loss of human life had jumped to slot one. Ambrose parted the Think Tank's blinds. They were still there, picketing Whitehall with crude cardboard signs lettered in predominantly red and black. The masses had gathered for the past two weeks; a daily relentless crowd, jousting their signs as if probing mangoes high on a tree. Today they wore red, the colour of choice among Trinidadians assembled for a cause.

Hunger strikes were in effect. Ambrose saw an old man faint and some from the crowd rushed to assist. But the picketing didn't stop; it grew more agitated, like a disturbed anthill. They were working class people. They were contented fighting for a cause, knowing that their financial security was protected by the unions, like umbrellas covering heads.

Alex burst into the office excitedly. He motioned the PM away from the window and passed a photograph of *The Dustbin Bomber* to Ambrose. "His name is Declan Foley," the MONS reported. "He belongs to the IRA and is wanted in connection with the murders of the British and American ambassadors to Argentina in '81 and '85."

Ambrose studied the picture. Foley had a pale face, partially hidden by a thick beard; the red-haired man looked sinister. Stapled to the back of the photograph was a dossier about the Irishman. "What the heck is a member of the IRA doing bombing the hell out of *our* city?"

"Beats me," Alex said. "But we got the intel from the DEA. Jake Pipes called it in himself... Apparently he recognised Foley even though he was disguised with black hair."

"Took him eighteen days to do that?" Ambrose asked with visible sarcasm.

The MONS shrugged. He had thought the same thing. "Analysis could take time."

"So where's Declan Foley hiding?" Ambrose scoffed. "And what was his port of entry?"

Alex hadn't figured that out. "We got reports through our call centres since Foley's face hit *The Tabloid*, but all turned up negative. CISTU even shook down an Israeli exchange student doing chemistry. We're also looking at the airport's video archives but no luck so far."

Ambrose muttered something then: "If these bombings are politically motivated why not choose government targets?"

"The use of pipe bombs doesn't make sense either." The IRA was notorious for engineering car bombs and homemade mortars. Alex stopped, adjusted his tie, then added: "Believe-you-me, if they wanted to send a more direct message they probably could. Remember 2001? The Irish Three? Those guys were involved with South American rebels. Soon after judges and lawyers began showing up dead. The bomb signatures were similar to known IRA members. CISTU has been coordinating with Interpol and the evidence matches Foley's patterns."

Ambrose sighed. He had scrutinised the bombings from every angle, considered the Opposition, known gangsters, local chemists and arsonists, but it had turned out to be the Irish Republican Army (IRA). *How?* It didn't make sense for the militia man to be operating in Trinidad. Most important, where the heck was he?

"Yesterday I spoke with the mayor," Alex said, interrupting a pensive Ambrose. "Guess who owns Damascus Cloths?" He didn't wait for an answer. "Hamad." He watched Ambrose's eyes widen. "That's not the only interesting part. The Hamad Group of Companies owns all seven stores hit by last month's bombings. Cathleen Fate was the manageress of one of the family's electronics outlets."

Aram Hamad. The Syrian was a major financier of the Opposition, supposedly Mark Lloyd's close pal. "A Syrian/Irish conflict?" It didn't seem plausible.

Alex passed a transcript over the table. "In late January the call centre had received a tip. The caller, David Alfonso, had reported a robbery and shooting at Damascus Cloths." Alex added: "He mentioned a high-ranking police officer at the scene, but never gave a name. Get this: the story never hit the press. Hell, we didn't even know about it."

"And we can't approach Alfonso to reveal more because of the call centre's commitment to anonymity?"

"Exactly," Alex responded moodily.

"How did we make a connection after so long?"

"We're able to give the call centre software parameters. Recordings can be searched using supplied key words. It was Kerwin Acres who suggested searches using the names of the attacked stores."

Ambrose's frown deepened. "Is it safe to surmise that Aram has lost something belonging to the Irish? Some insurance scam?"

The MONS shrugged.

"Possible links to the cocaine Mickey Samaroo mentioned?"

"It's a possibility not to ignore." His eyes followed the PM as he went to the fish tank and generously sprinkled flakes into the water, like a person putting too much salt into a pot. In a flash the meal was nibbled away then there were no more wafers of gold and green, only water, bubbles and an array of fish.

"Maybe Foley is a mercenary acting on behalf of some third party." Ambrose wondered aloud.

Alex waved his hand like a seesaw, "Sounds more like a job for the French. If drugs are the link then we should be expecting the People's Army."

The PM clasped hands as if in prayer and exhaled loudly into them; the warm gush of air did nothing for comfort. "Let's get some eyes and ears on Aram Hamad," he said finally.

Alex was already a step ahead.


AS PAUL learnt, *Alan The Diener* had fallen into a drain along the Priority Bus Route and broken his neck. The mishap occurred a day before Aram's henchman tried to contact the *corpse servant*. Another tunnel sealed, Paul thought, as light had begun to shine inside the realm of hope.

This had been two weeks ago and the Rose Cottage – Paul preferred the euphemism to 'mortuary' – wasn't proving to be an easy place to access, despite flashes of money rolled larger than Paul's hands.

There had been one woman, a Petal Clarke, who had been quite nice on the telephone, but skeptical when asked about Jane Doe. There was an authoritative air to the pathologist's voice that stumped Paul. He had erroneously assumed that the professional was a snobby, spoilt brat who would care for money rather than people – an existing trend in health care. He had been relentless in his bribery attempts, timing various shifts but never getting to the pocket of any.

Now, before Frankie's house – *where had he disappeared to*? – Paul got the premonition that it was time to bail out. *But go where*? Word in the underworld was that the Syrian had imported some heavy characters, mercenaries no doubt, to do the lifting. *They wouldn't do any good*, Paul thought, *just more disappointment for Aram*. Paul sighed. *It is best to flee, to run before I share the Syrian's inevitable fate*.

He thought of his sister in Philadelphia. It would be nice to go to her but her husband was such a fool. Paul thought of his childhood days in Beetham; he hated them. But he had made something of himself through Gregory Hamad's help. He owed the family and was committed to finishing the job.

Paul *steupsed* and lowered the car's automatic window. Before he could sound the horn, Frankie's voice beckoned. Five more intolerable minutes and Headley caved into the pleading voice.

INSIDE FRANKIE'S abode Navin waited, knife in hand, its tip pointed at the door. When the baldheaded man peeked inside, Navin didn't respond as planned. Later, he would blame it on the mere shock that Paul was so dark that he shone.

The delay gave Paul the opportunity to dart back to the car, with Navin and the midget in hot pursuit. Unable to grab his firearm, the baldheaded man turned and faced his unknown opponent. *Opponent and a half*, the thought flashed.

The Manager's orders were simple. *The Creole,* as Bharat had nicknamed Paul, was to be taken quietly and alive, a point he had recapped for Navin's sake. The plan would have worked superbly had Navin brought a gun and Raj not feigned diarrhoea. It was this lapse of judgment that placed the fearless man face-to-face with the more powerful Paul Headley who, with a loud grunt meant to instill fear, caught Navin's slashing right hand at the wrist and arched his body so that the knife wielder smashed into the back door of the car, shattering glass. No neighbour would peep past curtains at the noise; they had had enough of Frankie.

What Paul didn't foresee, as Navin went down, was the angry midget striking fast and hard from behind. Paul heard the savage scream one would expect of an insane man and felt knuckles skidding past his buttocks, making direct contact with his nuts. The henchman who possessed an enlarged right testicle felt the uppercut connect with this ball first. The hit was followed by a rough squeeze and twist, a motion similar to wet cloth being wrung dry. Paul bawled. A sharp abdominal pain erupted, not quite a cramp, but a pain which travelled as swiftly as recurring lightning to his head. His right leg buckled and he went down hard against the open car door. White dots, as tiny as pinheads, flashed before his eyes. His pain told him that to survive he needed his gun, but Frankie was up and over him.

Paul fell. On his knees he stood taller than Frankie but the midget, to demonstrate his allegiance to Bharat, had gone mad. It took more than three solid punches to Headley's temples to make him tilt like the Pisa tower, then a swift final blow toppled him. The spirit of survival told Paul to rise, but the midget packed mean punches to his groin. Paul drifted into unconsciousness, his last few thoughts touching the outskirts of Philadelphia.

Frankie's onslaught continued.

"WAIT! YOU'VE known me for two months and seven days and haven't noticed?" Leah was more hurt than disappointed. "*Shucks* man, Sean."

The driver was surprised. He looked away from the road. "I thought you didn't like that word?"

It was true. She saw the slang as offensive, the combination of two obscenities. Sean had mentioned it exactly a week ago in a telephone conversation, but it was mild enough and had successfully amplified her feelings. She retracted her hand from his leg and focussed on the dark road, sparsely spotted with incandescent headlights. She told Sean to do likewise. She checked her watch then sighed loudly. It was late. She should have been home hours ago. "Daddy going and kill me," she said unconvincingly, her mind still on Sean's inattentiveness. *He should know better*. She expected that he would have an eye for things she didn't highlight and an ear for things unsaid. It was love's guarantee and a man's duty to notice the things a woman did for him: fix her hair, straighten it, curl it, wear the dress he says he loves and secretly she doesn't.

The traffic was flowing steadily east out of Chaguaramas and although the car was fast the winding coastline roads prevented Sean from maximising the vehicle's power. *How the heck was I to know that Leah was missing the tip of her wedding finger*? She had been edgy since their departure from BiteInn; enough to spoil Sean's dinner. It annoyed him how adeptly she could recall precise dates and events. Sean's insensitivity angered him. "So what happened?" he cajoled, gauging the idiotic driver who insisted on hugging the car's back bumper.

Leah didn't answer. She watched the coast zip pass through the darkened windows. Wordlessly, a few minutes and potholes later, they approached the exit bend from Chaguaramas. The car ahead suddenly slammed its brakes. Cursing, Sean geared down. A narrow escape, but there was a slight thump from behind, so gentle that the airbags of Leah's award-winning vehicle didn't deploy. Still cursing his luck, Sean pulled the car onto the shoulder.

Leah, who had exited the vehicle, screamed.

DECLAN FOLEY moved swiftly. In seconds he was upon Sean and Leah. He was used to screams and even more proficient at silencing them. As a boy he had witnessed, on countless occasions, his father beating the daylight out of a lass he had married. To Declan, striking a woman was second nature. Blowing things up was his first. An effortless punch rendered Leah unconscious.

In a flash he was over on the driver's side. Foley pinned the door so that Sean stumbled back into the car as if performing a catastrophic flamenco. The attacker saw approaching headlights. He needed to be swifter. The first gun butt blow shattered the window. The second caught Sean on the side of his head, a loud snap as steel met bone. The attacker crouched and motioned as if speaking to the driver while four cars zoomed past. *Caribbean people. So busy.* Too busy to notice anything except their own affairs. The Irishman saw blood oozing from Sean's head, but the blow had been calculated; the man he had photographed over the past few days wasn't dead. Moving quickly, Foley flicked the headlights off and rushed to the rear car. The girl was already inside, slumped over the backseat. He spoke sharply to the driver and as suddenly as they had struck they vanished.

RAJ'S EMBRACE was real – cold, but real. So was the previous day's fight. In his arms Radica felt like a hostage. They were strangers; two pens in one drawer, one black the other red, each blind to the other's colour. She thought about Mickey. *Had Raj killed him*? She quivered and wished herself rid of the rough arms which wrapped around her neck like a leash. She craved gentle hands reserved for a lover's body. Mickey's hands.

Two weeks ago she had returned home with Randy. Raj had been a loving, caring husband but alas his efforts were in vain. She thought it unfair that he demanded two years of faults erased. 'Indiscretions,' he called it, not wishing to accept all the blame. He felt it was unacceptable a woman should cheat because of alcohol.

Trapped in his embrace Radica refused to relinquish memories of her being alone while her foolish husband drank with Lucky. Coupled with the alcohol were the traces of cheap perfume she found on his clothes. She would pretend she was asleep when he called out, contemptuous when he woke her to engage in intoxicated sex. He thought himself a man, yet couldn't give her a son. *The barren, useless mule*. She had always known it but he denied it, blaming her instead, like a child shifting error to a sibling.

Radica thought of the day she had met Raj, and cursed her luck. Lucky had introduced them, then left for a round of drinks. Raj, startled by her beauty, had played the cool hand, refraining from alcohol and using the best vocabulary and grammar his judgment allowed. It had taken two weeks to swoon her and as they made love for the first time, in the backseat of Bharat's car, he believed: *if I impregnate she marriage go follow*. Unlike a ball of dough Radica's stomach never grew round, but when Bharat had discovered the affair he insisted that they marry.

They did and on the heels of their marriage Mickey, out of luck and having lost his job as a forklift driver, came to live with them. He couldn't bear to return home to his parents and the big-hearted Raj had extended an open invitation. *Mickey Mouse*, the newlyweds called the man, then it became *Mouse*. It aptly described the quiet, unassuming individual who was Radica's faithful companion and confidant when Raj went drinking with his buddy. It did not take long for them to become lovers.

Trapped in Raj's arms, she smiled at the thought. Whenever Mouse's body had touched hers she would feel ecstasy mounting within her, like a crack which appears in a wall and violently widens. She had dropped the nickname and began calling her lover by his Christian name. Raj had noticed the change but thought nothing of it.

Radica reminded herself that her infidelity was not for cheap thrill but for the fulfilment of love, which she didn't care to conceal, like money behind her bra. She wanted to declare it from the rooftop but she couldn't, not with Raj around.

Her mind became filled like a sold-out football stadium and Raj's embrace served to increase her revulsion. She hated him. Confusion clawed at her mind and entered through opened windows she thought locked. She wanted to escape, to flee from the world she lived in, to one where there was nothing but Mickey, Randy and herself but her lover was dead; poisoned at the hand of an assassin.

Raj felt the agitation in Radica's body. "What happen to you, girl?" he asked aggressively.

She didn't answer. She unlinked from his hands and slid away. In silence she found sanctuary.

"Why you can't confess? *Eh* girl?" Raj stood and faced the blank Radica. "Look at me!" he barked.

She did, but her gaze wavered like a lit candle in the wind.

Raj wanted to hit her, to cripple the woman but kept his vibrating hands fisted tight at his side. *Radica have gall or two brass balls.* He knew her infidelity was real but wanted to hear it from lips pouted with resolve. Angrily he stormed out of the house, heading for the closest bar, leaving Radica to plot her escape.

LANCE JONES swore ambitiously. It wasn't a habit he practised regularly, especially in the presence of his stepson, but Sean's frantic knocking and bloodied head warranted the outburst. At the time the journalist had been authoring an article (he thought it a poor piece) on the recently initiated Government Mentor Programme, but he darted to the open door, in time to collect Sean who collapsed.

"What the heck happened?" He settled the boy in a chair and checked outside. His initial thought was an accident but the unfamiliar, expensive car looked undamaged. "Whose Audi?" Lance asked nervously. He looked at Sean and grimaced at the gash, uncertain as a rookie mechanic as to what should be done. In his career, he had investigated worse scenarios but none where he had been attached by an umbilical cord of emotion. From old western movies he knew the wound had to be cleaned. *Was it warm or cold water they used*? Lance couldn't remember and mixed hot water that had been prepared for coffee, with cold liquid from the faucet. "What happened?"

Sean hesitated as lukewarm water touched his head – he flinched. He thought of Leah and of the brutal attack on his life. When he had regained consciousness the enormity of his predicament stepped in groggily. He hadn't committed a crime, but already he felt like a criminal whose data was being plugged into iCitizen. It was this fear that had driven him home, hoping that Lance would be there. Now, he wasn't sure if his step-father was the one to speak to. *If he isn't, then who is*?

"So?" Lance enquired.

Sean closed his eyes at the sight of blood leaking down his shirt. Blood sickened him. As a child he could recall fainting from the slaying of a lamb. What could he say to his mother's husband? Sean began a choppy recollection of the incident.

"Hamad!" Lance exclaimed.

Sean had just started the story. "You know her?"

The journalist ceased cleaning the wound and stepped back, his mouth agape. "You mean this Leah… she's a Hamad?" He was more shocked than Sean. Disbelief engulfed him. "Father! Boy, you know who you dealing with?"

Sean didn't.

"Them Syrian does play real rough." Lance Jones had experienced an unpleasant run-in with Gregory Hamad after he had written an article on a suspicious factory burglary. He sat and began wringing the reddened cloth into a basin. When it was damp he dipped the fabric into a pot with fresh water and repeated the wringing process. "Do they know who you are?"

Sean shook his head; it hurt when he did. "*Nah*. I don't think so. I know the girl rich, that is why I was frightened to go to the police or the family."

Lance wasn't sure if his stepson had made the right move. The immediate problem was the car outside. The right thing wasn't always the best thing; Lance Jones' experience told him so. He had seen upright families suffer. He wondered: *what is the best thing to do?* It was unsavoury to be *hammered* into a corner. As a journalist it was his duty to give the people the truth, unedited and unrated. He knew that through the barrel of the pen the sword could be conquered and an era of prosperity proclaimed. In the face of these events the journalist wanted to protect his son. Even if it mean lying.

Sean wanted to rescue Leah. "Dad, I just can't leave her out there. I love Leah. Because I'm scared does not mean I want anything to happen to her." Love was supposed to be unselfish, but he didn't want to be harmed. He faced a tidal wave of fear.

The journalist weighed the situation. "Do you have a picture of Leah?"

"Yes. On my laptop." Sean was confused but trusted Lance. His stepfather would know what was best.

"Okay, let's go and park her vehicle at the university," Lance commanded. "Just do as I say, boy"

Twenty minutes later the task was done and both were back home. It took the journalist three hours to concoct the page three story. He signed it with the nom de plume, Lot Adams.

## 27  The bull pestle

ARAM WAS maddened at the news of Leah's kidnapping. He became a cursing, vulgar bomb. No longer was he symmetrical; his life had become a blur. Twisted. Jagged. Like a stone subjected to harsh weather. He had everything but nothing, should know all but didn't. Even the walls of the basement seemed closer; they weighed oppressively on his mind, like survivors in an overcrowded life raft.

He walked to the newspaper, scattered across the thick Persian carpet like a pack of unused cards. He pulled at the leaflets until he found the front page. On it was a recent picture of his daughter and a headline casually announcing her dilemma, as if it were a grand invitation to a warehouse sale. How was it that the newspaper had news of his Doll even before he did? Wasn't she supposed to be at home? Where was Paul? The Syrian's blood boiled hot, like oil prepared for pouring on Christian raiders of biblical days.

The photograph of Leah was unfamiliar. The graphic artist had done a poor job of cropping the picture. There was someone intimately close to his daughter, the face unseen. Was her camera upstairs? It wasn't in her car, discovered on the university's compound. If it was, the authorities weren't saying. When Aram had observed the slow methodical work of the police on the outskirts of the taped area, he concluded that every person in the country deserved the right to a private army. The men worked like sculptors, irritatingly slow, the results of their labour invisible to the Syrian.

Det. Marco had reeked of cigarettes and incompetence. Neither did the Syrian's promise of money contend within the spectrum of the man's duties. Aram had felt his powerlessness in the dismal university morning, blind to the piercing eyes of joggers and other curious folks aroused by the alien activity. In anger, Aram had fled and on his return home found the family gathered, praying as Sunni-Muslims should, but to no avail. Their prayers had gone unanswered, even in bringing Gregory home; his wife was dressed as a mourning Syrian widow would. Aram's wife was in the group, faint or drunk with grief. It didn't matter. Aram's office was his sanctuary, his place of claustrophobic refuge where news of failure had continuously engulfed him.

Behind biometrically secured doors Aram clutched the picture of Leah to his chest and cried. He needed strength, a power God alone could give, but his consciousness told him that a man in his position, a man who had succumbed to worldly vices, his prayers would never reach heaven. Still, he prayed for redemption, not for himself but for his family, for his daughter.

Aram felt strength that made him rise. He shuffled upstairs like a deflated gambler. In Leah's room he found his wife, a limp soul, on their daughter's bed. Aram wondered how many times his spouse had been in the room. She had never been especially attentive to Leah or maybe it was vice versa. They were two different women: one very materialistic the other simply Leah – not Leah *Hamad*.

Aram pulled and dug through drawers, undisturbed at skimming through Leah's personal effects. Finally, he found what he sought. He deciphered the mechanics of the electronic device and discovered pictures of Leah and an unfamiliar, non-Syrian profile. There was something about the face that seemed familiar, as mixed faces tend to look. *No*, Aram decided, *I do not know this man*.

Aram felt hot anger at his daughter's betrayal. The lies she had told. The promises, the hugs and kisses that had reminded him that she would always be an angel, his Doll.

All fibs. Her character dissolved before his eyes. The brief stint of disgust vanished, replaced instantly by hot shame. *Yet she is my daughter.* True, she had broken the family's code of love which should remain within the race, but matters like that were now inconsequential. Once she was safe, her failures could be dealt with.

Aram hurried to his basement and dialled Paul Headley. When the call failed, he summoned another contact Gregory had once provided.

THE BULL pestle is a curious weapon produced from the severed penis of a dead animal. The process takes time. The organ is soaked in oil, hung vertically from a height equalling the desired length and left to dry for two weeks. It then becomes rigid as bamboo cane and its application is simple: swing and hit. The first blow is rumoured to stiffen a man. The second has the victim dancing. The third causes the idiot to run for miles with bovine strides. For an added sting, the device is soaked in urine, one night before a flogging.

Bharat stooped and removed *Betsy*, a five-foot-long bull pestle, from a bucket of cow pee. He held it by a knot tied to one end and shook it so that droplets briefly appeared on the dusty floor of the vast storeroom.

Navin, who had been standing next to Paul Headley who was securely bound to a chair, stepped back as The Boss approached.

"You know what this is?" The Manager scowled at Paul, and when the bound man didn't reply, he looked at his henchman and said, "Like he do not know who *Betsy* is, Navin? You want to introduce him?"

Navin smirked. He had been waiting patiently to get his hands on Paul Headley, a man as big as Crapaud but definitely more skilled. Paul had inflicted a severe blow across his face and left a mark to prove it.

"Crack him one," Bharat ordered and extended his hand.

Navin swiftly dealt a savage blow to Paul's head, smashing the shades off his face, splitting his skin into two inches of pale white. Five seconds later, in hot rushes, blood cascaded down his face. The second blow landed across his chest, fracturing bone. Paul bellowed like fifty cows and defecated into a bucket below the chair.

"Like he shit himself yes, Boss," Navin chuckled

"That is a bull pestle you know!" Bharat boasted. "That is what gangs used to fight with long ago, and police *uses* to move with that." He turned to Paul who still shook violently on the chair. "Boy, shush *nah*! You will disturb my employees." Bharat looked around until he found a piece of cloth – it smelled like wet clothes left in a bucket for days – and stuffed it into Paul's mouth. "Hit him a couple more," Bharat dictated. "He will talk don't worry."

Navin smashed away and with each cruel blow to the chest, arm, legs and shinbones Paul jolted violently, but there was no escape. The restraints tightened around his wrist. Blood trickled down into the bucket. When the torturer delivered an overhead strike to Paul's shoulder he became still. His head slumped to his tattered shirt, his jacket long torn to shreds.

"Don't kill him!" Bharat shouted, more annoyed than concerned. "Look how you knock out the damn man." He wriggled his fingers and Navin passed *Betsy*. "How the ass he go talk now?"

THE CONTRAPTION is sadistic. It is made of wood that separates symmetrically into two, each piece an innocent looking model of a three dimensional rectangle. When joined, the pieces form a hollow box. It is designed to monstrously restrain the neck, like a rabbit's head trapped in a chain link fence. The crude device is four feet high; an adult has to kneel to fit inside.

When Leah awoke she was locked in such an apparatus. Terrified, she tried to scream but her neck was pressured by the wood which snagged the mobility of her larynx. Within the contraption her hands had some leeway. She pushed up on the wood, but no luck. She felt for her legs, her hands bruising against the un-sanded material. Careful to keep her head still, her eyes swept the cabin. *Where am I?* Then she heard music, a melody belonging to a genre she didn't recognise. *Irish music?* She thought of Sean. Numb to the pain she inflicted upon her throat, Leah began to cry.

TO SEAN Brown love excluded cowardice. The revelation dawned on him while seated in the international departure lounge on the eve of his great escape to the Big Apple, the brainwave solution of Lance Jones, stepfather, but it was a move that clashed fiercely with Sean's convictions.

An attendant with an American accent announced the departure of flight 522. Sean's couldn't stand; his legs felt like rubber. He wanted to find Leah, to set her free of whatever evil had beset them. His head still throbbed. The cap hiding his unstitched wound was uncomfortably tight, like undersized elastic pants on a blubbery waist.

The attendant repeated the announcement, calling for passengers belonging to group one only to queue at the boarding gate. Everyone stood, including travellers who had taken seats in an area designated for handicap passengers. Sean remained seated. Suddenly he remembered something. Despite the sight of the diminishing queue he browsed his laptop until he found an email, sent by Kerwin Acres, its subject: *'iCitizen gr8 job.'* Below the signature was a telephone number. Sean sighed and looked around. His eyes met the attendant's, but he quickly looked away. The boarding gate closed.

Hesitantly, Sean dialled the number. He negotiated. An hour later an irritable Det. Marco and Kerwin 'Ernie' Acres escorted him from the airport.

## 28   Dinner for four

THE NAME *Chief* tickles the woman. She smiles. She likes it. *Chief*. There is a certain power in it, not subtle, but of raw authority. *Cocky*. The slender woman takes the call outside. Inside are too many buzzing ears.

It's the synthesised voice again. She had spoken to *it* for the first time, two days ago, and the caller had become a persistent burden. She lights a cigarette and speaks casually, using a deep, masculine voice she has mastered. She dusts the ashes from her cigarette by applying her thumb like a lever to the butt rather than tapping closer to the ignited tobacco as women tend to. She smiles, enjoying the shift in power structure, experiencing a queer, sexual ecstasy regarding the caller's identity, his or her physical's structure, face – *he*. It is more exhilarating to imagine it is a *man*.

He asks the same questions, but she has no news for sale. She becomes agitated. She shows her frustration by speaking rapidly and rotating her hand in small angry circles, causing the pencil-thin cigarette to burn faster. Even the loud flapping of the national flag in the compound irritates her. She moves away but the noise persists.

She could only assume there is no government intelligence on Paul Headley and knows there is nothing on the kidnapped girl. If there was she would have known, she guarantees the caller. The call ends the same time her cigarette does.

Chief looks around, the way someone would when searching for a familiar face at an airport terminal. It is an unconscious habit she exhibits each time she is uncomfortable or believes she is being careless. She doesn't know it, but it is this habit which renders her a poor hand at poker. Her recent escapades worry her, but she tries to wave off her indiscretions, like one does an annoying fly. It was her practice to never communicate for more than a single day – two for the most – on the same prepaid mobile number and keep her communications limited to after office hours. But the players have become more demanding. For her it is not the money but the thrill of belonging to a world dominated by men. She tries to convince herself of this. She walks, still trying to evade the sound of the flag but careful to stay behind the white wall; she hides to avoid men.

Her inability to identify the caller makes her hesitate. *It could be a setup*, she thinks. *Why would the voice enquire of Leah Hamad and Paul Headley?* Days ago – *was it three?* – Bharat had enquired regarding Paul, giving a silly story (*cock and bull*) too inconsequential to recall. Chief knows Paul. She bites her lips at the thought of the tall, black, bald, muscular man and makes a sucking, non-sexual sound, as if she had licked a spoonful of honey and tasted instead concentrated lemon. Muscle-bound men (or any for that matter) do not interest her, neither does the function of their manhood. She sees man and his mind as a kid's pool, shallow at either end, its length unable to satisfy an Olympian gold medallist. She has no qualms when men die at each other's hands, but protecting her identity is as important as concealing her hidden lust for women.

More relaxed, Chief leans against the hitching rail and watches traffic crawl past, like grocery items on a conveyor belt. She lights another cigarette and takes a fierce, manly pull. She flicks the stub away when a raw, burning massages her oesophagus. The appearance of the vice intrigues her, but the scent reminds her of her father and his inability to function with paternal authority.

Chief convinces herself she is secure but finds little comfort. The waters need to be tested. She needs to see if the synthesised voice is real and not a hoax. She decides to arrange a dead drop, a down payment in good faith. If there is five thousand dollars waiting, she would play against Bharat. She pops a mint past sensuous, thick lips and re-enters Whitehall.

That night her phone would ring. When it did she would negotiate.

ARAM HAD aged two decades. It had been three days since Leah's captivity (*and not death*, he hopes) and already the forty-three-year-old had greyed significantly around the mouth and head. Before, it was about drugs, now it was just about Leah. *Or is it?* He imagined his daughter on one end of a scale and 1.5 tonnes of cocaine on the other. It was morally right that one should outweigh the other, but he saw the items as having equal importance. He sunk his face in his hands, aware of but not enjoying the curious, squishy sensation of his features being dragged beneath calloused fingers. His face bore a dull, jaundiced complexion, his height lessened by slumped shoulders.

The only catalyst to his senses was the telephone. Each time it rang he experienced unnerving flashes of hope and fear. He did not desire calls from well-wishers, but from his henchman and his daughter's abductors. His cellular phone rang. Aram stiffened at the synthesised voice. He thought of Paul, but the voice identified itself. Aram cursed. *Professionals.* Instructions were issued then the voice was gone.

Aram rushed out of the house and drove to Port of Spain, dismissing every road rule; he had a package to collect.

An unmarked police car followed the Mercedes.

MOUSE FELT like a caged animal. At the army base the nights were suffocating. A queer stillness pervaded, like the dark seconds before a tremendous dance act that would never come. Mouse appreciated the quiet moments, but he had been so long without Radica that he had lost count of days. In the safe house it was snail pace. Television and newspapers held zero appeal.

CISTU was good to him, particularly Bob who always had a good joke or riddle. Two days before Mouse had caught up with the private who gave him something to think about. In his thick Tobagonian accent he said: "I have a good one for you. A riddle, not a joke. As a boy I hear it from Mr. Jones... he dead now." Hope had noticed Mouse's impatience and said: "A man have a boat that can hold only two things at a time. He has to take a lion, a bundle of grass and a goat over to the other side, but the thing is, he must never leave the goat unattended, with the grass, or the lion with the goat." The riddle had briefly occupied Mouse but his thoughts soon strayed. Radica wasn't in his life.

Mouse left the kitchen and anxiously walked to the living area. "Bob," he said timidly. He was glad it was the private and not the sterner Sookram.

Bob Hope checked his watch. "Yes boy, Mouse. What you doing up at eleven in the night?"

The witness confessed. He missed his girlfriend. He hadn't spoken to her in ages.

Hope felt sorry for Mouse and regretted his isolation. "Listen," he said, "make the call brief. No more than two minutes. Here, use my cellular phone and keep this *below the white line*." Hope adjusted his phone's settings. "I blocking my number. Don't want that going through."

Mouse thanked the man profusely. Back in the kitchen he dialled, and when Raj answered, he almost hung up. "*Cuz*, is me... Mickey." He stayed silent. He wasn't sure what to expect.

"Mouse, is you? Is really you? Where you?" Raj asked. He hustled out of the bedroom where Radica was changing Randy's pamper.

Mouse, unaware that Lance Jones had published his *death*, fabricated: "I was in Tobago for a few days. Bharat was right, I needed to cool off. Listen, I don't have much time. You could pick me up in Chaguaramas? I meet some friends and we went fishing but the car shut down."

"Sure. Sure. No problem at all," Raj said excitedly. "What you want to eat?" He was thinking about Bharat. *Should I call him?*

Suddenly, it occurred to Mouse that for the past month he had been living on baked beans and sausages, food that had become unpalatable as rubber tyres each time he chewed on it. "Yes boy Raj, a good curry. We could make a cook. Meet me at twelve, okay, close to the entrance to the army base." His two minutes were up.

It was half-an-hour to midnight when Mickey Samaroo vanished like a shadow. The State witness had flown the coop, like so many before him.

MICKEY EMBRACED Radica. To the casual onlooker the hug could have qualified as one of friendship, but in it electricity flowed. A thrill snaked down into his loins. In the brief moment he savoured her familiar scent, but there was a stiffness about her.

Radica had been arranging the table when both men entered. Raj had left earlier ordering her to cook for an unexpected friend. She hadn't thought much of who it would be, but there he was – the *dead* man she had been flogged for and would take a licking for anytime.

She rushed into the kitchen and began biting her nails, hoping that Mickey hadn't admitted to their adultery. During their embrace, she had tried to relay the message, *Raj knows*, but Mickey had missed the warning signals tapped on his shoulder. What was to become of them she could not guess and so she waited for the right moment to warn Mickey. *I need to fix this.*

She delayed in the kitchen and Raj called out to her. After awhile he entered the cooking area and quietly, yet roughly, commanded her to sit with the guest. Look your man reach, he said nastily. There was no alcohol on his breath but he was still the same ass, she thought. Wordlessly she left and sat at the table, listening to Raj overturning pots and pans. He was looking for something. Raj was adept in the kitchen, much unlike her real lover. Radica felt that if she could sew together the best parts of both men she would have the perfect man, the Frankenstein of love. But seeing Mickey alive rekindled love she knew could never be extinguished. Just when she thought it was safe to say something, Raj entered the dining room bearing two large pots filled with curried chicken and dumplings, steam curling from beneath lids, displaced during rough handling. Raj was the last to fill his plate.

The State witness was relishing his second dumpling when Raj spoke: "Mouse, I want you to know that you have been dishonest with me."

Mouse looked at both adults, first at Raj then at Radica. She lowered her head and stirred dumplings on the white enamel plate, leaving skid marks in the curry. *Does Raj know?* Mouse swallowed food gone bland. "What you talking about boy Raj?"

"Mouse," his cousin said, licking food-stained fingers, "you don't need to play me for a fool. I know about you and Radica long time." Raj paused. "I waiting long time for my suspicions to be put to rest and *meh* prayers get answered cause you come back from the dead to answer." Radica was about to speak but Raj silenced her with a pointed forefinger which shifted to Mouse. Imitating Radica, he mocked: "*Mickey*, what you have to say? Why you so quiet? How you so *cargo-cargo*? *Yuh* real *poohar eh!*" Randy began crying feebly. Raj wanted to scream, to silence the child.

The last time Mouse had felt trapped was during his interrogation with Robert Marco and Kerwin Acres. Now, he knew the walls were crumbling. "Raj," he stuttered, putting down his spoon. He felt faint. "Yes. Yes! We had an affair. I so sorry," he murmured, but Raj waved feebly, like a sick old man.

Raj looked at his son who had stopped crying and had fallen asleep on the table. "Mouse you *dutty, stinking,* lying, cheating bastard!" he exclaimed. He had long accepted the event. What he could not digest was who the adulterer – *hornerman* – had turned out to be. *With Mouse?* The man was so inferior, so lame. Raj looked at the woman he was bound to only by a ring. She was a miserable wife yet he loved her dearly. Still, he wanted to lash out, to hit her. He felt blood draining from his body. *Is not even she who admit. The mother of me child. How could she?* Raj never imagined that confirmation would be so painful. Death would have been kinder; he thought about suicide and not alcohol.

He looked across at Mouse – *the blasted rat according to Bharat* – whose head lay on the table. *He can't even face me*. Raj wanted to forgive him but knew it wouldn't be easy. Still, the traitor was family, as cunning and deceitful as he was. Raj had sworn to Mickey's mother; he would protect the boy. As such he had kept Mouse's return from the dead secret from Bharat. Later, he hoped to purchase a ticket for Mouse's departure to Canada, using a fake passport. *With him gone I could work things out with Radica. If I wanted he dead he would ah done be floating in Caroni River*.

It was Lucky's input which channeled Raj's thoughts. 'Everyone deserves a second chance,' the older man had said from his rehab bed. 'Maybe our lives have become unmanageable but a higher power can restore us to sanity.' Lucky hadn't convinced Raj to give up the bottle, but he had left the younger man with a smile that stretched into his soul and dug deep to find the little good that still existed. Through his vertigo, sharper than a drunken stupor, he said, "Mickey Samaroo I forgive you. You is my flesh and blood." Raj licked the froth that had gathered around his mouth.

The pesticide with which Radica had laced the food was taking effect. Randy, being the youngest, had died first. Mouse never heard Raj forgive him. Radica dolefully observed Raj, regretting that she had met him before Mickey. She had not expected his forgiveness, but it didn't matter. Mickey was already dead and with her secret in the open, life would never be the same. She had foreseen Mickey's confession. She had thought: *no doubt I would end up on the streets*. She didn't want that. Neither did she want her child to be called *bastard*. Looking at the dying Raj she was convinced: *all ah we better off dead*.

Raj lunged from his chair. Clutching his chest, he fell over the table. Radica watched him. He had always been a tough man. Another burst of terror sent him sprawling across the dining room and crashing violently into the television set. There, life's screen went blank. Radica stared at his contorted body. *How pathetic*.

She embraced her dead child and began eating. Then she fumbled across and sat on Mickey Samaroo's lap. Death was a slow, painful, agonising release.

## 29   Giovanni's

INSIDE WHITEHALL an angry Alex Peters tossed *The Tabloid* at the PM.

"Where does this man get these stories?" Ambrose asked. The lines in his forehead deepened as he read Lance Jones' page three article: *Dinner for Four.* "Mickey Samaroo. Isn't he our hopeful?"

The distressed MONS nodded. "Guy disregards our protection programme and ends up dead. Imagine, those gangsters killed an entire family to get to this one man."

"And we're taking the beating for it," Ambrose said, reading on. "What about Ricky Love and Amrit Sankar?" he asked, feeling like he was enquiring about spare parts. CISTU was doing a good job of keeping the lid sealed. At least so far. "Where are they?" He was genuinely curious.

The PM wasn't cleared for such information. "They're safe. Maybe too safe. Their lips are as sealed as their whereabouts." Alex thought the rapists were being punched with kid gloves.

"And are they are legit?" Ambrose asked.

"Yes" Alex replied irritably. "Semen samples place each at the scene of Jane Doe's murder, but nothing links them to the Boodoo massacre. Our forensic team is good, it knows what to look for."

"Any other leads?"

"None that we can immediately follow," Alex regretted. "We can't work their families. The men are *missing* on their own accord."

"Any idea who their boss is?" Ambrose asked hopefully, to no avail. "Maybe we should release them with two million dollars less."

"Good idea, but they're more likely to skip the country than take us back to the mother ship."

"Maybe the mother ship will go looking for them."

"We can't work on faith like other prime ministers," Alex said. "Sooner or later we are going to have to react."

The PM caught Alex's hint. "It's almost one month since they've been in custody. You really think we should apply more pressure?"

The MONS smiled.

"Anything on Leah Hamad?" Ambrose asked, wiping the smirk off Alex's face. The story was on page five, still important, but no longer major news.

Alex shifted and fussed over lint on his jacket. He felt like a bearer of ill tidings. "The family isn't being very helpful either; you know, a clandestine bunch." Then, to compensate: "Their telephones are bugged, we're listening."

Ambrose sighed. Trinidad hadn't suffered a kidnapping in over two decades. So far the Hamads hadn't come forward or responded favourably to the authorities. Maybe they had their own private army. "Do you think she's dead?" He bit his lips and closed an eye, as if watching the climax of a movie that had suddenly become too scary.

Alex didn't commit an answer.

"And the boy?" It was a great disappointment to learn about Sean Brown.

"He's clueless. Never even saw his attacker." The MONS shook his head. "Poor guy." Alex, unlike Ambrose, could sympathise with Sean's actions. At twenty-five, he himself or his youngest son could have erred in like manner. What he didn't appreciate was Lance Jones' contribution to the ordeal. The journalist could face a long prison spell. The way things looked, his writing days seemed over.

INSIDE THE parcel are five thousand crisp American dollars. Chief smiles and flicks through the money with her thumb, enjoying the rustling sound, like the pages of a new book being flicked. She reminds herself that money is made of paper and rags and it isn't the reason she commits treason. Money is merely an added bonus. She admits, though, that the score is pleasant even if worrisome.

A knock resounds on the expensive mahogany door enclosing the facility. In the restroom the mahogany emits a sharp, pleasant odour which most attribute to a grape-scented air freshener hissing every two minutes. Chief responds politely. She pauses, her thumb still caressing the money. She listens. A male voice apologises and the shadow behind the door disappears. It is about the only quality she admires in men: the respect they have for the distressed female requiring urgent use of the john. She laughs at her tactic; it is as good as placing an out-of-order sign on the door.

Chief would never dare to make a dead drop in the *Ladies*. She knows women. They are more likely to waste time inspecting fine designs and *Giovanni's* commodes are second-to-none. Super would be an understatement. The restroom, grand as a five star hotel's, is comfortable enough for popcorn and movies. Women were more likely to apply makeup, complain about their date or gossip about the bartender who kept staring. They could do this for minutes. The *Ladies* is never private. Chief hates this. But men would simply pee, wash their hands, if at all, and leave to consume more beer. They would never ask another man to 'hoist my zipper.'

In the Italian restaurant the envelope was fastened securely to the base of the splendid marble counter supporting a tempered swirl glass bowl. In the package there is a note written in horrid upper case characters one would expect a doodling child or doctor to create. The note is short, requesting information on 'LEAH HAMAD.' The name is written neatest, traced heavily to emphasise importance. Next to the name 'URGENT!!!' is scrawled. Paul Headley's name is mentioned and information requested on the 'MAN' in the photograph.

Chief shakes the envelope and a photo falls into her hands; it is awkwardly angled but not blurred. Chief immediately recognises Leah's face. The other, she has seen before, somewhere important, but she fails to attach a name to the geeky 'MAN.' She promises herself that when the synthesised voice calls she would have valuable information on Paul Headley. She sticks the envelope in her brassière, massaging the American dollars, and quits the restroom.

THIRTY HOURS after Aram collected the parcel, the kidnappers called on the cellular phone they had provided. Had circumstances been different the synthesised voice which relayed instructions would have sounded annoyingly comical to the Syrian, but he listened. A financial demand was made for Leah's life, an inconsequential amount, nothing more than a few shillings below a rich man's carpet.

The caller's second request was simpler and grossly unnecessary: no police. Aram found himself agreeing with the caller – *is it the Irishman mentioned by the press?* – noting the service's inefficiencies with a nervous laugh, wanting to say more but not knowing what. He went silent. The reply was an electronic '*heh heh*.'

Aram almost screamed when he was given a Thursday appointment, nine days away. The third demand simply stated the drop-off site, a familiar but unexpected location. The caller re-emphasised the need to maintain silence: should arrangements go contrary, the girl would be as inconsequential as the money.

Aram wanted to believe the caller was bluffing, but couldn't chance it. This wasn't a game of cards; this was Leah, his life, his Doll. When the caller had ended the list of demands Aram requested proof of life. *Click*. The line went dead. Aram Hamad dialled his personal banker and spoke in Arabic. Then he called Chief using the STE.

ERNIE HUSTLED to the interrogation room with a digital voice recorder, the kind journalists thrust at interviewees. Robert looked up impatiently; it was the third time his interview had been disrupted. His shoulders assumed a questioning shrug. Ernie beckoned him into the conference room and pressed a green button.

"Arabic?"

The analyst nodded.

Det. Marco was paces ahead. He knew it was imperative to translate the conversation but lacked human resources inside CISTU to do the job. Stanley, a linguistic expert, could have done it but he and Frank were dead. *Damn it*. He left to make a telephone call.

Ernie entered the interrogation room. Sean was seated, his head shaven and stitched (six in all). Sean looked up and greeted Kerwin Acres, and again the analyst insisted on being called Ernie. The circumstances of their first meeting had been acknowledged as awkward but they had communicated in a manner which to Robert sounded like a discussion in tongues. The small, bare room did not disturb Sean and the two began speaking like marine scientists who alone could comprehend jargon such as 'red tide' and 'bathypelagic zone.'

Because Sean faced the door, he saw Det. Marco first. With a wink and thumbs up – both hidden from Robert – Ernie left and Robert resumed questioning. It was the third day of interrogation and he was at it alone, Ernie was proving to be most friendly and unprofessional with Sean.

"My answers can't change," Sean said when Robert asked who else was involved in the Leah Hamad incident.

The detective didn't believe him. In the early part of the investigation Sean had declared that he alone was involved. Then he had cracked and involved an imaginary friend. Then Lance Jones' name had surfaced. "Is there anything you can recall?" Robert implored. "Anything... anything that can help us? We need to know, Sean."

The software engineer bore the look of one warily contemplating marriage. "No. Nothing. I'm sorry." He imagined faces of villains from modern movies. Nothing.

He wanted desperately to help, to save Leah, but his throbbing head was blank. When offered lunch he declined. As he sobbed he wasn't sure he had done the right thing in responding to Ernie's email. Leah was still missing and Lance's claim on being contacted by an anonymous group regarding the girl's disappearance, had fallen through because of Sean's admission.

PRIME MINISTER Taylor was inflamed. "How can you tell a man not to negotiate for his child?" *Tacticians and strategists can be such insensitive...* The thought of a strong word eluded Ambrose. The leader's day had been long and tiresome.

Alex shrugged defensively. "Negotiate and it's going to become a lucrative trade. Obviously Aram is requesting one million US dollars to pay a ransom." The MONS had been reluctant to have DEA agent Jake Pipes and his foreign personnel translate the tapped conversation between Hamad and his banker. Alex wanted to keep the affair local but time didn't permit for such conflicts; Leah's life was at stake.

Ambrose understood Alex's contribution. He said so, but found it surprising that Alex had bluntly rejected negotiations – '*even if it is one cent*,' he had boomed. Perhaps it was because his children were all grown, hardened men pursuing tough careers in the army as their father had. But a young woman, while depicting more maternal characteristics, was often more emotionally attached to her father. Ambrose knew this. His teenaged daughter would consult him first, then he was expected on her behalf to appeal to Patricia. Ambrose thought: *maybe it's the reason why women seem to wed men who remind them of their paternal parent.*

"Sir... generally it is felt that if you negotiate you are going to get a happy ending," Alex reasoned, "but it is an obnoxious alternative. What we don't want is a criminal business venture being established. We don't want to become like Mexico or Columbia."

Ambrose conceded. Alex was an entrusted minister, a man his equal; joint, not better, judgment would prevail.

Ideas had to be meshed and thus far all the players weren't on the field. An important man had to be included in the equation. "What do you want to do? Call Hamad and tell him that we know what he's up to?"

The MONS shook his head fiercely. "No, that's not it. We can observe from a distance." He smacked a clenched fist into an open palm. "But we must strike. We must deal a heavy blow." He searched for words; he needed the right ones to magnify the depth of his intent. "Kidnappers *will not* be tolerated in Trinidad and Tobago."

Ambrose nodded. "Okay, but we're going to do it the proper way. I'll call Hamad."

Alex was satisfied, but didn't smile.

## 30 The water board

RICKY LO had been brought up on the word of God but, isolated in the windowless cell, he was beginning to doubt even *Jah's* existence. In his confusion he questioned his life on earth. At intervals, between the timeless minutes that slipped past in the small horrid room, he yearned death. Prison was the one place he despised, but he knew the inmate's life. It was better to be loyal and in prison than disloyal and free where Bharat could find him. He would have welcomed death but his drive for revenge, the drive to know who subjected him to this torture, gave him strength. Ricky Lo suffered in solitary confinement.

The three-by-five cell sank into darkness and Ricky was manhandled into handcuffs. He was roughly gagged, a hood swept over his face. He was shoved along until he came to a familiar room. He could discern Amrit sitting to his right. Ricky grunted, recognising his accomplice's foul scent. Amrit's reply was a feeble murmur as a familiar silhouette locked Ricky into a chair.

MINUTES LATER the door screeched open and the hooded Amrit perceived Ricky being unshackled. Ricky disappeared but the door was left ajar. From where Amrit sat, he saw into the bright room where shadows danced on the walls. An argument seemed underway. Suddenly, a scream pierced Amrit's ears. It was a shrill, horrible sound which jellied his mind. He rocked violently until there was a snap and the chair toppled over. From the prone position he still saw shadows. *Ricky must be the screaming mongrel*, he thought. *What the ass going on?*

Amrit's fear had come alive: the men had begun to play rough. He was dragged upright by rough hands despite his squirming and kicking. When he was shoved into the room, Amrit swore into his gag. Ricky Lo lay shackled to a board and a mysterious figure was pouring water over his face. Amrit began squealing like a piglet.

TWO ROOMS away, Ricky Lo heard the piercing scream which had jellied Amrit's mind. His vantage point was similar and he became fearful when he saw the eerie shadows torturing Amrit. Then he heard the sound of water. *Like they drowning he?* Ricky's fear escalated. Obviously the door had been left open for a reason. He was being made aware of what to expect and water was something Ricky thought himself incapable of handling. The frightened man prayed. When his head was shoved into the room he saw Amrit on the Waterboard. Ricky knew of the device; in prison he had heard rumours.

WITH WATERBOARDING a person is inclined on the back with the head downward, known as the Trendelenburg position. A cloth is placed over the victim's mouth and nose, and whether water is poured on the face in small or huge amounts, the gagging reflex elicited by the inclined position indulges the victim in an experience of drowning. The CIA had long proven the method to be more effective than dipping someone's head into a bucket filled with water.

Merv prided himself as a swimmer. His bronze, sleek, shaven body bore the symmetry of a man who kept busy in water. He had never experienced suffocation and the inhalation of water through his nostrils made him retch uncontrollably. The pouring stopped and the gag was removed.

"Did you touch him?"

It was a harsh voice which Merv didn't recognise. He wanted to break free but straining at the shackles didn't help. He felt the warmth of his blood seeping over the water when his wrists ripped. *Where am I?* The last thing he could recall was watching Phillip's naked body gliding through the crystal pool in his Diego Martin backyard. Now he was here. Something told him his survival depended on dishonesty.

Captain Rawlins gagged the man and again poured water. He was angry. His son had played right into the hands of a demon. *But neighbours were supposed to be loyal friends!* After an unexpected return home he had found Phillip being entertained by the pervert. *Was it the first time?*

Rawlins removed the gag after six seconds. Another denial. The pervert had stamina.

ONE LEVEL up, members of the assault team observed the waterboarding on surveillance monitors. Sookram was having a frenzied fit. "This isn't right!" he again declared. He voiced the unwritten fact that the purpose of the mountainside facility was to house criminal detainees, not to address personal vendettas.

"Why not?" Oxy asked. He was angry at the sailor. "Imagine your son naked in the neighbour's swimming pool. Not only that but the old, dirty bastard is masturbating." He motioned to the screen with his forefinger. "I would be doing the same thing if I was captain and so would you." He looked at the screen. Rawlins was pouring water on the pervert.

MERV'S SPIRIT broke. He had only undressed the boy, he confessed, nothing more, nothing more.

AMRIT SANKAR and Ricky Love heard the single shot. Seconds later, Amrit told Oxy everything. With Ricky dead, he didn't believe it made sense to keep a still tongue. He hoped it was the Rasta's denial and not admission that had claimed his life. If so, Amrit felt there would be another gunshot.

TWO ROOMS away Ricky disclosed everything to Sookram. The Rasta didn't want to face the water board. In the end both stories coincided. CISTU had killed two stool-pigeons with a single bullet. They had a name and one child molester less to worry about. Rawlins dialled the MONS and mentioned the ominous Chandra Bharat.

"WHAT'S THE word?" Ambrose asked when Alex Peters slipped into the Think Tank. He had been expecting the Minister of Finance.

Alex related the jail birds' tale; the confession had come as quite a surprise to him also.

"Chandra Bharat? The reformed Chandra Bharat?" Ambrose hadn't heard the name in decades.

Alex threw a manila folder onto the desk and it skidded over the polished surface to the head of government. "He was more active in his early days, doing jail time for trafficking marijuana, prostitution and possession of small arms. Apparently he paid his dues and became quite a generous gentleman."

Ambrose jogged his memory. "He also featured heavily in a land squabble that ended favourably for squatters."

Alex looked puzzled.

"Don't you remember?" the PM asked.

Alex didn't. He shook his frowning face.

Ambrose rubbed his forehead. "This ex-housing minister... Timothy Charles. He and Bharat clashed in a heated debate over a Las Lomas land controversy."

"Shit!" Alex exclaimed. He had missed that. "Didn't Charles die of a heart attack?"

"A bullet," Ambrose corrected. "Timothy survived a front lawn assassination attempt, but a heart attack later claimed his life. I'll say he was murdered, others will rival this, but they never found the shooter. In fact no effort went into apprehending anyone."

Alex muttered a single, slow obscenity which surprised the prime minister. "After that Bharat dropped off the scene. His profile declares that he owns a farm in Central Trinidad. Based on what the jailed men say if we strike we could expect to find money, cocaine and probably human remains in the pig sty. Bharat and three of his goons are

234

linked to the Boodoo Lane massacre. We know that Mickey and Raj Samaroo died in a murder-suicide fiasco according to CISTU investigations. There are two others: Lucky and Navin, first names or surnames we're not sure."

Ambrose thought of the deceased Minister of Housing. *Is Bharat responsible?* Four years ago Charles had openly criticised Bharat and Mark Lloyd. Two weeks after Charles resigned from Mark Lloyd's Cabinet he was attacked. *Heck! Crapaud, Bull, Jane Doe, Ravi, Ranji and Mrs. Boodoo. Mr. Boodoo? Timothy Charles? Who else?* Ambrose was convinced he had to get Bharat and his henchmen off the streets. "Who's going to make the arrests?"

"The police are out of the question," Alex said flatly. "We can't risk our intelligence being leaked. We still didn't know who Chief is. "The major problem we'll have is Bharat's army."

Ambrose concurred as he flipped through the gangster's dossier. Bharat was a zealous provider to different groups. To have overlooked him entirely was a horrendous oversight. "How then?"

"We're going to have to hit him hard and fast. In and out," Alex continued. "We know exactly where the drugs are."

Ambrose whistled. "There's going to be bloodshed."

"Mr. Prime Minister," Alex said, catching Ambrose off guard with the formality, "you must decide. Ask yourself, do you want to fight Bharat and his men in court? Do you want to chance them walking the streets again? Inside that file, Sir, you have the evidence."

Alex left.

One hour later when he revisited Ambrose, the head of government was occupied with Lisa Maharaj, Minister of Finance.

IT WAS the night before the exchange. Aram had already entertained the afternoon prayer session with his family, uncharacteristically leaving before it was over, and as they maintained vigil on the ground floor he sat, a bitter, contemplative man in an office once elegant.

The call with the prime minister had been a brief one, a mere *'check up.'* Aram was angry at Ambrose's choice of words. The Syrian had felt like a patient enduring a virus which needed to be monitored. *It would be better if the incompetent leader ceased calling*, Aram thought.

Using his heels as a pivot, Aram rocked his feet, thumping them repeatedly against two duffle bags filled with the one million dollars that could save his Doll's life. The solace was temporary. He turned on the television then switched it off. He knew he should sleep but couldn't, not while his daughter's life was at risk. He sat in the dark wondering about, but not worried by, his plan. Everything would be fine, Ambrose had guaranteed, Leah's safety was the government's priority. *What a foolish man.*

## 31   One shot one kill

HER MANICURED nails are long and painted. They clack loudly with each keystroke. Chief knows this disturbs her co-workers but they have never complained so there is no need to desist. She is on a website known as *caribbeanMeetUp*, a virtual social network for Caribbean people. It is here, days ago, she found the young man's online profile, complete with a photograph that looks years old. She marvels that people would open their lives to public intrusion. Obviously he operates under a false screen name. His alias is *Cyberduck*, and text messages she has sent have all been unanswered. She clicks *Send* and another message transmits.

The synthesised voice hasn't called since she received the note. She knows that the more information she has, the more money she will collect. *More the merrier*. Chief laughs and an obese secretary in the adjacent cubicle *steups*.

Alex Peters appears and she minimises the browser that eighty-five per cent of the world population uses. He compliments her and asks that the note – he waves as he speaks – be personally delivered to the COP. Jimmy the courier isn't here, she tells him, and unbelievably he requests that she takes it.

"It's urgent," he stresses. "Use my car." He smiles broadly and she barely conceals her pleasure at the thought of driving in luxury.

She accepts the key and envelope in a way that suggests she is used to such daily tasks. Outside, she finds the automatic transmission car – she was hoping it was manual – and exits Whitehall. Traffic congestion denies her the chance to test the vehicle's torque, and twenty minutes later she arrives at Police Headquarters. The car is heavily tinted and equipped with official licence plates reserved for government personnel. The policemen standing at the corner do not disturb her; they expect MONS Peters.

Her eye catches the glove compartment. Curiously she tests it. *Locked.* She stares at the keys. The first one works and inside she finds a black journal only. It is bound with a combination lock. She rolls the small metal knobs until the numbers align to the password on the MONS personal computer. *Bingo!* The journal opens, the pages flip over slowly until they rest on the last entry – *yesterday* – due to the stationed bookmark, 'from a loving wife Angela.' There is a sentence written, in the minister's neat, familiar handwriting. *Strange that such a big man writes so small.* It reads: 'Suggested a move to take out....' The incomplete sentence is accompanied by two illustrations, surprisingly well done, of a rat and a rum shop. Chief fails to decipher the message. *What a bloody weirdo the minister is.* She thumbs the pages. 'Amrit Sankar and Ricky Love.' She recognises the names.

Her attention is jolted by a police officer who knocks on the tinted glass. She replaces the journal, carefully, locks the compartment and exits the car. The policeman isn't expecting a female and fumbles, to the amusement of his colleagues who gape at the sultry woman. Their eyes linger on her body and they turn away to comment.

Chief hurries up three stories to Ken Thomas' secretary. Doreen, Chief thinks, is an ancient woman who should be at home in a rocking chair knitting with a dozen cats and grandchildren at her feet. Doreen compliments her pleasantly. She is upset, however, when the attractive lady insists that the envelope must be personally delivered. Doreen waves her away, pointing at a chair besides Ken Thomas' desk and warns the visitor to touch nothing.

The slender Chief sits and waits. Ten minutes turn into twenty. She is impatient but not bored. Her mind works on Alex's journal. Suddenly, it makes sense. She searches for her *special* cellular phone but realises that she has left it switched off at Whitehall. She knows Ken Thomas' Private Branch eXchange (PBX) password and once she is sure Doreen is occupied, she calls *bar rat* from the Commissioner's phone and warns him about the government's plan. Bharat agrees to have five thousand dollars deposited at *Giovanni's*. She hangs up and glances at Doreen who is busy sipping coffee and adjusting a dusty shawl. Her nose is buried too deep in the paper to notice that Chief has just arranged a dead drop.

Chief is anxious to leave but duty binds her. She notices a manila folder placed neatly on the Commissioner's desk. Keeping her eyes on Doreen, she teases it over with her forefinger. The folder is labelled iCitizen. Chief pulls at the edge of a photograph which reveals *Cyberduck. Sean Brown* is scrawled beneath the photo.

Chief recalls where she has seen him: he had been scheduled for an interview with Kathy Mills, Minister of Information Technology. Chief is elated at her fortune. She has scored twice today. She thanks some unseen power and when the fat, old man arrives she smiles pleasantly (to Ken's surprise) and leaves abruptly. *Time waits for no one.*

THE BUG, activated when Chief lifted the receiver to call Bharat, transmitted the conversation to a listening post disguised as an abandoned storeroom in the basement of Police Headquarters. Software scrambled the voice data using an asymmetrical key encryption algorithm and routed the traffic to the forensic lab in Mount Hope.

DETECTIVE MARCO, alone in his van, watched the Mercedes Benz turn onto the eastbound lane. Aram's car was magnificent, Robert thought. Sun glittered against its body. Robert radioed his position to Ernie at the forensic lab and moved forward, keeping the car ahead in sight. He had to. In it was one million US, payoff for the kidnappers.

The executive car zigzagged as if uncertain about its destination, until it came to the national stadium and parked.

Robert Marco waited. *Something's silly about this plan*, he thought. He sweated for half an hour, since the van's air condition system was broken. When the car pulled off he transmitted a second message to Ernie. It took forty minutes to Central Trinidad and another forty to San Fernando.

The Amerindians had dubbed the city *Anaparima* – 'Single Hill.' It is flanked to the north by the Guaracara River, the east by the Sir Solomon Hochoy Highway, the west by the Gulf of Paria and the south by the Oropouche River. To the sides of the hill there is evidence of open wounds inflicted by quarrying. From the park on the hill one could see the oil refinery which bolsters the city's and country's wealth. The Mercedes had settled on the hill

In the car park, at the hill's base, Robert switched vehicles. In the abandoned Ford a camera monitored the road, transmitting the feed in real time to a forensic lab computer which recorded to a redundant array of independent disks. Marco's *new* car was heavily tinted and undisputedly the most common in the island. To Robert's delight it was also equipped with an air cooling system, perfect for a stakeout. Robert cellular phone rang, startling him as he was about to radio his position.

"We have a problem." It was Ernie. He had been reviewing telephone conversations originating from the Commissioner's desk. "Chief is planning a dead drop with Bharat."

The problem was huge. "Blast it." Robert lit a cigarette.

Ernie had a plan.

"You're crazy," Robert declared. He swore again. He was in a quandary. "What about Petal Clarke?" The pathologist was indisposed. A car was coming. Robert needed to get back to work and Ernie needed an answer. "Okay… use Sean, but give only necessary details," he said and hung up. He wasn't certain if he was stupid or mad for agreeing with Ernie's crazy idea, but with resources tied they needed someone to oversee the dead drop. Robert Marco detailed the approaching car: 'green, two passengers, male driver.'

"*Roger*," squawked Captain Rawlins. The assault team had been camouflaged in the hilltop's brown, sparse terrain since 0000 hours. The car showed. "False alarm," squawked Captain Rawlins, "just two local tourists."

After two hours of false alarms Robert was furious.

IT WAS 1030 hours, about the same time Det. Marco started swearing in the surveillance vehicle. The sea rolled around *Dolly's* bows as white as milk, studded with bright sparkles of blue light. The milk curdled, then it was marble with clear black water in between as the vessel headed further west.

Aram was in the bridge, manning the same luxury vessel he had captained on New Year's Day. Next to him were two duffle bags laden with one million American dollars. The captain was dressed in a loud red sweat suit, sleeves rolled in a vain attempt to combat the oppressive heat.

Aram felt an emptiness as vast and deep as the waters below him. He thought of his wife. It was the first time they were collaborating in years; their daughter's life was at stake. They had done things together, like the honeymoon in Damascus, but he wondered whether they had ever passionately bonded. Even now as his wife played decoy on San Fernando Hill she was unaware of his location, his dealings, but as expected she had done as instructed. Aram was too preoccupied to notice a waving yachtie who considered *Dolly's* captain a snob in his big, expensive boat.

Knots later, Aram slowed the vessel and with difficulty moored the five-million-dollar boat against the jetty. Scattered across the landscape were poui trees, tossing bright yellow blossoms onto the island's red, dry terrain. To Aram the place was no longer beautiful. The instant he set foot on the land he knew that Leah was somewhere on Huevos Island. *Where are you, Doll?* He quivered.

AT 1700 hours the sun blisters the land. Anaparima's terrain is rough, decorated with boulders, some weathered into loose gravel that scatters all the way down to the centre of the park. Captain Rawlins and his three teammates are dressed in beige and brown, desert camouflage. Months ago they would have been frustrated, but now they are trained.

Their positioning is strategic, each man, even in the wide open, has his AOR. They are prepared for three hundred and sixty degrees of surprises. Should the battle go mobile their transportation is hidden nearby. Each man has water in his canteen. They wait.

The radio squawks. It's the first communication from Robert Marco since 1638 hours. Rawlins confirms. A grey car comes into view and parks close to the Mercedes. No sign of Aram. A Rastafarian lumbers out of the grey car. The driver, another Rastafarian, laughs hysterically at his companion's antics then fusses over a stem of marijuana, which, through Oxy's crosshairs, seems six inches long. The newcomers are loud and, oblivious of the idling luxury sedan, peek into it, like children looking into an arcade.

Sookram's voice comes alive over the radio and Hope transmits.

"Stand down," Rawlins orders. Something isn't right, but his gun remains trained on the men. "Stand down." It seems impossible that these two marijuana goons are capable of keeping a kidnapped girl secret for thirteen days. Maybe they are accomplices, sent to dig out moles, if any; they *can't* be anything more, Rawlins reasons. It is possible, and again he repeats the order. CISTU is to fire only if Aram, who remains in the car, is compromised. CISTU waits.

When the Rastas have had enough of the car – 'Check the rims! The tint! The *bling*! Oh gawd!' – they walk towards the swings and sit. The shorter, more excitable one sparks another joint.

The Mercedes suddenly pulls off.

"Without a driver! Man, this is some good weed!" Another long drag and the marijuana changes hands.

CISTU waits.

TONIGHT, THE dead drop is crowded. Men, ignoring their female companions, look up as she glides past, decked in a maroon dress which seductively hugs her waist and lies comfortably flat on her stomach. She is black, beautiful, blessed and gorgeous. Her strides are long and confident. She sees a familiar face and turns abruptly. Too late, she has been seen. She waves lightly, rolling her fingers like a pianist, and smiles. Men gathered at the oval-shaped bar compete to catch her attention. She ignores them and one tries to swoon her over – 'Come and chill out nah, family.' *The drunk fool.*

She pushes the main restroom door which sticks halfway then opens. The mahogany door to the Men's room does the same. The scent of the wood greets her and she reminds herself that she must purchase the grape-flavoured aerosol. Once the door is locked she places a matching velvet purse on the marble. She stoops. She feels. The envelope with five thousand dollars is missing. *Damn it!*

She composes herself and checks again. She waits and listens, her ear pressed against the door. The corridor is quiet. She darts out and quickly examines the other commodes. Three obscenities.

Chief storms out of *Giovanni's*. A rush of wind greets her. It is night and traffic flows lightly. She can see Whitehall, but is disinterested by the building; she perceives it as contemporary slavery. She calls Bharat. To do otherwise would be weakness. It would make her as vulnerable as Achilles' heel. The call isn't pleasant. Bharat's abruptness is scary, his crude language intimidating. He questions someone on his end about the drop (Chief hears the name Navin). The Manager is back on the telephone, speaking louder than before. He guarantees that the money has been deposited – as always, first stall on the right. She can picture his face in its anger, reflective shades hiding his ill-kept secret. Bharat's breathing, deep and violent, subsides. In the background she hears laughter.

The door behind opens and the sound she hears on the cellular phone is amplified. She shifts to let the person slip past, but there is no movement. She looks up and her bowels weaken with fear.

It is Bharat dressed in grey.

The velvet caressing her breasts shudders, the momentum accelerating with rapid, powerful heartbeats. She cringes under his inspection feeling like a peasant before a proud king. His scorn violates her. He strikes a match and shelters it with both hands, reminding her of a sensitive child protecting a butterfly. Within this vacuum a cigarette is lit. With shaking hands she mimics him. Fear subsides with each drag and the thrill is different. She knows her confidence is rising. Chief regains that cloak of dominance and laughs, puffs of smoke shrouding her.

Bharat smiles too. Chief mistakes it for a grimace. His lips fold, exposing gums darker than his complexion. As Chief flicks her stub she decides that Bharat is an expensive, horrid man, but she accepts his invitation when he opens *Giovanni's* doors and sweeps his hand like a butler, allowing her entry.

"You are mad to be here," she tells him in a coarse whisper once they sit. The table is to the centre of the restaurant. She feels exposed and unconsciously adjusts the 'V' so her voluptuous breasts hide.

Bharat scoffs. He finds her bumptious, the type of woman Ricky Lo would have loved. He lights another cigarette and asks about the government's plans for him. Meeting Chief was vital as Alex Peters' plan was disturbing. He wants to hear it first hand from *his* inside source. He wants to know everything. It is why he, and not Navin, is at *Giovanni's*. He knew she would have called when she didn't find the money at the dead drop.

She can offer nothing more. Chief thinks: *it is not wise for me to be here*. To offer nothing would anger him so she lies. She warns about a possible attack, how soon she cannot say.

Emile, a pimple-faced waiter, appears. Bharat orders *Montalcino*, fine dark wine, Italy's best, and one rum and cola. The waiter hustles away. He has never sold a bottle of the expensive wine; no one has.

"Amrit and Ricky?" Bharat asks. He dusts cigarette ash on the white table cloth.

Chief tells the truth. She gives the date of the journal entry where the names appeared. She adjusts the 'V' again. *The damn thing only sliding.*

"Same day they disappear," Bharat notices. He bounces his leg rapidly and his knee hits the table. Cutlery and ceramic rattle. He adjusts a displaced fork which becomes the subject of his attention. "Anything else I need to know?"

Chief shakes her head. They smoke in silence, gauging each other. Bharat stubs out his cigarette and grimaces. She is not charmed.

Emile returns, lifting the awkward silence. He is excited and clumsy, lacking the finesse of an experienced waiter. He drops the wine as he presents it. The bottle hits the table with a loud bang and topples over. There is a bright flash. The waiter swears but the bottle doesn't break. It would have been two months without tips to pay for the dark wine.

Fists folded, Bharat dismisses the waiter's apologies and pays promptly from a fat wad of blue notes. Chief watches the money disappear into his jacket. He gets up and smiles – that grimace again. He dips into his pocket, the same one with the fat bundle, and passes a white slip of paper. Chief is visibly disappointed but Bharat leaves her with the *Montalcino*. She crumples the IOU slip for one thousand dollars and dumps it on her way out.

THE JOB was supposed to be simple: 'in and out, that's all.' Take the photographs and leave, Ernie had said, and don't get caught. But at 1827 hours, Sean Brown was still propped on a stool at *Giovanni's* bar, a neat oval with a bustling crowd – *for a Thursday night* – that drank mostly local beer labelled in vibrant yellow and blue. Women swirled glasses of red wine, the cheapest *Giovanni's* had.

It is a bar where one, to sit, has to drink alcohol. The policy had grossly upset Sean. He thought it distasteful for an establishment to impose the rule of drink on customers. He had mentioned this to the barwoman, a chubby red-skinned female with hair greased onto her forehead and a neck with too much powder. *Giovanni's* policy, she stressed. Her response had been simple: 'Find another bar that does sell *seadrink* (sweet drink).'

But *Giovanni's* bar offered the best vantage point. Sean had been ordering cheap beer and water (at ten dollars a bottle) since 1300 hours. The beer had tantalised him. He was a young man, one month sober, trying hard to deny alcohol. At intervals he sniffed the green bottle, contemplating the taste of the *beastly* cold, defrosting brew. He bought one every thirty minutes to remain seated. He waited, hoping Leah would walk through the door each time it swung open, but it couldn't be. He thought of his stepfather but the kidnapped Leah was foremost in mind.

At 1430, the appointed hour, no one had come. Wait, Ernie told him, someone will show up. Sean ordered another beer. This one was more inviting. He stuck his tongue into the bottle, to the scorn of some very young women who looked like they had skipped school. The liquid was out of reach. The girls were aghast. One tried to break the ice, but Sean lamely responded in Spanish, '*no hablas mucho ingles ahora.*' They pointed at his beer and giggled at their inability to communicate with the '*Spanish guy from Venezuela.*' One commented that Sean was dumber than he looked, and their chatter swung to an upcoming Alternative concert. They enjoyed the future rather than the moment, Sean thought. *Maybe I have done the same with Leah.*

At 1715 hours (when Mrs. Hamad departed San Fernando hill in the Mercedes) Sean called Ernie. It was important, the analyst told him, and apologised for his indiscretion; Ernie had lied to Sean. He had informed him that his girlfriend was supposedly cheating and proof was needed; the clandestine meeting would be at *Giovanni's*. Earlier, at the forensic lab, Sean had recognised photographs of a younger, cruel-looking Chandra Bharat, Ernie's fabricated rival. Sean had given Ernie the incredible story of his encounter with Bharat, but the analyst had not looked as fascinated as the software engineer had expected. Sean had demanded the truth about the assignment but all he squeezed from Ernie was: 'Top Secret.' Sean had to get a picture of the woman only, if Bharat showed get one of him also. Maybe then, Ernie had bargained, Lance Jones' release could be negotiated.

Later, Bharat had entered *Giovanni's*. Sean checked his watch: *1800 hours on the dot.* It was as if the man had been standing outside waiting for the exact moment to enter. It was time to purchase another beer. Sean ducked low behind the Happy Hour crowd and ordered. When the lager came, his tongue touched the liquid. The beer was hot. He complained to the barwoman but she ignored him. Sean took it as a sign and ordered water – the discounted price was eight dollars; beer was seven bucks.

Cautiously, Sean peered past bobbing heads and saw Bharat sit. *Shit.* Ernie had not portrayed this; Sean had only to snap a picture of Chief. If impossible, visual identification was ample. There was nothing in Ernie's scenario about Bharat dining. The man, if he showed at all, would simply go to the dead drop then leave. There was nothing about him ordering rum and cola from a waiter who had just clocked in. In panic, Sean placed another call to Ernie. Voicemail.

Bharat sat motionless, sipping rum and cola. Sean saw him guzzle six drinks in an hour. Then the plot thickened. He recognised Chief, but not from the photographs he had seen. He knew her face. He had seen her before at Whitehall. She looked different. *She is more confident, more… pompous.* Sean looked at Bharat whose head turned as the lady in the maroon dress strode across the floor. A drunk, annoying patron hailed her. She responded with a wave but her face suggested menace. She disappeared into the restroom and Sean became acutely aware that he hadn't taken a leak for the past six hours. His bladder ached, fear flowing unchecked. He was trapped and still without a photograph.

Later, in the restaurant, Bharat's phone rang. Crouching, Sean looked as Bharat exited *Giovanni's*. The software engineer wondered: *do they really know each other? Did Ernie get it right?* Moments later, Chief and the gangster were seated and appeared to be in a heated discussion.

Sean looked on as a waiter took their order and came to the bar.

Emile, as his name tag read, was laughing. "A bottle of *Montalcino* please." The way he pronounced the brand and the barwoman's expression telegraphed that the wine was expensive.

"Go and give them the wine and come back for the *rum and coke*," she ordered, passing the four-thousand-dollar bottle.

Sean clapped the rookie waiter on his shoulder. He leaned over and made an offer. Sean watched Emile walk nervously to Bharat's table. The timing had to be perfect else all hell would break loose inside *Giovanni's*. Men like Bharat didn't test easily. Cautiously, Sean observed the waiter as he slid through the crowd balancing the *Montalcino* clumsily on a tray.

Meanwhile Sean requested a *'photographo.'* The girls willingly agreed; they loved foreigners and flash photography. As they settled themselves – fixing hair, adjusting makeup – the chubbiest asked Sean if he was a member of *caribbeanMeetUp*. *'No intendies,'* he replied.

Behind them the waiter dropped the four-thousand-dollar bottle. 'Bang!' There was a wave of turning heads. Sean snapped rapidly and no one noticed or cared, all eyes were on Bharat and Chief.

Sean saw that Bharat was infuriated and with difficulty stayed composed. Emile, apologising grandiosely, tugged, wiped and fussed at the spot where the customer's grey jacket had been stained with *Mostarda*, *Salmoriglio* and other condiments that decorated the table. Bharat paid and shooed the rookie away.

Emile rushed to the restroom, all part of the plan, imagining his grand fortune; with the cash he would be able to buy the latest game console. Sean watched as Bharat stood and passed Chief a note. Then, with a grimace, he left. Fifteen minutes later, Chief followed with the wine clutched to her bosom. Sean ordered another beer before Emile showed.

"Good work," Sean said, tapping the anxious waiter on the shoulder.

Emile wasn't interested in compliments. "Where *meh* money?" he demanded. His voice was a musical scale that trembled from deep bass to a fine treble. The money stuffed into his pockets, he asked: "Did you get the picture of your cheating girlfriend?"

Sean, ignoring the question, handed over three hundred bucks – CISTU money. He didn't think the waiter would have pulled it off, but at least he had the evidence secured in a miniature, *low-light* specialty device that looked like a common digital camera.

A BOWL of ice, two glasses, a soft drink and a bottle of rum. Glen cracked the seal, fixed himself a drink, passed the bottle to his friend and waited while Icepick, shocked, looked at him.

"*Wha's* that one?" the angry guest asked.

The glass was almost to Glen's lips when he stopped, the drink forming tiny waves by its unexpected halt. "How you mean Sunil?" Confused, he wiped off rum which had splashed on his neck.

"You is the host and I does always crack the seal!" Icepick exclaimed. "And stop calling me Sunil!"

Surprised, Glen stopped sucking his fingers. "So what wrong with that?" He downed the drink.

"Man, to hell with you!" Icepick shouted, "I gone!"

"Well go, you blasted killer!" Glen barked. He was vexed and watched the man skirt along the foliage.

Icepick stopped by the boat and cursed it, Mr. Jeremy, Fr. Big Head and Glen. Then the darkness swallowed him.

Glen thought: *more rum for me*. He was annoyed but managed a surreal chuckle.

## 32   The final confession

PAUL HEADLEY was in the hands of bad men. Over the past two weeks his earrings had been sliced off his ears and when all six were gone, Navin had enjoyed skidding a knife along Paul's bald dome. Aram's subordinate had spilt the beans the very day he had been captured yet he continued to be held prisoner. Paul had learnt that there were no human rights in Bharat's camp, just the sharp edge of Navin's blade and the stinging palm of The Boss' hand. Unrelentingly he had been interrogated about his employer's operations. His answers never changed, and the physical pain increased.

The door to the storeroom opened and Isabel entered bearing a tray. She looked around frantically, like a mouse sniffing for a cat. She rushed over to the chair where Paul was bound and winced. The African didn't look good. "*Señor*. You eat," she said anxiously.

Paul shook his head. He didn't care for food, just freedom, something she hadn't been able to offer – so far. "Let me go," he pleaded weakly.

"I cannot. *Señor* Bharat will kill me," Isabel said. She set the rice, black beans and plantain on a table near Paul. She was stupid to think he could digest solids. She held water to his lips, cupped a hand below his chin, and tilted the glass.

Paul sipped at the liquid. "Please call the police... please," he implored. His eyes were closed but it didn't ease the pain. His shoulders and wrists were raw from the handcuffs. "Call Derrick Seales." He muttered a telephone number.

"It is if he has gone mad," Isabel mumbled. She didn't know enough English to pacify Bharat's prisoner. "*Dos dias...* two days ago? *Si?* Since you come here. He put more guns by the bed when he sleep… Like he expect *mucho* trouble." Isabel had vomitted, but it wasn't because of the weaponry. Why, she couldn't tell Paul; she didn't possess that level of intimacy with this black man. At the sound of a horn outside, she slipped from the room, removing the items she had brought.

Paul Headley was alone in the darkness. He screamed. Bharat and Navin entered. There was the scent of stale urine and Paul cringed at the sight of his enemies and the sinister bull pestle they called *Betsy*.

DEATH VISITED Icacos. He walked down Lalla Trace, a long narrow strip lined with coconut trees and leading to a pleasant beach. Thirty years ago the road was sand and houses were wooden. Today, split-level concrete structures pushed the past further away. Times had changed. The population had grown, and cattle had lessened. *Ah, more people*. The Hooded Spectre chuckled.

None ripe for the picking, *Yama* (as the lord of death is known to Hindus) tossed his scythe on his shoulder and retraced his steps to the junction which formed a 'T' with the trace. There was the church to the right, but Death turned left. Gliding, he moved one hundred and fifty paces to a nameless road. He saw a man, cigarette dangling from his mouth, with a great round head and big white beard, cleaning fish in a bowl of water spotted with large yellow limes. *No, not this one*. The black hood glided on.

Then he saw Glen.

The stale-drunk man was raking fallen periwinkle flowers and leaves. From Death's awkward position it was impossible to see the small heaps the man had gathered, but as the cloaked figure moved along he noticed four, small mounds of dried leaves and stones. The man had a peculiar filth which Death savoured: the faint smell of alcohol evident despite the strong scent of fluoride; the red network of veins across his eyes, like a jellyfish's tentacles.

Glen looked around uncomfortably – everyone does when Death is near. He continued raking, stopping occasionally to glance around jittery.

The Grim Reaper was inches away.

Glen stooped and gathered a small heap, using the rake and his hand as a vise, and dumped it into a barrel. *For burning later*, he promised. Death waited while Glen gathered two more heaps. He moved quickly, like a man in a hurry to keep an appointment. The fourth heap was closest to Yama. Glen inched in and with the slightest touch of Death's finger the boat, which had snuffed out Mr. Jeremy's life, tipped over and fell on his son.

The clock began ticking. Glen had ten minutes to live.

LITTLE JOHNNY, an eight-year-old, was the only witness to the accident. He rushed over and found Glen pinned from the torso. Under his head periwinkles were squashed and red liquid oozed from the neighbour's mouth like bubbling lava. No stranger to plucking and gutting chickens, the sight didn't disturb Johnny. The sand swallowed blood. Glen mumbled something. It took a minute to understand and five to return, not with a rescue team which Johnny knew Glen needed but with '*Father Big Head*.'

The clock ticked. Four minutes left.

Awkwardly the priest knelt, ignoring the sand, blood and dead leaves which clung to his surplice and cope. He and Johnny tried to free Glen but it was useless. The fibreglass boat was too heavy. Father Dugan, gesticulating wildly, told Johnny to call all the strong men he could find. 'Hurry lad!' The priest gauged Glen. He didn't look good: a pale film coated his body and a jaundiced cloak covered his face. Fr. Dugan thought he should fetch water but didn't want to leave. He had to wait.

Glen clutched at the Irishman's vestments and tugged until the priest's ear pressed against his lips. Glen knew he didn't have long for his final confession. He spoke of the pictures he had hidden from the priest. With deep, painful gasps he stuttered about destroying the picture below the mattress. He had lain on it, broken it in error.

Dugan listened to the confession, a revelation of lies Glen had spoken so often on behalf of Sunil, a name the priest didn't know. The clergyman was not angry, but absorbed every word in sombre disbelief as the bloody lips quivered on.

"They is not all lies... Father. The events are true... I know so... now." He clutched the priest tighter. "There is drugs leaving Monday morning in... in... Sunil's car. Balkeran... Balkeran is the big drugs man in... Ica...cos. He... is... a... nasty man... who go dead just now. He have... *portrait* cancer. Pain.... Father... pain! Oh... Lord!"

"Who is this Sunil you speak of?" the priest whispered sternly to grasp the dying man's attention.

Glen didn't answer, but he was still alive. His empty eyes stared past Father Dugan's head to a shadow that had gathered. "Sunil," he said, and smiled. An agonizing sound curdled within his throat. He smiled again, death's smile. He wanted to say sorry for the argument they had last night, for not being a better friend. He found the heart, but not the strength, the words reached his lips, but died there. There was a low, mournful sound. A last effort. "Father, forgive me, for I have sinned," he gagged. Glen Jeremy's time had run out.

Father Dugan turned and saw Icepick standing, hand-in-hand, with little Johnny. Others would soon come.

Death's work was done.

## 33  Prime Minister Taylor's dilemma

BHARAT SHOWED up suddenly, just as Isabel was exiting the storeroom. "You *Spanish* fool you! I know you feeding he!" He struck her viciously.

Isabel didn't stay down. She darted for the bar where Sinatra's *My Way* blasted from the stereo.

Bharat followed. His world was filled with problems and the woman who should be supporting him was working against him. He recognised some of the Spanish obscenities she hurled at him along with glasses from the bar. "Who you cussing *eh*?" he barked, advancing menacingly. A glass for which he had paid one hundred American bucks, flew past his head. "You buy that *eh*? You little whore!" He trapped her against the bar and pressed hard into her pelvic area with his knee. His hands held her roughly, just above her elbows, giving her room to thump at his chest.

"You calling me a whore?" Isabel screamed. "Chandra, I pregnant with your child and you call me a whore?" Bharat heard, but the news did not affect him positively as she had expected. Isabel had chosen the wrong time.

Bharat's burdens had pushed him beyond sanity into a hemisphere of madness. He functioned, but couldn't think; he acted, but upon impulse. He had developed a compulsion for rage and though Isabel carried his child, he beat her savagely. The bar was destroyed. Splinters were everywhere.

He found a chipped glass and an unbroken bottle of rum. A drink revived his senses. He still had anger to unleash but Isabel was unconscious. He longed to punish something or someone. Paul Headley was still in the storeroom, he remembered. Bharat ambled in that direction.

SUNDAY, 1015 hours. Alex tossed the twenty-seven photographs Sean Brown had taken on to Ambrose's desk. Each picture viewed, the PM passed it to the President. The fifth picture shook PM Taylor. "Is this...?"

"*Yup*, that's Chief," Alex said. He had already recovered from the shock.

Ambrose had met earlier with the President and brought him up to speed. The meeting had been long overdue but the older man's recent triple bypass had excluded him from dialogue on national security. The head of state had a reputation for being fiery but declining health had chipped at his robust character. He approached new issues like a barefooted person tiptoeing near broken glass. "What's *she* doing with Bharat?" Michael White asked astounded.

"That's *the* inside source," Alex assisted.

Ambrose still hadn't recovered from the surprise. He was speechless. He started to say something then stopped. He scoffed. "We're being screwed over and over."

Alex looked at the man. It wasn't the best analogy, especially for Sunday, but the prime minister was right. "At no cost," Alex added, not offensively, but the words stung. "This isn't about politics, this is about war."

"Any word on Aram?" Ambrose enquired.

The President looked at the MONS.

"No," Alex said abruptly. "Neither about his daughter. Our intelligence has nothing for us. They both just disappeared off the face of the earth, it seems. The mother knows nothing about their whereabouts." He sighed. "It's a bloody fiasco."

"You think he has been kidnapped also?" the President asked crossly. Suddenly, he clutched at his chest.

Ambrose poured water from a glass jug and passed the crystal liquid via Alex.

"Possible, but who's going to pay the ransom? He signs the cheques," Alex replied, shrugging.

"And Bharat?" Ambrose probed.

"He's lying low in Central." Alex handled one of the photographs which showed a hostile Bharat looking at the waiter and the woman in maroon cringing. The gangster looked disgusted, as if he had soiled his expensive shoes in dog poop. Alex passed it to Michael. "We have no idea what she has told him and what she knows, but she's playing the field."

"She's a brave woman," Michael commented. "Shouldn't we have *moved* on her already?"

*Moved?* Alex wasn't sure if the President meant assassinated or arrested. He played it safe. "Some would say so, but we're monitoring her. She's involved with some low lives, men we've tried to nab and who have slipped out of our hands, no doubt because of her. We've retrieved information from Subscriber Identity Module (SIM) cards she purchased under the guise of *Sam Kingsley*. The analyst, that's Kerwin Acres–" he said this for the President's sake– "is doing the background checks. She has made more calls to bad guys than they probably do to their lawyers."

"Including Bharat?"

Alex nodded at the President. "Including Bharat. That's how we traced her. She called him from the Commissioner's desk phone."

Ambrose tossed the pictures onto the desk. It couldn't get any worse. "Lance Jones?"

"He's out of our hair for the moment. *The Tabloid* is hitting us with everything they've got, especially with the Hamads still missing. He is a major financier for the Opposition so you're not going to hear the end of that until things iron themselves out." Alex paused. It was time. "Sean Brown took these pictures."

"Sean Brown?" Ambrose was astonished.

Alex looked at the prime minister. "Resources were tight, we didn't have a choice."

Ambrose didn't complain.

The President wasn't pleased. "Does he expect compensation?"

"*Yeah*. Leah walks, and he and Lance Jones are in the clear." Alex hadn't yet agreed to the proposed terms but he had no fears, except maybe for the journalist.

"Cheeky guy," Michael added. "Fellow pulls a trick like he does and wants to walk away clean?" Then, calmer, he suggested: "But Lance Jones, he's a good guy."

Alex grinned. Michael White was entitled to his opinion.

"Chief... I still don't believe it," Ambrose said. He gazed at the last picture in the stack.

"That's the way it is," Alex said. He wasn't in the mood to pacify, but as angry as the prime minister. "She has cost us a lot, Ambrose, and come tomorrow she will be back in Whitehall doing what she does best." Alex paused so the words could sink in.

"And what's this?" Ambrose asked. He held up a manuscript which looked like it an old bank statement printed with a dot matrix printer.

"That, my friend, is fresh news," Alex said excitedly, "That's a transcript of a conversation between an *anonymous* informant and our call centres."

"What's it about?" Ambrose asked. He wanted the synopsis, he wasn't animated about browsing seven pages. Maybe later. He passed it to the President.

"Word on a quantity of drugs leaving Icacos tomorrow."

Ambrose looked squarely at Alex. "Verified?"

"Yes."

"Who called it in?" Michael White asked innocently. He was expecting a full name and address.

"A contact known as *Padre*," Alex responded. "The cargo is coming in by plane. Maybe it already has... we aren't sure."

"How can our radar technology help?" the PM enquired.

"Nil. It's *FUBAR*. We need to have that technology operational ASAP," Alex urged. "We can consider communicating with the Venezuelan Air Force, but we have no solid intelligence to share with them. Given our current relations they might not be willing to assist. The manuscript mentions a fellow named Jake who could be the cocaine recipient."

"Jake Pipes?" Ambrose guessed.

The President knew the DEA agent. "Are they working this guy... Baljan Balkeran?"

"If they are, they're not communicating with us," Alex admitted.

The Commissioner entered the Think Tank and Alex gave a ball-by-ball commentary on events.

Angrily, Ken took the offered transcript. "I wouldn't doubt it. There have been incidents when the DEA worked cases clandestinely."

"What if it is not our Jake Pipes?" Ambrose asked.

"What if it is?" Alex retorted.

"I wouldn't gamble either way," Ken snapped. "If we have this intelligence we have to work on it. Screw the DEA. If it is them then they should have involved the local authorities."

Alex took the lead. He didn't want to pressure Ambrose onto a specific path. He had tried the approach countless times and failed. He moved the conversation forward with a different approach. "Ambrose, the ball is in your court. You make the call, we do the leg work." The MONS smiled softly and waited.

The room became still, almost serene. The only motion was of the President drumming his chest.

The COP, rolling his tongue, waited.

Ambrose Taylor made executive decisions.

## 34   The Wet Affairs

EARLY MONDAY. Working class people despise the day but joggers welcome it. Port of Spain's air is at its freshest, less contaminated from the weekend relief of cars and trucks fussing in and around the city. The morning is wet; there had been a surprising burst of rain which kept a mass of the trainees away, but Alicia Sylvester reassures herself that she is different, totally committed, all *woman*, businesslike. She walks with her back straight; her strides are long and confident. She is dressed in black tights, cut just above her knees, and a tight yellow top which embraces voluptuous breasts and flattens out on her toned stomach. She has worked hard on her abdominals and are proud of them. She ignores the water which seeps through her sneakers and soaks her socks. The heaviness suits her efforts at further weight loss.

At January's end she had been fat, unsightly, unnoticeable, unwanted; work colleagues shunned her. At 0430 hours as she begins to jog, slowly at first, she is aware of men admiring her. Some greet her, but today she disregards their muscular legs and firm butts. She despises them as they pass with sweaty – *or dewy?* –backs and glistening biceps.

A red-skinned man glides past wordlessly. He is tall and not fat, but not Herculean either. His head bore a razor's edge. She has never seen this athlete and guesses his preference for weights over cardiovascular training. He does not possess the narrow frame of a runner; his broad, toned shoulders suggest raw power. But he runs nimbly for a man of his size. Unconsciously she begins tailing him.

Her mind strays and she thinks of the *Montalcino: indeed, it is good wine*. There is half left and she intends to enjoy it later. They say that wine is good for the heart, especially after meals. *Meals*. The thought of one causes Alicia to smile. Her food is bird bite portions of salads, a total of six per day. No longer does she gorge on junk. Food deprivation during Christmas had nearly driven her mad but she survived. At first she was terrified, but the results were encouraging and so were the compliments. She does not consider herself a woman seeking flattery, but being obese had taken a toll on her self-esteem. Now the landscape brightened as her physical contours took exquisite shape and she longs for vanity's satisfaction.

Another runner turns and greets her and she is delighted. Still, she maintains a cold mask. She knows it is this ego which could sink her. Alicia quickens her pace. She has done her homework and knows that she can burn up to three hundred per cent more fat by drilling her body early in the morning. Later, she promises, she would return to the Queen's Park Savannah to jog again, a total of three laps. It is the secret of her success. She has shared it with others, but no one so far can cope with her stamina. Alicia is hardcore. Alicia is a wo*man*. Alicia is Chief. She smiles.

It begins to rain, not heavily, but the droplets are fat, heralding the downpour to come. Alicia thinks of how dry March had been. Now, on the last day, there is rain. She runs hard, wishing to escape a drenching. The tall man looks back and hurries on, maintaining the lead. Alicia scoffs. *He has misread my intention. How typical.*

Suddenly, and fiercely, clouds burst and the rain is thick as if falling from the grey skies of a squall. Alicia sees only the runner and the imposing Whitehall ahead. It is her last lap. Before the sun is up – *will it be?* – she will have a smoke, shower and be showcased dressed for duty as Executive Secretary to the Prime Minister of Trinidad and Tobago. She navigates the final curve and slowly begins to zip past the runner who, so far, has proven to be elusive. Alicia is already drenched. Her goal is to overtake him before he reaches the limestone boundaries of Whitehall. Her chest is pounding, her feet heavy with muscle milk, but determination worked before and she is convinced it will do the same now.

OXY HAS plans for Alicia Sylvester. In the thick, white rain he slows and Chief gains ground. He could hear the thump of her sneakers hitting the puddles hard, the rapture of her breaths, short sharp bursts. Alicia is fast, but lacks the control of a true athlete. She moves alongside him. He can see her breasts cascading smoothly below the wet t-shirt. He teases her by quickening his pace but metal determination keeps Alicia moving, like a mean, lonesome outlaw, shot and hunted by Apaches but intent on crossing the Mexican border.

*Now*. Oxy slows and Alicia moves forward. The borders of Whitehall are three metres away. Chief wins. Exertion is evident as her palms fall to her knees. She inhales deeply to recover spent energy. She sees the feet of the man who has stopped to congratulate her. Jubilant, she glances up and confronts not a defeated face but the barrel of a gun.

Two shots; a *double tap*.

Chief drops dead, red gushing from the holes in her head. Blood forms a wide arc and engulfs Alicia Sylvester. It is smooth, like the dark, expensive *Montalcino* waiting at home.

DEEP IN the south, Icacos was experiencing a bright, cloudless day. Balkeran smiled. He had not felt so blessed in ages. His sickness had somehow subsided and his children were gaining their Masters – *or some kind of thing like that*. Business was good and things were about to get better. *1100 hours? In a few hours I richer*.

Gently, he told Icepick to decrease the car's speed. He enjoyed the wind in his hair, the sunlight on his face. It had been awhile since he had left his home and today's business gave him exceptional reason to do so. Riding in the trunk was one hundred kilos of pure Columbian cocaine.

Whiteman had migrated quickly to the gold phone. Balkeran had been introduced to Jake, beer in hand, by Sonnie – *thank goodness he dead* – and business had blossomed. The American pilot had become Balkeran's drinking *buddy* and replaced Bharat, the man who became too big for his boots; the man who had spat out the people who had always been there for him. The blind fool thought he was everyone's boss and other dons the subordinates. *Yes,* Balkeran thought, *I is a don. To hell with he.*

Balkeran looked at Icepick behind the wheel and pitied the fellow. To kill a man wasn't easy. Don Balkeran had never seen it occur since his operations were more relaxed yet he was regarded as an ironfisted ruler. Thus, he and Chandra Bharat had warred in the early years. *That is why he move back Central.* He visited, but each year Bharat had became more distant, colder, more abrupt. Visits decreased to one a year. Then none. But Bharat needed Balkeran; until recently, it seemed.

Balkeran had not been certain of what had brought about the change, but over the past three months his main source of revenue had steadily declined. Then Jake, the cash cow, had resurfaced. This first big buy motivated Balkeran to be on the drop. The pockets of all the right people were filled, the road was cleared of police and in Point Fortin an escort awaited.

Balkeran enjoyed the scenery Cedros offered while a grieving Icepick drove. *Still thinking about he dead partner, the dougla.* When they were almost out of the village Balkeran saw a familiar face, someone he hadn't seen in years, *Bumpy.* Balkeran ordered Icepick to stop the car and engaged in spirited talk with Bumpy. Balkeran's schoolmate invited him for a quick whiskey. One for the road, they laughed.

One drink would lead to two, then a bottle. Icepick waited in the car and thought about Glen. He wanted to leave, to return home to mourn, but he waited. *Today is a big day for meh boss.*

CHIP RIVERS, in the refurbished cockpit, cursed. He had chosen to launch the *Amity* on a day rain dominated. He was a sailor and loved any weather but deep down he had imagined a day of sunshine for the special event. The sky was pregnant with rain; heavy grey clouds hung low over the blackened waters of The Bocas. Chip, disheartened to sail further west, navigated until his compass pointed east to *Marina Ideal*. Sailing was slightly different to when Angie was on board: *still alone, but happier*. He had been glad to see her go, but worried that she hadn't yet returned to her family. Maybe she had run off with another sailor. *What did it matter?* Being alone and being with someone and alone was vastly different. He had realised this days ago, taking it as a sign when a native finally answered his call. Angie McKenzie-Rivers had deliberately given a wrong number.

Suddenly, to starboard, he noticed a vessel perched dangerously against rocks to the north of Monos Island. Alarmed, the sailor throttled closer, navigating skilfully until his smaller boat was alongside the vessel. Chip braved the rain and peered over. He didn't expect to see a body face down on deck. Chip noticed the dark stain and a pool of light, pinkish-red water which had collected at the bow.

Chip didn't think, he reacted. He rushed to his radio and with quick adjustments the device was on the international distress channel. "Mayday, Mayday, Mayday, this is *Amity*. Mayday, Amity. Position 10.7033 North 61.6881 West. Mayday Relay for vessel *Dolly* in distress, crashed into Monos Island. Dead caucasian male on board. I repeat, dead caucasian male on board. No sign of other passengers. Over."

A voice cackled over Channel 16. Chip repeated the coordinates, then confirmed: there was no other sign of life.

THE COAST Guard showed in full force. The helicopter came first and after a bout of circling, ropes descended over the unmanned vessel. Chip saw two CG cutters hustling to the scene, a mass of white foam in their wake.

Chip remembered the day he had been trapped in *Amity* and fear welled up in his stomach. He took a long hard swallow of nothing. *What if they decided to search Amity?* The vessel was clean, but there was still the notorious compartment. Chip saw three men rappel from the hovering helicopter, its blades emitting a guttural, thudding whoop. The men hit the deck, weapons cocked and unlocked. Quickly, two of them disappeared into *Dolly's* bowels. Chip strained his ear but didn't hear any commotion. He was curious. He waited. The masked men reappeared on deck with a young woman. Heavily-armed sailors on the decks of the cutters began clapping and although Chip was uncertain what had transpired he joined in the wet, standing ovation. The survivor was airlifted from the scene and Chip, hailed as a hero, entertained sailors who had boarded *Amity* to congratulate him on fine seamanship.

THE LAST three members of The Wild Bunch waited. They had been killing time for the past six hours in the stifling heat of the countryside. Each man was dressed casually with blue Kevlar vests strapped tightly to their bodies. Even with cold air blasting through the car's vents, it was uncomfortable seated with the devices.

Ken was at home with his boys. "Strange, all this hot weather here and it have real rain in town *eh*?" There had just been a report of stormy weather in the north.

"Yeah boy," Chinee said, "And like is real blasted rain." He had always been the vocal one in the group.

Snake grunted confirmation. He was as silent and deadly as the predator after which he had been nicknamed

Chinee, seated as driver, was the most impatient. "Like this thing not going down again or what?" He bounced his feet steadily, a habit Snake had always found incongruous for a highly-trained man.

"They will come," the Commissioner assured. He shifted. It had been long since he had worn a bulletproof vest. The muscles in his shoulders were stiff, his withered hand rested limply on his left leg.

Snake propped his elbows against the passenger's and driver's headrest, like a child anxious to reach a theme park. Ken reminisced about the cocaine cook they had clashed with and Chinee, his eyes vigilant on the road, chipped in humorously. Snake hissed.

The location of the impending ambush was at a sharp bend at the end of a needle-straight road, quarter of a mile long, where a car would slow. The men waited, with talk drifting in and out of the golden years; how times had changed. Ken felt an adrenaline rush. Their feet bouncing in unison, he and Chinee looked like performers in a leggy stage show.

Chinee suddenly cocked up. "Look them! Look them!"

"You sure that is them?" Ken asked, his fingers wrapping around the UZI between his legs.

Snake, peering through binoculars, confirmed the taxi's licence plate. Keeping low, he slipped out of the car. Ken followed. Chinee tumbled the war machine's engine and watched Sunil's Black Giant slowly approaching.

ICEPICK, CONFUSED by the war wagon's magical appearance, swerved and accelerated into the path of the metal missile. Balkeran had enough time to curse his mother-in-law. '*BANG!*' Steam erupted from under the bonnets of the stalled cars. What happened next neither Icepick nor Balkeran expected: automatic weapons were trust through the windows.

"Put your hands outside the car!" Snake ordered roughly.

Ken's weapon addressed the passenger. He cursed and a whitened Balkeran mimicked Icepick.

Chinee, shaken by the accident (he had expected The Black Giant to stop), stumbled out of the war wagon and rushed over. He called out and after Snake's monologue of obscenities, he was tossed a single key attached to a black loop. Chinee popped the trunk open. He exclaimed. He cut one of the bags and licked the white substance on his forefinger. It was good. "Bingo!" he called out to The Wild Bunch. "They didn't even bother to hide the damn thing!"

"What now?" Snake asked, sensing a tiny, harmless movement in the bushes. Like Ken he wanted to see the haul, but he had an offender to police. His hands were wrapped tightly around the weapon, his finger millimetres away from the hair trigger. He maintained a distance from the door, in case the driver decided to run for it. Not that he would reach far.

Ken scanned the road. No cars were in sight, no homes decorated the edges of the road. In either direction there was only lush green grass. The location was indeed strategic, void of people, empty of witnesses. He thought of Raul and Steve. Dead, their widows still grieving. He looked at his withered hand, a limp attachment, a blow which had sunk him into the murky waters of depression. He looked at Balkeran, a name whispered in shadowed circles, a man worse than scum, a face he had never before seen.

Snake and Chinee waited. It was like old times: Ken always made the calls. The Commissioner's gun was cocked, the safety off. He levelled it on the glassy-eyed Balkeran who was sobbing and pleading. He stuttered about a dog named Lady, a wife, five children, ten grandchildren, six great-grandchildren, a white partner in Toco, his beloved mother-in-law, great nieces and nephews, *portrait* cancer and diabetes. He didn't have long to live, he cried, three months max.

Ken Thomas felt no compassion. He looked into Balkeran's face. They were always quick to sob, quick to offer handsome bribes. Balkeran's three million sounded fine, but too evil to compensate for the brutality the nation suffered at the hands of drug lords. Chinee spoke, but Ken didn't catch his words; it sounded like a command to hurry up and kill the bastards. Seconds ticked on.

"Ken?" It was Snake who spoke. He remained poised to shoot, oblivious to everything but the target. Since The Wild Bunch had disbanded he had worked only with simulations in the Royal Navy and more recently with CISTU. This was real.

"Make the call, Ken!" Chinee exclaimed. He was still hovering over the trunk, hypnotised by the quantity. It was a big cocaine bust, the biggest he had ever been on.

Ken's eyes narrowed into a thin, mean slit. The moment was now, the road still clear. He tightened his one-handed grip on the UZI. "Cuff them," he ordered.

"Lucky bastards!" Chinee exclaimed. He assumed control of Balkeran.

Ken walked to the trunk. 'Bingo' was an understatement. Balkeran and his companion were facing life in prison. He looked as Chinee scrambled the crime boss on the hot pitch and roughly applied the handcuffs, repeating the Miranda Rights. He felt no pity at the sight of Balkeran being dragged to his feet The drug lord didn't look healthy. *He's probably my age. He was foolish to choose the wrong profession.*

It took two minutes to reconfirm plans. Ken Thomas, at the wheel of The Black Giant, led the way. Chinee and Snake followed with the bound prisoners.

FARMER DASS, an oldtimer who had been tying his prized heifer beneath the shade of an almond tree, had witnessed the incident. He ran home to tell his wife what he had seen, but she doubted him. Later he would tell the story at Bindu's Bar to a room filled with pensioners and young men: The Wild Bunch was back in town.

THERE IS no moon, only shadows which curl, twist, turn and dart across the orchard and its slopes. Rawlins lifts a fist and the three men halt. The night is still. After four miles through thick bushes CISTU reaches Bharat's palace. The compound isn't big, it is *vast*.

The soldier activates the NVD and surveys the scene. To the left is a splendid steel structure which houses oranges and vehicles. To Rawlins it is bigger than his Diego Martin home. To the right, about twenty-five feet away, is Bharat's dwelling, a house neither Ricky nor Amrit could have described in minute detail. Ernie had not been able to retrieve a blueprint for the structure. There was none; raw cash had built the house. Rawlins is disturbed that he is about to take his team into an unplanned combat situation, but CISTU is trained for the unexpected.

Oxy sees a flicker of light, on the ground floor, showing in the two inches between the window and the top of the curtains. He taps the captain on his shoulder.

"What do you think?" Hope whispers coarsely in the darkness.

"Can't see shit," Rawlins confirms. The view inside is blocked by dark, heavy blinds. The light goes off. The soldier hears a commotion and the barking of what could only be a ferocious dog. Rawlins cocked his MP5.

"YOU SPANISH fool you!" Bharat flung a glass which shattered against the door Isabel had slipped through. "Who the hell you think you is *eh*?" He darted outside. The woman had made him run all the way downstairs. "You think you could just leave me?" Unlike his first wife, Isabel had erred in telling him she was leaving so, now, he had a say: "You pregnant and you want to leave here with *my* child?" They were in the open yard, Bharat waving a gun in her face.

But Isabel did not shrink, neither did she experience nausea. Her mind was clear, she was leaving, yet she wasn't sure she wanted to. "*¡Imposible!*" she exclaimed. "You cannot call me a whore, you cannot treat me like... like *sheet* and expect me to stay!"

Bharat stopped in the centre of the paved plateau and ordered: "Woman, get your Spanish ass back inside before I beat you again." He shot the barking dog to show he was serious. *To hell with Mouse and the Samaroo family.*

Isabel grimaced, but didn't flinch. She didn't doubt that Bharat was capable of shooting her, yet wondered. She had had enough of his madness but something compelled her back indoors, some intangible force that was love, the feeling that she couldn't bear life if he wasn't in it. She didn't dare to test him.

Bharat dragged her upstairs, locked her in the master bedroom and pushed a heavy table before the door. He doubled back to the storeroom where Navin had been carving up Paul Headley before Isabel started her ruckus.

THE APPROACH takes time. Captain Rawlins moves slowly past Patsy, the dead canine, and continues slowly to the door. Very slowly. This is real, a matter of life and death. He knows if they engage in a gun battle it won't be blanks heading their way; it will be slugs designed to kill. Anticipation makes the door seem far, but soon he is upon it. Rawlins' earpiece cackles.

It is Oxy. An anticlockwise move finds the big man at the north of the compound, and from dense bushes he covers the team's entire approach through the scopes of a sniper rifle mounted with an NVD, the ultimate backcountry toy.

The captain looks at Sookram who nods. He is ready; so is Hope. The private reaches for the handle and gently depresses it. The door is open. He looks at his leader; it shouldn't be this easy. *Have we been made?* Hope steps out from before the fatal funnel and eases the door further. It swings inward and Sinatra's golden voice startles him

"Room looks empty from here," Oxy transmits from fifty yards away. He relocates twice and his intel is the same.

CISTU enters. No shots are exchanged.

Sookram, in his AOR, is surprised at the broken glass scattered across the room. A high whiff of alcohol permeates the room and the music is loud. Beyond the bar is a grand, marble staircase wide enough for two sedans to parallel park. The team inches forward, two men slithering along the walls, Bob Hope to the centre, panning in and out of his teammates' Areas Of Responsibility. His job is simple: support Sookram and Rawlins and not get shot. Apart from the music his trained ear hears no other sound.

The ground floor narrows and continues beyond the base of the staircase. Rawlins signals and both men stack up behind him. Slowly, they move on, each concentrating on retaining the element of surprise they still possessed. *Or does it belong to the enemy?* Along the wall are the entrances to three rooms. A quick peep. The kitchen is clear. Light shows below the second door. Suddenly there is a shrill cry.

OXY HEARS the noise of what sounds like a wounded hyena. *What the jail going on?* His earpiece comes to life and Rawlins barks an order. Oxy doesn't have time to enquire, only to act on instructions. Running low along the outskirts of the paved area he circles around the metal shed until he is twenty-five feet from the window where he had first seen the light. Instinctively, he looks up to the second floor. Peering through drawn curtains is a full, shapely, beautiful woman. She screams.

"WHAT THE ass is that?" Bharat asked. He looked at the knife-wielding Navin. "That is Isabel?"

What happened next neither expected. There was a loud explosion outside and a ball of flame shone orange through the thick, dark blinds. Confused, Bharat headed for the window.

"STAND BY, Stand by, Stand by... Go!"

Upon the order Rawlins hears the fire bomb explode. Oxy had done his part. Simultaneously Bob Hope brings down a Dynamic Hammer on the wooden door. With a smash the door swings inward and before it makes the maximum possible arc, Sookram flings a Flash Bang into the room. The space erupts into a bright flash and loud noise. Rawlins, pumped on adrenaline, is already inside. He gauges his surroundings and fires. He sees Bharat go down hard. Beside him the sailor fires into his AOR, the right side of the room.

A FALL averted Bharat's execution. He was moving to the window at the sound of the explosion but turned when the Dynamic Hammer slugged the door. The Flash Bang was tossed inside and the disguised men entered the room, guns blazing. As Bharat fell, a bullet whizzed past his face, shattering the left lens of his shades. *Are these Paul Headley's protectors?* If they were then Aram was a big fish as the Creole had warned. The Manager stayed where he had fallen as bullets slammed into glass, stone and marijuana bales. It wasn't an ordinary storeroom but the size of a small house, pleasantly suitable for Bharat's souvenirs hoarded throughout the years. He cursed when a crate of *Montalcino* exploded, sprinkling wine everywhere. He hated its taste. He bawled when the bust of a Frenchman, almost as short as Frankie, crumbled. His eyes widened when a miniature model of the Las Lomas housing project was ripped apart. Over-ripe mangoes he had received as tax from Boodoo Lane rolled freely on the floor.

Navin, who had stepped away from Paul Headley when the door burst open, wasn't as lucky as Bharat. Sookram's first shots from the barrel of the MP5 went wide – the sailor had aimed high, misjudging the distance between the man and himself. He quickly readjusted and depressed the trigger. Six rounds in rapid succession caught Navin in the chest. Navin's heart was punctured by the second slug which exited below the shoulder.

The shooting subsided but Bharat lay still. *Yes, I go play dead to catch corbeau alive then kill them.* He burnt with rage: *how dare they invade my life? Who dares to trespass and upset my privacy? My sweat and blood build this empire!* Bharat listened. There was silence. The attackers were waiting. He heard light movements then whispers he couldn't discern. The intruders were obviously communicating. He scanned the window behind him; it was almost fifteen feet away. He thought briefly about escaping but cursed the thought away. *What the hell? I is not a pansy. This is my casa.* He thought of Isabel upstairs. He had been stupid to lock her inside a room filled with enough guns and ammunition to eradicate a small village. Chief had warned of the impending attack but he had been careless, too preoccupied with Paul Headley and Aram Hamad.

A single shot plunged the room into darkness.

Bharat made his move.

Bob Hope, scanning the corridor and the room, saw Bharat pop up. He levelled for a shot, but held his fire. Bharat had wrapped his hand around the hostage, cradling his face against the man. *The baddie is smart.*

Rawlins had seen the movement and cursed his luck; it was impossible to fire with Bharat rising immediately behind the hostage. It was weird to see the target snug against the captive, cursing, defiance shining like his left pupil in the display of the NVD.

"Is he you want?" Bharat screamed into the darkness. His fingers sunk into Paul's mutilated flesh like a tiger pawing a zebra. "Drop all you weapons or I will kill this son-of-a-bitch dead." He pressed *Baby* into Paul's head causing the feeble  man to grunt. Despite all the shooting Headley was still alive which suggested to Bharat that Aram had sent mercenaries to rescue his top muscle. Bharat knew that his escape depended on keeping Paul alive. It was ironic that all along he had threatened to murder the man. "I will kill this Creole, all you hear?"

Rawlins began to sidestep. "Go ahead."

"You sure?"

"Positive. Kill him"

Bharat's head exploded, the bullet exiting through his left eye. Beyond the window, Oxy had done as ordered through his earpiece.

The Manager died on Paul Headley's shoulders. Ninety seconds had elapsed from the time the firebomb had detonated to the moment of Bharat's death.

FIVE MINUTES later the entire building was cleared without further resistance, except for a single shot fired after the Remington had removed the hinges and lock to the master bedroom. Isabel was dead; suicide. The scenario would bother Sookram for a long time. Oxy commented that it was a covert mission and the fewer witnesses the better but the sailor wasn't appeased.

The three men hustled along the corridor to the room where they had left Hope.

"He's dead," the private said solemnly. He was stooping beside Paul Headley.

"Did he say who he was?" Rawlins asked.

"Never did." The Tobagonian stood. "He didn't stand a chance." Contemplatively, he bit his lip. "Those bastards really punished him." Hope was glad he was CISTU.

"Okay," Rawlins said sharply and pulled his team together. "Let's finish this." They headed along the corridor to the third door which opened into a small room adorned with religious statues.

"You sure this is it?" Oxy asked. It didn't seem likely. The room was large enough to house one person comfortably.

Rawlins navigated a labyrinth of clay until he came to the back of the room. The wall was recently painted but the fresh, crude, concrete work was evident; it flaked easily when the captain brushed his gloves against the surface. A frame charge could have worked, but the Dynamic Hammer did justice. Concrete fell inwards to reveal a hidden room filled with packages.

"Shit!" Rawlins exclaimed. "That's a lot of cocaine."

Sookram, who had cleared the room of its artifacts, peered inside. "*Shucks*," he swore. Rawlins hadn't lied.

"Do we proceed as planned?" Oxy asked.

Rawlins looked at the big man and shook his head.

It took another three minutes to douse the house and only when they were back in the yard, safely away from the structure, did the team hear the approaching helicopter.

Rawlins gave the order. "Burn it to hell," he commanded and the youngest man, Bob Hope, struck a match to the gasoline trail.

It took seconds for the house to explode into a ball of fire.

"That would work as a great Flash Bang," Oxy commented dryly, shielding his eyes from the towering blaze.

Within seconds CISTU was aboard the helicopter heading north. They quietly watched the orange inferno until it faded from view.

## 35   Stitched wounds

THE FOLLOWING day, April 1st, *The Tabloid* printed tales of murder, death, destruction and triumph. There was no front page photo, only the words 'No Joke' in White On Black (WOB).

The first story was about two unidentified men who, weeks after an autopsy, would be identified as Ricky Love and Amrit Sankar, the felons responsible for the murder and rape of Angie McKenzie (the journalist had uncovered her maiden name only). The second was a peculiar one, almost funny, about a character called Merv who had gone raving mad. He claimed he was kidnapped by the CIA, tortured, drowned, shot and returned to life. The unidentified source who dropped him off at a mental hospital was supposedly paid fifty dollars by the institution.

It was the page three story which gripped Sean, the one about Leah. The Lance Jones article hailed a yachtie, who wished anonymity, as the rescuer of Ms. Hamad. On board the vessel *Dolly* was a dead body, an Irishman identified as Declan Foley, the Dustbin Bomber and IRA member. Sean swore softly. The article revealed that the local authorities had initially thought the man to be Mr. Hamad, but up to press time the Syrian was missing. The Coast Guard commander confirmed that his men were investigating and that sea patrols were diligently scouting the north coast in search of the millionaire. The commander declined to speculate on Aram's fate.

"Mr. Brown." The voice was timid.

Sean responded. It was Petal Clarke who, according to Ernie, was one of the best damn doctors and pathologists in the country. She signalled for him to follow and led him along a sanitised corridor with rooms on either side. Here the antiseptic atmosphere was thick.

At room 101 she stopped and faced Sean. "Mrs. Hamad left but you don't have much time. Two minutes max, so hurry."

Sean nodded. Above the room number was a small, square window. He peeked inside and in the dim light he saw Leah  covered from neck to feet, a thick layer of bandage wrapped around her throat. *Is she asleep?* Guilt stabbed at Sean; he felt responsible for her condition. Petal urged him on. Reluctantly he entered the room and a cool current of air greeted him. Medical equipment beeped, their coloured, fluctuating readings in plain sight. The low hum of the air-conditioning was oddly comforting.

Balloons and get-well-soon cards decorated the room, giving it the appearance of a child's birthday party. Sean gripped the bed's cold metal rails and sobbed silently. It was painful to see the woman he loved wrapped like a mummy with IV tubes strung along the bed and disappearing below the blanket into her hand. He couldn't interpret the vitals displayed on the machines, but was relieved that there were no threatening beeps.

Leah stirred. She moaned. She opened her eyes and found Sean. She smiled; it hurt, but she smiled again. *At last I am safe.* She cried. A few days later she would explain that the tears weren't of sadness but of relief. She wanted to promise that she would never become angry at him again. She wanted to tell him that her fingertip was missing because her Papa had accidentally slammed a car door on her hand. She wanted to tell him she had first seen his name on his laptop and that she loved him since. She tried to apologise but Sean gently stopped her. Together they sobbed. Sean stroked her curls lightly and repeatedly whispered the magnitude of his affection. Leah asked for her Papa, but Sean had no answer. He leaned over her and shook his head sadly.

Rest, he told her, and removed an object from his shirt pocket. In it was a ring. "I love you," he whispered, and kissed Leah's forehead.

Petal entered and tapped her wristwatch.

He nudged the box under the blanket and into Leah's open hand then left room 101.

With Sean gone, Leah drifted into a sedated sleep, her fingers wrapped around her future commitment.

"DO YOU know where you are?" Aram's interrogator wore army fatigues and a moustache bigger and thicker than his. His eyes were a deep and unreadable brown.

Aram shook his head. Bound to the chair, he had been severely beaten. Today was just another day of suffering, he thought.

"My friend, you are in Columbia... just off the Pacific, guest of the People's Army." He spoke as if the mosquito-riddled tent, the colour of dark foliage, was a palace filled with fine treasure, women and alcohol; the sort of place a man would desire. He pointed north. "Your home is in that direction, very, very far away from here." He walked over to Aram. In his hands he toyed with an unlit cigar and a cigar cutter. "Do you know who I am?" He smiled slowly and thoughtfully like a professor asked to reiterate the solution to a problem.

Aram's lips were parched, his mind unwillingly to order his tongue. But he thought he knew the answer: he was the one man who had enough resources to extract him from Trinidad and bring him so far via the sea without interference.

The interrogator leaned over and spoke into Aram's ear, his voice a rough whisper, "I am Fidel Cortez and you, my *friend*, you have lost something belonging to me. A most unfortunate incident." He stood and addressed the only sentry and witness to the event: "Won't you say so Pablo?"

"*Si*," the Guerrilla Commander replied, "most unfortunate." As scheduled Pablo had returned to the camp a day ago. Señor Cortez had been waiting anxiously on the cargo which Pablo brought. As it turned out, two birds had been killed with one stone: Declan Foley of the IRA was dead and Pablo had been able to nab the Syrian mobster. His daughter was of no importance; Aram had to be hooked and Leah had served as good bait. It was unlikely that fingers would be pointed to FARC; not that it mattered, but the job of kidnapping Aram Hamad wasn't in the direct interest of the guerrilla group, merely a small favour to Cortez, a key financier of the People's Army.

Foley's name was stamped on a bullet three months ago when he, high on cocaine, fondled Garcia's woman and confronted the embittered Guerrilla Commander. Pablo marked time, denouncing the red-haired Foley as sloppy, a man who mixed business with pleasure, stout and cocaine. When he attempted stubbornly to rape Leah Hamad, Pablo intervened, not with his fists but with a gun, conveniently blaming Aram for the gaping hole in the Irishman's head. As a bonus the US one million ransom money went to FARC along with Señor Cortez's vessel which had transported Aram into Columbian territory; small bonuses, but nevertheless welcome benefits.

Aram murmured something which Cortez missed.

"Speak up you fool!" Cortez demanded, and landed a wicked blow on Aram, splitting his skull.

"He said *Leah*," Pablo offered. "That's his daughter." He whispered to Cortez in Spanish.

Fidel looked contemplatively at Aram and with a nasty tone said: "Your daughter is dead. *¡Muerte! ¿Comprende?*" He tilted Aram's face until their eyes met and with added venom repeated the words.

The Syrian sobbed. He wept. He cried for Leah, his Doll. He had failed her. There was no strength left to respond. The walls had crumbled and were burying him alive. He whimpered and resigned himself to his fate. His shoulders sagged and his legs buckled. There was nothing left worth living for. *It is over.*

The Columbian don recognised the expression.

Pablo Garcia passed a machete and somewhere, deep in the Cuaca jungle, Fidel Cortez executed Aram Hamad.

# Epilogue


## *Woodford Square, April 2nd*

"'I HAVE cherished the ideal of a democratic and free society in which all people live together in harmony and with equal opportunity.' Liberty, an ideal forged into humanity, an innate mantle we possess despite our creed and race.

Citizens, let us cease to see ourselves as different. There is no East Indian, African, Chinese, Caucasian, Syrian or Mixed race. We are one people, one nation, one community, born of one soil, nurtured by one faith, guided by one law.

The strength of a nation is not in one man, but in all men, a responsibility which we clasp together, red, white and black, and uphold rightly, proudly, to the sky and beyond, where possibilities are limitless.

We are the sculptors of the future. In us is a fire, that Trinbagonian fire, which distinguishes us from the world, a light for all to follow, a beacon to those in darkness.

Brothers and sisters we are soldiers of peace, justice and the ideal of democracy.

Let me give you my version. I see one nation, one people, one hope, one glory. I see children of one mother, one father, brothers and sisters of different colours, but of one heart. I do not see olden days when things *were good*. I do not wish for the past but for a future in which days *are* golden. I see not a vision, but a reality for our beloved country, Trinidad and Tobago.

May God bless our nation."

- Prime Minister Ambrose Taylor

FICTION

"An excellent depiction of the underlying reality of the nexus between the illicit drug trade and daily life in the Caribbean. An experience in my reading of the work was the constant pause to reflect on how close art was to reality."

- Darius Figueira, author of *Jihad in Trinidad and Tobago*, July 27, 1990'

When one tonne of cocaine goes missing, Trinidad and Tobago is thrown into a state of disarray. Bombings and kidnappings occur and Prime Minister Ambrose Taylor and his team must respond to the security threats through conventional and unconventional means. The race is on for the drugs and not only the government, the Syrians, East Indians and Africans find themselves involved, but also the IRA.

U.S. $18.95
ISBN 978-1-4401-2222-4

9 781440 122224

90000

iUniverse®
www.iuniverse.com